And so it begins...

Sure enough, after the initial surge, the mob, resembling some obscene monster, backed away from the line, and the confidence that they had displayed began to be replaced with fear. The grim reality of swords versus clubs, of bottles versus shields and armour, began to sink in. You could see it in the face of the townsfolk; the sudden look of terror as they realized what was about to happen. Gerald was glad. They would retreat, and the already tense situation would be over. The troops would have stopped the mob, and things would return to normal. All that changed in an instant.

As the crowd began to cautiously back away, the captain found his voice. "Kill them!" he screamed. "Kill them all!"

Gerald looked up with horror at the captain's orders. "My lord, the people are dispersing, we should hold the line!"

Captain Walters had a wild look in his eyes. His fear had overcome him, and he glared down with rage at his sergeant.

"Do as I say, Sergeant! Kill the stinking peasants!"

Gerald heard a yell come from the soldiers, and suddenly the terror they had held in for so long was unleashed, and they surged forward. This was no organized manoeuvre, but a mad rush at the enemy, many of whom had turned their backs to run. It was too late to stop it. The captain was yelling and screaming incoherently at the men.

The sergeant stepped forward, determined to stop the madness, but collapsed to the ground, his leg giving out beneath him. He sat, stunned for a moment, staring at the pool of blood forming around him. He'd been cut in the assault, but the numbleaf and adrenaline had prevented him from feeling it. Now, he was bleeding out, too weak to do anything but look on in horror as his life ebbed out of him.

"How did I get here?" he wondered. "How did my life culminate in bleeding to death in this stinking street, of all places?"

～

Also by Paul J Bennett

SERVANT OF THE CROWN

Heir to the Crown: Book One

PAUL J BENNETT

Fourth Edition: May 2020

ISBN: 978-1-7751059-3-0

This book is a work of fiction. Any similarity to any person, living or dead is entirely coincidental.

Dedication

There is an old saying that it takes a village to raise a child. This book, in fact, the whole series, has been developed over many years. I owe a debt of gratitude to a great many people, without whose input, the final story would not have taken shape.

This book is dedicated to the following people:

Brad Aitken and Jeff Parker, who brought the characters of Revi Bloom and Arnim Caster to life. Amanda Bennett who was my first Beta reader, and laughed at all the right moments as she read the original draft and later, the final draft. Ian Bennett, Katie Brintnell, and Brad Aitken who volunteered to be beta readers for my next to final draft. Christie Kramberger who did such an excellent job on the book cover with help from Chris Kramberger.

Finally, to my wife and editor, Carol Bennett, who helped inspire and support me through the long days of writing, rewriting, and what seemed like endless edits. You are my inspiration.

Kingdom of Merceria

Prologue

WALPOLE STREET

Summer 953 MC*
(*Mercerian Calendar)

~

The sun was hot, and for what felt like the tenth time that morning, he removed his helmet to wipe the sweat from his brow, absently flinging the moisture from his hand. He cursed the heat yet again as the stink of the slums curled around his nostrils, causing him to gag. Even as he stood, someone emptied a chamber bucket from a second-storey window, the contents splattering to the ground. The waiting was agonizing, particularly with his old leg wound throbbing painfully. The men stood with their backs to him, waiting for the mob to appear while beside him, the captain, Lord Walters, sat upon his steed surveying the street as if it held some hidden secret. The line of men stretched across the road from the tavern on the right to the general goods store on the left. The shopkeepers had already barricaded their doors by the time the troops had taken up their station, fearful of the coming bloodshed.

It had been a harsh winter, and the last harvest had been one of the worst in years. The city was starving, and the poorer sections of town had risen up in protest. This morning, word had come from the Palace ordering the troops to prevent any rioting from making its way into the more prosperous areas of the capital, Wincaster.

The soldiers stood with weapons drawn, relaxed but alert. Sergeant

Matheson wiped the sweat from his forehead again. It was far too hot. Tempers would flare; there would be trouble, he could feel it in his bones.

The captain, tired of watching the street, looked down at his sergeant.

"Sergeant Matheson!" he said in an overly loud voice.

The sergeant looked up at the lord and noticed he was nervous by the man's eyes shifting back and forth. He was trying to sound confident, but the cracked voice betrayed his fear.

"Have the soldiers move closer together!"

Gerald Matheson had been a soldier almost his entire life. For more than twenty years, he had served his country, mostly in the Northern Wars. Now, he was here, on the street, being told by an untried officer how to conduct his men.

"Yes, my lord!" he replied back.

He knew there was no use in arguing, so he gave the command, and the soldiers moved together. After carrying out the manoeuvre, they did not entirely cover the width of the street, leaving their flanks exposed. Gerald had thought of forming a single line, but a shield wall needed men in a second rank to help support it. Here he was with only twenty men, stretched across the road in a sparse double line. A company was fifty soldiers on paper, but the realities were far different here in the capital. With the crown holding the purse strings, most were lucky to have thirty men. On top of that, with sick and wounded, his company could barely scrape together twenty at any one time. He looked up at the officer and knew that Lord Walters failed to grasp the danger of their situation.

He glanced over at the far end of the line and immediately realized it was sloppy. He cursed under his breath, now he would have to walk over there to see to it himself. He wondered if he should take his numbleaf, but decided against it; better to be in discomfort and alert than to have his senses dulled. With the first step forward, his leg threatened to buckle as the unwelcome but familiar shooting pain returned. He stopped to catch his breath as he examined the line, trying to hide his weakness. His hand instinctively sought out his belt pouch, and he withdrew a small, pale green leaf. The line was still facing forward; no one was watching him. He looked at the small leaf in his hand and was overcome with guilt knowing that each one cost him dearly. The bulk of his pay funded the relief he now sought. He was tempted to put it away, but he knew he would welcome the relief the leaf would bring. He popped it in his mouth, looking around conspiratorially, lest anyone see his actions.

He quickly chewed the leaf, and as soon as the skin was broken, he felt the effects. The slightly minty taste enveloped his mouth, and then the blessed numbness soaked into his limbs. His leg no longer pained him, but he knew his senses were dulled. He cursed the Norland blade that had wreaked so much damage. Looking back towards the line, he saw that Henderson was still out of place, and he began moving again, hobbling down the line to stand behind the man.

"Henderson," he said, "move forward, you're in a battle line, not a brothel."

The man moved forward, and the sergeant stared at him a moment.

"Where's your helmet, man?" he demanded.

Henderson looked back at him and blushed, "Left it in the brothel, Sergeant."

The soldiers around him laughed at the joke. The man had likely sold it for some coins to buy drink, but now the mistake could very well cost him his life. The laughter died down. They were good men, but inexperienced in combat, and he wondered, not for the first time today, if they would do their duty. He knew they were nervous; he must keep them occupied so they wouldn't focus on their fears.

In an undertone, he uttered, "All right lads, when you see the mob, I want you to spread out to your left. Never mind what his lordship says."

The muttered response indicated they understood. He casually strolled over to the other end of the line and repeated the same command. Confident that everything was taken care of, he marched back to the captain and stood beside him. The officer's horse, already skittish, shied away from him while the rider tried to maintain control over his mount.

"It's cursed hot out here today, Sergeant!" his lordship said, trying to sound calm.

"Yes, my lord," he answered.

The officer was nervous; he was trying too hard to appear nonchalant. For a captain who barely spoke to his social inferiors, he was positively chatty. Gerald had stood with officers behind a line before. Lord Fitzwilliam of Bodden had an easygoing attitude towards his men. His capacity to entrust his sergeants to carry out orders had inspired their loyalty, but that was the frontier. Here, in the cesspit of the kingdom, the quality of officers was limited to those who spent most of their time socializing with the elite rather than training.

He stood still and waited as the sun grew hotter. Noon was approaching, and his right leg began to ache again. Had the numbleaf worn off already? Each time he sought relief with the remedy, it was less effective, and now he could barely get a morning out of a single leaf. He hobbled back and forth behind the men to try to hide his unease, knowing the pain would return shortly. He had reached the end of the line and turned, beginning to retrace his steps when he heard a noise in the distance. He stopped to listen; a dull roar echoed through the streets.

"Shields!" he ordered as he made his way back to the captain. "They're approaching, my lord!"

"Steady men," the officer commanded, rather unnecessarily. The soldiers stood at the ready, shields to the front, swords held up, braced to receive the enemy. Gerald would have hoped to form a proper shield wall with their shields interlocked, but the men here had no such training.

Two blocks down, a swarm of people rounded the corner. They strode confidently, brandishing clubs, daggers, and even broken bottles. There were old men, young men, women, even children in the crowd yelling and screaming. When they saw the soldiers lined up across the street, it was as if a tidal wave was released. The mob surged forward, increasing their speed. He saw the soldiers begin to shift.

"Hold your positions!" he yelled.

The last thing he needed was the soldiers to break and run. He drew his sword and walked behind the line, peering over his men's shoulders to see the oncoming mass of humanity. It was the job of the sergeant to make sure soldiers didn't run from battle. In the North, he was confident that every man would do his duty, but here, there was not the same level of dedication.

"Wilkins, lift up that sword!" Gerald shouted. "Smith, plant your feet properly, or you'll be knocked down."

He distracted the men, made them think about what they were doing rather than focusing on the mob. The officer was yelling something, but he didn't give a damn.

"Here they come, steady… steady… hold your ground!"

The mob slowed, then stopped short of the line, jeering at the soldiers that barred their way. He couldn't blame them. The king had been brutal in his suppression of past riots. The crowd was hungry and desperate, and he knew desperate people would do desperate things. Somewhere in the throng, yelling started; he watched people trying to gather the courage to attack.

"Don't do it," he said under his breath, "don't throw your lives away."

"What was that, Sergeant?" said the captain.

"Nothing, my lord, just keeping the men in line," he lied.

The noise in front grew more intense, and then suddenly, bottles and rocks were being thrown. Most hit the shields doing no damage, but Gerald saw the poor bloody fool Henderson take a hit to the head. The man collapsed like a rag doll, and then the anchor at the end of the line was gone. The yelling intensified. He knew it was only a moment before the crowd attacked. He moved as quickly as he could to Henderson's position and dragged the fallen man back from the impending onslaught. A sudden primal scream emanated from the middle of the press of people, giving them the courage to surge forward. He stepped over Henderson's body quickly, grabbing the man's shield as he drew his own sword just in time.

The rioters hit the wall like water breaking against rocks. A thunderous sound erupted as bodies slammed into the wall of soldiers. The line moved back at least a foot and a half, but it held. He knew that if they could only continue to remain steady, the crowd would give up. He didn't want to have to kill these people. He silently prayed for them to retreat, but they clawed and stabbed with their makeshift weapons. The soldiers occasionally struck back with their swords, but mostly they hid behind their shields, trying not to be hit themselves. During the war, a soldier who didn't fight back was considered cowardly. Here, he was thankful, for perhaps blood on both sides would be spared because of their inexperience.

Sure enough, after the initial surge, the mob, resembling some obscene monster, backed away from the line, and the confidence that they had displayed began to be replaced with fear. The grim reality of swords versus clubs, of bottles versus shields and armour began to sink in. You could see it in the face of the townsfolk, the sudden look of terror as they realized what was about to happen. Gerald was glad. They would retreat, and the already tense situation would be over. The troops would have stopped the mob, and things would return to normal. All that changed in an instant.

As the crowd began to cautiously back away, the captain found his voice. "Kill them!" he screamed. "Kill them all!"

Gerald looked up with horror at the captain's orders. "My lord, the people are dispersing, we should hold the line!"

Captain Walters had a wild look in his eyes. His fear had overcome him, and he glared down with rage at his sergeant.

"Do as I say, Sergeant! Kill the stinking peasants!"

Gerald heard a yell come from the soldiers, and suddenly the terror they had held in for so long was unleashed, and they surged forward. This was no organized manoeuvre, but a mad rush at the enemy, many of whom had turned their backs to run. It was too late to stop it. The captain was yelling and screaming incoherently at the men.

The sergeant stepped forward, determined to stop the madness, but collapsed to the ground, his leg giving out beneath him. He sat, stunned for a moment, staring at the pool of blood forming around him. He'd been cut in the assault, but the numbleaf and adrenaline had prevented him from feeling it. Now, he was bleeding out, too weak to do anything but look on in horror as his life ebbed out of him.

"How did I get here?" he wondered. "How did my life culminate in bleeding to death in this stinking street, of all places?"

ONE

Youth

SUMMER 922 MC

I t was a gorgeous, hot summer day, and a ten-year-old Gerald Matheson ran through the field with the energy of youth. Ahead, through the long grass, he saw Calum's tail poking above the tall blades as he wandered left and right, hot on the trail of something. With the seeds planted, there was little else that needed to be done. He had taken their dog down to the stream at the far end of the woods to see if the fish were biting. The warm sun had soon caused him to drowse off, and now he must hurry back to the farm for dinner. He knew the woods would slow him down, so with youthful enthusiasm, he ran across the field that straddled the north end of the trees, the longer, but faster route back.

He stopped to catch his breath, recognizing he would soon be within sight of the farm. Once he rounded the edge of the woods, the rest of the journey was all downhill. He called out to Calum, but the beast was ahead of him barking, no doubt tracking a hare or field mouse. Drawing a deep breath, he continued on his way, confident the dog would manage to catch up with him, as he always did. He slowed his pace to conserve his strength, finally clearing the long grass. Ahead the dog was standing in an open area, barking at something to the south. He slowed to a walking pace and began to look around cautiously. Was some creature lurking in the woods? Were there wolves about?

Hearing the whinny of a horse made him gather that the farm must have some visitors. No doubt a patrol from Bodden was in the area, checking up on them. He cleared the northern edge of the woods and turned south, towards the farm, catching a whiff of something in the air - smoke. He gazed off to the south, suddenly freezing, paralyzed by the sight that befell his eyes. Off in the distance, his family's farm was engulfed in flames.

The thatched roof of the house was burning furiously while a group of men overran the homestead. Two held torches while they walked along the barn and used them to set fire to the roof. A third man stood nearby, holding the reins of the horses, while a fourth had his sword drawn, ready for action.

Gerald's eyes went wild, for on the ground were two bodies, and he knew in an instant they were his parents. He was frozen with fear, watching in horror as the barn lit up in flames.

Calum growled, running forward towards the men, but Gerald, looking on with horror, could only watch as the dog bore down on the attackers. The man with the sword turned at the sound, waiting while Calum closed the distance. He struck the beast down with a single swing. All Gerald heard was a sudden yelp, and then Calum too was among the dead. The man by the horses yelled, and suddenly Gerald was snapped out of his trance.

"Over there," the man shouted, pointing at Gerald. "Get him!"

The two men carrying the torches threw them into the barn on the way to their horses. The warrior with the sword started jogging directly towards the young lad.

Gerald turned and ran in panic. He heard the sounds of horses behind him. Cursing, he changed direction, crashing into the woods. He knew the forest well, recognized all the paths and obstructions. Using the forest for cover was his only chance to survive. Through the dense underbrush he went, feeling the sting of branches as they whipped across his face, but his fear drove him. In his haste to escape, he had not been paying attention, and now he found himself in an unfamiliar part of the woods. He cast his eyes about, looking for identifiable landmarks and found none.

Closing his eyes, he tried to fight the panic for the second time this day, for this was no time to lose his head. He opened his eyes and looked about, his sight resting on a broken branch. I must arm myself, he thought. He had visions of fighting off his pursuers but quickly came to the conclusion that he would be severely outmatched.

He realized sprinting as fast as he could was not the solution. He struggled to steady his breath, to lessen his chance of detection. What should he do? Where should he go? He closed his eyes again and concentrated on taking controlled breaths.

"Think it through," he thought, "I've got raiders looking for me, they have to be from Norland. Where will I be safe? Bodden Keep, it's my only chance."

With his plan formulated, he plunged back into the undergrowth heading south towards Bodden, aware it would be a long journey, but he felt it was his only hope. He headed farther south, no longer sure of the distance travelled. The light was beginning to fade, and he needed to find some shelter. The sounds of pursuit had long since faded, but he was aware he could not go back. Completely exhausted from his flight, he finally halted, confident that they would not find him, but now the challenge was to survive the night.

Off in the distance, he thought he heard the faint sound of running water, so he made his way towards it. Sure enough, he came across a small stream, and he knelt, thankful for this small mercy. After drinking his fill, he sat down and surveyed the area. There was a large tree that had long ago fallen, its trunk supported on one end by its upturned roots, the other sprawled across the ground. Nearby were some smaller, younger trees, and he began to break off their branches. Laying these across the fallen tree's trunk, he formed a small shelter. It wouldn't keep him dry if it rained, but it just might hide him from wild animals. Walking around, picking up more branches from the ground, he spotted some mushrooms. He had always hated how his mother had made him help in the kitchen, but now, he thanked her, for he knew these mushrooms were safe to eat. Once washed off in the stream, he hungrily devoured them. All that was left to do this horrible night was to crawl into his makeshift shelter and fall into a fitful sleep.

The early sunrise spread through the forest, the sun's rays striking Gerald's face through a gap in the sticks, waking him. Crawling out of the shelter, he looked to the south as he drank thirstily from the stream. He remembered there was a stream near Bodden and hoped this was the same one. He stayed close to the water's edge as he walked, keeping an eye out for more mushrooms.

He came across a parchberry bush along the stream. Once again, he was thankful for his mother's knowledge of the land, for she had warned him against eating them. He smiled at the memory. They were not poisonous, she had said, but they would fill him up, not leaving room for dinner. Gathering a small number and tossing them into his mouth, he quickly realized how they got their name. They absorbed all the moisture from his mouth, leaving him feeling as if he had a mouth full of wool. He spat them out in disgust and kept moving.

The sun was now nearing its height, and he stopped to rest, sitting on a rock that jutted out into the stream. Off in the distance, he heard a snort and froze, straining his ears to hear more. Sure enough, another snort came his way and then the sound of something moving through water. He ran to the water's edge, ducking behind a tree, watching and listening carefully.

Horses could be heard long before he saw them. There were six men in the group, all warriors. The leader was wearing a chain hauberk. As they drew even with him, he saw the coat of arms of Bodden upon the man's saddle. Gerald staggered out from the trees.

"My lord!" he cried out. He heard the rasp of steel as two of the men drew their swords.

"Hold," the leader said, raising his hand in the air.

The horses stopped, and the man looked down at him, "Are you the Matheson boy?"

Gerald was bewildered and stood, mute, looking at the man.

"We've been looking for you. We saw the smoke from the farm yesterday. It's all right. I'm Lord Richard Fitzwilliam, one of the baron's sons." He held out his hand and used his fingers to beckon him forward.

Gerald moved closer and looked up. The lord before him was young, not much older than Gerald himself, but the finely made armour he wore had seen battle. He sat upon his horse with the ease of someone bred to the saddle. Gerald looked at the other horsemen and witnessed their instant obedience. This was a man that commanded respect. As Lord Richard offered his hand, the frightened boy met his gaze and recognized the kindness in his eyes. Richard pulled him up to his horse, and he took up a seat behind the lord.

"You're lucky we found you. There are all sorts of nasty things in these woods."

"My parents," Gerald sputtered, "they were killed by raiders."

"We know. We've been there."

"We need to bury them," Gerald blurted out, "we can't leave them to the animals."

Richard Fitzwilliam looked to the horseman on his left, then began to turn his horse around.

"Very well, we'll return to the road and make our way back to the Matheson farm. You're lucky to be alive, boy. What's your name?"

"Gerald, Gerald Matheson."

"Well, Gerald Matheson, let's go give your parents a proper burial, shall we?"

One of the men with him spoke up, "Is that a good idea, Lord? There may still be raiders in the area."

"The choice is mine, Sir Walter. The Mathesons were loyal tenants. I know my father would like them seen to."

Riding on the back of the horse, Gerald was surprised that it took them so little time to return to his farm. Thinking back to the previous day, he came to the conclusion that in his fear, he had indeed lost his way, going in circles in his haste to escape the raiders. His first view of the farm was devastating. Looking around, it was obvious that the raiders had disappeared, but their destruction could be keenly seen. The house and the barn were both smouldering ashes, the livestock either gone or burned as well.

They buried his parents behind the ruins of the house. Lord Richard Fitzwilliam was kind enough to say some words over their graves. Gerald noticed that the knights who accompanied the lord were not impressed by his thoroughness. They grumbled as they gave poor Calum a grave, but they did as they were commanded. As the afternoon wore on, they finished their task then began the trip back to Bodden.

"What's going to happen to me?" asked Gerald.

"My father will find something for you to do, perhaps work in the kitchen?"

"That's woman's work," said Sir Walter, "better to put him to work in the fields."

"He's a bit young for fieldwork," said Richard, "perhaps we'll put him into the stables. You ever looked after a horse Gerald?"

"Yes, Lord. We had a plough horse at the farm."

"Well, there you have it then, we'll put you in the stables. They'll look after you."

TWO

Under Siege

SPRING 925 MC

It was late in the summer, and the stables always needed constant attention. Horses came and went at all hours of the day and night, leaving Gerald constantly tired. In addition to mucking out the stalls, he had to saddle and unsaddle the horses when needed. Just when he finished one, another would require his attention. It seemed to go on forever, and his muscles ached with the strain. He finished with the shovel and sat down on a small stool by the entrance, a cool evening breeze evaporating the sweat from him.

"Are you hungry?" a voice asked.

He looked up to see a young woman with long brown hair tied neatly behind her back, her dress covered by a white apron. She was holding a small wooden platter on which sat some bread and small pieces of meat.

"Is that for me?" he asked in disbelief.

"Cook sent me to bring you some food. She said you hadn't eaten all day."

He looked at her face, her brown eyes staring back.

"I'm Gerald," he said at last.

"I know, I've seen you around. I'm Meredith, and I work in the kitchen." She stepped closer, holding out the platter, "There's some pork and bread here if you like."

He took the plate, keeping his gaze on her all the while. There was something mesmerizing about her eyes as if they were drawing him in.

"Thank you," he said, but for some reason, he felt awkward. He looked down at his platter and gently took a piece of meat, popping it in his mouth. This was a rare thing, the food still hot and moist!

Meredith giggled, and he looked at her, mad that she was mocking him, but then he saw the smile on her face and realized the silliness of it. He smiled back at her.

"Delicious," he said, "do you want some?"

She stepped closer and took hold of a small piece of bread, lifting it carefully with two fingers. Gerald watched her nibble at it, gently biting the piece as if it were a fine delicacy.

"It's just bread," he said, laughing, "it won't bite you."

"I know, I'm making it last."

The moment was interrupted by a call from the kitchen, "Meredith, get your arse back here, there's work to be done."

"When you're done, bring the platter to the kitchen," she said, turning to leave.

"Will I see you again?" he asked.

She turned back to smile at him, "Definitely."

He watched her leave to return to her duties, forgetting how tired he was. His thoughts were soon interrupted by the appearance of Lord Richard Fitzwilliam. The young man had returned from patrol and came through the gate with six soldiers. Gerald popped another piece of meat in his mouth and set the plate down, knowing he would be far too busy to eat now. Lord Richard dismounted quickly, and Gerald ran over to take the reins. Usually, the lord liked to look after his mount himself, an act his men thought was absurd, but today he seemed agitated.

"Can I take your horse, Lord?" Gerald asked.

Lord Richard looked to the gate, ignoring his stable hand. "Get that gate closed and man the walls." The soldiers in the Keep started running to their posts as a horn sounded.

"Get yourself to the cellars, Gerald," he said, "the Keep is under attack."

"I can fight," pleaded Gerald, "give me a sword, Lord, and I'll show you."

"No, Gerald, you're only thirteen. Your time to man the walls will come, but not today. Get to the cellars and make sure the kitchen staff are safe. You're far more use to us protecting the women and children. Can you do that for me?"

Gerald looked up at the lord, a surge of pride flowing through him.

"You can count on me, Lord," he said.

"Good lad," said Lord Richard, "now hurry up, they'll be here at any moment."

He made his way into the Keep, but as he was about to descend the steps to the cellar, he heard sounds from above. The stairwell here was circular and extended from the cellar to the top of the Keep. Curious, he made his way upward, eager to see what was happening. The door at the top was open, and he peered from the stairs, trying to remain hidden. He spotted a group of soldiers standing by the north wall of the Keep. They had baskets with stones in them, and there were some archers, occasionally loosing off an arrow or two. Off in the distance, he heard sounds, drawing him out from his hiding place. He crept up to the battlements to see the view and gaped.

There were hundreds of men swarming over the ground, with some carrying ladders as arrows whistled past them. Off in the distance, he noticed someone riding an impressive black horse, his cape streaming behind him as he galloped across the battlefield, followed by a group of horsemen. There was a banner bearer, but he couldn't make out the flag. This was more than raiders, he thought, this was a Norland Army, come from the north to take Bodden. He heard yelling to his right and shifted his gaze. He recognized Lord Richard, magnificent in his chainmail, shouting to the men on the roof.

"Get those stones over here, they're hitting the wall. Sir Henry, take five men and reinforce the gatehouse." He grabbed the knight, "You must stop them. If Bodden falls, the whole kingdom will be open to them."

When Sir Henry rushed past with a group of men, Gerald jumped out of the way.

"You," roared Lord Richard, and Gerald looked up to see the lord looking directly at him. "This is no place for you, boy, get below to the cellar!"

Gerald turned in fear and ran down the steps.

Sitting in the damp cellar, Gerald felt the cold seeping through his clothes as he listened to the sounds of fighting echoing through the Keep. The baron had begun the construction of an outer wall, but it wasn't yet complete, giving the enemy easy access to the inner yard. By the sounds he heard above, the fighting was in the Keep itself. Gerald tried to judge the action but to little effect. He had never been in a battle before and couldn't tell what the noises portended. Huddled by the door, nervous sweat dripping from his brow, he felt a hand touch his forearm and looked to see Meredith.

"It's all right, you know. The baron will protect us. Besides, we're in a keep, what could go wrong?" she said innocently.

He felt his heart nearly leaping out of his chest. He wanted to tell her plenty could go wrong, but as he looked, he saw the fear on her face, and he wanted to make her feel safe.

"You're right. We should probably get some rest. We're likely to be down here for some time. Besides, once the battle is over, I'm sure everyone's going to want to eat, then you'll be busy."

She sat down next to him, laying her back against the wall. She started to doze off, slowly leaning towards him so that her head finally rested on his shoulder. Gerald wasn't sure what to do, so he sat still, afraid to move, lest he disturbed her sleep.

He must have nodded off, for when he opened his eyes again, everyone had moved. Meredith was now talking to the cook on the far side of the room. He stretched his legs, trying to get the stiffness out of them, listening carefully. The sounds of battle had died down, and the silence unnerved him. He heard footsteps approaching, not the measured footsteps he would expect, but rather, the frantic footfall of someone in a hurry. They came closer, and then the door flew open.

The man in the doorway looked massive to Gerald. He was wearing leather armour of some sort, with a fur collar and shoulders. A one-handed axe dripping with gore entered the room before him, and Gerald noticed he had a long knife sheathed on his belt.

His sudden appearance stunned the entire room, freezing them all. The man took a quick glance around, then moved towards Meredith, a lecherous smile crossing his face. He strode past Gerald, either oblivious to the young lad on the floor or did not see him as a threat. The cook stepped forward, placing herself between the intruder and the girl, but she was pushed aside heavily, flung against the wall, sinking to the floor. Meredith screamed, and the sound awoke Gerald from his inertia. The intruder grabbed Meredith's wrist, forcing her to her knees by twisting her arm painfully.

Gerald jumped to his feet, fear driving him into action. Hidden from the man's gaze, he moved swiftly, stepping forward and grasping the handle of the man's knife. The Norlander whipped around, backhanding the boy, the force of the blow spinning him around and sending him crashing to the floor.

Thinking the opposition defeated, the brute turned his attention back to Meredith, but it was his undoing. Gerald had taken the sheathed knife from the enemy's belt while he took the blow. Now, he rose to his feet again, anger overtaking reason. He roared a challenge and struck, his untrained arm guiding the knife through the air in a side strike. It penetrated the man's left forearm, cutting deeply. Gerald took a step backward as the man howled and turned on him, releasing his grip on the girl. Gerald saw the gleaming axe arcing for his head, but he had succeeded in his mission to divert the attention back to himself. He had nowhere to go but to step back, where he tripped on a pile of baskets. As he fell to the floor, the light above him was blocked out by the huge man who cast a foreboding shadow over him.

The axe was raised, ready to deliver an overhead strike, but Meredith jumped on the man's back, screaming. She wrapped her legs around his waist, putting her hands over his face, trying to gouge his eyes out with her nails. He staggered, trying to free himself of his unexpected burden. His foot caught on the uneven floor, and he tumbled forward towards where Gerald lay. Gerald couldn't move in time. He was only able to hold the knife in front of him, hoping to defend himself. The crushing weight of the two bodies as they fell forward knocked the wind out of him. The intruder let out a groan, and then stopped moving. The blade had struck true, and Gerald had been lucky, for when the man impaled himself, it drove the knife handle into the floor, narrowly missing the young lad. The weight of the body crushed him against the stone floor, and the room started to swirl.

He felt a tugging as the body was dragged off of him. Lord Richard was there with a guard, and together they hauled the body from him.

"Are you all right?"

Gerald gasped, trying to get his breath, "Just had the wind knocked from me, my lord," he said.

"He saved us," Meredith gushed.

Gerald looked at her, he had reacted with instinct, but now that it was over, he felt light-headed, and the room was still spinning. He tried to sit up but merely flopped to the side.

"Easy there," said Lord Richard. "Sutton, go and fetch the surgeon. No wait, we'll take him there directly. Grab his feet."

He felt himself being lifted by the armpits while someone carried his feet. The whole room swam before him and then went black.

Gerald awoke sometime later, in a bed that was soft and comfortable, completely unlike his own in the stables. He heard voices talking, but they were quiet as if muffled by something.

"It's remarkable," said a voice that he recognized as Lord Richard.

"Nonsense," said Baron Edward, his brother, "the boy was lucky."

"He stood in the face of fear, that's something not easily taught."

"Ridiculous, send him back to the stables."

"He's wasted in the stables. I see something in him, Edward, a spirit if you will. There are grown men that would have run from that fight. Something about him tells me he'd make a good warrior."

"Complete and utter nonsense. You're a dreamer, Richard, this is the real world."

"Still," said Lord Richard, "I'm going to give him a chance."

"It's your decision, Brother. You're the one who will be responsible for training him."

Then there was only silence, and Gerald shifted his head to better listen. He opened his eyes to see a well-furnished room and wondered, for a moment, if he had died and gone to the Afterlife.

"He's awake," said a voice beside him, and he turned to see Meredith. She was sitting in a chair near the window, and as he watched, she rose and strode towards him.

"Where am I?" he asked, still trying to focus.

"You're in one of the guest rooms in the Keep. Lord Richard had you brought here to recover. You hit your head when the Norlander fell on you. You're quite the hero you know, you saved us... and me." She leaned over him and placed a kiss on his forehead. "You'll always be my hero," she said in a quiet voice.

She was smiling at him, and it felt infectious. He was suddenly aware that he, also, was smiling like an idiot, but he didn't care. He heard the door open then looked over to see Lord Richard with his elder brother, the baron.

"Well," said Baron Edward, "you had us all worried there for a while." He turned to his brother, "Richard, now that he's recovered, let's get him back to work, shall we? We can't have him lingering around here."

Edward turned, leaving the room, no doubt a busy man. Lord Richard remained, walking over to the bed.

"How are you feeling?"

"A little light-headed," Gerald answered. "What happened? Who was the man that I killed, my lord?"

Lord Richard sat on the foot of the bed, "He was a Norlander. A small group of them used ladders to get in from the east wall while we were busy fighting on the north. We were hunting them down, but he managed to evade us. It's a lucky thing you were there. You saved the women from... well, let's just say you saved their lives."

Gerald tried to sit up while speaking, "I must get back to work, Lord, the baron said-"

"Never mind what my brother said, he's only been the baron for a few months, he's just overcompensating. You need some rest, you took a nasty wound."

"I just banged my head."

"Oh, you did more than that." He unbuttoned the shirt that Gerald was wearing and showed him the massive bruising on his chest. "You were lucky. The surgeon says it was amazing you didn't break any bones. No, you'll stay here until I say so."

Richard looked knowingly at Meredith then back to Gerald, "I think it's wise if we have someone to keep a close watch on you. Can you think of anyone who would be willing to do that?"

He looked back to Meredith, who was smiling and nodding.

"Very well, it's decided. I'll leave you to rest under the watchful eye of Meredith here, and I'll get Cook to send up some broth for you. Probably best if you don't eat too much solid food for a few days."

"Lord?" said Gerald, not quite comprehending.

Lord Richard smiled as he explained, "You're bruised all over, Gerald, and what goes in, invariably comes out, if you know what I mean. It might be uncomfortable for you to, well, eliminate your waste."

"Eliminate my what?" he asked.

"You know, shit," he said, turning red. "Honestly, you really should try to increase your vocabulary."

"My what, Lord?"

"Never mind."

Lord Richard sat a moment longer, watching as Meredith took a damp cloth to wipe Gerald's brow.

"I think we might move you out of the stables, Gerald. It's time you learned some other skills. What do you say about learning to fight, become a soldier?"

"I would love that, my lord," said Gerald, "but I don't have a sword."

"Don't worry about that, Gerald, I'll see to it you're fitted out. Maybe I'll even train you myself, no sense in someone else mucking it up."

Gerald didn't know what to say. He was suddenly overcome with emotion and fought hard to hold it down. Ever since the death of his parents, he had lived in Bodden. Lord Richard had looked out for him, despite his brother's opposition. He felt an overwhelming sense of duty to repay the kindness, to become the best soldier he could.

THREE

The Offer

SPRING 928 MC

~

It was early morning, and Gerald rolled over in his bed. Beside him, Meredith, heavy with child, rested comfortably. He sat up quietly, trying to make as little noise as possible, for he had early guard duty and must be ready before the sun rose. Meredith stirred as he dropped his legs over the side of the bed.

"Are you off to work?" she said, sleepily.

"Yes, Fitz has me in charge of the early watch," he whispered. "You should go back to sleep, my love."

She smiled at him in the dim light, "I shan't sleep much with this baby of yours inside me. She kicks like a horse."

He placed his hand upon her stomach, "There, there, little one, stop troubling your mother."

As if by magic, the baby stopped moving, and Meredith sighed in relief. "Come back soon, we'll miss you."

"Nothing but duty will keep me from you. I'll bring some food back from Cook so you won't have to prepare anything to eat. I'm sure she'll insist on coming herself, she positively dotes on you."

"Well," she replied, "it's good to have someone dote on you. You should know, Lord Richard's picked you as his favourite."

It was true. Lord Richard had taken it upon himself to train Gerald personally, just as he had promised after the attack. It had been three years, and Gerald was now a muscular sixteen-year-old who had filled out. He was in charge of a watch, an unheard of honour for someone so young.

Even the soldiers appeared to respect him. He trained mercilessly, but always found time for his wife. They had been married barely two seasons, but already she was with child. Lord Richard was most congratulatory, unlike his brother, the baron, who was less so, "A wife makes a man weak," he had proclaimed.

Gerald had to disagree. A man who had something to fight for fought with a strength and vigour that was unmatched.

He stood up, pulling his chain shirt over his head, and then leaned over the bed to kiss Meredith.

"You be careful today, we don't want you overdoing things, you need your rest."

Meredith disdainfully replied, "Oh, for Saxnor's sake, my mother was washing dishes the day I was born. The women in my family are strong." Just as she finished her statement, the baby kicked, and she grimaced, "All right, maybe there's some merit in resting."

"Can I get you anything on the way back from my shift?"

"You could see about scrounging some of those spicy sausages from the kitchen," she suggested.

"Your wish is my command," he declared, bowing deeply. "I shall raid the kitchen and bring back a bountiful supply of said sausages."

She laughed, and Gerald thought again how beautiful she looked, especially with a smile on her face.

"Now, get to work, young man, there's guarding to be done."

"I am ever your servant," he bowed gallantly.

He finished dressing and grabbed his sword and shield from the chair. He took one last look at Meredith, then left the room, ready to carry out his duties.

Bodden Village surrounded the Keep that bore its name. Gerald had arranged lodgings over the Blue Swallow Tavern, due to its proximity to the Keep and the fact that its solid walls kept out much of the noise of the customers.

With only a short walk to the guard house, he quickly relieved Sir Martin of the duty of watch commander. Usually, only the knights commanded the watch, but Gerald had been given the honour by Lord Richard. Being the younger brother of the present baron, he had the responsibility to look after the troops while Edward saw to the running of the barony. This arrangement worked well for the Keep as Lord Richard was much more of a military man than his brother.

Gerald began his shift by checking on the sentries, making sure they were performing their duties, which consisted mainly of being on the lookout for raiders. It was a ritual that they grew tired of hearing, but Lord

Richard had taught him that routine was the best way to ensure the proper performance of a soldier's daily duties.

Gerald was very dedicated to his position as a watch commander and made sure that he performed all duties with the utmost care. These included reading any orders left in the log book. While reading the watch book, he mentally thanked Lord Richard, or Fitz as he was always telling Gerald to call him, for he had insisted that Gerald learn to read and write. Baron Edward had thought the idea ludicrous.

"Of what use are letters to a soldier?" he had asserted, but Fitz had insisted. It had allowed Gerald to assume the duties of watch commander when a position became available, and he was thankful for the increase in pay that came with it, particularly now, with a child on the way.

Today's log contained a note from Lord Richard instructing him to go and pay a visit to the baron at the end of his shift. He chuckled at the simplicity of the note. Only Fitz would write something like this down in the log, for the express purpose of ensuring the log was read. Other entries were typically along the line of 'nothing of import', 'all quiet', or even 'nothing to report.'

He was kept quite busy, and by noon he was surprised by Sir Andrew, who was ready to take the next watch. He handed over the log book, detailing all he had done since taking over from Sir Martin. Sir Andrew listened patiently but looked particularly bored by all the formality.

On his way to the meeting, he remembered that the note had mentioned going to the map room. Gerald enjoyed the view from this room as it was the highest in the Keep, enabling a person to see the entire barony.

He arrived in time to see the door open. Lord Richard was just leaving, and he looked angry but stopped when he saw Gerald.

"Take some advice, Gerald, refuse the offer," he said, then stormed off without explanation.

Confused, Gerald paused in the doorway, and then knocked on the door frame.

"Ah, Gerald, come in," commanded the baron. "I've been going over the accounts for the barony, and we need to produce more food. Your family were farmers, weren't they?"

"Yes, my lord," he answered.

"Ever thought about becoming a farmer again?"

"I can't say that I have, my lord," he replied.

"My brother tells me you've been doing well as a soldier," the baron continued, "but a barony without food can't last long. I'd like to make you an offer. You become a farmer, and I'll give you the land and equipment to maintain it. You'll have help to get started, of course, and the other farmers will teach you what you need to know."

Gerald looked at the baron in disbelief. Could this be some sort of trap?

"I'm not sure I understand the offer, my lord."

"It's simple. You would become my tenant, and a portion of the crop becomes the property of the barony, while the rest is yours to sell or use as you see fit."

It was an attractive offer. Farmers could make a decent living, but it would be a lot of hard work. "How much would you take?" he asked.

"Hah!" said the baron. "A man that understands his duty, just what I like."

They spent some time going over the details, with Gerald insisting on getting it down in writing.

Gerald left the room, the title to a farm securely in his pocket. He ran into Lord Richard as he descended the stairs.

"Did you take my brother's offer?" asked Fitz.

"Yes, Lord, it was too good to ignore. Why?"

"These are dangerous times, Gerald. The Norlanders are more frequent in their raids of late, and I believe it could be unsafe out there."

Gerald bristled, "I can take care of my family, Lord."

"My dear friend," Lord Richard responded apologetically, "you mistake my intentions. I only wish the best for you and your family."

"Then command me to stay, Lord, and it shall be so."

"That is a decision you must make yourself."

"But you don't agree with it?"

"You are a good friend, Gerald, and we don't always have to agree. Although I don't like this situation, I will support you in whatever way I can. You may trust that I will always keep an eye on you to keep you and your family safe."

Shame at his attitude suddenly overcame Gerald as he relaxed his stance, "I'm sorry, Lord, I thought-"

"Don't let it vex you. You've served me well these last few years, and you deserve a life of your own. Now, come with me," Richard commanded.

"Where are we going?" asked Gerald.

"Well, it wouldn't be prudent for you to show up at home without some wine to celebrate. Let me give you a bottle of my finest."

Gerald made a face as he asked, "Wine, my lord? Couldn't you make it ale?"

"Hah!" said Fitz. "I should have known. So be it, a large jug of the finest ale. We have much to celebrate."

FOUR

The Loss

AUTUMN 932 MC

T he day was hot, and he was sweating profusely, but he knew he must bring in the harvest. He sliced with the scythe, causing yet another clump of wheat to fall under the blade. He bundled the cut wheat and carried it to the cart, then paused to catch his breath.

Nearby, Sally, now four, sat and watched her father while playing with her straw doll. Her brown hair reminded him so much of his wife. He thought of Meredith, back at the house, no doubt preparing the mid-day meal.

Gerald was a happy man. He worked long hours, and the work was tough, but satisfying. He always returned to the house with a smile on his face as his eyes met those of his wife. His thoughts drifted to the warmth of her body pressed against his, and he felt truly blessed.

His thoughts were interrupted by Sally, who stood up and pointed to a distant spot, "Horses are coming, Daddy."

He looked past her to see a group of horsemen. He recognized Lord Richard leading, his distinctive coat of arms emblazoned on his surcoat, followed by a troop of six horsemen, no doubt just a patrol. At first, he could only make out Sir Rodney, but as the group drew closer, he recognized most of the other men.

"Gerald, good to see you in fine spirits," greeted Fitz.

"My lord, it's good to see you. Can I offer you a drink?"

Lord Richard smiled at the friendly greeting, "A kindly offer, but I think we're all right." He leaned down from his horse as he drew closer. "The truth is, this lot would drink your house dry," he chuckled at his jest, but Gerald recognized a look of concern behind his eyes.

"Well," continued Lord Richard, "who do we have here?" He dismounted from his horse, his men stopping their forward motion, knowing what would come next. "Is this the fair maid, Sally?" he asked.

Sally giggled and held her arms out for a hug. It was a ritual that they both enjoyed. Lord Richard always found time to stop and talk to Sally. He lifted her up in his arms.

"My, you're growing like a weed. I could swear you've grown a head taller in the last week alone." He placed Sally onto his saddle, "How about you look after my horse while I talk to your father?"

She smiled and began to stroke the horse's neck.

"Gerald, I wonder if I might have a word with you," he used a quieter voice to indicate the need for privacy, then began walking away from the horses.

Gerald followed him as he got out of earshot of his men.

"My brother, the baron, has, in his infinite wisdom, decided to reduce the patrols. I'm afraid they won't be coming out this way as often. I told him it was a mistake, but he's always been driven by cost, and he wants to maximize his profits, so he's let some of the men go."

"Let them go? You mean he's reducing the garrison?"

"Precisely. I know it won't take long for the Norlanders to get wind of it. You'll have to be alert, there's likely to be trouble. I'll get a patrol out here as often as I can, but you're a fair distance from the Keep."

"I understand, my lord," said Gerald. "Don't you worry about us, we can take care of ourselves."

"Glad to hear it, though I'd rather you were back safely in the Keep."

"But the baron needs the wheat," stated Gerald, "not to mention the pigs I've fattened up for him."

"Well, we'll have to have a feast at the Keep in your honour, and see how they turned out."

"You won't be disappointed, Lord," beamed Gerald.

"I never am with you, Gerald, I never am," he said, turning back to his men. "Now, I need to get my horse back before young Sally here, rides off with him."

He lifted her from the saddle and passed her to her father, "You'd better take her, Gerald, before I steal her away."

He smiled at his friend's jest.

"Aye, my lord," he said, "then I'd have to explain the whole thing to her mother."

Fitz settled into his saddle and looked down at his protege, "Remember what I said, Gerald, don't take any chances."

Gerald nodded as they rode off.

"Horses are going?" asked Sally, looking at him.

"Yes, Sally, the horses are going, but they'll come back and visit again, don't you worry."

It was dark outside when Gerald suddenly came awake. The wind was blowing, and he heard something crashing. Rising to his feet, careful not to wake Meredith, he walked over to the window, where he opened the shutters to gaze out the back of the house. In the dim moonlight, he noticed that part of the fence around the pigsty had come loose.

He cursed as he quickly put some clothes on. Losing a pig was more than just annoying, it represented a substantial investment. He was counting on its sale to help fill his coffers for the winter months.

He made his way round to the back of the house and looked over the fence. Sure enough, an animal had knocked down the cross beam and escaped, leaving the others in their pen. Now, he must hunt the creature down, or forgo the coins the beast would garner.

Looking to the east, he made out a faint light on the horizon. Fair enough, he thought. The sun was starting to rise, and it shouldn't be too hard to find the wayward pig once morning broke. He quickly repaired the fence, then gathered some rope and grabbed a bite to eat while he waited for dawn.

The trail was relatively easy to follow, so he soon found himself crossing the fields in pursuit. The creature must have been running, for the distance he had already travelled was impressive. The trail was lost shortly after heading into the woods. After making his way through the thick underbrush, he concluded that the cursed pig must have entered the stream. Walking up and down the banks, it took him some time to find where the creature had emerged on the other side. Finally, he came across the fugitive laying in the sun in an open glade.

Creeping up on it slowly, he quickly realized that the care was unnecessary, for it was fast asleep. He slipped the rope around its neck, giving a silent prayer of thanks that he found the pig at last. Waking the animal, he was reminded that a stubborn pig is not easy to move. It was only by prodding its rear that he managed to get it moving at all.

Now, his early morning search was becoming half a day's task. He had to travel back to the farm in small bursts. The pig was stubborn and reminded him of Sir Rodney in his temperament.

It was close to noon as he rounded Riley Woods to see his house off in the distance. The pig took a moment to lay down in the sun again, and Gerald cursed once more. He looked longingly at the house, wishing he could just pick up the pig, and then noticed that something was wrong. There should be smoke coming from the chimney, as Meredith baked during the early day to avoid the heat. A sense of foreboding came over him, and he dropped the rope, abandoning the pig to the sun. Racing across the field, his lungs burning with the effort, he called out to Meredith, but there was no answer. Dread filled his heart.

Rounding the corner of the house, he came to the front door in such a hurry that he almost tripped over what was there. Meredith lay in the doorway, a dark stain beneath her, her skirts lifted around her waist. Kneeling down to help her, he almost slipped on all the blood that covered the entranceway. They had slit her throat. He beheld the scene in horror, unable to fully comprehend what was in front of him, his mind refusing to acknowledge it. He lifted her head, trying desperately to call her back from the Afterlife, but it was too late.

It felt like his heart had been ripped from his chest. Just breathing was an insurmountable effort. He crushed Meredith's body in his arms, silent tears streaming down his cheeks, all thoughts gone from his mind. A sound from the long grass broke through his sorrow. He lay her down and ran towards it, hoping against hope that Sally was alive.

The grass moved as he spread it to reveal his daughter, lying motionless in a pool of her own blood. She let out a whimper, and he realized she still lived, but as he went to lift her into his arms, he saw that her attackers had slit her belly, and even now, the life ebbed out of her.

She looked up at her father, her mouth moving, but then her eyes glazed over and her head flopped to the side before she spoke. Gerald stood for an eternity, staring in disbelief at the body of his only child, Sally. He raised his head to the sky and screamed in anguish as he fell to his knees, his beloved daughter cradled in his arms.

So many thoughts tore through his mind. Fitz had warned him about raiders, why had he left them alone? Guilt surged through him, and then, quite suddenly, he decided that he must make these murderers pay. Calmly, he carried Sally inside the house and lay her gently in her bed. The raiders had ransacked the place, but he barely noticed.

Fortunately, they had done a poor job, and he reached beneath the bed, pulling out his sword and scabbard. It had been four years since he had wielded it, but now he would feed the blade with the blood of the men responsible for the murder of his family.

He lovingly placed Meredith on their bed, kissing her cheek for the last time. Turning from her final resting place, he drew his sword and left the house, intent on avenging their deaths. He knew he would not be returning home. He didn't deserve to live, having failed to protect the only people who meant anything to him. He would sell his life to fuel the vengeance needed to bathe the enemy in blood.

The murderers didn't make any effort to hide their tracks as they left the devastation behind them, making their trail easy for Gerald to follow. With the sun sinking in the west and nightfall soon to be upon him, Gerald heard sounds of a camp in the distance. He scouted around the area, waiting for the darkness to come and hide his approach. Soon, the glow of their fires would tell him exactly where they were, and then they would all die.

The first raider was an easy kill. Gerald's blade penetrated his back as he was pissing against a tree. The last thing the man saw was a blade appear out of his stomach before he fell to the ground amongst his own piss and blood. His silent death allowed Gerald to move into the camp undetected. The rest of the attackers were sleeping on the ground in makeshift bedrolls. He stabbed down quickly, puncturing the first one's throat, his victim's eyes rolling open as he choked to death. Gerald took a step forward, his blade seeking yet another man's death, but the raider had heard his companion choking and tried to roll out of the way. He screamed as the blade pierced his side, but was still able to fight. Gerald knew he had lost the element of surprise, but no longer cared. He would seek his death as he executed as many of them as he could.

The remaining raiders ran towards him, yelling. He struck one down with a vicious overhand strike to the man's head. He felt a blade hit his left arm and shook it off. He spotted a new blade coming from the right, and his training took over, blocking the swing, deflecting the blade to the ground, opening the attacker up to Gerald's next manoeuvre. He raised his sword to slash at the man's chest and felt the edge slice through bone, causing the man to stumble back, cursing.

Gerald screamed fearlessly, rushing towards a group of three men. He swung at one who tried to avoid the blow by back-pedalling and then tripped and fell to the ground. The second, much taller one, struck Gerald, and he felt the blow glance off of his shoulder. He ducked under the other's arm, stepped forward and bashed with the hilt of his sword. Blood spurted across his hand as he felt the nose collapse beneath the strike. He slashed wildly to his left, and the blade struck flesh again, but he couldn't keep track of all the combatants. He felt something hit him from behind, knocking him to his knees, but he struck out again, a different target yelling as he severed the fingers from their hand.

Shouted orders swirled around him, but all he could think about was revenge. His anger fuelled him, giving him the strength to continue the fight. Again, and again, he hacked with his sword. He was no longer fighting, merely flailing about with inhuman strength. He swung once more, but discovered there was no one to hit. The raiders had all backed up, encircling him. He had no escape route.

They taunted him. Some stabbed at him with spears, while others threw bottles at him. He felt something hit his head, then blood started to pour down his face. He looked to the ground to see glass shards of the bottle that had done the damage. Wiping his face with his arm, he charged towards his enemy, but then everything suddenly turned upside-down, causing him to fall forward onto the forest floor. He felt rough hands grab him and then all before him went black.

Pain. Searing, agonizing pain. This must be his punishment for failing to protect his family. He opened his eyes, trying to see through the crusted blood that almost glued them shut. His arms and legs were tied behind him around a large tree trunk, the ropes cutting off the circulation to his hands and feet, leaving his limbs twisted painfully against the bark.

Light appeared off in the distance, the coming dawn. He gathered he must have been unconscious for some time. Slowly, as his eyes adjusted to the sun's rays, he began to see the row of bodies that lay nearby. He had killed six raiders, but their companions were preparing to avenge their fallen comrades. There must have been two dozen men in this band. Now, half a dozen stood in front of him, readying their bows. Behind them, he could see others, tending to their wounds.

"Let them see how a Mercerian dies," he thought. "I will not give them the satisfaction of begging for my life."

He heard the snap of the bowstring as the first Norlander let loose with his arrow. The thud beside his ear told him how close the shot had been. Gerald glared at the man. A second shot nicked his left arm, and he spit in disgust. He glowered at the raiders in defiance, but it had little effect. They were mocking him, deliberately missing. He would soon begin to suffer from multiple small wounds. It appeared they would enjoy killing him slowly.

Twelve shots were loosed at him, all close, but no severe hits. They stood laughing at him, then came forward to retrieve their arrows and hit him, pummelling his stomach with punches. One struck his face repeatedly, and his eye immediately began swelling while his cheek bleed from a cut. Even his teeth were loosened in his mouth from the impact of the blows.

Their leader called them back, knocking his arrow. He took careful aim, and Gerald's uninjured eye was looking directly at the tip of the shaft. This shot would be the last, he thought, and then he would descend into the Underworld a failure, to forever pay for his mistakes.

He waited, tried to calm his beating heart, but he couldn't take a deep breath, his ribs hurt from their beatings. The bowstring was pulled back, ready to shoot when a yell came from behind him. The leader turned, and suddenly there were horses in the clearing. Shouting came from all directions, followed by the clash of steel, and then an eerie silence fell over the woods.

Footsteps approached. Gerald could not turn his head but heard the crunch of branches underfoot. A face loomed in front of him, but he couldn't focus his eyes.

"Gerald, are you there? Speak man," it was Fitz speaking.

He felt weak, he wanted to cry out, "Let me die!" but the words would not form in his mouth. He felt the tug as someone began cutting the ropes that bound him to the tree, and then he fell forward, unable to control himself.

Fitz caught him, lowering him gently to the ground, a concerned look on his face.

"Don't speak, Gerald, we have you. You'll not be travelling to the After-life today."

Hours later, they were back at the Matheson farm. The patrol had happened across the raider's trail, following it to find the bodies of Meredith and Sally inside. Only fate had led them to the clearing in time to save Gerald.

Now, they watched the house burn. Gerald had insisted on using it as their funeral pyre, and Lord Richard, surprisingly, had agreed. His life here, his happiness, was dead. Now, he only sought to kill those who took his life from him.

He turned to face Fitz, who watched the blaze as it engulfed the roof.

"I swear to serve you, Lord Richard," he pledged, "until I can no longer hold a blade. Until the end of my days."

"My brother is the baron, Gerald. You'd have to swear to his service, not mine."

"No, my lord, it is you I will serve. My old life is gone, all that's left to me is war."

Lord Richard looked solemnly at his friend, "Very well, Gerald, I will accept your oath."

FIVE

Second Siege of Bodden

SUMMER 933 MC

A tremendous crash shook the whole Keep. Bits of dust and plaster rained down on Gerald as he made his way to the map room. He cursed the Norlanders and their damn siege engines, wondering how much longer the defenders could survive under the constant bombardment. The Norlanders wanted Bodden, and they were throwing everything they had at it. He thought back to his first siege, eight years prior. This army was larger than anything that had attacked before, he thought, someone in Norland was spending a lot of time and effort to take this Keep.

He arrived at the tallest point of the structure, the map room, which overlooked the entire barony. Baron Edward was standing at the table where a large map of the Keep and surrounding area was laid out. His brother, Richard, stood beside him while the Knights of Bodden looked on. Lord Richard noticed him and motioned him over with a nod of his head. As Gerald approached, the baron's brother stepped back from the table.

"Have you any new information?" he asked in a quiet voice.

"I'm afraid not, Lord," Gerald replied. "They've still got six of the catapults and a sizable number of rocks stacked nearby. It's only a matter of time before the wall comes down."

Fitz snorted, "I told my brother as much, but he's convinced it will all end well."

"Is there something you want to say, Brother?" demanded the baron, turning at the discussion behind his back.

"Yes, my lord," replied Fitz. "The catapults continue their pounding, and they appear to have lots of rocks at their disposal."

"I see," retorted the baron. "In other words, there's nothing new to report."

"Might I suggest, Lord, that we send out a group to attack the siege engines? Surely without them, the invaders will be forced to give up the attack."

Baron Edward straightened his back and looked around the room at his knights.

"My brother would have us risk all on a foolhardy plan." He turned to face Lord Richard, "The men are needed to garrison the wall. If we'd had time to finish its construction, it might be a different story, but we have to deal with the issue at hand."

Fitz was stubborn and spoke up again, "Then let me take just a handful of men, Brother. We will destroy the catapults, or die in the attempt. We can't just sit here waiting for the wall to come down!"

"No," roared the baron, "I forbid it! We must prepare a counter-attack when they attempt to enter through the breach. Sir John thinks it likely the wall will collapse near the well. They'll try to storm the breach once it's down. We'll prepare defences, throw every combustible we have at them, burn them when they try to force entry."

"But, my lord-"

"Don't 'My lord' me, Richard. My decision is final." He paused and took a deep breath. "Richard, I know you mean well, but we cannot risk it. My way is the best, if we can decimate their attack, we can sue for terms."

Richard looked at his brother as if he'd been slapped in the face.

"Terms?"

"Yes, Richard. Terms. It's clear at this point that we can't beat them, and our messengers failed to break out to get aid. We must gain favourable terms to ensure the safety of the people. I have more to consider than just the troops. Do you understand?"

Lord Richard nodded, "Very well, Edward, it shall be as you have commanded." He turned to Gerald who, caught unawares, almost leaped to attention. "Come along, Gerald, we must see to the defence of the wall."

Gerald followed his mentor out as the discussion in the map room moved on to other matters.

They had descended the first flight of stairs when Gerald spoke up, "So, when are we attacking the catapults?"

Lord Richard stopped suddenly, surprised by the younger man's words.

"'WE' are not attacking the catapults, that is a job for me, alone. No one else can disobey the baron's orders."

"Begging your pardon, Lord, but you can't do it alone. Besides, you're to be married in a few months. Someone must keep you alive, or are you having second thoughts?" Gerald added with a slight smile.

"Don't be absurd, Gerald. You know that I can't wait to marry Lady Evelyn, and I shall do my best to remain alive."

"Really, Lord? One man against the entire Norland army?"

"Yes, all right, I concede the point. Still, you're likely to get into a lot of trouble over this."

"I swore my life to your service, Lord. I do not carry that burden lightly."

Lord Richard placed his hand on Gerald's shoulder.

"Thank you, Gerald, that means a lot to me. Now," he said as he continued his descent, "we must make some plans."

It was near midnight when they met by the main gate. Gerald was standing among a small group of men as Lord Richard approached.

"What's this?" asked the nobleman.

"A few volunteers, my lord," answered Gerald.

Lord Richard scowled, "You men must return to your posts, this is treason."

"No, my lord," declared Gerald, "this is desperation. We all know what will happen if the Norlanders get into Bodden. No woman in Bodden will be safe from their ravaging. These men are willing to give their lives to defend their loved ones. Can you deny them that?"

Fitz looked at the group gathered in the darkness. Each member looked back at him with a defiant gleam in their eyes. There were four men, in addition to Gerald, and now he stepped up in front of each one, looking them over carefully.

"Fletcher, I should have expected you. How's the wife?"

"Much better, my lord. Thanks to the surgeon."

"Excellent," continued Lord Richard, "let's hope your son stays out of the way of horses in future. We can't have your wife throwing herself in harm's way all the time."

He stepped forward to look at the next man, "William Blackwood, you old rogue! I suppose you're here for the glory?"

The man nodded back.

"Harold Cooper, I'm surprised to see you. Why did you volunteer?"

The man blushed deeply.

"He's recently met a young lady," proclaimed Gerald, "and wants to impress her."

Fitz chuckled, "I suppose that's as good a reason as any."

He looked to the last man.

"Roger Graves, I see you're much recovered."

Graves nodded. He'd recently gotten arrested for being drunk and fighting in the tavern. He had just finished his punishment; three days in the pillory, and he was, no doubt, trying to make amends for his behaviour, for he had become a social outcast due to his antics.

"Very well, I can see you're all rogues, but that is what is called for. Now, let's get started." He looked about dramatically before continuing, "Let us head to the guest rooms."

Gerald was confused, "The guest rooms, Lord?"

"Yes, it's on the south side of the Keep. We can lower ourselves outside the walls by a rope, and the shadows will conceal us. Besides, anywhere else, and we risk being seen by our own men. Being arrested before we can even begin would be embarrassing!"

Gerald grinned, "You've thought this out well, my lord."

The older man looked back, a smile on his face, "I have, indeed."

"There's just one thing you've forgotten, Lord," Gerald offered conspiratorially.

Lord Richard stared back, confusion written on his face.

"Forgotten? What is it I've forgotten?"

"This," said Gerald as he smeared mud over his lordship's face. "We have to hide your lily-white face, my lord, else the enemy will see us coming from miles away."

The men around him snickered quietly.

"I knew I had you around for a reason," complimented Fitz. "I should have thought of this myself. Come along, we have work to do."

It took the band of infiltrators some time to lower themselves from the Keep. Upon landing, they carried no torches, lest the enemy see them, and covered themselves liberally in mud to hide their appearance as an extra precaution. The very darkness that kept them concealed also hampered them, leaving Gerald feeling that they were stumbling around. He had spent a significant portion of his adult life at Bodden, thought he knew every acre, but creeping along in the darkness, he found new experiences with uneven ground and unexpected rabbit holes.

They began their sortie going eastward, paralleling the southern wall of the Keep, until it was out of view, and then headed north. In the distance, the torches surrounding the catapults were visible. The six large siege engines had been firing continuously for hours, so much so that the rhythmic cranking of the winches had become general background noise to all within earshot.

Now, as they crept closer, came the most dangerous part of their mission, for they would soon be in the area lit by the torches. They crouched in a shallow ditch and unsheathed their weapons. Fitz was beside Gerald and leaned in close.

"You take Blackwood and Fletcher," he whispered, "move around to the east end of the catapults and work your way west. I'll take Cooper and Graves and strike from the west. The catapults are in a straight line. Start from your end and work your way towards us. There's plenty of torches around. You understand what to do?"

"Aye, my lord. The pig grease they use to lubricate the gears should burn nicely. They'll have a hard time putting out the fire."

"Be careful," Fitz warned, "it can spit, and we don't want to set fire to ourselves."

Gerald poked his head up over the ditch.

"Get ready to go, my lord. I'll tell you when it's safe."

He stared at the enemy catapults, watching the sentries as they moved. Norlanders were not a militaristic society, they were raiders, nothing more. The concept of organized patrols was foreign to them. He observed two men wandering the near side of the camp, close enough to cause problems should any of the Mercerians be noticed. He waited for the furthest man to turn his back, then waved Lord Richard and his group forward. He watched them disappear into the darkness, turning his attention to the two remaining guards. Dropping back down into the ditch, he pulled Blackwood and Fletcher towards him.

"We'll have to take out the sentries," he whispered, "or we'll never get to the catapults."

"Let me go first," offered Blackwood. "I'll take out the man on the right, you two watch the other. If he looks like he's seen me, rush him."

Gerald agreed, pulling the shield from his back. He watched Blackwood disappear in the darkness, crawling parallel to the guard to get closer. A moment later, the man was swiftly silenced, falling to the ground with a muffled cry.

The second man turned and started to walk back towards the first. Gerald rose from the ditch and began moving forward quietly, his sword and shield held at the ready. Fletcher rose behind him, following his path forward. The second guard continued on his route, which was bringing him closer to their position, then something made him look in their general direction. The man's eyes went wild as he perceived their presence in the dark, and then he unslung his battle axe.

Gerald cursed under his breath, increasing his speed, careless of the noise it might make. He struck a solid blow, but the enemy parried it, causing a considerable clang to ring out as the two weapons met. To his left, Fletcher successfully attacked the man's other arm, a small cut appearing, glittering eerily by torchlight. He heard a clash of steel to his right and realized that Blackwood had encountered additional resistance, but all his attention must be devoted to the fight in front of him.

He shield-bashed his opponent, forcing him back, then lunged forward with his sword. He felt the point sink in, but his adversary was fast, and it only gave the man a surface wound. His enemy returned with a vicious overhand blow, but Gerald raised his shield just in time to feel the axe bury its blade deeply. Pushing the shield forward again, he felt the weapon release. He swung low with his sword, but the man knew his business and jumped back, protecting his legs from damage.

Knowing time was of the essence, he realized he must reach the catapults as promptly as possible. He waited for the next blow, parried it with his sword, then drove the edge of his shield into the man's chest. His opponent staggered back, and he continued to push forward, kicking the sentry's knee out from under him as he advanced. Falling prone to the ground left his adversary wide open for Gerald to drive his blade through his chest. A brief glance told him Blackwood was fighting to his right, some twenty feet away. The first catapult was directly ahead, and three men lifted a rock into the catapult's bucket, unaware of the danger that lurked nearby.

Gerald rushed forward, slashing one in the back. His target let out a scream of agony and fell to the ground, causing the other two to drop the rock. The remaining soldiers looked surprised but recovered their wits quickly. By the time Gerald had pulled his blade from his target, the others had drawn their weapons.

He parried the first clumsy strike but felt another attack on his shield arm. The sword created a ringing sound as it scraped across his chainmail, saving him from serious injury. The force of the blow left his arm numb, and he nearly dropped his shield. He slashed out with his blade at the man on his left, then used the hilt of his sword to smash the second man in the face as he drew it back. He felt blood on his hand and knew he had done considerable damage. He heard Fletcher coming up behind him.

"Grab the torches!" he shouted, turning back to the skirmish.

It took him only a moment to realize the man with the shattered face was running away. He ignored him and swivelled towards his second target with his sword already in motion, feeling the blade dig deep into his opponent's flesh. Pushing his blade forward, he unexpectedly felt a sharp jab in his chest. His opponent's sword penetrated his chainmail, then it continued scrapping painfully along his ribs. The discomfort was intense but served to focus his attention solely on this encounter. He immediately withdrew his sword and stabbed again before a defence could be mounted, leaving him with one less sword to defeat.

He looked around, trying to gather a sense of what was happening. Fletcher was holding a torch trying to light the greased gears. The fat was starting to bubble, and he had no doubt it would soon be alight. Standing at the second catapult in line, he saw Blackwood fighting a man at the first one. Many of the catapult's crew had fled in terror at the start of the fight, but he heard yells echoing around the enemy camp. They would not have long before the soldiers mounted a counter-attack. If they wanted to make this a successful foray, they must act without delay.

Hearing fighting to the west, he looked over and saw flames engulfing the far catapult. Light framed the figure of Lord Richard swinging his sword, as one of his men carried a torch to the next target. He wheeled to the right to see Blackwood, bleeding from his arm, holding a torch to light the first siege engine. A group of three men were running towards him, and Gerald moved to intercept.

He growled as he rushed forward, forcing them to take notice of him. Two turned to face him, while the third continued on. The first charged, but Gerald quickly blocked with his shield. So busy was he with this action, however, that he failed to see the other strike him. The blade bit into his arm, piercing his chain shirt and caused a shock of pain to travel up his arm. His sword dropped from his hand, and he swore as the man struck again. He rotated his shield skillfully, then pushed out, forcing the man back. His sword was now by his feet, so he stamped forward, pushing the edge of the shield towards his opponent. The man grudgingly stepped back, and Gerald crouched to retrieve his weapon.

As his hand grasped the hilt, the next blow glanced off his shield, making contact with his helmet. Knocked to the ground, he automatically rolled, desperately trying to avoid the expected flurry of attacks. He heard a groan as he saw Fletcher's sword strike the man beneath the armpit, collapsing his enemy.

Fletcher helped him to his feet, "We must hurry, there are more coming."

Gerald looked up and down the line. Three of the catapults were starting to burn, two at their end, and one down by Fitz. Blackwood came up beside him, brandishing a torch, a body behind him still burning from a strike.

"This way," commanded Gerald, "Fitz needs our help."

They travelled to the west, towards the third catapult. Blackwood started to light it while Fletcher stood watch, but there was no opposition. In the areas not illuminated by the flaming catapults, the darkness created mass confusion. The attack had come suddenly, taking the enemy by surprise. Now, they ran around in the dark, fearing a full-scale assault.

Gerald ran past the third catapult looking for Lord Richard. He could see something happening near the fifth siege engine, then a sudden clash of steel drew his attention. He came around the catapult to see Lord Richard on his knees, his shield held above him to stop the rain of blows that were descending upon him.

Gerald struck swiftly, stabbing an attacker in the shoulder as he ran by. Holding his shield in front of him, he ploughed into the next target, sending the man sprawling to the ground. A solid thrust with a sword finished him off. Lord Richard peered out from under his shield and struck with his sword, the blade cutting out the final assailant's legs from beneath him. The man fell with a horrifying scream and was finished off with an efficient stab. Cooper ran up to them, bleeding heavily from an arm wound, a burning torch held in his other hand.

"We've fired the first two catapults," he shouted, then fell to the ground, an arrow protruding from his back.

The whistle of more arrows flying through the air was all it took for Fitz and Gerald to duck behind the catapult.

"Graves?" said Gerald.

"Dead. Took a spear to the back, the bastards."

Another volley of arrows whistled by, but it was evident they were shooting blindly.

"We must get back to the Keep," declared Lord Richard. "Our work here is done."

"Fall back," hollered Gerald, hoping the others would hear him.

He glanced about and saw Blackwood and Fletcher by the third catapult. He waved them off and watched them run back towards the Keep.

"Come on, Lord," shouted Gerald above the noise of the roaring fires, "we need to get out of here."

Fitz nodded in agreement. They rose from the cover of the catapult and ran as if the very Guardian of the Underworld was after them, their shields on their backs for some degree of protection. Arrows whistled past them and thudded as they struck the ground. Gerald felt two hit his shield, but he kept running, pumping his legs with all the energy he could muster. They left the lit perimeter of the catapults and were engulfed in darkness, finally able to slow their pace. Off to the left, he heard Blackwood as they turned, diving into the same shallow ditch they had used when they started their mad escapade.

Gerald lay back, his lungs aching, desperately trying to pull in enough air. He heard yelling in the camp and could tell from the confusion, that the enemy had lost sight of them. He caught his breath, and then suddenly the sky lit up as a massive fire erupted on the northern wall of Bodden. Gerald looked south, saw the shadows flickering across the open space, and instinctively knew what had happened. While they were burning catapults, the enemy had assaulted the wall. Baron Edward, true to his word, had lit the combustibles, and now a massive fire engulfed the half-finished north wall of the Keep.

The screams of the dying echoed across the ground. Lord Richard, his face lit by the flickering light, swore.

"The wall," he yelled, "we have to help!"

They rose as one, each man knowing his duty, grasping their swords and shields as they moved in unison towards the terrible scene of carnage. The smell of burnt flesh assailed their noses as they closed the range. It was as if they entered the very Halls of the Underworld itself, as they made their way forward.

The fire had erupted suddenly, the force of it flinging stone far and wide. Rubble was strewn across the ground impeding the Norlander's retreat from the wall. A group of perhaps a dozen bore away someone on a makeshift stretcher, a nobleman no doubt, but the small group ignored them.

It took them some time to reach the remains of the wall. Rubble from the blast formed a ramp to the breach. They climbed it slowly, the rock tumbling beneath their feet as they took their steps. Soldiers were stripping armour off the dead, even women and children had rushed forward to find loved ones or recover valuables, but they ran off at the sight of the four warriors.

The returning quartet mounted the top of what was left of the wall, to look directly into Bodden itself. The explosion had spread into the village and set fire to two of the buildings. and left a dark smear on the ground where some inhabitants had been blown back by the force of the explosion. The survivors staggered around, some clutching their heads as blood dripped from their ears.

Standing still, examining the carnage, Gerald was overwhelmed by the damage that had been inflicted. He slumped to one knee as a sense of dread overtook him. Hearing the crunch of broken stone, he looked up to see Sir James approaching.

"My lord?" the knight said.

His face was covered in soot and grime, but Gerald could still see the sorrow upon it. Lord Richard turned towards the intrusion, his face still holding a look of horror.

"What is it?" he demanded.

"I'm afraid the baron is dead, Lord."

"Dead?"

"Yes, my lord. He lit the fire when the enemy topped the wall. No one expected it to erupt the way it did. There was a tremendous noise, and then the wall was engulfed."

"Where is his body?" demanded Lord Richard.

"Blown to oblivion. I fear there's nothing left of him," Sir James apologized.

Lord Richard stood in disbelief, his head still trying to make sense of the devastation before him.

In a sombre voice, Sir James declared, "You are the baron now, Lord. What is your will?"

Gerald could see the pain of his brother's loss in Lord Richard's face, but Fitz was a practical man and knew that he must take action now, for there would be time later for mourning. Lord Richard looked around, the fires still burning, lighting his face with an eerie glow.

"Place guards on this wall, but I doubt they'll attack again. We've broken their will."

As he talked, he became more animated, and Gerald watched the energy return to the man. Gerald heaved himself to his feet, and Fitz turned to him.

"Gerald, see that this wall is shored up as best you can. Sir James?"

"My lord?"

"You will take orders from Sergeant Matheson here. Do as he says."

"He's not a noble, my lord," objected Sir James.

"He has my complete confidence to carry out my will," Fitz barked back, "and I am the new baron, correct?"

The knight backed down. The new baron might have unusual ideas, but he was Lord of Bodden now.

"Of course, my lord," he replied apologetically.

"Then do as I say. Gerald, when you've got this secured, meet me in the map room. I have something else to attend to first."

"Aye, Lord," he replied and started giving orders.

It was dawn by the time he made it to the map room. Fitz was standing by the north window, staring out at the remains of the Norland camp. The enemy had left in a hurry, for the explosion at the wall had been devastating to both sides. Perhaps they would have continued the siege if the catapults had been intact, but now the ghostly siege engines stood alone, the charred remains still smoking in the early morning light. Gerald stood beside him, gazing out the window.

"I don't remember burning all six catapults," he reminisced.

"We didn't. The Norlanders set fire to the others as they left. They're much too cumbersome to take on a retreat."

There was a moment of silence as they both took in the view.

"So, we won?" Gerald was not convinced that this outcome was truly a win, looking at the carnage below them.

"Yes," agreed Fitz, "but at what cost? We lost some good men, my brother among them."

"What do we do now, my lord?"

Fitz looked Gerald directly in the eyes as he commanded him, "You take what horsemen we have, and you harass the Norlanders all the way back to the river Alde. Don't let up on them, keep them running, but try not to engage them unless necessary. I'm putting you in charge of the troops, Gerald."

"My lord?"

"You heard me, you're my Sergeant-at-Arms from now on."

"Sergeant-at-Arms?" queried Gerald.

"It's an old position, rarely used these days. You will be the senior soldier in this garrison. You report only to me, and you carry my full authority. If anyone tells you otherwise, you come to me."

His face softened, "You have earned it, Gerald. I've never seen a more deserving soldier. If it were within my power, I would knight you, but I think my solution is the better one. After all, if you were a knight, you might have to leave Bodden to serve the king, then I wouldn't have you around."

Gerald looked at his mentor in disbelief. Was this a jest? The seriousness of Fitz's face told him otherwise.

"I would be honoured to be your Sergeant-at-Arms," he acquiesced solemnly.

Baron Richard Fitzwilliam smiled, "Excellent, my dear friend. Now, let us have a small drink to celebrate, and then you must be on your way."

"On my way?" Gerald's look of confusion broadened Fitz's smile.

"Of course, to harass the retreating enemy."

Fitz walked over to a side table and poured two goblets of wine. Gerald followed him and took one, raising it in a toast.

"To the new Baron of Bodden," he said, "long may he rule."

"And to his Sergeant-at-Arms," added Fitz, "long may he live."

They both took a deep drink of the wine and then spat it out with a look of disgust.

"Oh, dear," grimaced Fitz, "I forgot how bad my brother's taste in wine was."

SIX

Wounded

SPRING 952 MC

Gerald adjusted the straps on his saddle in preparation for another long day riding around the Keep. The king had decided to visit Bodden, and for three days he had been run ragged looking after the royal troops. Now, the king himself was being a royal pain, insisting on a tour of the land. No doubt the knights enjoyed all the attention, but Gerald saw all the work that was required of a royal guest, and he was not impressed.

On this warm spring day, a guard detail was needed to escort His Majesty, along with the baron, of course. The king would take a dozen of his knights with him, but it would be improper not to escort them all the same, so Fitz had called upon his Sergeant-at-Arms to organize the escort. He had settled on a dozen men, to match, man for man, the king's guard. He thought this would avoid any insult, but should be more than sufficient to deal with whatever they might run across. Six of his men were knights, only proper considering the royal status of their visitor, but for the other group of soldiers, he decided to forgo the fancy armour of the knights. He settled, instead on his toughest, most capable warriors.

Now, they all waited in the courtyard, ready to ride out at the baron's command. Gerald looked again at his small entourage. Most knights he seldom had any time for, but his soldiers he trusted with his life. After years of service, he knew he could count on them. William Blackwood sat uncomfortably on his horse, chewing some blackroot. Beside him was Richard Fletcher, looking about impatiently. Dawes, the bowman, and young Harris were next in line, rounded out by Hamlin and Fitzwilliam.

Lady Beverly Fitzwilliam was the spitting image of her mother. Her helmet hid her long red tresses, but her infectious grin was evident. Gerald had trained her at the behest of her father, and she had taken to it like a natural. At the ripe old age of seventeen, she was fully armoured and ready to fight, having proven herself on the battlefield. Now, she sat on her Mercerian Charger, waiting to move out. Gerald nodded as their eyes met, and then turned at the sound of approaching footsteps. Baron Richard Fitzwilliam looked at the assembled men in appreciation.

"I see you've picked our finest," he noticed, his eyes resting on his daughter. "Now, let's ride over to the other stable to meet His Majesty's knights, shall we?"

The escort fell into step as the baron mounted his waiting horse, trotting through the stable entrance to where King Andred and his knights waited. The king was chatting amiably with his guard captain but stopped when he saw them approach. The Realm's Monarch was an imposing man at an impressive six feet tall with unusually broad shoulders. His midnight black hair stood out among his men, and his well-trimmed beard gave him a chiselled look. He looked up as the baron's troops appeared.

"Baron, you've an excellent body of soldiers there, are we expecting trouble?"

Gerald looked over his men again, not sure if the king was mocking the baron. He saw Lady Beverly adjust the chin strap on her helmet and he wondered what King Andred would say if he realized a woman was guarding him. The column began to move, startling him out of his reverie and he silently cursed himself for not paying closer attention.

They left by the main gate, heading west. Baron Fitzwilliam had taken pains to bring the farms closer to the Keep in recent years. Attacks like the one that had killed Gerald's family were now uncommon. He fully expected this tour to be over quickly, for although Bodden claimed a large expanse in the name of the crown, the reality was that all the people were nearby, while the rest was simply wilderness.

The king's wish to travel west to see the land dashed any expectations Gerald had for a quick outing. Had it been within Gerald's power, he would have advised against it. It was a regular patrol route, and on occasions, they had found Norland raiders in the area. He knew, in his heart, that not all Norlanders were vicious, but the raiders who came across the river were a lawless rabble, and they must continually be on guard against their predations.

He dropped back as the column made their way across the land until he was riding beside Beverly.

"Keep your eyes wide open, Lady Beverly. I have a sense that the

Norlanders might be up to mischief today. I'd like you to stay at the rear. If there's to be trouble, they'll likely strike us from behind."

"That's fine by me, Gerald," she replied. "I don't much like the Royal Knights anyway, they're full of themselves."

Spurring his horse forward, he caught up with the rest of the party, where Fitz was chatting up a storm with the king, but Gerald ignored them. He was constantly scanning the tree line, watching for any signs of trouble.

At noon, they all stopped when the king dismounted. One of his knights produced some wine, and all the knights toasted the king. Gerald was not impressed with the royal knights. Yes, they were undoubtedly of the finest houses, with breastplates containing ornate gold details that showed off their wealth, but they were an undisciplined bunch, a constant problem with soldiers of their ilk. Knights came to Bodden all the time to seek out fame or glory in combat. It was always the same, and it was a lot of work to form them into battle-hardened warriors. They came to the frontier as spoilt younger sons, but they returned as disciplined veterans once he was done with them.

Gerald did his duty, had his soldiers take watch while the elites had their wine. Finally, after what seemed to be an interminable length of time, they remounted. The column headed off again, this time to the northeast and soon they turned to return to the Keep. As they turned south, Gerald thought he saw something off in the distance. He stopped, letting the others ride past. The ground here was undulating, and it was sometimes possible to get quite close to something before it would be revealed. He waited a moment longer, then saw the sun reflect off metal.

"To the north, raiders!" he screamed, turning to gallop back to the column.

Beverly, hearing him, turned in her saddle at the cry, while the other soldiers looked back over their shoulders as they rode.

He halted in front of her, "Look, Beverly. Your eyes are better than mine, what do you see?"

He noticed even she strained to make out details, her hand held above her eyes to block the sun.

"Damn, there must be almost two hundred of them. We have to tell Father."

"Maintain your position and keep the back of the line moving, I'll go tell the baron. The enemy won't catch up with us for quite a while."

He rode to the front of the column, but Fitz had already taken control of the situation. The Keep was visible in the distance, all they had to do was maintain their speed. He dropped back behind the king's knights. One of them turned in the saddle and saw the cloud of dust to the north. The man

panicked, there was no other word for it, and suddenly he and his companions spurred their horses forward.

Knights were typically superb fighters, but ill-disciplined. The inexperience of this group led them to react out of their nervousness, rushing
forward as fast as their mounts would carry them. The anxiety was infectious, and the other horses, sensing the fear, likewise started to gallop. Even
so, there was no real threat. The Keep was in the distance, and even a slow
trot would be sufficient to see them to safety. The sound of a horn changed
all that. The note was clear, and Gerald recognized it instantly. A group of
Norlanders erupted from a copse of trees to the west, and Gerald wheeled
his horse.

"You there," he commanded the ones nearby, "to me, we've work to do."

They headed west, towards the horsemen who were erupting from the
trees. He drew his sword as they approached, and Blackwood nearby,
roared a challenge. Gerald rode past the first Norlander, swinging his
sword in a reverse blow at eye level, ducking as a blade whistled over his
head. He struck the rider on his side, feeling the tug of his sword as the
blade bit. His horse carried him past his first opponent, to the next, and he
swung again, an overhand strike that collided with the enemy's sword as
the rider tried to parry. The weight of the blow knocked the blade aside and
dug into his foe's shoulder, tumbling him from the saddle with a scream.

Gerald twisted in the saddle as a spear lunged at him, causing it to
glance off his chainmail instead of impaling him. Lifting his shield up
quickly, he brought the edge down on the spear and heard the splinter of
the wood as the weapon broke. Now he was in close, stirrup to stirrup. He
kicked out at the horseman's leg, heard a groan of pain, then stabbed with
his sword. There was no room for fancy moves in this encounter. He
hacked with his blade, feeling it penetrate the leather armour of his opponent. A spasm shot up his arm as the man expired, and then he quickly
withdrew the blade as blood gushed up his sword and splattered his
armour, but he had no time to take notice. He wheeled his horse to the left
and slashed out with his sword. The oncoming horse shied away from his
blade, the rider clinging on tightly as his mount lurched sideways. A short,
efficient jab in the side left the man clutching at the wound, his fingers
sliced as he grasped the blade. Gerald, pulling the blade out, heard the man
gurgle something as he fell from the saddle.

All about him, he listened to the ring of steel on steel while he glanced
around. Blackwood had just finished one off, and Fletcher was trying to
stab another in the back as the enemy rode away. It had been a short,

bloody battle. Fletcher was bleeding from his arm, but it didn't look serious. His thoughts returned to the king as he looked back eastward. The colour drained from his face when he saw the king's horse stumble and go down, its rider tumbling from the saddle. Hearing new sounds from the east, he spied a new group of raiders closing on the fallen king, but he was too far away to help. A lone rider on a Mercerian Charger was drawing close to the king. Instantly, he knew it was Beverly. He must trust in her abilities, and do what he could from where he was. With the king down, the original group would now be able to overwhelm the Mercerian Ruler. He raised his sword high in the air.

"We must save the king," he shouted, and then pointed his blade at the group approaching the king from the north.

He spurred his horse onward, desperate to intercept the attackers, his men following behind him. The mass of raiders looked like a swarm of ants crawling across the landscape. On Gerald rode, the horse straining to reach the enemy in time. Suddenly they were right in front of him, and he yelled defiantly. He swung his sword and urged his mount into the mass of men. Soon, he was surrounded, curses greeting his ears. He struck out randomly and felt the blade bite into something. He screamed at the top of his lungs, knowing he had to get their attention away from King Andred. Unexpectedly, his horse stumbled, and a sharp pain shot up his right leg. He heard a snap, and looked down to see the head of a spear buried into his leg, pinning him to his horse. His mount reared, then fell to the ground causing everything to tumble around him. He instinctively tried to jump, but his impaled leg twisted painfully beneath the horse as the creature landed on top of him.

He screamed out in agony as the head of the spear snapped again, releasing his pinned leg, but tearing his skin open further, blood gushing out of his leg. His horse was writhing in anguish, but there was nothing he could do but try to roll to safety as another spear jabbed down beside him. His horse's thrashing subsided as it drew its last breath. All around him, horses hooves tried to trample him. Blocking with his shield, he felt the wood split with the force of the beast above him, then stabbed up in a blind fury and felt blood spurt all over him. The creature reared, trying to get away, and the rider fell, hitting his head on a rock when he landed, a look of disbelief frozen on the dead man's face.

Gerald dragged himself across the ground, trying to get out of the way, but there were too many opponents. He cast away his damaged shield and sat up as best he could, blocking yet another blow with his sword. He knew he was doomed, knew he had thrown his life away when he charged the enemy. He suddenly thought of Meredith and Sally, and a calm overcame him. He would join them soon in the Afterlife, and all this pain and anguish would be over.

He saw the blade coming towards him and tried to brace himself for the sweet release, but he had been a soldier for far too long. He instinctively raised his left arm to block the blow, felt the blade brush across his chain-mail sleeve, then struck back with his weapon. His sword slid across the enemy's blade, slowed but not stopped by the crossguard. The man swore as the blade dug into his hand, releasing his weapon as he moved away, his horse bearing him to safety.

Gerald felt something strike his head, the blow ringing in his ears. His vision started to blur, and he called out, "Meredith!"

"'Fraid not," said a voice, and suddenly strong arms were lifting him to safety.

"Get him out of here," said Blackwood, and Gerald felt himself flung over the back of a horse. He grasped the saddle with all his remaining strength as Fletcher's horse galloped clear of the fight, the cacophony of battle following, serenading him into unconsciousness.

The smell of putrid flesh assailed his nostrils as he awoke, bile rising in his throat. His stomach churned, and he turned his head to try to catch a fresh breath of air. Slowly, he became aware that he was lying on a blanket on the ground, the sounds of injured and wounded all around him. He tried to take in the rest of his surroundings, but could only turn onto his side and vomit. A reassuring hand touched his shoulder, held a bowl to his mouth, offering water. He took a sip, tried to focus. Above him stood the Keep's surgeon.

"Don't move," the surgeon gently laid a hand on his shoulder. "You've taken a rather nasty wound. You're back in Bodden."

"The king?" Gerald sputtered.

"Safe, he's resting."

"What happened?" he asked, still trying to focus his eyes.

"This man pulled you out," the surgeon answered, looking to his left.

Gerald turned his head to look but then darkness started to close in again.

"Easy there," he heard William Blackwood say, "you had us worried for a while."

"I'm alive?" he was astounded, and a little saddened.

"Either that, or we're all dead," retorted Blackwood.

He heard a slap as someone hit his benefactor's arm. A face loomed before him, framed in red hair.

"Gerald, can you hear me?" the reassuring voice was familiar, but he could not focus, saw only a blur.

"It's me, Beverly, you're safe. Father's going to move you to a more comfortable place. Try not to move."

He heard her voice but his head swam again and then everything went black.

He awoke to clean sheets and a soft bed. Opening his eyes slowly, the room gradually came into focus.

"He's moving, my lord," remarked a female voice.

"Thank you, Margaret, please fetch some fresh water."

The recognizable form of Lord Richard Fitzwilliam loomed over him.

"How are you feeling, Gerald? Can you hear me?"

His throat felt dry as he tried to speak, so he nodded instead.

"Let's get him sitting upright."

He felt arms lift him, then someone pushed pillows behind his back to prop him up.

"You had us worried, Gerald. It was touch and go there for a while."

"Where am I?" he rasped.

"You're in Bodden Keep. You've suffered a grievous wound."

"My leg?" queried Gerald, his eyes widening in alarm as he remembered the fight.

"It's all right, the surgeon managed to save it, but I'm afraid it'll never be quite the same."

Gerald's mind whirled. If his leg was damaged, his fighting days were over, once again changing his whole life.

As if reading his mind, Baron Fitzwilliam spoke up, "Now, you just relax, Gerald. We're going to send you to Wincaster. I've written a letter to the Royal Life Mage, and we're hopeful he'll heal you, especially after all you've done."

"The king?"

Fitz looked to the other side of the bed and smiled, "It seems a young warrior stood over the king and saved his life."

Gerald, confused, turned his head. Beside him, he saw Lady Beverly, grinning.

"Rest, Gerald," she used her words to calm him. "You'll be good as new once the mage sees you, then you can join us back here in Bodden."

Gerald allowed himself to sink back into the pillows. Perhaps she was right. In a few months he could be back here doing what gave his life purpose

SEVEN

Return to Walpole Street

SUMMER 953 MC

Gerald awoke to the smell of burnt flesh and smoke. Was he finally in the Underworld? He opened his eyes, letting them adjust to the brilliant sunshine that fell over the carnage surrounding him. His sight blurred. He had trouble identifying where he was, but felt the pressure of cobblestones beneath him. Shaking his head, everything came abruptly into focus. He was lying in the street, with bodies strewn about him. He remembered seeing his blood spilling out onto the ground, so he looked down at his right leg. Someone had tied it off with a tourniquet and then must have moved him from his previous position, for he spied the large blood stain where he had fallen.

As he tried to sit up, a sharp pain lanced through his leg. He looked down at the blood-soaked rag and was convinced he would have to have it amputated. He stopped, pausing a moment on his elbows, inhaling deeply and then sat upright. HIs head seemed to spin a little, and so he took another calming breath. He noticed more dead bodies nearby, mostly men, but also a few women and at least one small child, perhaps no more than eight years of age. He conquered the urge to vomit at the sight and continued to survey his surroundings.

The fighting had moved farther down the street when the soldiers were released from their line. He saw smoke coming from the tavern, and knew that it would soon be engulfed in flames. He could only hope that it wouldn't spread to the other buildings, or there would be a massive conflagration.

He tried to stand, but his wounded leg would not hold his weight. Cursing under his breath, he looked around for anything that might be able to help him. He soon spied a broom propped against the wall outside of the shuttered bakery. It was some twenty feet from his location but felt like a mile in his present condition. He lay back down and rolled over onto his stomach, then began to drag himself towards it. The pain was excruciating, and he stopped, gulping in air to dissuade the contents of his belly from once again attempting to make an appearance today. Inch, by agonizing inch, he pulled himself forward and slowly, ever so slowly, the broom grew closer and closer. Soon, it was within his grasp, and he grabbed the wooden handle in a death grip. He fought off a third wave of nausea and then decided enough was enough. Reaching into his pouch, he withdrew another small leaf. The numbleaf brought almost instant relief, but he knew he must be careful not to push it too far, for although the pain was gone, he could still bleed to death.

He used the broom to help him get into a sitting position. Outside the shop was a small box, and he hauled himself onto it, then sat, his back against the wall while he tried to think things through. From the sounds of it, the company was running rampant. There was little Gerald could do to control it, but somewhere the officer must still be giving orders. He must find the lord, and try once more to convince him to stop the bloodshed.

He looked at the broom and, deciding it could make a temporary crutch, he glanced around for something to chop the pole to a more useful size. He was surprised to see someone had returned his sword to his scabbard, and he withdrew it, using it to cut the broom handle to a slightly shorter length. Now, came the moment of truth, for he must attempt to stand. He braced himself for the arduous task, and then used his good leg to push his back up the wall, raising him to a standing position. He tucked the broom handle under his right arm, thinking it might support him, as his right leg was useless. Slowly, he stood and allowed the makeshift crutch to take the weight.

He took a tentative step forward and discovered his leg was dragging. He adjusted his gait by lifting his hip higher, then the useless limb could swing forward on its own. He was rewarded with some progress as he attempted a few steps. He hobbled back to the wall and picked up his sword in his off hand. It would be awkward, holding his weapon as well as the broom, but he would at least have protection. He moved experimentally, ten feet forward, ten feet back. He adjusted his grip on the broom and hobbled some more until he found the best combination.

He was about to congratulate himself when he heard a woman's scream. Struck by dread, he tried to rush forward, only to stumble. He used the crutch to stop his fall, and it pushed painfully into his armpit. He cursed to himself, he must slow down, pace himself. He moved towards the alleyway, then turned into it to see a woman being pushed to the ground by a soldier who loomed over her, fumbling with his belt.

Gerald was outraged! He stepped forward intending to strike the man with the hilt of his sword, but as he swung, the broom came out from under his arm. He fell forward, hitting the man on the back and clutching at him to arrest his fall. They crashed to the ground, but luckily the woman rolled to the side.

"Get out of here," he screamed at her, "save yourself!"

His weight pushed down on the soldier, and the man had grunted as he hit the ground. His opponent rose to his knees, while Gerald struggled to get into a sitting position. The soldier turned, and his eyes went wild with recognition. It was one thing to attack a woman in an alley, it was quite another to strike one's superior. The soldier scrambled to his feet, a look of shame on his face. He offered his hand and helped Gerald to his feet.

"Sorry, Sergeant," the soldier said, with an apologetic look on his face. "I got carried away."

This was no time for a lecture, Gerald thought, he must take action.

"Start gathering up the rest of the men, call them back to the line."

"Yes, Sergeant," the soldier agreed, his discipline returned.

"Have you seen Lord Walters?"

"He's on the next street over," he replied, pointing down the alleyway. "He's had us breaking into the buildings to root out the rabble."

"Never mind that, gather what men you can and form a line at the end of the street. If you find anyone looting, stab them."

"Sergeant?"

"You heard me. No looting is to be tolerated. You understand?"

"Yes, Sergeant. What are you going to do?"

"I'm going to talk to the captain. I'll join you shortly. Smith, isn't it?"

Smith smiled, pleased at being recognized, "Yes, Sergeant."

"Well, wipe that smile off your face and get to work."

He wasn't happy about leaving Smith to his own devices, but he had no choice. He must find Lord Walters to stop this madness. He took a moment to check his leg. He must be careful not to cause more bleeding. He steadied himself, and then proceeded to move down the alleyway, his sword once again gripped in his hand. Crouched behind a rain barrel at the end of the alleyway was the young woman. She turned as he approached.

"Oh, thank you, sir," she said, gratefully. "I don't know what I would have done if you hadn't shown up."

"Stay where you are," he instructed her, "it'll be safer here. I'm going to try to stop this madness."

"You're bleeding, sir. Let me help you."

She ripped the hem off her skirt and began bandaging up his leg.

"What's your name, sir, if I may be so bold as to ask?"

"My name is Sergeant Gerald Matheson, from Bodden."

"I knew you was different from the others," the woman said. "You've the look of a gentleman about you."

Gerald snorted, "I have been called many things over the years, but a gentleman is not one of them. What's your name?"

"Marcy, sir." She finished wrapping his leg and tied off the ends. "There, that should hold you."

"Thank you, Marcy. Now, stay here and hide behind the barrel. If the way looks clear, move down the street, but stay to the side of the road. The first building you can get into, you get inside and hide, understand?"

"Yes, sir. Thank you, sir," she said.

Gerald moved to the end of the alley and gazed out at the street beyond. He spotted Lord Walters, still mounted on his horse, sitting tall, waving his sword around and screaming orders. The captain had a wild look on his face, and Gerald could tell the lord was thoroughly lost in battle lust. He had seen it before, usually in the knights that came to Bodden to test their mettle in combat. It took training and discipline to overcome that fear, and more than one young knight had gotten carried away in battle, often to their detriment. He remembered a young knight named Simon who had charged recklessly into a group of Norlanders, only to be riddled with arrows. He shook his head. There was no time to think of the past, he must concentrate on the present.

He staggered out of the alleyway, moving directly to towards the captain. The officer either didn't see him or ignored his approach. Gerald was suddenly there, right beside him.

"Lord," he declared, "it's over, the enemy has fled. You have the victory."

The officer turned to him. "We must kill the filthy traitors!" he spat out.

Lord Walters was wild-eyed. Gerald tried to grab the horse's bridle, to gain control of the beast, but the horse, excited by his rider, reared up unexpectedly. Lord Walters, caught by surprise, let out a shriek and fell, landing heavily on the cobblestones, his horse bolting off, with Gerald diving out of the way in a desperate bid for safety. As he landed with a thud, he could still hear the officer screaming. He got to his feet, pulling the broom back under his arm.

"Stop this madness!" he hollered, desperate to get the officer's attention.

Lord Walters kept up his diatribe. "You filthy traitor!" he yelled. "I'll have you hanged for this!"

Gerald stood straight, moving forward to stand over the man, his sword in his hand.

"This ends now," he said with finality.

EIGHT

Wincaster

SUMMER 953 MC

L ord Richard Fitzwilliam, Baron of Bodden, looked out the window, silently gazing down onto the well-worn streets of Wincaster. He was deep in thought, and though his eyes looked outward, he ignored what they saw. He stood stroking his beard and thinking, not at all aware of the outside world. He remained still for several more moments, and then made his decision. He turned from the window and strode to the door, opening it. Outside stood a young woman, clad in the glittering armour of a knight of the realm with the coat of arms of Bodden emblazoned on her breastplate. As was typical in the Palace, she wore no helmet and carried no shield, but her sword hung from her belt. He knew that she was more than capable of using it.

"Beverly," he said in a kindly voice, "come inside a moment, I need to talk to you."

"Yes, Father," she replied dutifully, stepping into the room as her father stepped back. She looked as though she knew something was about to happen, and closed the door behind her, turning to face him.

"What is it?"

He looked at her for a moment. With her red hair and angular face, she looked so much like her mother. But where her mother had had a soft look, Beverly's was hardened. Life at court as a knight had been tough on her, but she had been resolute and determined to earn her spurs the old-fashioned way. As proud of her as he was, now was not the time to speak of it. There were more urgent matters to discuss.

"I am about to have a meeting with Lord Barrington and Lord Montrose. You know of them?"

"Yes," she replied, "Barrington is one of the king's advisors, and Montrose is the Earl of Shrewesdale, one of the king's strongest supporters."

"No doubt, by now, you've heard of the massacre at Walpole Street?" he said.

"Yes, though I don't know all the details."

"Tell me what you know," he gently prompted.

"Lord Walters lost his head and let the troops massacre the townsfolk. If he had not died in the assault, they would have dismissed him!" Her disgust was evident.

"Well, that's true, but it looks like his family wants a scapegoat, someone to blame for the blunder."

He watched her face for a few moments, knowing his next words would sting, "They want to blame his sergeant, Gerald Matheson."

"No, that can't be!" she said. "You know Gerald would never condone such a thing!"

"You and I both know that Gerald Matheson would never support such an action, but I'm afraid that they want a scapegoat. This meeting, I hope, will avoid any public humiliation for him, but I fear his military days are over."

"But that's not fair! He served you for years, for Saxnor's sake! He trained me, taught me to use a sword! He's been a mentor to me!" Beverly said, incensed at the very idea that someone should blame such a distinguished warrior.

"I know that, and believe me when I say I will do everything I can for him. I owe him much. Save for his wound, I would have kept him on at Bodden. The king's life mage could have been more cooperative and healed him, then he would have been returned to us, but you know how the king is. Wants to keep all the magic to himself. I sent him here to recuperate, with letters to Marshal-General Valmar to ask for his intervention, but to no avail. Instead, he assigned him to this local company, and now we have to deal with the results."

Beverly grimaced at the mention of Valmar.

"You must learn to hide your emotions, my dear. Valmar is a powerful friend of the king."

"Valmar is incompetent," she growled. "We both know that you should have been made marshal-general."

"Be thankful I was not," he replied, "or Bodden would be someone else's responsibility, and the north would have surely fallen by now."

He was not prone to bragging, but he knew his abilities, and he was confident that no one else could handle the defence of such a vital location.

"So, what is it you want me to do?"

"I want you to be present for the meeting, stand inside the door, just observe and listen. One day you will succeed me, and you need to be able to handle yourself diplomatically."

She scoffed at the thought. "I cannot inherit the title, Father. You know that!"

"True," he replied, "but when you marry, your husband will inherit the title. Everyone at Bodden respects you, and they'll do as you say." He smiled as he reminded her of this. "Marry a weak-minded man, and you will control the barony!"

She smiled at the jest. Her father had a way of making even the most distasteful news palatable.

"Now," he continued, "take your position outside the door. When they arrive, show them in and remain inside the room rather than returning to the hallway. They will probably ignore you, but it will keep them on their best behaviour."

"Because I'm a woman?" she asked, already starting to bristle.

"No, because you're a witness!"

She had only returned to her station in the hall for a few moments before she was opening the door for the distinguished guests. Lord Fitzwilliam turned to greet his visitors.

"Your Grace," he greeted the Earl of Shrewesdale.

"Good to see you, Fitz," said the earl with a false sense of familiarity. "You know Lord Barrington, of course?"

"Of course," he replied, nodding at the other visitor. Barrington was from a noble line, beneath the baron's social status but was said to have the ear of the king. "Can I offer you gentlemen a drink?" he asked.

"Yes, that would be wonderful!" said Barrington. Fitz turned to the table to see that Beverly had already begun pouring the wine into beautiful Elven glasses, and then she brought them over silently. Barrington looked startled when he realized it was a woman wearing the armour, but the earl feigned indifference. They each took a glass.

"To the king!" they chanted together and drank heartily.

"What is it you wanted us here for Fitz?" enquired the earl.

"I was interested in the Walters' affair," he said noncommittally, trying to sound only mildly interested.

"I believe Barrington can better inform you, than I," responded the earl, swivelling his gaze in the direction of his companion.

"Pretty much what you would expect," he began. "Walters' family has influence, and they want someone to blame for the fiasco. It stains the family name to have this massacre associated with their line. Someone has to be held accountable. It should be a simple matter to blame it on his sergeant. We can then execute him for treason, and the incident will be soon forgotten. The people will have their scapegoat, and the Walters' family will have their honour back. All loose ends tied up nicely, I should think."

He seemed very happy with his plan and drained his glass to emphasize the finality of it. He held his glass out to the side absently, waiting for it to be refilled. Baron Fitzwilliam hid his disgust at the very idea and turned to hide his true feelings. He gazed out the window to give himself time to gather his thoughts.

"A solid plan, were it not for some small details," he said.

A look of worry crossed Barrington's face. He had been confident of the plan, and now he was being told there was a problem. Lord Fitzwilliam was well known and well-liked by the people. It was said he could persuade any crowd. He was also Barrington's social superior, and he dared not break the rules of etiquette. He continued to wait until he could stand it no longer.

"Such as?" he urged.

"Just rumours," Fitz continued, "but there are numerous accounts that the sergeant was seen trying to stop the carnage and pull the soldiers back under command. There's also the matter of his record on the frontier, which was exceptional."

"But..." Barrington stammered, "someone must be made to pay! We can't have people going around killing nobles!"

Shrewesdale was unusually quiet. No doubt he knew where this was heading and was waiting for Fitz to show his hand.

"That's all well and good," continued the baron, "but the mob more than likely killed Lord Walters and we have no way of finding out who is responsible."

"I take it," interjected the earl, "that you have a solution to propose?"

"Of course, Your Grace, I think I have a solution that would fit every-one's needs. I propose that we place the blame on a military unit out of control. As punishment, dismiss the sergeant from the army, then find him an out of the way job, far from Wincaster where no one will ever hear from him again. The family will retain their honour, after all, since their son was dead, he couldn't control his soldiers, could he? It also stops us from publicly executing a man who has served the king loyally for years, while still getting him away from prying eyes!"

"Excellent," uttered the earl. "We can ship him off to one of the Royal Estates, out in the middle of nowhere. Does he have any skills?"

"I believe he was a farmer before he joined the army," supplied Fitz.

"Perfect," the earl replied with mock joviality. "We'll send him to Uxley, the king never goes there anymore. It's just close enough to Wincaster that we can keep an eye on him, but far enough away that he can't cause problems. What position do we give him? Guard? Stable hand?"

"I should think that groundskeeper would be more fitting to his talents, my lord," suggested Baron Fitzwilliam.

"Groundskeeper it is, then." The earl downed the rest of his drink. "You have solved a problem for us, Fitz," he congratulated. "I shan't forget it. The king will be pleased."

"I am honoured to have been of service, Your Grace," he replied, bowing slightly.

"I shall inform His Majesty that the matter has been dealt with and have Marshal-General Valmar cut the orders," said the earl. He turned towards the door and stepping forward, placed his glass on the table. As he did so, Beverly opened the door, standing out of his way.

"Come along, Barrington, we have details to execute." He made this last statement as he began to leave the room.

Barrington, caught unawares, desperately downed what remained of his refilled wine glass and hurried to catch up, placing his glass tottering on the edge of the table as he left. The glass wobbled slightly, then fell from the table, saved from crashing to the floor by the dexterous hand of Beverly. She closed the door as the two nobles left, the sound of their distant footsteps still echoing in the hallway.

"That was neatly done, Father!" she said.

"I wish I could have done more, but these are dangerous times, and it's best not to push the king's favour these days."

It was three days later, that Lady Beverly Fitzwilliam met her father at the Queen's Arms. He was sitting outside, watching people walk by, a tankard of dark ale on the table beside him. A serving wench made her way to the table and laid down a plate of bread and cheese beside him. He was appreciatively looking over the plate as his daughter came towards him.

"You look pleased with yourself!" she noticed the grin on his face.

"Ahh, Beverly my dear, so pleasant to see you. Come and try some of this delicious cheese." This last statement was made as he popped a piece into his mouth. "A most excellent Hawksburg gold!"

She sat down waving to the server to indicate that she would have the same ale her father was drinking.

"I don't know how you can stand that, it smells awful!" She wrinkled her nose as the aroma wafted towards her.

"I must admit that the taste far exceeds its smell!" he said.

The server brought her a dark ale and wandered off. She waited until the server was out of earshot.

"What news?" she hastily enquired. "Has everything been arranged?"

"Yes. Even as we speak, Gerald is en-route to the Royal Estate at Uxley, where he will take up the position of groundskeeper. We have kept him safe!"

She visibly relaxed. She had been convinced that something would go wrong, but now, as she sat with her father, she could finally take a deep breath. The constant plotting and currying of favour at court was exhausting. One always had to look over one's shoulder, and be careful when talking, lest eager ears were listening. The relaxation abruptly ended with her father's next words.

"Now, we just need to get you a position at court!"

NINE

Settling In

SUMMER 953 MC

Gerald awoke with the sudden movement of the wagon hitting a pothole and jarring his body. He winced as his leg cried out in agony while he struggled to keep a calm demeanour. Fortunately, the man beside him paid no attention as the wagon kept moving. He thought of taking more numbleaf, but his supply was getting low. He imagined the rare plant was hard to come by this far from the Capital, best to save it for when he needed it.

The trip to Uxley had been arduous. It had been one wagon after another, for he could not afford an actual carriage to travel in. The ride had been bumpy, and he was finally on the last leg of his trip, aboard a wagon belonging to Uxley Village's saddle maker, a man named Sam. The man was disgustingly cheerful and had talked Gerald's ear off all the way to the Royal Estate.

"Shouldn't be long now," the man said. "This road bends around a bit up ahead, and then we should have a clear view of the Hall. Ever been out this way before?"

Gerald rubbed his leg and then answered, slowly, "Not really. I travelled through the village on the way to Wincaster, but I've spent most of my life in Bodden."

"Bodden? That's on the frontier, isn't it?" asked Sam.

"Yes, far to the northwest."

"Is it dangerous up there? I hear the Norlanders are always raiding."

"Yes," answered Gerald, exasperated by the endless questions. "The

Norlanders are constantly trying to steal from us. Occasionally they mount a full-scale attack."

"I take it you've seen some fighting then?"

"You could say that," Gerald replied, then lapsed into silence, hoping the man would stop talking, but it wasn't to be.

"Is that how you were wounded? Your leg, I mean?"

"Yes," an annoyed Gerald continued, "though it was made worse in the Capital. I took a second cut to the leg stopping a riot."

The driver nodded as if that cleared up everything.

"How much longer till we arrive?" asked Gerald, eager to be finished with this enforced companionship.

"We're almost there," the saddle maker continued. "In fact, we're right beside the grounds now. Everything to the east of here is the Uxley Estate."

Gerald looked at the wide-open fields in surprise.

"Where are the crops?" he asked.

The saddle maker smirked, "You won't see fields farmed around here. The Hall was a retreat for the Royal Family, a place for them to get away from the Capital. It used to be a favourite place for the king to hunt, but it's all quiet now. Though I dare say, there's a healthy yield of weeds about." The man laughed at his jest, then continued, "The grounds run for acres, but most of it's still wilderness, covered in trees and whatnot. There's an extensive hedge maze behind the Hall. It was said to be a favourite of the queen, but I hear it's overgrown now."

"Why's that?"

"Well, when the king took up with his mistress, he stopped visiting. The staff now does little more than just prevent the house from falling apart. There hasn't been a royal visitor in years, as far as I know. I'm told the king's mistress prefers the warmer weather to the south."

They almost bounced out of their seats as the wagon struck another pothole. Gerald landed at a slight angle and pain shot up his leg, causing him to hold his breath against the throbbing.

His host continued his discussion without interruption, "What is it you're here for again?"

"I'm the new groundskeeper," he supplied. "I suppose they need someone to clear away the weeds."

"You don't seem very happy about it."

"Nonsense," said Gerald, sarcastically. "I'm overwhelmed with excitement."

"I imagine it'll keep you busy, at any rate. It's a vast estate."

With a bark from the back of the wagon, the saddle maker's dog poked his head between the two men in front.

"Jax is excited. He doesn't come up here very often."

Gerald absently pat the dog's head, "Does that mean we're almost there?"

"Yes, just beyond the large elm tree there, is the main gate. From the gate, there is a road that heads straight to the Hall, forming a loop at the door, you'll see."

"Your dog certainly likes attention," Gerald observed.

"Who, Jax? He loves it. He just thinks he's a small dog in a large dog's body," he chuckled.

"Well, he's certainly a large dog," said Gerald.

Gerald saw an immense archway as they approached the gate, crowned with a wrought iron top. The two large sides of the gate stood open, but it was clear they hadn't been closed for years, as evidenced by the weeds tangled among the vertical metal gates. In days gone by the Hall must have been an impressive sight, but now the entrance, rather than being an ornate roadway lined with neatly trimmed trees, was a mass of weeds and unkempt bushes.

The house, however, was another story, for although it was only two stories high, the exquisite white stone used to make it stood in stark contrast to the unkempt roadway. The wagon pulled up in front of the door and halted.

"Here we are," announced Sam with a smile. "Good luck to you."

"Thank you," said Gerald. "I appreciate the ride."

"If you ever find yourself in the village, look me up," offered Sam. "I'll buy you a drink."

"That's kind of you," replied Gerald noncommittally, slowly lowering himself from his seat. "I'll keep that in mind."

His feet hit the gravel, and he only remained upright by holding onto the side of the wagon. Sam passed him his crutch, and he nodded his thanks. The house looked immense, but he could see the signs of negligence now that he was close to it. The windows were dirty, and the shutters showed where the paint was flaking off.

He moved slowly to the back of the wagon to get his belongings while Jax ran across the top to meet him. He patted the dog a final time as he retrieved his bag. It was hard to be annoyed with such a friendly beast, and he found himself smiling. He tapped the wagon with his hand, and Sam started moving out. As Gerald watched him drive off, he was filled with remorse for he had been rude and petulant. The man had only been trying to be helpful.

He tucked the crutch under his arm and walked towards the stables, the gravel crunching beneath his feet. The smell of horses wafted in his direction, pulling his mind back to Bodden. Gerald had never been an accomplished horseman, not like Fitz or his daughter, but he could ride when needed. As he approached the side door, his right foot struck an over-sized piece of gravel and pain lanced through him. He stopped to catch his breath and waited for the familiar throbbing in his leg to quiet down. He poked his head in the doorway to see a man brushing down a horse, steadying the beast with his hand on its shoulder.

"That's quite a horse," he greeted the man.

The man looked up from his work, "Yes, this is Blade, he and his brother pull the wagon."

It reminded Gerald of the knights' horses in Bodden. They were of a similar size, but where a knight's horse was trained to fight, this creature appeared to be docile. He stepped through the doorway, careful to avoid hitting his foot on the slight incline.

"I'm Gerald Matheson," he said, extending his hand. "I'm the new groundskeeper."

The man placed his brush down on a nearby stool and walked over, extending his hand in reply, "Glad to meet you. I'm Jim Turner, the stable master." He looked Gerald up and down, sizing him up. "I have to say," he continued, "I'm a little surprised. It's not like we've had a groundskeeper in the recent past, and, quite frankly, you don't look much like one."

Gerald wasn't quite sure how to respond. Was this man mocking him?

"Not that it matters much, half the staff here is completely unnecessary. Can I ask how you got the job?"

Gerald cleared his throat, "I was recommended by Lord Richard Fitzwilliam, the Baron of Bodden."

"Indeed," the man appeared suitably impressed, "and what, might I ask, did you do for the baron?"

"I was his Sergeant-at-Arms for many years."

"Well, welcome, Sergeant Matheson, to Uxley Hall. If you just let me get Blade here settled, I'll take you up to the Hall." He said as he picked up his brush. "Have a seat," he indicated the stool off to the side, "I'll only be a moment."

Gerald sat, grateful for the chance to rest his leg. It was aching again, and he considered taking some more leaf but decided against it. He would have to have his wits about him for he was soon to meet his new employer. Being drugged up on numbleaf was probably not his best option for the coming situation.

He watched as Turner walked the animal out of his stall, and handed the reins to a stable boy. It was remarkable how compliant the creature was. He had seen knights struggle with controlling their mounts, but very few had this kind of relationship with a horse. He remembered Baron Fitzwilliam.

There was a man who was comfortable around horses, a skill he had imparted to his only daughter.

"This way," the stable master indicated, "I'll take you to the servant's entrance around back."

Gerald dutifully fell into step beside the man, who was gracious enough to walk slowly so that he could keep up.

"The Hall has a dozen or so staff, but for the most part, we're not very busy. The king doesn't visit here anymore."

"Yes," said Gerald, taking an interest, "they mentioned that in the village. Why is that?"

"The king has many estates," the stable master continued, "and I hear he prefers to spend his time at court among the wealthy. There's not much here at Uxley Hall to maintain his interest."

As he was talking, they walked down the side of the sizable building. Gerald looked up at the stonework, seeing the fine craftsmanship that had built the place, but it looked like it had not been maintained in years with broken shutters, cracked bricks and a multitude of filthy windows. He thought he caught a glimpse of someone at one of the windows, out of the corner of his eye, but when he focused his gaze, he could only see a curtain falling back into place.

"So, the place is empty?" he said.

"Not exactly, but there's little to do here. You'll find there's an overabundance of staff, and the work is not too strenuous. I expect you'll spend most of your time cutting the grass and trimming the hedge." He nodded towards the vast maze they could now see around the back of the Hall. It was indeed a hedge maze, but the corridors were difficult to see. It had plainly not been trimmed in many years and was now a riot of branches and leaves. If he had wondered what he would do to keep busy, the state of the grounds answered his question.

"Here is the servant's entrance," said the stable master, indicating a large wooden door. "We use this whenever we enter or exit the Hall, unless of course, there are visitors, but the king hasn't come in many years."

He opened the door as he spoke, and entered the building with Gerald in tow. They walked into a small hallway with coat racks on the wall on one side, and a small bench one could sit on while removing boots on the other. He beckoned the new groundskeeper to follow him. There were two doors visible, and he nodded to the closest one.

"Through there is the kitchen, and the door at the end leads to the servant's dining room. Follow me."

They turned to the left and entered a large room, with ovens along the outside wall and a large work table in the centre. Cabinets and shelves were scattered throughout the room along with a sink, the latter having a hand pump for water. The kitchen was a busy place. Turner introduced the staff that was present in a whirlwind of names. There was Mrs Brown, the head cook, another named Mary, and a teenaged girl named Sarah, who he rather gathered was the scullery maid. Two more women sat at a smaller table nearby, and he struggled to hear their names over the noise of the kitchen. Gerald nodded as they were introduced. He was not likely to remember them all, but he was confident he would learn them in due time.

"Now," the stable master continued, "we'd best take you to see Hanson. He's the steward, although he also acts as the head servant when necessary. You can leave your bag here, and we'll get it on the way back."

They went out the other side of the kitchen into a hallway which led to the front of the house. They walked no more than ten feet to a doorway on the left that opened to another, shorter hallway.

"He's in his office, down this way," announced Turner.

They stopped at the door, and the stable master knocked three times.

"Come in," responded a firm voice from inside.

Turner opened the door and waved Gerald inside.

"I've got the new groundskeeper here, a Sergeant Matheson."

An old man sat behind an enormous wooden desk, his thin hair combed over a mostly bald pate. His face was clean-shaven, revealing a wrinkled countenance. The steward had stacks of papers on the desk and was using a quill, which he dipped absently into an inkwell then scratched on the parchment in front of him. Gerald stood in front of the desk, as any good soldier would.

Hanson waved his hand absently, "Have a seat, I'll be with you in a moment. You can go Turner."

"I'll wait for you in the kitchen. When Hanson's done with you, come and see me."

Gerald nodded in understanding, and then sat on the wooden chair, eager to be off his leg. He looked around the room to see ledgers, no doubt used to keep the accounts. Baron Fitzwilliam had insisted on doing his accounts himself, a rare practice amongst nobles, but it was far more common to have someone like Hanson do the work.

"Now," the old man's voice startled him out of his reverie, "this is a Royal Estate and to work here you have to have proof that you're reliable. You have your letter of introduction?"

Gerald reached into his tunic to carefully pull out his letter and passed it to Hanson. Hanson slowly unfolded it, as if he might accidentally damage it. He watched the old man's eyes move as he looked over it.

"A most handsome recommendation!" He appeared impressed with the words written upon the paper. "It seems the baron holds you in the highest esteem."

"I served Baron Fitzwilliam for many years," Gerald proudly replied. "I owe him my life, several times over."

"He makes the same statement regarding you, though I daresay we have little use for a soldier."

Gerald felt the crushing weight of disappointment building. "I was told I was to be the new groundskeeper," he interjected hopefully.

"Oh, yes, I see it here. We shall put you to use, have no worries, though I suspect with that leg of yours, keeping the grounds well-groomed will prove... burdensome."

Gerald sat back in relief, "I'll do my best sir. I want to be useful."

"I'm certain you will if this letter is any indication."

Hanson rose from his desk, "Well, I should let you get settled in. You'll be staying in the groundskeeper's cottage, Turner can show you where it is. You're free to eat at the Hall, Mrs Brown can tell you when the meal times are. Of course, you can take care of your own meals if you wish. The cottage has a small fireplace, but I'll let you figure that out for yourself."

"When do I start work?" asked Gerald, rising from his seat.

"Work? Oh, there's no hurry. Give yourself a couple of days to settle in. You can start when you feel you're ready. After all, there hasn't been a groundskeeper around here for years."

He had walked around the desk as he talked and now he held out his hand, "Welcome to Uxley Hall. I think you'll do fine here."

"Thank you," Gerald said, returning the handshake.

He showed himself out and made his way back to the kitchen. Turner was teasing the two young girls and turned as he entered.

"There he is, just the man I was speaking about. You'll be lodged in the cottage, I understand?"

"Yes, so Hanson told me."

"The groundskeeper's cottage is out behind the stable. It's a bit run down, but roomy enough. And of course, you'll need firewood. We have plenty of that to spare. Come on, I'll show you the way." He glanced over at a young man who had just entered the kitchen. "Ned, lend a hand and carry Mr Matheson's bag."

Ned strolled over to him. He had a cocky look about him, with his tousled hair, which fell over his face, obscuring his eyes. Gerald glanced at his carry bag sitting on the floor. He just had to see the lad's reaction when the weight of the bag dawned on him.

Sure enough, the young man grabbed the drawstring, expecting to heft the bag over his shoulder easily. Gerald was highly amused. The look on

Ned's face was priceless. Not only did he underestimate the weight, but his lackadaisical approach led him to overbalance slightly, and he stumbled. A titter of laughter burst forth from the two girls at the side table. His face flushed red, and then he made a more determined effort to lift the heavy bag, unaware of the chainmail that lay within. He drew it up awkwardly and slowly eased it onto his shoulder. The weight was obviously uncomfortable to him, but he refused to admit it. Gerald turned, hiding his smile from the young man, and followed Jim Turner out of the house.

They walked partway back to the stables, then turned to the right, cutting through a small wooded area, only a few yards in depth. Here, in a clearing, was the cottage. It looked like a single room dwelling, with a door in the middle, and a window to either side, though both were currently shuttered. The thatched roof was in disrepair, but Gerald had fixed those before. At the one end was a small shed, which, no doubt, held the groundskeeper's tools. The stable master opened the door, having to shove it harder than expected when it stuck slightly. Inside was dark, but the light from the doorway was enough to see the interior; a fireplace sat opposite the door, while to the left was the living area and to the right was the bed. There was not much room for anything else, but Gerald didn't mind. As a sergeant, he was used to sleeping in a small room in Bodden Keep. He hadn't had this much room since his farming days.

"This will do very nicely!" he muttered, more to himself than to either of the others. He turned to Ned, effortlessly lifting the bag from the young man's shoulder and moved into the room, dropping the bag on the bed.

"I'll get Elsbeth to bring you some linen for your bed, and I expect you'll want some towels and such," offered the stable master.

"Thank you, Jim. I'll drop by the Hall for dinner after I've unpacked and settled in," he replied.

The stable master, with Ned in tow, left him to his thoughts. He opened the shutters on the windows, and a fresh breeze blew into the room, disturbing some dust. He wandered over to the bed and sat down, fishing in his belt pouch for the numbleaf. It had been a busy day, and his leg was aching. He placed a leaf in his mouth, chewing it quickly and the pain subsided. He lay his head down, intending to rest for only a few moments, and fell instead, into a deep sleep.

TEN

Strange Events

SUMMER 953 MC

The sun was high in the sky, and he saw Meredith and Sally running through the long grass. Gerald called to them, and they turned, but as he moved towards them the sky grew cloudy, and blood began pouring from his wife's neck. Sally called out. He watched in horror as her stomach split open and her guts spilled onto the ground. He tried to stop the horror, tried to pick them up, put them back into her, but they ran through his hands like water.

Gerald awoke in a sweat, gasping for breath. It had all been so real. He looked around, eyes wet with tears, and saw the sun streaming through gaps in the shutters. It was morning. Would the dreams ever end, he wondered? Would he ever be free of the guilt?

Stumbling out of bed, he hobbled over to the table where he poured some water into a bowl. He fully intended to splash the water on his face, but the previous day's activities had left him drained of energy. He took a breath and plunged his head into the water instead. The coldness of it cleared his mind, and he withdrew his face, letting the water run down his shirt. He resolved to get to work quickly, for he was not a man to sit by and do nothing.

He wandered out to the shed to see what he had to work with and found a large assortment of tools in various conditions. Some were obviously well kept, but others appeared to have been neglected. He decided a trip to the local blacksmith would be required before he could begin any work. It was easy enough to have the stables prepare a horse and wagon, and he spent the morning watching the local smith sharpen and oil some of the rustiest of the tools.

By the afternoon, he had returned, and he set about his self-appointed tasks. First, was the long grass which grew on either side of the roadway. He grabbed the two-handed scythe from the shed and immediately found a new problem, for he could not walk with his crutch while he held the large, awkward tool. He ended up dragging it in his left hand while he stumped along to the grass. The next challenge was to stand while using it, for he could barely stand without his crutch. It wasn't until he fell, painfully, that he decided against cutting the long grass. Perhaps, he thought, he could pull weeds, for he could sit on the ground to do that simple task.

It was not to be. Gerald lowered himself to the ground, but needed to kneel, and his right leg would not bend properly. He sat on his backside, but then didn't have the reach he needed to do the job properly. A curse escaped under his breath. Surely there was some work he was able to do, for he refused to believe that he was a helpless cripple. He looked around, searching for something that he might be able to accomplish.

His eyes passed by a hedge in front of the Hall and then fell upon an old bucket near the overgrown flower bed. He grabbed some shears and hobbled over to the hedge, picking up the bucket on the way. He placed the bucket on the ground, upside down, and used it as a stool, stretching his leg out in front of him. It put him at a decent enough height, and with some slight adjustment, he found he could sit relatively comfortably while still being able to use the shears. The work would be slow, but at least now he could do something.

Sometime later, his back sore from the effort, he returned to the cottage. He opened the door to the shed and noticed that something looked amiss. He looked carefully at the contents, then realized that some of his tools were missing.

"Someone from the house must be using them," he mumbled to himself, "and why shouldn't they? It's not like I own them." He closed the shed and headed towards the Hall, for mealtime was fast approaching, and he had slept through the first meal of the day.

He made it a point of asking the staff who might have borrowed his tools, but only looks of bafflement met his gaze. No one claimed to have used them, and when he returned to the cottage sometime later, the mystery remained unsolved. He was just about to enter his new home when he thought to check the shed. Low and behold, the tools had been returned!

He shook his head, "You're imagining things, Gerald," he mumbled, "next thing you know you'll be talking to yourself."

He collapsed into a chair, his leg aching once again and placed a small, thin leaf in his mouth, chewing it absently. The relief washed over him almost instantly, and he relaxed. There was a lot of work for him to do, but little rush to do it. Tomorrow, he resolved, he would get back to work on the hedges and see how they turned out. Once that was out of the way, he would see what else he was capable of doing.

He had wanted to get up early, for the lifetime of his military service he had risen before sunrise, but now, in this lonely, forgotten place, his body refused to work. He awoke, cursing and swearing as a thin stream of sunlight penetrated his shutters, cutting across his face, mocking him with its glare. He suspected it was the numbleaf causing him to sleep so long and swore again not to take any more. It was an expensive remedy, and he realized his limited supply would not last much longer.

His body was lethargic, and he had to will himself just to get out of bed. He doused his face with water for the second time in as many days and forced himself out of the little cottage. It was a sunny day, and he felt the warmth of the sun on his face, drying the water as he looked around. Gathering up his tools, he made his way back to the Hall where he knew he had left the bucket. He decided he would work for a while, and then grab something to eat in the kitchen.

He was soon lost in his work, sculpting the hedge to a more uniform shape. It wasn't until a shadow fell over him that he realized someone was watching. He looked up to see Hanson, the old steward, staring at him intensely.

"It looks good," he observed. "You've a talent for it."

"Thank you, sir," Gerald responded proudly, adding the last word almost as an afterthought. He was used to taking orders from a noble, but to be talking to a superior who was a commoner was new to him.

"Have you done this type of thing before?" the old man enquired.

"No, but I've spent many a day cleaning out the crops. Mind you, that was more than a few years ago."

"I can imagine," the old man continued, "that it takes a lot of patience."

"Yes, something I learned as a sergeant. Training recruits was a very…" he struggled for the right word, "intriguing experience."

Hanson chuckled, "I imagine it was. I sometimes wish we could take a firmer hand with the servants, but I doubt it would make a difference."

"You have trouble with the servants?"

"This is a Royal Estate and, as such, only the most trustworthy individuals are taken on as servants."

"I would think that gives you the pick of the litter, doesn't it?"

"You would think so, but occasionally it goes to their heads, and they begin to feel superior."

"Well, you don't have to worry about me, I tend to keep to myself."

"I'm not worried about you, Gerald, your reference letter speaks volumes. You know, you surprise me."

"How so?" asked Gerald, interested in learning his reasoning.

"You could have retired here, lived in the cottage, eaten at the house. No one expects you to actually work."

"It's not my style to accept charity, sir. I wish only to make an honest living."

Hanson nodded wisely, "As do many of us, at least the older ones. When you're done here, what do you intend to do next?"

"Hadn't thought about it," Gerald responded honestly. "I suppose I'll come up with something."

The old man smiled as he suggested, "I thought that you might tackle the hedge maze. It's been abandoned for years, and you can barely enter it now."

Gerald nodded, "That's a good idea. I can trim it up using the same technique."

"You'll need a ladder for the upper levels, but you ought to be able to lean on it, I should think," Hanson suggested.

"The maze it is then," smiled Gerald. "I always like a challenge."

"Excellent. When you finish that, you can direct some of the younger servants to trim up the grass. There's no lack of capable backs, and I'm sure you can give orders."

Gerald nodded, feeling much better about himself, "Indeed I can. I look forward to it."

The old man extended his hand, "I think you're going to work out well here Mister Matheson, very well indeed."

Gerald shook Hanson's hand earnestly. It was nice to feel useful.

The maze presented its challenges, and to prepare, Gerald strolled around it as best he could. It was a good seven feet or more in height and filled much of the backyard. It would take him several days, he was sure, perhaps even closer to a week or more to tame it. The lower reaches appeared to be easy enough. For the mid-height section, he needed to get a taller stool from the Hall. For the upper levels, he would need the ladder that Hanson had suggested.

He approached the trimming of the maze as he would a battle plan. Determine the desired result, then create a strategy that made for a positive outcome. He decided to work on the outside of the maze first, starting on the northern side. The first step entailed beginning with a small section, no more than ten feet in length. He must start with trimming the ground level, proceed to the middle region, then use the ladder to cut the top. Once the section was complete, his next step was to move on with military precision. This three-layered format allowed him to stretch his leg rather than spend hours in one position.

He started working on the hedge the next day and was soon making progress. It took some time to get into the rhythm, but he found that by making some slight alterations to his position, he could avoid the incessant ache that had become his constant companion.

It was near noon when he decided to take a break. Descending the ladder, he sat on the ground, stretching his leg out in front of him. He unwrapped the kerchief to reveal the cheese and meat that Cook had prepared for him. He bit into the spicy sausage, letting the flavour roll around his mouth.

He was just about to swallow when he heard a sound, and his soldier's instincts told him to freeze. Off to his right, he picked up something moving. He looked in that direction but saw nothing out of the ordinary. He was on the northern face of the maze, looking to the west. He knew that if he turned the corner, he would be at the entrance. He held his breath, straining to identify the strange noise. He heard it again, a rustle, and decided somebody must be in the maze.

Annoyed by this intrusion, he got to his feet, hastily swallowing his mouthful of food. Crutch tucked firmly under his arm, he made his way, as quietly as he could, towards the entrance to the maze. He neared the corner and paused, listening once again. He heard no sounds, so he cautiously peered around the edge to get the shock of his life.

Sitting at the entrance to the maze was a massive dog. Gerald had seen dogs before, they were a common enough sight. He had even seen the big wolfhounds that nobles favoured in the Capital, but this beast put even those large animals to shame. The creature was the size of a pony! It was lying on all four legs, its front protruding from the maze.

It turned its head to look directly at Gerald, and the man stood perfectly still, while he tried to decide what to do. The dog looked like a mastiff, its face filled with loose, wrinkly skin. Gerald let his breath out slowly and calmed himself. He looked over at the creature who was no more than four paces away from him. The dog's face was scarred, and he was immediately reminded of Bodden. He remembered an event, years ago, when soldiers had been found betting on fighting dogs. Baron Fitzwilliam had been furious. He remembered the dogs they had found had born similar scars to the one that now sat before him. What had he discovered? Was someone fighting this creature? Or was he here scrounging for food?

He was suddenly conscious of the sausage still held in his other hand, and he almost laughed out loud. He tossed the meat towards the beast, and it landed just in front of it. The creature sniffed the meat carefully, then grabbed it quickly in its massive jaws. In the blink of an eye, it disappeared down the dog's throat. It ignored Gerald and looked about, scanning the yard as if searching for something, licking its lips.

Gerald, free of its gaze, withdrew back around the corner of the maze. He returned to where he had been working and wondered where the dog had come from. Gathering up the rest of his meal, he hobbled back to the entrance, but was disappointed to find the creature had disappeared. Did he imagine it? He started to doubt himself.

Slightly shaken by the encounter, he decided to return to the cottage for a rest. Leaving the ladder where it was, he made his way back home, stopping at the shed to find the usually latched door swinging open. He looked inside, noticing that a trowel and small hand rake were missing. His first reaction was to fume, but he took a deep breath. The tools belonged to the estate, and he needed to let go of his anger.

He returned his tools to their proper place, closing the door to the shed, then turned to go into the cottage. He made his way to the bed, plucking a book from the bookshelf as he did so. He sat on the bed, his back leaning against the wall, his legs extended in front of him, and began to read. Though he sometimes struggled with words, he found books, in general, to be very interesting, particularly when they dealt with soldiering. Soon, his eyesight began to blur, and after reading the same paragraph three times, he nodded off, the book falling into his lap.

A banging noise woke him, and he was instantly alert, for years of working on the frontier had kept him sharp. He realized that the sound he heard must have been the shed door and he leaped off his bed, forgetting for the moment his bad leg. It gave out beneath him, and he scrambled to steady himself. He cursed as he grabbed the edge of his bed, his leg twisting painfully.

His damaged leg would not stop him this time. He grabbed his crutch, and was soon outside, making his way to the shed, determined to discover the culprit. He rounded the corner of the cottage to see the shed door closed, just as he had left it. He yanked it open revealing the tools exactly where they should be, including the missing trowel and rake. He looked around, desperate to spot some sign of the thief, but to no avail. Whoever had returned the tools was long since gone. He turned around to the shed to close it back up and froze. The ground was still damp from an early morning shower, and he noticed a footprint of a huge dog in the mud

He stared at the print for several moments before shaking his head.

"Don't be stupid," he muttered, "a dog's not going to use a trowel."

He scrutinized the area for signs of a Human footprint, but none fell within his view, and he soon grew weary of searching. With the adrenaline wearing off, he felt the soreness of his leg sapping his energy, the lethargy from his morning romp returning. Without the numbleaf, the effects of his wounds were ever present.

At mealtime, he avoided all mention of the beast, lest they think him crazy. He asked about the maze, but Hanson told him there was no map. He had thought of looking down on the maze from the second floor of the Hall, but again the old steward said that the maze was so badly overgrown that the path was not distinguishable.

Later that afternoon, he returned to continue his work. Disappointed, but not surprised, Gerald made his way to the entrance armed with food, in case he once more encountered the dog. The way in was thick with over-grown branches. He began by cutting away the largest offending growths, piling them by the entrance to burn later. He worked steadily, using the bucket and chair to ease the pain of his leg, and soon saw a marked improvement to his surroundings.

He stopped trimming, and as best he could, he gathered the cuttings to put into a pile, then he noticed marks on the ground. There were two parallel ruts, not very deep, about two feet apart, giving the appearance of something dragged along the ground. These grooves immediately reminded Gerald of a wooden frame pulled behind a horse. Caught up in the mystery before him, he abandoned his work to investigate.

The ruts led farther into the maze, and he ducked under the branches to move deeper through the labyrinth. Enough light filtered through to see his way, but the branches here were wild and tugged on his sleeves as he made headway. More than once he had to stop to extricate his crutch from the tangle of branches that interfered with his progress. He had spent enough time in the north tracking down raiders that he knew how to follow a trail, and thankfully the parallel marks were relatively straightforward to follow. Whoever had come this way knew where they were going, but were not trying to cover their tracks.

Eventually, he came across an open area, the centre of the maze. It was five yards on each side with two entrances, the one he now stood at, and another to the left. Directly opposite him, against the far hedge wall, was a simple stone bench. Weeds grew unhindered here, but to his right, he spotted a patch of ground that had been cleared to reveal three rows of recently turned over dirt.

Moving into the clearing, he noticed a watering can sitting nearby. Some water was still in it, the rest obviously having been poured onto the dug-up area. It dawned on him that someone must have planted something, but his mind struggled to determine who would do such a thing. He moved around the area looking for anything that might give him some clue as to who was responsible and groaned when his lame foot struck an object among the weeds. He let out a curse that would turn a Holy Father crimson and looked down. The glint of metal revealed two tools at his feet, hidden within the bed of weeds. The trowel and hand rake!

"So," he muttered, picking up the tools, "you've been using my tools again, but this time I've found your secret hideout!"

His musings were interrupted by the sound of rustling branches, and he turned quickly, wincing at the effort. He registered movement out of the corner of his eye, looked at the entrance, but nothing was visible. It occurred to him that it might be prudent to leave the area, so he moved back to the entrance, only to hear a low growl. Again, the branches moved to give way as the monstrous dog appeared. The creature's head was even with his chest, and he quickly calculated that the beast had several pounds on him.

Gerald froze in place. He was not scared, but his experiences told him not to move, not to bring attention to himself. There was nowhere to run, even if his leg had let him. He was trapped here, blocked by a creature that he had no doubt, could kill him if it wanted to. Time stood still while Gerald observed the creature. Its ears picked up unexpectedly, then it turned suddenly, disappearing back into the maze.

Gerald let out a sigh of relief, making his way to the bench. If truth be told, he was a little weak in the knees from his unexpected encounter. Perhaps, he thought, he should carry his sword from now on. Somewhat shaken by the ordeal, he retraced his steps to the entrance of the maze, only to realize that in his haste, he had dropped the very tools he had discovered. Not to worry, he thought, whoever took them would return them, of that he was sure.

It was evident to him that someone was using the maze as a private garden, but he couldn't fathom why? There were far more accessible areas that were suitable for growing plants. He put all thoughts of it out of his head, returning to work on the entrance.

. . .

By the end of the day, the opening to the maze had been cleaned up nicely with the first corridor now neatly trimmed, along with the outside wall. He marvelled at the progress he had made, taking pride in a job well done. He wandered down the corridor, but as soon as he made the first turn, it became overgrown again. More work for the future, he thought to himself. He took the clippings back to the cottage where he started a bonfire to burn them. Pulling out a rickety wooden stool, he sat upon it while he fed the flames, drinking some cider as he worked and tried to stretch out his right leg.

The cider and the chair soon relaxed him, and his thoughts turned to the people here. They were decent enough but appeared reluctant to interact with him. He was an outsider, that he understood, but they were more distant than he had expected. Only Hanson, Turner and the cook seemed even vaguely interested in talking to him. Perhaps in time, he thought, he would win their trust.

The next morning saw him busy. The Cook, Mrs Brown, sent him into the village with a cart. She had arranged for him to pick up some plants from Mary Sandlewood, a local farmer's wife, herbs to replant in a small garden near the kitchen. He took the offer of Sam, the saddle maker, to join him for an ale at the local tavern, then made his way to the Sandlewood farm. It was a bright day, and as the sun rose, he could feel its warmth. Soon, he was sweating as he rolled the cart up to the farmhouse. He saw a young girl, perhaps ten or eleven years old, run towards him and call out as he approached.

"Mother," she called back to the house, "there's a cart here!" She slowed her pace as Gerald brought the horse to a halt. "Are you from the Hall?"

"Yes, Mrs Brown sent me. I'm here to get some herbs."

An older woman came out of the house. She was slightly stocky of frame and had on a well-worn apron with her brown hair tied loosely behind her back.

"Mrs Brown?" she asked.

Gerald nodded, "She told me you'd be expecting me."

"I've got what you need over here," she said. "Come this way, and I'll show you where they are."

He climbed carefully down off the cart and followed her around the back of the house where a small garden sat.

"I have what she needs here," she said. "Molly can help you load them up. I've got some small clay pots, but I'll want them back when you're done."

Gerald was impressed, "You must do this a lot, to have pots. I don't think I've seen them outside of the city."

Mrs Sandlewood smiled, "Well, most of the village folk come to me when they need herbs, and the extra coin doesn't hurt."

With the help of young Molly, they loaded the plants into the back of the cart. He gave her the small bag of coins Mrs Brown had provided and was soon on his way back to the Hall.

His trip completed, he pulled the cart up to the side of the house to unload his cargo. He carefully laid the potted plants on the ground and took the wagon back to the stables, returning to the garden plot after stopping by the cottage to pick up the tools he would need. Upon arriving back at the garden, he began taking each plant out of its pot and placing it into a small hole that he dug up with his spade. He was almost done the first row when he came up short. He was missing two of the plants. He examined the first row of ginger root and counted the plants. He knew he had purchased twelve, yet he had planted only ten. He looked over the still potted plants, and with a shock, realized that not only was he two ginger root plants short, but several other pots were missing as well. He resolved to look into the matter but must finish planting those he had first.

Sometime later, he placed the last blackroot plant into the ground. He was filthy with dirt and headed back to the cottage to wash up and return his tools. When he opened the shed door, he saw that more tools were missing. The culprit must be tending to their garden back in the maze!

By Saxnor's beard, this was the final straw! It was one thing to use his tools, but it was quite another to steal his plants! He made his way to the cottage where he strapped on his sword and grabbed a knife, tucking it into his belt. He looked at his chainmail armour hanging on the wall, wondering if he should don it. He could make out the newer links that had been used to repair it over the years. It was not the prettiest suit of armour he had seen, but it had saved his life on more than one occasion.

"I'm being silly," he said out loud, "it's only a dog."

He left the armour hanging on the wall but decided to keep the sword and knife. He was just about to exit the room when he remembered he had food, some leftover cheese. He took the knife and cut off half a hand's worth of cheese, wrapping it in some cloth.

"What dog doesn't like cheese?" he thought out loud.

He made his way to the maze. He hadn't had the opportunity to do any more work on it, but the entrance was still empty. He crept into the labyrinth, treading carefully, trying not to make any noise. He had a hard time remembering the route to the centre and had to backtrack several times, but eventually found the plot he was after. Peering around the corner, he saw a small girl, perhaps six or seven, carefully digging up the ground and placing a plant in it. Across from her, the large dog was lying quietly until it saw him, then it raised its head and growled.

The girl dropped what she was holding and ran for the hedge wall opposite the entrance, crawling through the bottom by squeezing her small frame between the bushes. The dog stood up and growled again. Gerald put his hand on his sword hilt as it advanced. The dog approached slowly, allowing him time to compose himself and think. He removed the cheese from his satchel and, holding it out in front of him, unwrapped it, then placed it in the palm of his hand.

The great beast stopped just short of him, nose up to the hand holding the food. Sniffing, it let out a huff of air. Gerald flattened his hand, moving the cheese closer to the animal, watching it lean forward a tiny bit more, and then gently taking the treat. It stood, eating it, occasionally looking at Gerald, who started to relax. He inched ever closer to the animal, taking care not to move suddenly, lest he startle the creature. He reached out tentatively, touching the top of the dog's head, rubbing it ever so slightly. The dog's ears suddenly perked up, then the dog sat down, and lay on all four legs. Gerald bent halfway to scratch the dog's head, pleased that the dog let him. Now that he could see it up close, he was once again astonished at the scars visible through its fur. Old wounds covered the dog, and only a dog that fought in the pits could be so badly marred.

He was feeling sorry for the creature, when it suddenly decided to lay down on its side, thus presenting its stomach. The dog wanted a belly scratch! Gerald relaxed and started rubbing the dog's belly, noticing the dog's collar. It was old, and quite worn, but had a small brass plate on it, similarly worn and tarnished. Engraved upon it was 'Tempus'. This must, he thought, be the dog's name.

"Tempus," he said aloud. The dog responded by sitting up and looking at him. "You've had a tough life from the looks of it." He moved closer, leaning on his crutch, scratching the dog under the chin.

"Looks like we're both old and scarred. How did you come to be here of all places?"

A small voice came from the hedge, "He's my friend, don't hurt him!"

Perhaps overcome with fear for her dog, the little girl stepped out from between the branches. She was about three and a half feet tall, wearing a rather worn and dirty green dress that fell just past her knees. Her feet and legs were covered in dirt, while her long blonde hair was matted. Her blue eyes peered out from behind the hair that fell in front of her face with an intensity he had seldom seen in one so young.

"You hurt him, and I'll hit you!" she said bravely, her quivering voice betraying her bravado.

The conviction in her voice touched Gerald.

"I'm not going to hurt him. I was just petting him. He's very nice," he said, trying to soften his voice so as not to sound threatening.

He straightened up, backing away from Tempus while keeping his hand outstretched to the side to show he meant no harm. The girl advanced timidly. She was clearly devoted to the creature, but still scared. She came up beside Tempus and placed a protective hand on his back. It was almost comical for, even with the dog sitting, the girl had to reach up to touch him.

"My name is Gerald Matheson. I'm the groundskeeper at Uxley Hall." He waited for her to acknowledge his words with a slight nod. "Who are you?"

"Anna," she answered. "I live here."

ELEVEN

Anna

SUMMER 953 MC

H e had expected to find a servant, perhaps one of the stable boys or maids, but to find a small child was entirely unexpected. His mouth gaped open as he struggled with what to say.

He finally settled on, "Is this your garden?"

The child nodded but said nothing more.

He pointed to the plants as he spoke, "You planted these?"

"Yes," was all she replied.

"You're the one that's been using my tools," he realized, his frustration rising.

He had dealt with children before, but not in years. Was the child touched in the head? Did she not understand she was stealing?

"The tools belong to the estate," she informed him.

He felt like her eyes were boring into him and found it slightly unnerving.

"You stole those plants," he accused.

"I needed them," she whispered.

He could feel his temper rising, and raised his voice, "You can't go around stealing other people's property, that's theft."

His temper was threatening to erupt. He had dealt with difficult people before, but now this strange circumstance, along with the constant agony his leg, combined to overwhelm him.

"Saxnor's Balls!" he shouted in irritation.

He immediately regretted his outburst, for the girl's eyes began to tear up. He had been a brute, and he was annoyed at himself. His leg was on fire, his face was flush, and he needed to catch his breath. He limped over to the bench, sitting down, breathing heavily. What was wrong with him? Why was he like this? He sucked in a big breath of air, held his breath then let it out slowly. He took out a small leaf and bit into it, feeling the relief flood through him. He closed his eyes as the calmness spread, and then he opened them again. The girl was still there.

"I'm sorry girl, I shouldn't have yelled."

"Anna," she reminded him gently.

"Anna," he repeated. "Tell me, how long have you lived here?"

"All my life," she replied timidly. She was standing close to Tempus now, her arm trying to drape over the dog's neck.

"And you planted...," he swept his arm theatrically at the plants, "these?"

She stood up straight, brushing the hair from her face, "I did!"

He rose to his feet, moving closer to the small plot, examining it in more detail.

"Do you know what that is?" he said, indicating one of the plants.

She shook her head.

"It's blackroot, and it's going to die. You haven't dug the roots in deep enough. These are plants, not seeds."

Anna came closer, leaving the dog behind. He eased himself to the ground and sat beside the row of herbs.

"Hand me that trowel. We need to re-plant these."

She gave him the tool, and he drove it into the dirt.

"We need about a hand's length for blackroot, otherwise it'll dry up. It's a thirsty plant. Now, we'll move the plant into the new hole."

He dug out the root carefully with his hands and placed it in its new home. It was awkward, reaching across to do the work with his leg stretched out to the side.

"Now," he continued, "push the soil in around it. That's it, not too tight."

She was moving the dirt carefully. Gerald watched her, and a lump came to his throat. It reminded him of what life could have been like with Sally, but that part of him had been buried for years. He felt tears welling up and coughed to save face.

"Like that?" she indicated.

He cleared his throat, "Yes, that's it, now you try the next one."

She took the trowel and drove it into the soil. It appeared large in her small hands. Moving the tool once it was embedded was more difficult, and he saw her struggle, her young muscles not quite up to the task. He was about to say something when she heaved and the trowel came free, spraying dirt into the air, mostly into Gerald's face. He spat out the dirt, wiping it from his eyes to see her standing with an absolute look of horror on her face.

"Tastes just like I remember it," he smiled, "not as good as Cook's scones though."

She giggled unexpectedly, and he was reminded of his own daughter's laughter. This was too much! He couldn't take the resurfacing of his old memories. He struggled to rise to his feet.

"That's it, just keep doing that till they're all done." He planted the crutch firmly under his arm, "I have to go now."

She looked up at him with a sad look on her face, and he felt his resolve melting. A tear formed, he felt it as it ran down his face, moistening his beard.

"What's wrong?" Anna gently laid her hand on his arm.

"Nothing," he bit back. He'd done it again, overreacted. "It's nothing to do with you."

He stormed out of the maze as best he could. Turning as he left, he saw her standing there, watching him. Were there tears in her eyes, too? The maze was but a blur before him as he was weeping openly. He stopped, leaning against the hedge wall, overcome with fierce wracking sobs. He wanted to control himself, but it was all too much. He had never properly mourned the loss of his family. He had taken revenge, had plunged himself into his soldiering. He had faced men in combat, fought incredible odds, but never had he been as unnerved as he was by this small young girl.

He had fled into the maze in such a rush, he was unsure of the way out. He looked skyward as if Saxnor himself might guide him. Why must he suffer so much? He had lost his parents, lost his family, and lost his life as a soldier. Must he be forever tormented by the memories as well?

He needed to drown his sorrows. It was past time to get back to the cottage and let it all become a blur. He felt a small hand softly grasp his.

"It's all right," she volunteered, "I know the way out."

With a dulled mind he let her lead him out of the maze. It was like a dream, the numbleaf making it even more surreal.

"There's a water trough over by the wall. We can wash up there."

She led him to a bench, and he sat, while she dipped a small tin into the water, carrying it over to him. He rested, spellbound, too drained to care, as she carefully washed his hands.

"What's this?" Anna said as she knelt onto the ground.

He watched as she picked up a small leaf, inspecting it, horrified as she moved to put it into her mouth.

"NO!" he shouted, slapping it from her hand.

She let out a small scream, and the massive dog advanced towards him, growling menacingly. Once more, the tears came to her face, and yet again he felt incredibly inadequate to this task.

"It's dangerous," he explained, "you shouldn't do that."

"But you chew it, I saw you."

"It's numbleaf. It's for pain," he defended his actions.

She placed her hand on her dog's head, calming the brute instantly.

"Is it your leg?"

"Yes," he responded.

"How'd you hurt it?"

"It's an old war wound. It was made worse in Wincaster. Some days I can barely walk on it."

She was staring at his leg, which he had stretched out in front of him.

"You need something to stiffen it so that it can take the weight."

Gerald looked on in disbelief. How could one so young come up with that?

"I've seen something like that before," she offered.

He couldn't believe his ears, "You've seen something?" By Saxnor's beard, how could she have seen something to brace his leg?

"In a book, in the library. There's a drawing of a man with a thing on his leg."

"A brace?"

"Yes, a brace. Wait here," she ran off, leaving him bewildered.

A short time later, Anna returned, struggling to carry an oversized book under her arm.

"Here it is," she dropped the tome into Gerald's lap.

She sat down beside him, her short legs dangling in the air. She leaned across him and opened the book, flipping through the gold edged pages. It was an illuminated book, its pages rich with illustrations. She stopped flipping, stabbing her finger in the centre of the page.

"There you are! I told you I'd seen it before."

Gerald looked on in amazement. There, before him, was an illustration of a man, perhaps a Dwarf, with a brace of some type on his leg. He scanned through the text. Luckily, it was written in the common language of the three kingdoms.

"It's a picture of Kargol the Strong," he explained, "a Dwarven hero."

"You can read that?" her eyes widened incredulously.

"Yes. I had to learn to read to become a sergeant."

"Really?"

"Well, not really. You don't have to read to be a sergeant, but the baron insisted. Can you read?"

"A little, but the big words are hard to understand. Maybe you could teach me to read better?"

"I'm not a teacher," he refuted.

"But you were a sergeant, you must have taught other soldiers," she said, sitting up with anticipation.

"True, but they weren't little girls, and I wasn't teaching them to read."

"Please show me. No one else here will do it. I think they all hate me."

She was swinging her feet back and forth beneath the seat of the bench "Why would they hate you?"

She stopped her fidgeting as she spoke, "No real reason, I just don't think they like having me around, I... get in their way."

"I'll think about it," he surrendered. "But I'm tired now. The numbleaf has taken all my energy. I need to rest."

He got to his feet a little unsteadily and tucked the crutch under his arm. Anna was cradling the book.

"I bet if we took this to the saddle maker, he could make you a brace."

"Perhaps, but that's for another day."

He hobbled back to the cottage and collapsed into his bed. It had been an exhausting day.

As Gerald awoke, the sun was setting, casting its ever-growing shadows across the cottage. Either his imagination was playing tricks, or he heard a knocking noise. He listened carefully, definitely a knock coming from the door. He rose from his bed, using the wall to support him as he made his way to the door. He swung it open to see young Anna standing before him, holding something behind her back, a large grin on her face.

"I brought you a present," she beamed.

"A present?"

"Yes, another book from the library." In a flourish that only a young child can get away with, she revealed the book she was hiding. "It's about soldiers. I thought you'd like it."

Gerald looked at the embossed letters on its cover.

"The Proper Employment of a Shield Wall with special instructions pertaining to its deployment in battle," he read aloud. Someone called General Phillip Baines wrote it. The name was somehow familiar to him, but he couldn't quite place it.

Anna continued, "General Baines was the king's general back in 864 when we fought Westland. He served King Robert."

"How do you know that?" he was astonished at her comprehension

"There are notes under some of the pictures. There's more in the pages. Can you teach me how to read them?"

"All right, but let's start with something a little easier. This book is rubbish anyway, I remember Fitz mentioning it."

"Who's Fitz?" she asked.

"Er... Lord Richard Fitzwilliam, Baron of Bodden. I used to serve him before I was injured. Now, let's sit down at the table before my leg gives out." He moved to the table, retrieving a book from the shelf on his way.

"This book is a better place to start, it was written by the baron and tells of the Northern Wars. Besides," he patted the book, "General Baines wouldn't know a shield wall if it hit him in the face." Anna giggled, and Gerald felt calmer than he had in a long time.

The warmth of summer had given way to the coolness of autumn, and the estate was alive with hues of red and gold. Sam had managed to rig him up a brace, and now he moved about without a crutch. The leg was still stiff, but now he could use a swing of his hip to push the leg forward.

Most of his time was spent trying to rake the leaves which seemed to appear from nowhere to clog up the walkways. These leaves would be carried in his wheelbarrow to a pile where he would make a fire each evening after dinner. There, Anna would visit him, and he would have her read. He found that she learned quickly and very seldom would he need to repeat a word. Sometimes, she watched him work in the afternoon where he would be weeding the flower beds or the vegetable patch. She would talk to him about all sorts of things. She had an inquisitive mind and liked to question every detail of the work he did to better understand it.

He was happy to have the company, for the rest of the staff only interacted with him on the rare occasions that he was in the Hall, usually only at meal times. He had been at Uxley Hall now for almost three months, but he still felt like an outsider. Perhaps, he thought, they didn't like him or thought he wasn't up to the job, but Hanson, in his manner, had assured him he was doing well.

It was a chilly, slightly windy day as Gerald made his way, wheelbarrow in hand, to the pile of leaves he was assembling near the cottage. As he tipped the barrow to allow the leaves to join the growing mound, he heard Anna and Tempus approaching. The young girl was always quiet of foot, but Tempus had taken to howling a welcome on coming to the bonfire. The large dog came over to Gerald, waiting for his traditional head pat, his tail wagging affectionately. Anna was standing nearby, nervously shifting her weight from one foot to the other, waiting to say something that she deemed meaningful. He put the wheelbarrow down, and turned to Anna, petting Tempus absently on the head as he looked at her.

"Did you scarf some pastries from Cook again?" he asked in mock seriousness.

She looked confused then realized he was kidding and broke into a grin. "No, but I've got something exciting to share!" she burst out. The excitement was very evident on her face.

He waited a moment and then interjected, "Which is?"

"Oh!" she said. "I think I've found some angelroot! You have to come see!"

Gerald frowned, studying her face to see if she was making a joke. "I doubt that. Angelroot doesn't grow around here, Anna. It requires a wet soggy area. Besides, how do you know what angelroot looks like?"

She looked taken aback by his statement and straightened up to give her answer in a most authoritative voice, "Angelroot bears a white flower with a cluster of small seeds. The flowers are quite small, and are bunched together in a grouping approximately the size of a man's hand." She looked very pleased with her answer.

"That description," he replied, "could be any number of plants."

"Yes," she continued, unfazed by his reaction, "but they bear leaves in the shape of a three-pronged spear."

Now, he was intrigued. He had seen angelroot before, his wife would brew a tea from the leaves, but it was notoriously hard to find.

"Where did you see this?" he said, trying to sound only vaguely interested.

"Down near the grotto. I was taking Tempus out for a run, and he ran down a long hill and, and-" she was now rushing out her words in her excitement.

"Slow down. You're talking too fast for an old man like me to follow!" he cautioned.

"Sorry," she took a moment to collect her thoughts. "I was chasing Tempus down the hill, and I slipped. I fell flat into some grass, and when I lifted up my head, I saw the white flower. I ran all the way back here to tell you. Isn't it exciting?"

"Yes, but do you know what angelroot is for?" he probed.

"I heard Cook telling Elsbeth, the maid, that she would brew her an angelroot tea if she could. Not sure why, though."

"Well, that's because it has some healing properties. It has to be brewed into a tea just the right way," Gerald explained.

"So what's it used for?" the young girl asked.

"Well, it's for..." suddenly Gerald realized what he was talking about and became flustered. "It's for women who... well a woman who is ..."

"Is what?" she asked innocently.

"Well, it's for lady pain," he said, fumbling for an answer.

"Lady pain?"

"Yes, you know, er, that is, it's for when a lady or I mean when a woman has, well you know," he blustered. He was getting embarrassed, and his face was turning red.

"No, I don't know, I don't understand!" she seemed really frustrated at his hesitancy to answer her question.

"You should probably ask Cook about it. Girls who have grown up and become women use it. I'm sure she can tell you more about it." He was beet red by this time.

"All right," she said, and that was the end of the discussion.

Before she could raise the question again, he quickly asked, "Can you show me where you found it?"

"Yep, follow me, Master Groundskeeper!" she gestured with a sweep of her hand.

"After your ladyship," he responded with an exaggerated bow.

She let out a small giggle and skipped off, her loyal dog running by her side, with Gerald following. A little later, they were in the northwest corner of the estate near the grotto. The ground here was lower than other parts of the land with poor drainage. There were long grasses and bulrushes in abundance. The ground was soggy and squished as he walked, threatening to soak Gerald's feet thoroughly. He wished he had thought to change into some heavier boots.

Anna led him down a rough trail and showed him where she had fallen. He could still make out the crushed grass where she had rolled down the hill. Sure enough, he spotted the distinctive white flower and three-speared leaves of angelroot.

"Should we pick it, Gerald? Maybe we could surprise Cook!"

He scrutinized the plant before turning to her. "Or we could bring a pot and transplant it. Then we could grow our own. We just have to make sure we give it plenty of water."

"Oooh," she gleefully exclaimed. "I didn't think of that, that's an excellent idea. Maybe if we look around, we can find some more?"

They spent some time roaming around the vicinity searching for more plants. They had found three more plants when Gerald crouched down near the base of a tree. Anna ran over to see what he had discovered. She found him carefully examining something.

"What is it?" she implored. "Did you find more angelroot?"

"No," he replied, "something a little more interesting, come and have a look."

While she wandered over, Gerald found a small stick, about half an arm's length long. He used it to scrape the base of the tree, where a green coloured moss with flecks of blue in it grew.

"This," he said, "is what we call warriors moss."

"Oooh," she remarked, not understanding but excited nonetheless. "What does it do?"

"Soldiers use it to cover a wound that turns bad. It absorbs the pus and prevents the gangrene from spreading."

"Do they drink it in a tea?" she asked.

"No, it's usually mixed with something to give it some substance, even mud will do. Then it's applied as a paste over the wound. Sometimes it's covered with a cloth, just to hold it in place. You must be careful picking it, there are similar mosses that can be extremely dangerous. Come closer and watch as I run this stick through it. You'll see flecks of blue as the sun hits it, that's how you know it's warriors moss."

She observed him, eager to learn. He handed her the stick, and she poked and prodded the moss until she was convinced she would recognize it anywhere.

"Can I take some back to the Hall? I know the library has a book about herbs, it would be fun to see if it's mentioned."

"We can take some back. I'll use a rag to wrap a small sample up. It won't keep long as it'll dry out and then be no good after a while."

He gathered a small sample, and they resumed the hunt for the angel-root. They poked their way among the taller grass, for this is where the plant grew naturally. Tempus thought this was great fun and helped by rolling in the long grass whenever they stopped to look at something, undoubtedly trying to make it easier for them to see the plants. By the time they were done, they had located seven plants.

They were so immersed in their exploration that they missed the call to dinner. They realized this when they returned to the cottage to get some pots. Luckily, Gerald had some food in the cottage so they didn't go hungry. Later, as the sun was beginning to sink, they sat around the bonfire, eating cold pork and bread. Lined against the cottage wall were seven little pots, each with a small white-flowered plant bearing three-speared leaves.

TWELVE

A Visitor is Coming

AUTUMN 953 MC

I t was partway through October, and the days were getting cooler. Gerald was, once again, gathering the leaves that seemed to come out at night, obliterating the raking he had done the day before. He now wore a light coat, though he knew the work would soon find him sweating and he would, naturally, have to remove it. He began working on the roadway that led to the Hall. He had a wheelbarrow with him, but he had to cover the leaves with a tarp every time he placed them within, or else the wind would blow them back out again. It was mindless work, but he didn't mind, it kept him busy.

He had just dropped the leaves off for burning and was returning to begin another round when he saw Anna running towards him, her faithful companion cantering behind her. So excited was she that she hadn't taken the time to put on a shawl. She stopped in front of him, shivering from the cold morning air, but her face was keen with excitement.

Almost as soon as she halted she burst out, "Did you hear the news? The queen is coming to Uxley!" Her eyes were lit up, and her smile was infectious.

Gerald paused, leaning on the rake and looked at her. He turned his head to examine the estate and the mass of leaves that was wearing him down. All he could think of was the work he would need to do to make the place presentable.

"Did you hear me?" she burst out again. "The queen! She's coming to Uxley Hall!"

It was hard to see her enthusiasm and not smile, and so after a moment, he relaxed and let her infectious grin spread to him.

"That's terrific news," he replied. "Just when is this grand event to happen?"

Her reply came out almost before he finished speaking, "She's coming on Tuesday and staying for a week. Isn't it great?"

"It certainly sounds like it will be interesting," he responded, "but if the queen's coming, I've got a lot of work to do. Look at all the leaves!"

She cast her eyes around the entrance road. The roadway was choked with leaves in hues of red, brown and gold.

"We can help!" she said, enthusiastically.

"We?" he replied, doubt written all over his face.

"Tempus can help, too," she explained earnestly.

"Tempus doesn't rake leaves," he said, "he rolls in them, remember?"

"But what if he pulls the wheelbarrow? He's a large dog. He can carry stuff."

"How would a dog, even one of Tempus' size, pull a wheelbarrow, Anna? It just wouldn't work," he explained.

She looked at her dog, her eyebrows knotted in a furrow.

"Couldn't he pull a cart or something? We could give him a harness like a horse, and have him pull a cart. Then we could use the cart like a wheelbarrow!" This last statement was made with pride.

It was indeed an intriguing concept. Tempus was huge, the size of a small pony, damn, even a large pony. It wouldn't take much for a saddle maker to rig up a harness. After all, dog carts had been used for generations. Having a cart made that he could pull might be a bit trickier, but perhaps there was a pony cart they could use. He was considering the situation silently, looking at the large dog and trying to figure out how it might be done when he was interrupted by the girl's voice.

"What do you think, Gerald? Will it work?"

"You know," he paused for a moment, "it just might. I have to go into town later today, and I'll talk to Sam to see what he thinks. As long as it doesn't take too long, I believe we'll give it a try. When did you say the queen was coming?"

"Next Tuesday," she replied.

"It's Wednesday today, so that gives us a few days, at least. I tell you what, if we can get this idea working by the end of day on Friday, we'll give it a try. If we don't have it working by then, we'll have to get to work without it. What do you say?" he said, looking at her, gauging her response. "Do we have a deal?"

"Deal!" she responded.

"Excellent!" he replied, holding out his hand.

She stared at his hand. Her face looked perplexed, and the inner turmoil could be seen as she fidgeted slightly. Finally, she extended her hand and stood, their hands about two feet apart.

Gerald stepped forward and grabbed her hand, shaking it. "It's a deal then. We'll seal it with a handshake."

He witnessed her small mind finally grasping the situation. She looked quite proud of herself.

"Now, if you can convince that dog of yours not to roll around in the leaves, we have some work to do before lunch. You'll need to go get a rake from the tool shed, but before you do that, you need to go put on something warm, it's far too chilly out today for you to be wearing just that dress!"

"All right!" she turned to run back to the Hall. "I'll get changed and grab a rake. Come on Tempus!"

The huge dog lurched upright, sending leaves scattering and galloped off towards the Hall, following the little girl who was tearing across the lawn in excitement.

All Gerald could hear in the distance, fading as she got farther away was her yelling, "The queen is coming! The queen is coming!"

The afternoon sun found Gerald walking into town. He had considered taking a cart, but he told himself that he was getting soft. A walk into town would do him good. The trees were throwing their golden leaves in front of him even as he walked. It was quiet here, only the distant sound of the occasional bird or the rustle of the leaves disturbed his thoughts. He was thinking about the royal visit. What did he truly know about the queen?

He was aware that Queen Elenor had married King Andred many years ago. The union had produced two sons, Henry, the oldest, and Alfred, along with a daughter, Margaret. Margaret was the youngest, and she would be somewhere around twelve. Everyone knew the king had a mistress, and the queen had not been seen at court for many years, except for sporadic events. It was speculated by many that the king had tired of his queen after the birth of their last child, as his mistress had appeared on the scene shortly thereafter. It must be hard, he thought, to be discarded in so public a manner. He felt sympathetic towards the queen but realized that he knew very little about her.

The king was not known to be a pleasant man, and Gerald's experience of the monarch at Bodden bore that out. He had never spoken to him directly during that time, but he had spent enough time with his retinue to be able to form an opinion. He remembered the monarch as an obstinate man, seldom interested in the opinions of others. Perhaps the rumours were not true, the poor always complain about the rich, but then again he never heard a bad word about Baron Fitzwilliam, so maybe a portion of it was true. He could imagine the wrath of the king being something that one would want to avoid. He supposed that the queen was lucky to have only been banished from court.

He thought on this in some depth. More on his mind, however, was how the queen would view the estate. He had convinced himself that he wanted the grounds to look perfect. He certainly couldn't make them perfect in the short time he had, but he wanted her to feel as though some considerable effort had been made to make the place presentable.

He was deep in thought when he heard a twig snap. He halted immediately, his soldier's sense alert to the possibility of ambush, instinctively reaching for his weapon, then remembered where he was. He felt foolish for not carrying a sword, then cursed himself, for he was acting irrationally. He was in the middle of the kingdom, safe from Norland Raiders.

He stood quietly for a moment, then resumed his walk. Was he hearing things? He thought there could be bandits in the area. They had been seen from time to time. Then again, he was only a groundskeeper, poor pickings for thieves. He kept walking, willing himself to calm down. He eventually took a deep breath and let it out slowly, then quickened his pace slightly and set his mind to the task at hand, continuing on his way. The road took a slight turn, and began to descend, revealing the village of Uxley in the distance. His friend Sam's workshop was opposite the stables at the very beginning of the town, just before the bridge that spanned a stream. The village proper was just beyond that, with the bulk of the Old Oak Tavern nestled beside the massive tree that gave the place its name.

As he strolled down the road, he heard a bark, and Jax came running towards him. Sam looked up from where he was sitting to take note. He appeared to be oiling some leather, and upon seeing Gerald approaching, he placed it on the bench next to him before getting to his feet. Jax was running around Gerald in circles, excited to have a visitor.

"Gerald! What brings you to town?" said the saddle maker, extending his hand.

"I've dropped by to see you about something, perhaps over a drink?"

"I've got just the thing, come with me."

They entered the saddler's workshop and crossed to the small room in the back where he lived. He grabbed a mug from the shelf and placed it beneath an earthenware pot with a spigot on it, turning the tap to reveal a golden cider. Gerald smelled the richness of the aroma that wafted towards him. Sam handed him the mug, taking another to pour himself a similar amount.

"Tuck that into you."

"Mmm, smells good," Gerald said as he took a deep breath. "I see you've been busy brewing again."

Sam prided himself on his apple cider. It was believed by many to be the best around. He even sold some to the tavern.

"Yes, I've managed to make a few… adjustments. What do you think?"

Gerald took a deep swig, it was a dark nectar, and the fruitiness warmed him.

"Delicious, it has just a hint of something, very nice. If it's not a secret, what did you add?"

The saddler smiled conspiratorially, "Hazelnuts, but if you tell anyone, I'll deny it."

Gerald laughed, "Don't worry, my friend, your secret's safe with me."

"Now," interrupted Sam, "much as I like your sparkling personality, what is it you came to see me about?"

The old groundskeeper took a swig of cider, relishing the taste as it warmed him to his toes.

"I wanted to get your ideas on a type of harness."

"For a horse, I assume?"

"No, for a huge dog," he said this with all seriousness.

Sam looked like he was just told a joke, but Gerald's serious face convinced him otherwise. "Well, a dog harness isn't too hard to rig up. I've made dog harnesses before. Whose dog?"

Gerald took a pause, drinking more cider to allow him time to formulate his words. "It's a very large beast, up at the Hall. Taller and more muscular than Jax."

The saddle maker considered this for a moment. "Doesn't sound too hard, I can rig up a harness relatively quickly. I assume this is for pulling something?"

"Well, that's the other part. I want the dog to be able to pull a cart. A two-wheeled type, for carrying things, not people though," he added the last part quickly, not intending to confuse the matter any further.

"Well, I'm not very busy at the moment. I can work out a basic harness and rig, but I'd need to take some measurements. Now, if we can - hold on a moment," Sam said, moving to the door where outside Jax was barking loudly, alarmed at something.

. . .

Gerald followed Sam, and the two of them made their way outside. They watched Jax running around in circles near the edge of the tree line, barking his head off. He could faintly make out a low growl coming from the trees.

"Looks like Jax has found something interesting," Gerald said calmly. "Maybe we should take a look."

Sam nodded his agreement. He re-entered his workshop and came out a moment later, with a pair of knives, one of which he handed to Gerald. "Can't be too careful, there's all sorts of wildlife around here. Come on."

As they got closer, Jax suddenly stopped running and laid his front paws down, his tail wagging in the air. A moment later, Tempus ran out of the tree line, barking.

A young voice said, "Tempus, NO! Stop!"

Sam was startled, but Gerald had to stop advancing and bend over, he was laughing so much. This gigantic dog and Jax were running around each other barking and yapping, both wagging their tails. The saddle maker looked confused. He could see this enormous beast with his own eyes, yet Gerald was laughing his arse off. Gerald stopped laughing and straightened himself up.

"Come here, Tempus. You too, Anna, I know you're in there!" he yelled out.

Tempus barked and ran towards Gerald, Jax following along behind. Anna shyly made her way out of the wood line.

"This," said Gerald, indicating Tempus, "is the dog I wanted the harness for, and that little girl over there is Anna. She looks after Tempus, or Tempus looks after her, I haven't quite figured that out yet."

Tempus came right up to Gerald, allowing him to pet the massive dog's head. Jax was still running around barking happily. Anna came forward shyly, her head held down, her long golden locks hiding her face almost entirely.

"Anna, say hello to Sam," said Gerald, "and this is Jax."

"How do you do, sir," muttered Anna, a guilty look on her face.

"What are you doing in town?" Gerald pressed.

"I came to see you get the harness made. I didn't mean any harm."

"Why didn't you just ask to come with me?" he gently prodded.

"I'm not supposed to go to the village. I could get into trouble."

"Don't worry, we won't tell anyone."

"I tell you what," interjected Sam, "how about we get you some nice apple cider, and you can watch me while I measure Tempus. Do you think you would like that? I bet we can have a harness made up in no time."

Anna nodded. She followed Sam and Gerald back into the workshop, hesitating slightly as she entered. The workshop was dark compared to outside, but as her eyesight adjusted, all the tools in the room became visible. Her eyes widened in amazement, and Gerald realized that she was observing each item, each little tool or object as if the whole room were foreign to her.

It only took about half the afternoon to rig up a harness. Luckily, Sam had an old harness that he adjusted for the bulk of Tempus. The cart proved to be a little more troublesome. Gerald was talking about how his wheelbarrow took forever to wheel back and forth when Sam came up with the solution. He ended up using two wheels from old wheelbarrows. These he fixed to a single axle and had the frame in place in no time. So impressive was his work that Willard Harvey, the blacksmith, and Henry Prescott, the stable master ended up getting involved. By the time dinner time rolled around, there was quite a serviceable little cart rigged up to a new harness for Tempus.

Realizing the time, Gerald suggested they all go to the tavern for some food, but Anna looked terrified, afraid she would be in trouble if she didn't get home. He acquiesced, and Sam offered them a lift. By the time it turned dark, they were riding back to Uxley Hall in Sam's wagon. Gerald and Sam sat in the front seat with Anna between them. Jax and Tempus were lying in the back with the new cart. Gerald invited them in for a bite to eat and they all headed over to the cottage, leaving Sam's wagon near the stables. The harness and cart were wheeled over to the tool shed, with the harness hung up and the cart set just outside. Gerald pulled out some bread and cheese he had been saving, and then put a pot of water to boil, tossing in some meat and vegetables.

They began talking as the food cooked and continued well into the night. Anna soon fell asleep, so Gerald wrapped her in a blanket and took her back to the Hall. He caught a blast of trouble when he arrived with the young child in his arms. No one at the Hall knew where she had gone and they were all in a tizzy. He couldn't understand how they would ignore her so much, yet be so upset at her absence. He shook his head. He had long since given up worrying about the strange behaviour at Uxley Hall.

He returned to his cottage and bid Sam and Jax goodbye. As they headed off, he turned in for the night. He had experienced an enjoyable afternoon, more fun than he had had in a while.

The arrival of the queen was far less of a spectacle than Gerald had expected. He was cleaning up the side of the house when he heard the carriage approach, the distinctive sound of its four horses, easy to discern.

The horse's hooves struck the cobblestones, and the sound echoed throughout the Hall. Upon hearing the noise, he walked to the front of the house to observe.

The carriage was richly decorated, accompanied by servants who rode on the back. It was painted jet black with gold accents, the passenger door emblazoned with a coat of arms, and the driver and footmen dressed in expensive clothes. Gerald watched as Ned, the estate's young servant, rushed forward to open the door. A small step swivelled down out of the carriage into position, and he watched, fascinated, as the queen exited the coach. A glimpse of her brown hair was all he saw before she covered it with the hood of her cloak which only partially blocked his view of her ornate purple dress. She stepped down to the ground with grace, making her way to greet the servants, who were lined up in front of the door. She waited halfway there, turning to look back at the carriage. Another figure emerged, a child who could only be her daughter, Margaret. Although he could not hear the conversation that transpired between the two, Princess Margaret looked bored and petulant, clearly not wanting to be present.

Princess Margaret walked over beside her mother, and the two of them proceeded down the line of servants, saying nice things and complimenting each of them. The servants looked pleased, and as they arrived at the end of the line, Hanson welcomed them and, by his gestures, invited them to enter the Hall. The queen disappeared from view along with the princess, leaving the servants to fall in dutifully behind.

Gerald wondered where Anna was? He remembered how overjoyed she was with the thought that the queen was coming, but now she was nowhere to be seen. Perhaps, he thought, the queen did not like to see little girls running around the estate?

He did not see the queen again until the next day when he was in the backyard, digging out an old bush that had died. It was warm for a change, and she was wearing a blue and white dress without a cloak. Her hair was tied in long tresses, accented with silver wire making her a striking woman for her age, but she had a sense of sadness to her face. She wandered out the back door and stopped when she saw the old hedge maze. It briefly brought a smile to her face, and then she turned and strode back to the Hall.

That evening, when Gerald went to the Hall for dinner, he was given his plate of food and told it was best if he ate at the cottage. He objected, but the cook insisted and said there would be a special dessert tonight and that she would send a servant with some for him. The queen is particular, she said and left it at that.

The third day of the queen's visit he saw her once more. This time he was working on the front gate, which had become entangled by weeds. He was hacking away at them and paused to catch his breath. Far off, at the front of the estate, he recognized the queen. She had come out front with a smaller person wearing a green dress with a yellow kerchief over her hair. They were talking in low tones, and he couldn't quite make out any words at this range. It was a private discussion, which was made more evident by the manner in which the queen kept glancing around as if she feared someone might overhear. He assumed that she was talking to her daughter, the princess, but something looked off. He didn't recognize what it was, but it set his mind to wondering. He tried to ignore the feeling and got back to work on the gate.

He finally cleared the gate, allowing it to swing freely, and made his way back towards the cottage by way of the stables. He decided to cut through them, intending to come out the back way where his home lay. As he approached, he heard a young girl's voice. He thought it was Anna, but upon listening more, the voice sounded older. Entering the stables, he was unexpectedly faced with Princess Margaret. She had just ridden in, and the stable master was taking the reins, as a stable boy helped her dismount. She was wearing a blue dress, similar in style to the one her mother had been wearing earlier in the day, but less ornate. She saw Gerald enter, briefly noticing his presence but ignoring him. She remarked how much the stable stunk, and then stomped off.

He didn't think much about it at the time, but later, as he sat eating in the cottage, he realized that if Princess Margaret had been out riding, the queen must have been talking to someone else. Who was this mysterious girl in the green dress?

He didn't see the girl in the green dress anymore, but two days later, he heard the queen was leaving. He watched from the stable as she and the princess exited the Hall. Once again, the servants were standing in line. This time the queen ignored them, walking straight to the carriage. She bid her daughter to enter the coach and then, with only a brief glance at an upstairs window, climbed into the carriage. There was the shortest of delays, then the driver cracked the whip, and the horses began trotting out. It appeared the queen was leaving early. This did not bode well for the staff.

Gerald avoided the other servants until dinner, hoping this time he could talk to them, and find out how the visit went. He heard a sobbing noise as he was just about to go into the servant's entrance. Following the sound, he found Anna sitting in the back garden on a stone bench. She was wearing the same green dress that was on the child the queen had been talking to a few days earlier. Could the queen have been speaking to Anna?

He came and sat down beside Anna, trying to figure out how to comfort her. "Anna, is everything all right?"

"No," she choked out, "everything is not all right! Everything is terrible. I hate this place. I wish I'd never been brought here."

She clutched the end of her dress, and he saw where the lining had caught on a bush or something. She was absently fingering a small tear in the material. He sat in companionable silence for a moment or two and thought of what to say. As he was doing this, Mary, the scullery maid, come out of the servant's entrance and came over to them.

"Cook says to tell you that dinner is on the table. You two need to get washed up before coming in for dinner," she said, oblivious to Anna's inner turmoil.

"I ripped my dress," the sad little girl squeaked out.

"Not to worry," the maid retorted, "you'll get another one next year when she comes back. You make it sound like the Underworld has opened up before you!"

Gerald was incensed by the callous treatment Mary was dishing out but held his tongue. Something was going on here that he was not seeing.

"What's that supposed to mean?" he asked, perhaps with a little more venom than he had intended.

The maid was quick to make amends. "Forgive me, Master Groundskeeper. I merely meant the queen always brings a fresh dress for the princess when she visits. That one won't fit her much longer, anyway, at the rate she's growing. Now, you'd best get inside before Cook loses her temper." She disappeared back into the house.

It felt like a slap in the face as he comprehended the enormity of the word he had just heard, 'Princess?' He turned to face Anna, and suddenly things began to make their way through his addled head.

"Anna?" he asked softly. "Are you a princess?"

She nodded slowly, not daring to speak.

"And the queen is your mother?"

"Yes," she muttered. "She only visits once a year. I thought that maybe this year she'd take me back, but she left early. She doesn't want anything to do with me!"

As she let out the words, tears began to flow in great sobs. She instinctively turned to Gerald and hugged him. He held her gently, feeling sad at the way her mother had treated her.

He moved to place her at arm's length. "It's all right, Your Highness, you'll be fine."

"No, I won't," she stammered. "Don't you see? Everybody treats me different. Nobody wants me, all they see is a spoiled little princess."

Gerald became acutely aware that Anna was not just a little girl, she was a member of the Royal Family. There could be huge ramifications for any actions he took with her. Even allowing her into town could suddenly become an enormous problem. He stiffened in his seat, suddenly aware of the deep water he had been treading.

Anna looked at him. "See, even you treat me different now. Just because I'm royalty, everyone hates me."

He saw that she was right, and yet he acknowledged to himself that even a child needs a friend, not a courtier.

"You're right," he finally agreed, "people do treat you differently, but I'm still your friend, Anna. You'll get through this, I promise. And besides, you have friends."

"Who," she responded. "Who do I have that are friends?"

"Well, for a start there's Tempus over there. He looks anxious."

She cast her eyes over at her faithful dog. He seemed to see the worry in her eyes and wandered over to her, nuzzling her affectionately. She buried her face in the massive neck and cried.

"I wish I had never been born!"

"Anna!" Gerald shouted. "Don't say that. You're a wonderful person. Besides, we still have to work on the maze garden, prepare it for winter. You don't want all that work to go for naught, do you?"

She withdrew her face from her dog and looked at him with a determined expression. "I suppose that's true." She looked as if she was almost admitting to the inevitable fate.

"Good, cause I'd hate to have to do all the work myself. I'm getting old you know."

That brought at least the hint of a smile to her face.

"Let's get you cleaned up and get some dinner into you. I bet Cook's made something special tonight," he tempted.

He stood up and held out his hand. Anna placed her hand in his, and they began to walk up to the Hall, Tempus following slowly behind. She took a few steps and stopped suddenly, bringing Gerald to a halt.

"Gerald?" she begged. "Make me a promise."

"Anything you like, Princess," he responded.

"Can we still be friends, like before?" she asked.

"Of course," he responded.

"And can you just call me Anna, not Your Highness or Princess?" she pleaded.

Gerald stooped to her level to answer, "Yes, Anna, I promise you."

She smiled and hugged him.

"Thank you," she said in a much more matter of fact manner. "Now, let's go get some food before it's all gone."

They wandered up to the Hall to the waiting dinner table.

THIRTEEN

The Seasons Pass

WINTER 953/954 MC

I t took some time for Gerald to become accustomed to Anna's parentage. To him, she had always been the little girl with the dirty feet, and he couldn't quite come to grips with the fact that her father was the King of Merceria.

He was sitting in front of his nice warm fire of an evening in the middle of winter, some mulled cider in his tankard. He had been reading with the oil lamp by his side but had found his attention wandering. He was thinking of Anna, and how he could help her, but every time his mind began to work on the problem he would get caught up in her situation. He just couldn't understand why she was treated so badly by her own family. He was reading a book that Baron Fitzwilliam had sent him a few months ago. It was about the Royal Houses of Merceria. He had been such a fool not to have reasoned out Anna's identity. Obviously, Fitz knew, so why hadn't he seen it for himself. He let out a sigh and turned the page. The illuminated book contained a drawing of King Andred, the current ruler, and, he had to remind himself, Anna's father. Holy Brothers had carefully made the hand-crafted book in Wincaster and, unlike most books, Fitz had paid the brothers to illustrate it.

The ink drawing of Andred was remarkable, showing off the man's black hair and short, cropped beard, just as Gerald remembered it. He examined the picture carefully, trying to see a resemblance to Anna, but he just couldn't. The blonde-haired girl looked nothing like him.

He held his breath for a moment when he realized what he had just discovered. He skimmed back through the book, finding the king's ancestors. All of them were dark haired and dark eyed. He remembered when Queen Elenor had visited in the autumn. She also had darker hair, and he was told, brown eyes. He shook his head and looked again in the book, suddenly grasping what was before him.

As it dawned on him, everything fell into place. The isolated location, the rare visits from the queen, even the fact that the king and queen were seldom seen together. It was undeniable now, Anna was the daughter of the queen, but King Andred was not the father. Now he understood why she was shunned. The king wanted nothing to do with her, never even publicly acknowledging that she existed. The poor girl was a nobody. Worse than a nobody. Not only was she denied her position in life, but she was also actively shunned, hidden away like a mad dog.

The very thought of it disturbed him deeply. He liked Anna, was beginning to think of her as a daughter. He was furious that she was treated in such a callous manner. He resolved to give her a life, to allow her to experience things like a regular child.

Hearing a knock at the door, Gerald smiled. He recognized Anna's light tapping instantly. He wandered over to the door and opened it, peering out into the snow. He ignored her presence and looked directly over her head as if she wasn't there.

"That's funny, I thought I heard a knock on the door."

Tempus barked, and Anna said, "It's me, Gerald, down here." She waived a mittened hand in front of his face.

"Well, bless my soul," he declared with an exaggerated expression. "So it is. Come in, come in. Warm yourself up by the fire."

She stepped inside the cottage, careful to bang the snow from her boots. She was carrying something behind her back. She carefully removed her coat, hat and mittens, hanging them on a hook by the door. She waited until she thought he wasn't watching to return the item behind her back. She waited for him to look at her after closing the door.

He decided to let her enjoy her fun. He looked at her and asked, "Anna, is something wrong?"

"No, Gerald, I brought you something," she said, producing a cloth-bound gift that was several feet in length.

"Is this for me?" he asked. "What's the occasion?"

"It's close to midwinter," she stated. "It used to be tradition to give gifts to family members at midwinter, and since I don't have a family, or at least a family that cares, I thought I would give you a gift."

Gerald was touched. She handed him the wrapped item. It felt like it was made of wood and was not too heavy.

"Let's go to the fire to unwrap it, shall we? Why don't you go over to the apple cider and grab yourself a cup, and don't forget Tempus, too?"

The dog had become a regular visitor, and now there was always a bowl on the floor for him. Anna poured herself some cider and then poured some into the bowl for Tempus. Gerald sat on his chair in front of the fire and examined the wrapped gift. It was tied with ribbon, and he could see where her small hands had struggled to tie the knots. He waited until she was seated, then he began to unwrap it with great deliberation.

Inside, was a beautiful oak walking stick. It was highly polished but worn. It was capped with metal at its tip and the handle, likewise, had a solid metal knob.

"This is wonderful, Anna. Where did you find it?"

She smiled, "I found it searching around the Hall. It must have been there for years just waiting for you. I know you have the brace, but I see your leg still bothers you sometimes, so I thought this would help."

Gerald was deeply moved. "Thank you, Anna. This is very kind of you."

For the first time, in a very long time, he felt genuinely thankful. He felt valued as a friend. It was almost like having a family again. He rose and gave her a hug. She clung to him, and he realized how truly ignored this poor girl was. Anna released him and sat on the floor beside Tempus. Every evening after dinner, she would come over to the cottage to be tutored in reading. She had made remarkable progress and was a very quick learner. Gerald sat in thought, mulling over an idea.

"You should try it!" she said.

"Yes, let's give it a try," he agreed enthusiastically, standing up. He held the stick in his right hand and walked up and down the room. The curve of the knob fit his hand perfectly, and the cane was just the right height. He knew this would help immensely.

"Look at that!" He was exaggerating his enjoyment just a little. "A perfect fit! An excellent gift, why, along with the brace you'd never know I had a bad leg."

Gerald returned to his seat. Anna was sipping her cider and absently leaning against Tempus. He was big enough that it was like he was a sofa. Her dog warmed her back with her front heated by the fire.

"I thought," he said, after a moment's hesitation, "that tonight we might try something a little different."

Anna perked up. "A new book?" she said, eagerness in her eyes.

"No, I thought we might do something a little different from reading a book."

"What?" she asked hurriedly. "What are we going to do?"

He paused for dramatic effect before speaking, "I thought we might build a snowman!"

"A snowman?" she asked. "What's that?"

"It's a man, made of snow. You roll up the snow into balls and..." he saw that she was not comprehending. "Come, get your coat on and I'll show you. We used to make them all the time up in Bodden."

They both suited up for the cold, and soon the enthusiasm had spread to Tempus.

"We'll need some sticks for arms and some stones for his eyes and nose."

Anna had no idea what they were going to do, but she was fascinated. They trundled outside, and Gerald made sure to grab his new cane. Moments later, they were rolling snow into big balls to build the snowman. Anna had never played in the snow, never being allowed out in the winter. She now found the cold exhilarating. They rolled up the bottom of the body, then made smaller balls of snow for the upper body and head. Gerald had to lift the body and head up as it was too heavy for Anna. He pointed to some sticks lying at the edge of the trees and asked Anna to go and get them.

She wandered over to the sticks and selected two of them. As she turned to come back, Gerald threw a snowball at her, startling her.

"What was that?" she asked, looking questioningly at him.

"A snowball. Haven't you ever made a snowball before?"

"No, how do you make one?"

Gerald smiled, "Come here, and I'll teach you."

He showed her how to pack the snow together using his hands, and they threw some into the woods. Tempus thought this was great fun and tried to catch them. They ended up tossing them for him until their hands were almost frozen. They didn't finish the snowman, but they were laughing when they returned to the cottage to warm up.

"That is the bestest present ever," said Anna.

Gerald smiled at the wording. Now was not the time to correct her grammar.

"You mean the snowman?" he asked.

"No, the snowballs! I've never seen Tempus so lively!"

They both laughed. Anna smiled at Gerald and leaned forward conspiratorially. "I have an idea."

Gerald leaned forward, acting as a co-conspirator. They were both having far too much fun.

"What?" he asked.

She almost whispered, "I saw Cook making some mince pies earlier today. I say we do a kitchen raid and snarf some."

"All right, I'm in, but we have to plan this carefully."

He went over to his bookshelf and withdrew a bound volume. He took it to the table and opened it, beckoning her over as he did so. Anna moved to the table. The book was simply bound paper. Gerald had used it on occasion to make some notes. He had tried to sketch flowers and herbs, but he didn't fancy himself much of an artist. He turned the book to a fresh page and took out some charcoal.

"Now," he began, "the kitchen is located at the back of the Hall."

As he spoke he sketched out the floor plan. Hours later, they were still at it, making plans and corrections to his sketches. It would be a proper operation that was never carried out. He realized this when he looked over to see she had fallen asleep at the table. He bundled her up and took her back to the Hall for the servants to tuck her in. The great kitchen raid would surface again in the coming months, but they never did quite manage to pull it off.

The bitterness and cold of winter had turned milder and finally warmed into spring, then spring naturally turned to summer, and Gerald could not remember nicer weather. It was on a warm day in the middle of the summer that they decided to walk the estate. Remembering the adventure last year of the angelroot, he made sure to wear waterproof boots. He had a backpack which he had used for years in the army. Now, it held food and some extra water. He had packed some sausages, and Cook had generously packed some tasty meat pies for the expedition. Anna was straightening her pack while Tempus sat and watched.

They had planned the trip for weeks. A circumnavigation of the estate would take most of the day. They had spent three evenings poring over maps of the grounds to pick the perfect route. Anna was very good at reading maps once Gerald explained them to her. She had a sharp mind, with a knack for noticing trivial details. They had thought about checking the old well for water, but in the end, they decided it would be too much work, as it was still boarded up. They settled for taking their water with them. Anna had managed to sneak some pastries away from Cook, as she often did. Gerald had concluded that Cook kept these out on purpose for her to take, but he didn't want to spoil her fun. Even Tempus was ready to go. In the spring, they had travelled to Uxley Village and paid Sam to make a simpler harness for Tempus. He could still pull the cart, this had proved itself useful many times over with the spring planting, but his new harness was simpler and let him carry a couple of saddlebags.

They had decided that they should look for herbs while they were walking the estate. Anna had produced an ancient book from the library. In it, were sketches and notes on different types of herbs. Gerald knew some of them, albeit with different names, but the book had been fascinating to both of them. They had pored over it for almost two weeks, searching around the immediate vicinity for some of the more common types. They had decided against taking it with them for it was far too valuable a book to risk damaging, but Gerald had written down descriptions of some of the plants. Anna's handwriting was getting better, but she was meticulous and slow when it came to her writing.

They left the cottage just as the sun was coming up. They would start by heading east, towards the furthest extent of the estate. The entire property had a fence around it in theory. In some places, it was a stone wall, principally near the Hall, while at other locations it was a simple wooden fence, meant only to mark the edge of the grounds. There were numerous places where there was no fence at all. This allowed a generous amount of wildlife to enter the estate grounds.

Gerald had become accustomed to his brace and cane, and he could now walk the grounds, confident in his ability to keep up. They cut across a field, the early morning mist still clinging to the ground. They heard Tempus bounding ahead of them, occasionally chasing after a rabbit or a squirrel, but he never strayed far. He had little chance of catching the creatures, for in his saddlebags was his metal bowl and some metal plates that Anna had taken from the Hall. They banged together noisily when he ran, scattering the wildlife in multiple directions ahead of him.

If one were to draw a map of the estate, the Hall would be in the southwest corner, so when they reached the eastern extent, they turned north, following the wooden fence that marked the borders.

They kept up a steady pace, but Gerald made sure they took breaks to drink some water. This included Tempus, who would amble over when he was called. It was almost noon by the time they decided to stop for lunch. They were near the northeast corner of the estate, as far as they could reckon. The rise here had a good view of the area, so they made their way up the hill, its top surmounted by an open field. They unpacked a blanket from one of Tempus' saddlebags and laid it on the ground, then proceeded to bring out lunch. The view from here was spectacular! The Hall was visible off in the distance, a small white mark on a green background. They became aware that the maps they had been using were either very out of date, or very inaccurate, but that was part of the fun. They felt like they were on a voyage of discovery.

Sitting on the blanket having just eaten their meat pies, Anna opened the small pot and withdrew two pastries, passing one carefully to Gerald. Tempus lay nearby, as usual acting as the back of Anna's chair. Gerald looked over at Tempus, he was such devoted dog. It was remarkable how much the two of them got along.

"Anna?" he asked, interrupting her careful deconstruction of the pastry. She had a knack for pulling them apart as she devoured them. "How did you and Tempus meet? You've never told me."

She finished off the pastry, carefully licking each finger clean

"I came to the estate when I was really young," she started, "but I don't really remember that. I remember not knowing him. I think I was three, at least that's what Hanson says. I remember some sort of nightmare. There were men with skeleton faces. They broke into my room and tried to kill me. Then I remember hiding under the blankets and screaming. Tempus charged in and killed them. He saved my life. Ripped their throats out. Mrs Henderson, my old nanny, was furious at the mess, blood was everywhere. She said that Tempus was dangerous, and should be put down, but I said no, he had saved my life. Hanson agreed, and after that, he would sleep in my room. He's actually supposed to sleep on the floor, but after the servants leave, I invite him onto the bed." She grinned as she talked. "He's always been there for me, and for a long time, he was my only friend. Until you came along, that is. The other servants were always too scared to be my friend. That's why when I met you I didn't tell you who I was. I was afraid you would be scared of me."

"He really is your best friend," Gerald marvelled, "and he loves that bone you brought for him."

She turned slightly to pet him, and Tempus moved his massive head towards her, temporarily forgetting his bone. The adoration was evident for all to see, from both of them.

"So where did he come from. Dogs like Tempus don't grow on trees?" he asked.

"I'm not really sure. I looked for his type in the library once. I think he's a Mastiff. A Kurathian Mastiff. Does that sound right?"

Gerald recognized the breed, though he had never seen one before Tempus.

"Interesting," he mused. "Kurathian Mastiffs are trained as warrior dogs. They specialize in bringing down horses. They say they can bring down a full warhorse, even armoured, but I've never heard of one in Merceria before."

"I don't know how he came to be in Merceria, but the king likes to fight dogs. Tempus made him quite a lot of coins in the pits and so, when he got older, he was honourably retired."

"Funny," said Gerald, "I would think that he would retire him in Wincaster if he were fond of him. Isn't that where the king usually lives?"

"Yes," said Anna, "but the king likes his mistress better, and she hates dogs."

You could see the bitterness in her face when she spoke of the king's mistress.

"But he's mine now, aren't you Tempus!" she said, burying her head into his neck.

Gerald mulled over the conversation. There was no doubt in his mind that Tempus was capable of killing a man. He was exceedingly gentle with Anna, but he could imagine him becoming vicious in a fight. He liked Tempus, and Tempus liked him, but most of the rest of the staff found the ugly brute distasteful. Their words, he could tell, upset Anna, but Gerald didn't see an ugly brute, he saw a veteran of fights who pledged his life to protect the princess. There were knights, he thought, that would do well to emulate him. The staff would have been horrified at the carnage he had inflicted, he had no doubt. War, for Gerald, had always been a fight to the death. You don't play games in war, he had learned, you do what you need to do to survive. Perhaps he saw a simpler version of himself in the great dog.

A thought flicked through his mind and brought him out of his musings. "Did you say earlier that the men had skeleton faces?"

"Well, not real skeleton heads. They had hoods covering their faces with skeleton faces painted on them. We saw that after they'd been killed. Hanson pulled the mask off one of them. They were just men underneath."

Gerald told himself he must look into this for something bothered him about the whole affair. He believed Anna's story, but couldn't figure out why someone would want to kill a small child, or why they would wear such strange garments. He was musing on just this topic when Anna drew his attention to the sky. Clouds were beginning to roll in and threatened rain. They packed up what was left of their lunch, resolving to return to their base camp, their name for the Hall. Their operation had been carried out successfully for the most part, and they decided that the rest of the estate could wait.

They cut across the estate diagonally, making their way back scarcely in time to avoid the storm. It was just starting to spit as they entered the Hall. They left their packs and boots in the entrance hall, and Anna asked if he wanted to see her library. She was obviously very proud of this, so he agreed.

He had not spent much time in the Hall, its size was overwhelming to him. She led him into the main hallway, then up the grand staircase. They turned to the left, continuing on to the north wing near her room. The building itself faced west, with the north wing to the left as one was looking at the front of Uxley Hall. Anna had a bedroom and a playroom, but very close nearby was her pride and joy, a children's library.

It was chocked full of books, though one could hardly call them children's books. She had, she told him, taken most of these books from the king's library, over in the south wing. He never visited, so she figured it was safe to do so. She had books of all types. Many were history books, but she also had books about animals, plants, even books about Elves, Dwarves and other races. She had not read them all, she said, but she was working on it.

The size of her library overawed Gerald. This single room was larger than his cottage, and yet it was filled with books. Anna pulled out some of her favourites and began showing him. It was like these books were her friends. She positively lit up when she talked about each one. Her exuberance enthralled him, but soon, the long walk and warm air began to take its toll, and he nodded off. He was shaken awake by a concerned servant. Anna had become worried and had called out for help. Now, a distressed Ned was leaning over him, offering a glass of water.

They got him to his feet and escorted him back to his cottage. He was tired. Anna carried his cane and saw him tucked into bed still wearing his clothes. He fell asleep as she read him one of her favourite stories.

FOURTEEN

The Tutor

AUTUMN 956 MC

A nna had just turned nine and winter was fast approaching. This autumn was colder than most, with a wind that seemed determined to penetrate Gerald's coat. Once again, he was cleaning up the estate. There had been a brisk wind overnight, and branches were scattered everywhere. He was working on the line of trees at the entrance road when he became aware of someone watching him. He stopped what he was doing and turned to face a well-dressed man, of medium build, with neatly trimmed hair. The man was beardless but had thick sideburns, which he kept cut to perfection. His clothes were of good quality, but not so well made as to identify the man as a noble. He had the look of a well-to-do middle-class merchant, perhaps, or more likely, a scholar. Gerald had taken in the man's visage for only a moment when the visitor spoke.

"You there," the man demanded, "do you work here?"

It seemed like a stupid thing to say. Did the man suppose that Gerald just decided to visit and clean up the yard? Of course, he worked here! Instead of the retort the man deserved, he just sighed and replied politely.

"Yes, the name's Gerald Matheson. I'm the groundskeeper. Is there something I can help you with?"

The man's look of disdain was apparent as he spoke, "I am here to see a Mr Hanson, whom I believe is in charge. You will take me to him at once."

Gerald instantly took a dislike to the man, but Lord Fitzwilliam had told him once that all people should be treated equally until they reveal their stupidity. He was sure it wouldn't take long for this man to carry out the task.

"Certainly. And who might I say is here?" Gerald enquired.

"William Renfrew," the man responded as if he should recognize the name.

"If you'll come this way, Mr Renfrew, I'll take you to see the steward."

He dropped the sticks and began walking towards the Hall as fast as his bad leg would let him. As a sergeant, he had to deal with people with superior attitudes quite often. Usually, they were knights, but anyone with coins could turn into a person with an overblown feeling of their self-importance. He set a brisk pace, confident that the man would be hurrying after him. He felt satisfaction knowing that the visitor would be sweating by the time they arrived.

He led Mr Renfrew through the great hall, then turned to the north, leading him through the servant's wing until he arrived outside of Hanson's office, officially the clerk's room. He summoned up his best sergeant's behaviour and rapped on the door, waiting for the thin voice of Hanson to bid him to enter. He opened the door and stepped into the doorway, stopping to block the visitor.

"I have a Mr Renfrew here, sir. Shall I bring him in?"

Hanson sat, stooped over a large ledger filled with writing, his hands stained with ink, discarded quills littering the table. Gerald had seen books like this before, they were the ledgers for the estate. When he was in the army, he had to track every expenditure and see to the payment of the troops. Baron Fitzwilliam would regularly inspect the books, but he was pretty sure that no one had ever needed to check the meticulous work of Mr Hanson.

Hanson looked up from his ledger. He sighed and put the quill down on a blotter, closing the book and clasping his hands together in front of him.

"Bring him in, bring him in."

As Gerald stepped aside to allow the newcomer entrance, Hanson added, "Do stay, Gerald, I would have a word with you afterwards. Now, what can I do for you, Mister..."

"Renfrew, William Renfrew."

Once again, the man waited expectantly, as if his name would invoke some measure of respect. Hanson looked him up and down. The old man's eyesight wasn't what it used to be, but he could still manage a harsh look if he was unnecessarily interrupted.

"And to what do I owe the pleasure of this visit, Mister Renfrew?"

The look of surprise was evident on Renfrew's face.

"I've come from Wincaster," he said as if that explained everything. He waited for a moment, and when it was evident that Hanson still did not understand, he continued, "I am the new tutor to the princess. I am here to teach her how to read and write, as well as etiquette and proper behaviour."

Gerald felt offended and spoke out of turn, "The princess already knows how to read and write!"

"Really," said Renfrew, sounding offended, "and who, may I ask, carried out this task?"

"I taught her myself!" Gerald responded, perhaps a little more vehemently than he intended.

"Impossible!" the tutor replied. "We cannot have a princess of the realm instructed by a country bumpkin! I must teach her the proper ways of royalty. I am horrified at the thought."

Gerald could almost feel the man sneer in contempt. He was about to offer a retort but bit his tongue, it would do no good to antagonize him. He was here to tutor Anna, Gerald must get used to him.

"I have here a letter of introduction from the Royal Palace in Wincaster," Renfrew said, producing a folded letter with the Royal Seal holding it closed. He passed this across to Hanson, handling it as though it was made of crystal, and he was worried about breaking it.

Hanson gingerly accepted the paper, closely examining the seal. He reached into his desk drawer and withdrew a small knife, which he used to remove the wax. He carefully unfolded the paper to read its contents. The room remained silent as Hanson read. His eyes reached the end of the document, and then he appeared to study it some more. He looked back up at Mister Renfrew, locking eyes with him.

"Your letter of introduction is well received, Mister Renfrew, but says little of your purpose here. It only references that you are here to provide your services. Would you care to elaborate?"

Renfrew seemed to warm to the challenge, becoming more animated as he spoke, "I am here to train the princess in the ways of the court, sir. How to behave in civilized society, and make sure she will make a suitable bride one day."

"And how, precisely, do you expect to do that?" Hanson said.

"I aim," the visitor continued, gaining confidence, "to start with the basics. I shall ensure that she has a proper understanding of the elements of conversation and reading. I must test her comprehension, and increase her vocabulary to a state that is suitable for a royal."

"I see," Hanson stared down at the letter which was still in his grasp, "and when would you expect to start?"

"Immediately," the man announced, almost too quickly. "It is imperative that I begin as soon as possible. You must take me to the princess so that I can start assessing her!"

Hanson stared at him. Gerald could tell he was not happy with this. It would mean another name on the payroll, and Hanson already spent much of his days balancing the books.

Hanson finally broke the uncomfortable silence,"If you would be so kind as to wait outside Mister Renfrew, I just need to speak to Mister Matheson for a moment."

Renfrew appeared pleased with himself. "Of course, sir, I shall await your pleasure in the hallway."

He turned and exited the room, closing the door behind him. Gerald noticed that the man had more of a spring in his step and no wonder, he had just gotten the upper hand. Hanson indicated with his hand that Gerald should have a seat. This would be an informal meeting then, thought the groundskeeper.

"Gerald," the old man opened with, "I understand you and Anna get along very well," he raised his hand to still Gerald's objections, "and I don't have a problem with that. I know that the rules say we are not to get attached to the princess, but you and I both know that's not in her best interest. I have purposely not told Wincaster about your relationship with the girl, and yes, before you ask, I have to send in monthly reports. Don't worry, I won't breathe a word of it, but I want you to do me a favour."

Gerald tensed, was he being threatened, or was this simply the old man's request for help?

"I would like you to introduce Mister Renfrew to Anna. I think it would soften the blow coming from you."

Gerald was going to object but saw the reasoning. He nodded in agreement.

"You may not like this…," Hanson gazed down at the paper again, "tutor, but he is here at the behest of the king, or at least someone at the Palace. Take him up to the library, and I'll have Sophie ask Anna to meet you there. Perhaps it will give Mister Renfrew some time to wipe the smug look off his face."

"Of course, Alistair, I'll do all I can to help."

He shook Hanson's hand and opened the door to the hallway. Renfrew was standing outside, leaning against the far wall. He looked startled when the door opened and quickly straightened up.

"Please come with me, Mister Renfrew, I will take you to the library. The princess will join us there shortly."

He led the tutor back to the great hall, taking a shortcut to pass through the dining room. They made their way up the grand staircase and then to the children's library. The shelves were stocked full of books, and Renfrew began to peruse the titles while they waited. Gerald was quite familiar with the library and yet was still impressed by it. Renfrew had other ideas, however.

He looked over the titles, muttering, "Oh, my, this will never do," and, "this will have to go."

The door opened, and Anna entered the room.

"Your Highness," said Gerald bowing.

Anna almost giggled when she saw his serious face, then she remembered that someone else was present.

"And who do we have here?" she asked, trying to sound as imperious as she could.

Renfrew turned to look at her, "William Renfrew, at your service, Highness." He bowed deeply. "I am here as your new tutor. I am instructed to teach you the skills of reading, writing and etiquette."

Anna looked genuinely surprised. "I already know how to read and write, Mister Renfrew. I-"

"With all due respect highness," Renfrew interrupted, "that is for me to decide. It is important for a member of the Royal Family to learn how to behave. A royal is expected to be aloof, separate from the common man."

Gerald could hold his tongue no more.

"Horse shit!" he said. "A royal needs to learn how to lead, not be stuck up."

Anna suppressed a laugh. Gerald could feel his face turning red.

"With your permission, Your Highness," he said with exaggerated politeness, "I shall retire from the room. I am afraid I may have upset your delicate nature."

Anna appeared to like the game.

"Very well," she said, "you may return to your duties."

As Gerald moved past her, she whispered, "I'll tell you all about it later."

It was dinner time before he saw her again. He had just sat down at the dinner table. Hanson, as usual, was at the head of the table, and the other servants sat around in no particular order. As was customary, the seat at the opposite end of the table was left for Anna if she chose to use it. He could tell as soon as she entered that she was not happy. Her lips were pressed tightly together, and her brow knitted in frustration. She sat down at the end of the table, a vacant stare in her eyes, not saying anything. Everyone looked around at each other and then at Gerald. They all knew that he was close to Anna. They wanted him to see what was bothering her. He finally gave in and asked the question everyone wanted him to ask.

"How was your day today, Anna?"

"Terrible!" she spat out as if she was tasting venom. "Renfrew treated me like an idiot. Had me reciting the alphabet and spelling words like dog and cat. I swear the man is an imbecile!"

Nobody wanted to meet her gaze, they had never seen her this angry before.

"And then he had me walk around with a book on my head. Told me it improved my posture." She turned to face Gerald directly. "You have to help me, Gerald, I can't stand it!"

"I'm not sure there's much I can do, Anna. He's here on orders from the Palace. I'm just a groundskeeper, and I can't tell him his job. Besides, if I spend more than a few moments with him, I'm likely to punch him, and then where would we be?"

The last statement, at least, made her smile.

"Give it a few days," he continued, "perhaps he'll mellow a bit. He's trying to do what he thinks is necessary to make you into a princess."

"But I don't want to be a princess, I just want to be me. I was having fun before he came along."

"Still, you must give him some time. He'll realize soon enough that you can read and write. Besides, you never know when you might have to carry a book on your head, it's a useful skill," he said, smiling at her, and sure enough, she returned the smile.

"All right, I'll give it a try, but I'm not too happy about it."

At this exact time, Cook came in with the main serving, a generous plate of Mercerian pudding with thick cuts of meat and a heavy gravy. Her eyes went large. Gerald knew this was one of her preferred meals. He looked over at Cook, and she winked back. Mrs Brown always knew when to cook Anna's favourite. With the meal brought in, everyone tucked in. The table was generally like a free for all, with hands reaching across each other to snag the best slices of meat. Hanson took charge, making sure to serve Anna first. She dug into her meal with gusto, soon forgetting the events of the day. Gerald had come to like these meals. When he first arrived, the staff had been distant, more guarded, but the shared experience of being at Uxley Hall had created a bond between them, and to Gerald, they had become a family. In some cases, a mildly dysfunctional family, but a family nonetheless.

As they were all finishing up the last of their plates, Anna spoke up, "Gerald, are you making a bonfire tonight?"

"I suppose I could, I've got lots of loose branches ready to burn. Why?"

"I thought maybe we could all go and have a sing-along. Mr Turner can play the fiddle, and Sophie is a really good singer. We could all have a campfire sing along. You can teach us some songs," she said with a hopeful tone.

She leaned slightly forward, placing her elbows on the table and trying to look cute, but only partially succeeding.

Gerald laughed, "All right, a campfire sing-along it is, but I have to warn you the only songs I know are of a more mature nature." This elicited laughter from the table. Looking around at the staff, he was aware that there would be lots of work to clean up from dinner. "Let's all help Mrs Brown clean up, and then maybe she'll bring along some desserts."

Mrs Brown looked very pleased. It was well known that she always had pastries available as they were big favourites with Anna. The table erupted in a flurry of activity. Events of this nature did not occur very often, and soon all the dishes were cleared away. As the staff had engaged in this whirlwind of clearing, Gerald noticed that Hanson appeared a little pale. He walked over to the old man and placed a hand on his shoulder.

"Are you well, Alistair? You look a little pale."

The old man looked up at Gerald with appreciation in his eyes. "Just getting old, Gerald. I'm afraid I shall have to pass on the singing tonight. Perhaps another time?"

"Of course, you're welcome anytime. Do you want some help getting to your room?"

"No, no," Hanson shook his head, "I can make it there fine by myself. You run along with the rest and have some fun." He looked across at Anna who was waiting patiently. "The princess looks like she could use some."

The old man rose from the table and headed off to an early bed. Gerald heard a commotion in the kitchen, and he and Anna wandered in to see an astounded Cook watching the other servants, even the stable boys, washing up the dishes and plates. They had made her sit down and were singing a bawdy song while they worked. The song was about a minstrel who seduced women, and each verse told of a wench he targeted. Every time they got to the end of the verse, Charles would pinch one of the maids, resulting in a shriek of laughter.

Soon, the kitchen was squared away, and the troupe wandered outside, heading towards the cottage. Gerald had gathered sticks and brambles earlier in the day, and it only took a moment to start the fire. The yellow flames soon licked their way through the pile, the bonfire growing in intensity quickly. As the flames leaped higher, Jim Turner produced his fiddle and was started sawing away at a jaunty pace. The maids commenced dancing around, enticing the men to join in. Even Cook got into the spirit.

Anna was laughing hysterically as Mrs Brown, led by Owen Bellamy, was strutted around the fire.

Gerald had seen plenty of bonfires in his time, but this was magical. Never could he remember people just enjoying themselves so much, not worrying about what the next day might bring. It warmed his heart to be in such company, and he could see Anna taking it all in, watching every face and beaming with pride. These were her people, her family, and she fit right in.

The party lasted well into the night. Gerald ended up carrying Anna back to the Hall, as he had on multiple occasions. He had told her numerous times that she needed to go to bed, but she didn't want to miss all the excitement. With the help of Sophie, he carried her to her room, laying her on her bed. Sophie pulled the blankets over her, making sure she was comfortable. They didn't worry about changing her for fear she would wake up.

"Let her sleep," Sophie had insisted. "It won't hurt her to wear her clothes to bed. It's not like she hasn't done it before."

They waited until Tempus had made himself comfortable on the bed by her feet, then tiptoed out of the room. Sophie carried the candlestick that lit their way, with Gerald following just behind her. The young girl stopped suddenly causing Gerald to lightly bump into her. He had been looking back into Anna's room and now turned to see what the problem was. Standing in the hallway, his hands on his hips, was Renfrew. He had a stern look on his face, and his fury erupted on Sophie.

"What is the meaning of this!" he said in a loud voice, not quite yelling, but intimidating her all the same. "How dare you treat the princess like this!"

In all likelihood, he had not seen Gerald behind Sophie, for Renfrew raised his hand to slap the young maid across the face. The girl visibly flinched as the hand came crashing towards her, stopped at the last moment in Gerald's firm grip. Gerald stared at the man and grinned. In the flickering candlelight, the groundskeeper must have looked terrifying with his full beard and unkempt hair.

"Give me a reason, Renfrew," he threatened, "and you'll know what it's like to be slapped."

Even in the dim light, he saw Renfrew pale. The man turned and ran down the hallway, not saying a word. Gerald looked at the young maid. "It's all right Sophie, you're not in any trouble. You can head off to bed."

She curtsied slightly and ran off back to her room before the wicked Mister Renfrew could harass her again. Gerald stood for a moment thinking, he had probably just made a big mistake and hoped Anna would not pay the price.

The next morning Gerald was up early. One of the ditches at the back of the Hall had become clogged up with leaves, and he needed to free the flow of water for drainage. It took most of the day to clean up the mess; the wet soggy leaves proved tenacious in their ability to cling together, refusing the efforts of his rake. So busy was he that he didn't even break for lunch, only completing his arduous task when he heard the dinner bell ringing. He had been so consumed with his task that he hadn't noticed the time of day.

He made his way, exhausted but pleased with his efforts, to the servant's dining hall. He was careful to remove his boots, which were caked in mud and water-logged leaves, leaving them in the rear entryway. Arriving at the dining hall, he found most of the staff already in place. He sat down and smiled at Cook as she put hot soup in front of him, its aroma drifting up to pleasantly tickle his nose and tease his stomach which suddenly decided it was hungry. Everyone else had already started their meal, so he dug in. It was after he had eaten a few spoonfuls that he realized that Anna was missing.

"Is Anna not joining us tonight?" he asked Hanson.

Mrs Brown let out a small sob and rose from her chair, quickly exiting to the kitchen.

Hanson looked at Gerald with a sad face. "I'm afraid the princess will no longer be joining us for dinner, Gerald. She will be eating in the formal dining hall, as befits one of her station."

"Let me guess," Gerald frowned, "this was Renfrew's decision."

Hanson nodded, too upset to speak. The whole mood of the table was down, standing in stark contrast to the enjoyment of yesterday. Gerald put his spoon down and made to rise, but Hanson, who was sitting right beside him, placed his hand on his forearm and spoke.

"Don't, Gerald, you'll only make it worse for Anna."

Gerald was shocked and saddened but heeded the old man's advice.

"Anything else I should be aware of?" he asked.

It was Sophie who spoke up, "She must wear a proper dress from now on, and is not allowed to go outside."

"What about Tempus?" Gerald asked.

"He's not allowed in the room with her during the day," Sophie added.

"Poor girl," added Hanson, "she must be lost without him."

"This is ridiculous!" fumed Gerald. "There must be something we can do."

He looked around, but everyone either shook their heads or looked away in shame. There had to be something that Gerald could do, but he was at a loss as to what that would be. He managed to finish his dinner but didn't taste any of it. He made his way back to the cottage and found himself restless. If the truth be told, he had become so used to Anna's visits that now that she wasn't there, he felt lonely. He had only had a few close friends during his life and even fewer that were still alive. He decided to read a book, to take his mind off of things, but every time he opened a book, he remembered how he had used it to teach Anna how to read. He had accepted his loneliness before, but now that he had experienced friendship again, he felt its loss ever more keenly.

It was late when there was a knock. Gerald's heart leaped a little with hope as he made his way to the door, but he was disappointed when he opened it to reveal young Sophie's face.

She almost whispered as she spoke, "Gerald, you must come with me. Anna wants to see you, but we have to be quiet. She'll meet us in the trophy room."

Gerald had no clue where the trophy room was, but he put on his boots and coat and followed.

The south wing of Uxley Hall had a sun room, a large room with many glass windows. It was added more than 150 years ago by the Lady of the Hall. It had seen little use since but provided a second entrance to the rear of the Hall. It was to here that Sophie brought him. They entered the room, and Gerald noticed furniture covered in sheets. The large glass windows, which must have cost a fortune, were thick with dust and the room had not seen a cleaning for many years. The door they entered through was on the south side of the sun room, for the room itself jutted out from the bulk of the house, evidently added long after the original construction. Along the same wall, but inside the central portion of the Hall, was another door which Sophie indicated with her hand.

"Go through there," she said, pointing to the door. "It leads to the old mud room, across from that you'll find the trophy room."

He nodded his thanks and made his way through the door. The mudroom must have, at one time, been a rear entrance. It was sparse of furniture and reminded him of the entry to the servant's quarters, except the bench was of finer quality, and there were some paintings on the wall. He stopped to check his boots, but they were long since dry and free of leaves. He opened the door at the other end of the room and entered the trophy room. As he stepped in, he felt a chill pass over him. Eyes stared down at him from heads mounted on the wall. He could see a bear, elk, even a boar head, all staring down at him with their lifeless eyes.

Gerald had never been impressed with hunting trophies. Perhaps he had learned this from Baron Fitzwilliam, for the baron had no problem with hunting for food, but had little patience for trophies. Gerald remembered an occasion where one of the knights, Sir Michael, had bagged himself a stag of which the knight was quite proud. He brought just the head back to boast of his prowess, and the baron saw him enter the Keep. Lord Fitzwilliam was furious. He had scolded the man for the kill. It had no purpose, he said, he had not even brought back the meat. He made the knight bury the stag while the other knights watched. Gerald had asked him about it later, and the baron had revealed his belief that all things must live in balance. If they fall out of balance, he had said, nature will find a way to redress it. The words had stuck with Gerald throughout his career, and so now he looked on the trophies, not as objects of wonder, but of disgust.

He was reminiscing about this very thought when he heard the click of a door handle. He turned to see Anna entering. She was in her nightshirt and robe, and when she saw Gerald, she ran over and hugged him. Even Tempus seemed to smile, though thankfully he didn't bark or else the whole Hall would have been awoken. She hugged him for a few moments then finally let go, a big smile on her face.

"I'm so glad you came, Gerald. I was worried you wouldn't show up."

Gerald returned the smile and patted Tempus on the head. The great dog sat down on the rug, and Anna crouched down beside him, absently rubbing his back.

"It's terrible!" she announced with gusto. "The man's a tyran, tran, no tian…"

"Tyrant?" Gerald offered.

"Yes, a tyrant," she confirmed. "He won't even let me out of the house, and poor Tempus is stuck all by himself."

"I'm afraid there's little I can do, Anna, and I hate to say it, but it may be all my fault. I had an altercation with him when he tried to slap Sophie, and now he's taking it out on me, through you." He was crestfallen that he had caused this sad situation.

Anna looked at him with wisdom that seemed to transcend her young age. She placed a hand on his forearm and looked up at him. "It's all right, Gerald. It's not your fault. He's the one that's being the… what's the word I'm looking for?"

"Horse's ass?" he offered.

She giggled out loud and then quickly covered her mouth to keep quiet. Even so, a small chortle escaped.

"Yes, definitely that. I think Renfrew's face looks like a horse too. Maybe I should call him horse face."

"No, Anna, that will only make things worse. What time do your lessons finish?" he asked.

"Not till dinner time, and then he sits in the king's library and makes me read after I've had my meal. He makes me sit in the formal dining room, all by myself, and have the servants bring in the food. Just for me! It's so unfair! He tried to get Tempus to leave while I was eating, but Tempus wouldn't have any of it, would you boy," she scratched Tempus under the chin as she said this.

"I can't think of any way to rectify the situation, Anna, but I'll continue to think about it. In the meantime, do you think you can sneak back here? I'll come here each evening about this time. Renfrew must be in his room by now. At least we can talk, and you can share your day with me. I'll try to bring you some treats from Cook tomorrow."

"All right," she agreed, "but can you take Tempus during the day? He doesn't like to be alone, and at least I'll know you're taking care of him. You can bring him back into the Hall at dinner time. He'll know where to find me. I'll send him to the kitchen in the morning. You can find him there when you go for breakfast."

"All right, I'll do that. Now, I have an idea," he whispered conspiratorially.

Anna leaned in to hear the plan.

"I think we should commence Operation Shadow," he said, knowing that Anna enjoyed making plans. "We need to observe Mister Renfrew and gather as much information about him as we can. Remember, a good commander must survey the enemy before he attacks."

"Aye, General," Anna responded with a mock salute. "Operation Shadow is underway!"

FIFTEEN

Lord Brandon

AUTUMN 956 MC

Lord Robert Brandon, Baron of Hawksburg, was an educated man. There were some who thought him among the most intelligent in the kingdom. It was for this reason that he had found his way onto the Royal Council, and specifically found himself in his current position. His skill at mathematics had proven useful to keeping accounts. For the last three years, his courtly duties were to oversee the expenditures, hires, and contracts pertaining to the eight Royal Estates that were scattered about Merceria. All, in fact, save the Royal Palace itself.

The Royal Estates were each run by skilled individuals who looked after the day to day concerns. It was Lord Robert's responsibility to tally the accounts when they were submitted each month. On this day, one of the first of the new winter, he was examining the books for the Royal Estate in the Glowan Hills, one of the king's favourite places to relax. The books were impeccable, as they always were, and he dutifully transcribed the numbers into the master ledger. It was not the most exciting position, but Lord Brandon prided himself on doing more than just being a noble.

He finished copying the numbers and gave the ink time to dry. Closing the tome, he reached for his glass of wine. He brought the chalice to his nose to smell the aroma, leaning back in his chair to savour it. He was just bringing it to his lips when there was a knock on the door.

"Come in," he invited, and the door opened to reveal one of the Palace runners.

"These messages just came in from Uxley, my lord," the messenger announced as he walked into the room.

The runner was about to place them on the table when Lord Robert spoke up, "Give them directly to me Charles, and I'll look at them right away."

"Yes, my lord," Charles replied, dutifully placing them into the baron's hands. "Can I get you anything, Lord?"

"Yes, thank you, Charles. See if you can rouse me up something from the kitchen would you? I'm feeling a bit peckish."

Charles turned to leave, and the baron added, "On second thought, forget the food, Charles. If I remember rightly, you've got to get home for your daughter's birthday, don't you."

Charles was always surprised by the baron's thoughtfulness. "Yes, my lord, thank you." He left the office, closing the door quietly behind him.

Lord Robert examined the satchel placed in his hands. He opened the flap to see three letters, each sealed with wax. Two were familiar looking, probably the monthly ledgers, the third looked more like a personal letter. He put aside the books to examine the message. The seal looked very ordinary, no coat of arms, hence it could not have been from a noble. He noticed it was not addressed to anyone, so he saw no reason not to open it. He grabbed his slim dagger and sliced the seal off the document, carefully unfolding it.

The letter was written in a hand he did not recognize. Typical correspondence would have been authored in Hanson's sure hand. This writing was far more elaborate. Intrigued, he read further.

18 October 956

My Lord,

I must report that the education of the Princess is proceeding well. So well, in fact, that I have found it necessary to increase the expenditure for books due to the rapid progress that she is making. I trust this will meet with your approval under the circumstances. After all, we cannot deny the best education to a member of the Royal House.

On another note, I must bring to your attention the efforts of one of the staff at Uxley Hall who, I feel, is having an unhealthy influence on Her Highness's progress. This groundskeeper, a most uncouth man by the name of Gerald Mathe-son, opposes me at every turn.

I trust, my lord, that in the interest of the crown, you would consider termi-nating this man's employment at Uxley Hall immediately.

Your faithful servant,
  William Renfrew

Lord Brandon was astounded. In his years of looking after the estates, he had never seen such a request. He reread the letter to see if he had made some mistake. Who was this William Renfrew and who was Gerald Mathe-son? And, perhaps more importantly, what princess was he talking about. He knew Princess Margaret was wintering in Wincaster. Was someone impersonating a royal?

He laid the letter aside and opened the accounts for Uxley Hall. He recognized Hanson's neat hand, though it was getting weaker, for the man was aging. He quickly glanced over the numbers. The expenditures had taken a sharp increase in the last month, and Hanson had noted the arrival of a tutor, with a plea to release more funds due to the added expense.

Lord Robert was perplexed but thought it through. Every staff member of a Royal Estate had to have a letter of personal reference which was stored here, in the Palace. He rose from his chair, making his way over to the bookcase that held all the relevant documents for Uxley Hall. Sifting through them, he easily located the two he was searching for and carried them back to his desk.

Perhaps William Renfrew had a legitimate complaint, but Lord Robert would not condemn a man without a proper investigation. He read over the first document he had retrieved. It was a note of reference for a William Renfrew, a Royal Tutor. It praised the man in no uncertain terms, but the wording bothered Lord Robert. It was ill-written, and the frightful grammar made him wonder who it was that had written such a note. His query was satisfied when he reached the end. It was signed and sealed by none other than Marshal-General Valmar. He found it curious that a general should recommend a tutor. Surely the king or queen should make such a statement? The baron disliked Valmar. The marshal-general had made no secret that he wanted a title, but Robert wouldn't let that sway his decision.

He picked up the second letter and read it. It was a well-written docu-ment extolling the virtues of Gerald Matheson, a valiant soldier who had served his country well. It was signed by Lord Richard Fitzwilliam, Baron of Bodden, and held his seal which Lord Brandon instantly recognized. Lord Richard had married Lord Robert's older sister many years ago leading the two nobles to become good friends.

Lord Robert decided he would talk to Fitz and find out more about this Gerald Matheson, and then he would be able to determine whether or not the man should be dismissed. He placed the letters aside and turned back to work. It was a matter of half an afternoon to transfer Hanson's numbers into the official ledger. By the time he was done, it was late afternoon and, knowing Lord Fitzwilliam was in town, he decided to try to track him down at his favourite haunt, the Queen's Arms.

Soon after, carrying the letters of reference in a satchel, he arrived at the tavern. The place was busy as the cold snap had driven all the customers inside. A nice roaring fire warmed him the moment he stepped through the doorway. It was packed and the smell of ale and roasted food made Lord Robert hungry. He pushed through the press of people, glancing around at the customers. As expected, Lord Richard Fitzwilliam, the Baron of Bodden, was sitting in his usual seat away from the window and close to the sounds of the kitchen.

The man appeared to be eating a hearty stew. A tankard of some sort sloshed as he absently picked it up, spilling a small amount onto the table. Lord Brandon made his way to the table, and Fitz looked up, seeing him as he approached.

Fitz stood up and extended his hand. "Robert, splendid to see you! Sit down, man, have some ale!"

He waved at the server to get her attention, indicating he wanted two drinks by holding up his tankard and then two fingers and pointing to Lord Robert.

"Good to see you, Fitz!" said Lord Robert. "You look well. What have you been up to lately?"

"Oh, you know," he responded cryptically, as he always did, "this and that, nothing to bore you with. And how have you been, my dear fellow?"

"I've been well, though I miss the family. I'm hoping to get home before the midwinter festival. I haven't seen the children in months."

Fitz smiled. It was always good hearing from Robert for he was a good friend. Even after the death of Lady Evelyn in childbirth, Robert had kept in touch.

Lord Robert continued, "That reminds me, did I hear that niece of mine is back in Wincaster? I thought she was down in Colbridge?"

Fitz made a face before answering, "Shrewesdale, actually, and I'm afraid it was not the best of times for her. Still, she's back in Wincaster now. I'm trying to get her to learn more about court life, but you know how it is. She's a knight, and it's hard for her to be accepted."

Lord Robert understood thoroughly. Beverly Fitzwilliam was a capable woman. She would not take to the bad example of nobility that was the Earl of Shrewesdale.

"Say, I have a thought," Lord Robert offered, "why don't you send her up to Hawksburg? I know Mary would love to see her niece and I'm sure Aubrey would delight in spending some more time with her cousin."

Fitz smiled again, "An excellent idea! It'll do her good to see a noble that does his job well."

The server arrived with two more tankards of ale and Fitz dropped a crown into her hand. She was about to go and get change, but the baron gestured for her to keep it. They savoured the hot ale, Lord Brandon feeling the warmth go all the way to his toes.

"Are you taking your work home with you?" enquired Fitz, indicating the satchel that Lord Robert was carrying.

Lord Brandon put his tankard down, remembering why he had sought his friend out.

"I did come here to ask you about something. I had a letter come across my desk today from Uxley Hall."

Fitz was immediately interested. Typically he would guard his interest, but Robert was his brother-in-law.

"Go on," he urged.

Robert retrieved a document from his satchel and handed it to his friend.

"This letter came to me with the accounts. It mentions some things that confuse me. See what you make of it."

Fitz read over the letter. Not trusting his eyes, he read it over a second time, then carefully handed it back.

Robert broke the silence. "Am I missing something? Princess Margaret is in Wincaster, so who is this mysterious princess at Uxley?"

Baron Fitzwilliam leaned in closer and kept his voice low, "I recall years ago a rumour that the queen had a fourth child, do you remember?"

"Yes," responded Robert, "but wasn't it dead at birth?"

"There were persistent rumours that the infant survived, but it was said there was some type of birth defect, and the child was hidden away. I suspect we may have discovered this missing child."

Lord Brandon could scarcely believe his ears. He fished about in his satchel, pulling out Fitz's letter of recommendation.

"I presume you wrote this," he said, handing the sheet to his friend. "What can you tell me about the man?"

Fitz read over the letter quickly, before responding, "The man has served me for years. I would trust him with my life, or my daughter's, to be honest. He is completely trustworthy. If he is interfering in some way, I can only conclude that this Renfrew character is up to something."

Robert nodded his head, he had expected as much. "I completely trust your judgement, Fitz. Now, let me show you Renfrew's reference letter."

He retrieved the last document from the satchel and placed it into Fitz's hands. Fitz read the letter and stared at it for a while, digesting its meaning. Valmar! The very name upset him.

"I have to make a decision on this, but I'd like to investigate further. Have you any suggestions on how I might proceed?"

Fitz looked at him for a moment, then a smile crept across his face.

"I'll tell you what, Robert, let me take care of this for you. I think you'll find that your little problem at Uxley might present its own solution in due course. Do you think you can hold off on a decision for a few weeks?"

"Certainly," Robert responded. "Anything for you, Fitz. But I better take the letters back, they'll need to stay in the Palace."

Fitz handed them back. "Of course, Robert," he agreed.

They sat and chatted for some time, mostly about their families. It was well into the evening by the time Lord Brandon returned to the Palace to turn in for the night.

Baron Fitzwilliam, on the other hand, had work to do, so he made his way to the knight's barracks. It was typical that the knights who served the crown were billeted within the Palace, and Lord Fitzwilliam had visited the place on many an occasion. He arrived at the stone building to see the chimney pumping out smoke, the mouth-watering smell of meat greeting his nose. He opened the door. Inside the single room was a group of seven knights sitting around a table playing cards. He knew the beds were upstairs along with the officer's quarters, and so up he went, leaving the knights wondering who this mysterious visitor was. At the top landing was an office, with a door, and a series of beds laid out in rows.

He knocked politely on the door and was greeted a moment later, by a feminine voice.

"Come in," it responded, neutrally.

He opened the door. Dame Beverly Fitzwilliam was sitting at a desk writing in a journal of some type. She looked up to see her visitor.

"Father!" she said, a smile on her face. "I didn't know you were back in Wincaster. How have you been?"

"Very well, my dear," he said proudly, looking around, very impressed with her new promotion. "I'd heard you'd become the section commander. Excellent work."

"Only by virtue of most of them being illiterate."

"Still," the baron added, "it does well for your career. You're making progress."

She wrinkled her nose a little. "Not really, Father. Since I've returned from Shrewesdale, I've managed to alienate most of the knights. They're all such... I can't find the words to describe them."

"You're used to being around fighting knights, Beverly. These knights are more like courtiers, knighted for their family name more than their ability."

"Yes, but I was knighted-" she began

"For your ability," he quickly interrupted. "You saved the king's life! Of course, had he known you were a woman he probably would have changed his mind." He remembered with pride that fateful day and chuckled. "I can still remember it. He promised to knight you on the spot. I think he was shocked when you took your helmet off, but then he couldn't lose face, so he had to go through with it. You earned it, Beverly, don't let anyone ever tell you any differently."

"And how did you find Shrewesdale?" he prompted, though he already knew the answer.

"Terrible. The earl is a... man dedicated to his pursuits."

"Impressive," acknowledged Fitz, with simulated shock on his face, "you're learning to be diplomatic."

She looked at him carefully, recognizing the sparkle in his eyes.

"You didn't come here just to see me, did you? You're up to something. What do you need me to do?"

He returned her studied gaze and smiled, "You know me too well, my dear. Tell me, you had to guard Princess Margaret a few years ago, do you remember the name of the tutor she had?"

"Hard to forget," she said. "His name was Renfrew. I had to slap him for making a lewd suggestion."

"To the princess?" Fitz was aghast at the very thought.

"No! To me!"

Fitz laughed, "I'm sure that if you slapped him, he'll not soon forget it, though why the king would employ such a man in the first place is beyond me."

"According to the princess, he was frequently drunk," she said, "and he had a thing for the ladies, though they seldom returned the sentiment. He had an overinflated opinion of himself."

"Thank you, Beverly. I believe you have filled in the last piece of the puzzle. I have to go now. I need to write a letter immediately to Gerald Matheson."

"Gerald? How is he involved with Renfrew?" she queried.

"I'm afraid I don't have time to explain it all right now. Much of it I'm still figuring out, but if you meet me tomorrow for a luncheon, I'll tell you all about it."

"Agreed," she said, happy to find any excuse to get away from court.

Fitz walked over to Beverly and hugged her, then held her at arm's length to look at her.

"I'm very proud of you Beverly, and your mother would have been as well. Tomorrow then, the usual place?"

"Of course, Father, but perhaps I'll wait till you've had time to finish that smelly cheese."

Baron Richard Fitzwilliam left her office with a laugh and a smile, but by the time he reached the ground floor, he was deep in thought. He had much to do, but first on the list must be a letter to Gerald to help straighten out this problem at Uxley Hall.

SIXTEEN

Hanson

WINTER 956/957 MC

The first snow at Uxley had settled on the ground. Gerald felt the cold penetrate to his very bones as he walked over to the Hall. It was morning, and he had decided to join the other servants for breakfast. He was always welcome, of course, but often remained in his cottage so that he could eat at his leisure.

He entered the servant's hallway and was removing his coat and boots when he saw young Sophie. She was passing him on the way to the kitchen.

When she saw him, she spoke in a friendly manner, "Hanson wants to see you in his office when you get a chance."

He made his way through the kitchen, grabbing a plate and a couple of scones, dripping with honey. He navigated his way through the others that were pestering Mrs Brown for more food and made his way to Hanson's office. He knocked respectfully, entering upon hearing Hanson's voice, still carrying the plate. Hanson waved his hand to indicate he should have a seat. Sitting down, he observed the man at work. As usual, he had his quill and ink out and was poring over papers, bills most likely, making entries into the ledgers that recorded all financial transactions for the Hall.

Gerald was the first to break the silence. "Scone?" he offered.

Hanson looked up from a letter he was perusing. "No thank you, Gerald, just let me finish this, then we'll get down to business."

Gerald finished off the second scone while he waited. Hanson was a dedicated man, and he hated to interrupt the clerk's work. Gerald looked around the room observing the neat ledgers that lined the bookshelf, one for each year that the Hall had existed. Uxley Hall was old, he knew, but it had largely fallen into disuse under the current king. It had, as they say, seen its heyday and was now an old, forgotten relic of the past. He couldn't help but feel that the staff here was also, in some ways, relics of the past. Perhaps it was just as well that they had all ended up here.

The old steward finished making his entries, and then carefully blotted the pages to dry the ink. He held the book up to the light, satisfied that all was well, he closed it and placed it to the side. He looked up at Gerald, who, upon seeing the book closed, had focused his attention on the old man.

"It might surprise you to know," said Hanson with no preamble, "that you have some powerful friends." He waited for a reaction.

"I do? That would be a surprise to me," retorted Gerald.

"Well, I know of no other man by the name of…" he looked at the letter on his desk, "Gerald Matheson here, do you?"

"Of course not, sir," he said, not sure where this was going.

"Today I have received a package from Wincaster, not an uncommon occurrence. They have sent coins, of course, and a receipt indicating that they received my last reports. I was rather surprised to see some other correspondence in the satchel." Hanson lifted the letter before him and held it out to Gerald. "It bears the seal of the Baron of Bodden. Very impressive!"

Gerald was surprised but took the letter. He had served the baron for years, had even received some books from him, but he never expected to get a letter. Was this a summons? A rebuke perhaps? The look on his face must have spoken volumes.

"You look shocked," Hanson said. "I'm not surprised. After all, it was the baron who provided your reference for the position here." He smiled at Gerald in a friendly manner, before continuing, "But in any case, you won't be able to read the letter by staring at it. Open it up, man, see what's inside!"

Gerald broke the seal and unfolded the paper. It was indeed a message from Baron Richard Fitzwilliam of Bodden, for he immediately recognized the handwriting.

25 October 956

My Dear Gerald,

I bring you the joy of the season and wishes for a prosperous new year. I under-stand that you have been doing well for yourself at Uxley Hall. I hope this message finds you in good health. I have been rather occupied of late in Wincaster, having found myself busy handling all kinds of correspondence. These include such mundane topics as requests for funds, requests for titles, and even for favours from a rambling tutor. It was on that very matter that I find myself putting ink to paper, for I have recently read a letter from a man named Renfrew. He was appointed to Uxley by Marshal-General Valmar, Head of the Army. If you should run into him, remember he is an important man, but he is not a noble, so ensure that you use the proper title.

Beverly is doing well these days and is often taken to quoting her favourite writings. I believe one of her favourites is:

"What is a man to a noble? And yet to a royal, even a noble is a man."

I must admit I rather like that one. I cannot, of course, be aware of everything that goes on in Merceria, I can barely keep up with Bodden's affairs. I trust that you can soldier on and do your duty with full diligence.

Your friend,

Richard Fitzwilliam,
   Baron of Bodden

The baron's seal was on the bottom of the document beside his signature. It was a cryptic message, and Gerald couldn't help but feel there was some hidden meaning to it. He read it a second time, and it began to dawn on him. He looked up at Hanson, conscious that he had been pondering the letter for some time.

"I think, sir, that I have a solution to our problem."

Hanson looked back, relief on his face. He still looked pale, but that had become his daily countenance.

"If you'll come with me, I think we can straighten out this whole Renfrew business."

Hanson smiled, an expression that was rare these days.

"By all means. Where are we going?"

"To see a royal," said Gerald, standing. He opened the door for Hanson. "Where would the princess be at this time of day?" he asked, knowing that the steward was aware of everything that occurred at the Hall.

"They would be in the king's meeting room. It's this way, follow me."

Hanson almost had a spring in his step as he led them to the south wing towards the great hall, stopping a moment to open a hidden panel beneath the grand stairs.

"Servants entrance," he said, and continued into the corridor. They eventually came to the meeting room, and there, Hanson stopped for he was breathing heavily and was sweating profusely.

"Are you all right, Alistair?"

Hanson took a moment to catch his breath before speaking, "I'm fine, let's get it over with."

He opened the door to the meeting room. Inside, Anna was standing in front of the desk, at which Renfrew was seated. She was balancing a book on her head and reciting a poem of some type. At the sound of the door opening, she turned, and the book slipped from its position to crash to the floor. Renfrew looked irritated by the interruption, but Gerald cut him off.

"Your Highness," he began.

He was about to say more, but suddenly he felt Hanson grab his arm for balance. He looked at the old man, his previous words lost.

"I can't see properly, everything is-" Hanson slurred, then the whole side of his face went slack. His right hand, which had gripped Gerald's arm, went limp, leaving the old steward to fall suddenly to the floor.

"Hanson," Anna cried and ran to his side.

Gerald knelt beside the man, trying to loosen his shirt. He was murmuring incoherently. Gerald glanced about, desperate to help his old friend. Renfrew was still sitting at the desk.

"Use the bell pull!" he commanded.

Renfrew reluctantly got up, making his way to the corner where the silken rope hung. He tugged on the rope, and a distant bell sounded.

"Help me get him onto a chair," ordered Gerald, straining with the weight of Hanson.

Anna moved a chair closer, and they managed to get him into a seated position. It seemed to be taking an agonizingly long time for the bell to have its usual effect. Gerald knew that in moments of crisis, time had a mind of its own. He heard footsteps approaching, then a yell to get others and soon more of the servants were there. They all gathered around Hanson as Gerald checked his eyes, which had rolled back into his head. While they looked to Hanson's health, Renfrew made what was perhaps his greatest mistake, for he chose that precise moment to speak up.

"Well, carry him off then," his hand waved them away. "We don't need the old man taking up precious time."

Anna turned on him with a sudden fury. "Shut up!" she yelled, then pointed at Renfrew. "Tempus! Guard!"

The huge dog lunged towards the tutor and stopped short, growling menacingly. Renfrew turned pale, backing into the wall. The rest were too busy to deal with the tutor at this time. There were far more important things needing their attention.

"Let's get him to his room, and into bed," a fretful Anna tried to lead the way.

By now, most of the servants had arrived, and the anxiety level had only increased. In the end, it was Gerald who took control of the situation. They laid Hanson onto the floor, on a small rug in front of the desk. Then he had four of them lift it by the corners. In this way, they made a makeshift stretcher and carried him, albeit awkwardly, to his room. Soon, they had put him to bed. He was not conscious, and he was deathly pale, with his face still distorted. No one knew what had befallen the kindly old man, but Anna was insistent that they keep a watch on him night and day.

Renfrew, wisely, was not seen for the next few days. Anna helped keep watch over Hanson. She had Gerald organize shifts to ensure someone was always present. They made him as comfortable as possible. They spoon fed him, but he made slow progress. Once he regained consciousness, he could only speak with considerable effort in a slurred voice. His right side appeared almost frozen.

Gerald went into Uxley Village seeking help, but it was not promising. Mrs Sandlewood, who grew herbs, sent some to help him relax, but the consensus was that nothing could be done but make him as comfortable as possible.

Mrs Brown was a total wreck, in fact, the entire staff were on edge. Everyone knew what would happen when a servant could no longer do their duty. He would be turned out.

It was four days before Hanson was finally able to articulate words. The ordeal had rightfully terrified him, but all he could do was apologize.

"I'm sorry, Your Highness, I have let you down," he slurred.

Gerald saw Anna tearing up, but she stubbornly fought back the tears.

"Nonsense, Hanson," the princess said, "you have done your duty. It's time for you to rest. We shall look after you. You shall always have a place at Uxley Hall, regardless of your health."

The old man looked to relax after that and slept more soundly. Anna made it a point to talk to the rest of the staff who gathered outside the door. They were waiting with bated breath, expecting the worst of news.

"I know you're all worried about Hanson," she said, struggling to bite back her tears. "He has looked after this Hall for many years and now it is time for the Hall to take care of him. We will not turn him out of this house. We will look after him and care for him as he is one of our own." It was a strong statement coming from a small girl. Gerald was impressed. "But now," she continued, "it's time for him to rest and for the rest of you to get back to your duties."

No sooner had the last of the servants left the hallway when Anna turned towards Gerald, throwing her arms around his waist and hugging him while the sobs came out in a river of tears.

The next morning, Mrs Brown came to talk to Gerald. He was in Hanson's room with Anna and Tempus, and he noticed her nervousness.

"I'm beggin' your pardon, Gerald, but we have a wee bit of a problem," she said, wringing her hands as she spoke. Anna looked up from where she sat beside Hanson. Gerald turned to face the cook.

"What is it?"

"Well, you see..." she was struggling to find the words. "We need some supplies and, well, Hanson would usually release the funds."

"I see," said Gerald, even though he didn't understand. "Can't you just take the coins you need?"

"Oh, no," she objected, "you have to account for everything. It's the books, you see."

"Of course, but I don't have the authority to issue coins, Mrs Brown," said Gerald.

The cook looked positively crestfallen.

"I do!" Anna unexpectedly interjected. "I can release the funds, I'm a princess, aren't I?" She looked towards Gerald. "Can you read the ledgers, Gerald?"

He thought for a moment, before speaking, "Shouldn't be too hard, I've handled soldier's pay books before. Shall we go and have a look?"

Anna nodded. They left Hanson in the care of Mrs Brown while they went to the clerk's office. Gerald had the foresight to retrieve Hanson's key. The old man used to keep it around his neck on a string, but it had been lying on his bedside table since his illness.

Once in the room, it didn't take Gerald long to find the most recent ledger. He then retrieved the small lock-box from Hanson's desk drawer, using the key to open it. Inside was a tidy sum of newly minted Royal Crowns. Anna walked around to stand beside Gerald as he opened the books. She saw the numbers with small entries for amounts. It was she that first noticed that Hanson's last entry had indicated a significant increase in the funds for the estate. The coins must have just arrived. Gerald carefully pulled out two crowns, then, after a brief pause grabbed a third.

"This should cover Cook's expenses for the next few days, I should think," he said.

Anna was watching intently as Gerald dipped a quill in ink and entered the expenditure. He had picked an amount consistent with the previous entries and was about to sign for the entry when he realized he had a problem.

"What's the matter, Gerald?" Anna asked.

"I can't sign for this expenditure, Anna, I don't have the authority."

He was half tempted to sign anyway and curse the bureaucrats, but he knew such things could come back to haunt him in the future.

"I'll sign it," declared Anna determinedly.

She grasped the quill in a firm grip and re-dipped the end in the ink pot. She tapped it lightly on the blotter and then, in a neat, delicate hand, initialled the entry.

"Can you show me how these numbers work?" she asked.

"Certainly, but let's get the coins to Cook first, shall we?"

Gerald tugged the bell pull, and moments later, Charles arrived. They asked him to bring Mrs Brown back to the office. The look of relief on her face as she accepted the coins was evident to all. She thanked them profusely as she departed, and the two of them were left looking at the book.

"Now, this," explained Gerald, using his finger to point out an entry in the ledger, "is how we show an item of expenditure..."

They spent hours poring over the books until Anna was sure she understood. The arithmetic she found straightforward, only the format confused her at first. Using a blank paper, Gerald gave her an exercise where she would buy seeds, grow them, then sell them and calculate the profits. He had her note all the entries that would be costs and then calculate the profit at the end. By the time they were done, she had completely mastered the concept. It wasn't until they were interrupted by Sophie that they realized they had spent all day working on it.

The next morning, as Gerald arrived for breakfast, Mrs Brown told him that the princess was in the clerk's room. He snagged two bowls of porridge, some spoons and headed over to the office. As he entered, Anna was kneeling on the chair behind the desk, looking at papers she had opened. He showed her the porridge, putting the bowl down in front of her. She grabbed the spoon and began eating.

"I found Renfrew's letter of recommendation, yours too," she said. "Baron Fitzwilliam certainly thought highly of you."

Gerald smiled between mouthfuls.

"So I gather. He recently sent me a letter." He was reaching for it from his pocket when he remembered he needed to talk to Anna. He paused, "There's something I wanted to talk to you about, Anna, but events... well, they got us off topic."

"All right, what is it?" she asked.

Gerald took a breath. How did he approach a child about such a serious subject. He knew she was very bright for her age, so he decided to let her figure it out for herself.

"I'd like you to read this letter, Anna. Lord Fitzwilliam wrote it, and I only just received it."

He handed her the letter which she unfolded, reading through it.

"Is he trying to tell you something?" she asked.

"I think so," he said cautiously. "The quote is from one of his favourite books. It was written by a Shrewesdale poet. They even made a play from it. Do you understand the reference?"

She knit her brow as she stared at the words. "What is a man to a noble? That's easy, a man here refers to a commoner. They must always follow the word of the noble."

"Yes," prompted Gerald, "and the rest?"

"Well," she mused, "and yet to a royal, even a noble is a man, seems to indicate that just as a commoner must follow the word of a noble, so must the noble follow the word of a royal?"

"Exactly!" said Gerald.

He could see her mind at work, and a moment later, he saw the recognition of the meaning in her eyes.

"So Renfrew has to do what I say," she exclaimed triumphantly, "because I'm a royal!"

"Precisely. Of course, that means you'll have to talk to him. Do you think you can stand up to him?"

"I don't know, Gerald. I'm afraid, I've never done anything like that before."

She looked pale and fearful. He walked over to her chair and lifted her up, putting her down so that she was sitting on the desk, the better to meet her gaze.

"Sometimes we have to make hard decisions, Anna, even though we don't want to. Shall I tell you a story of something I had to deal with when I was young? Maybe it'll help you."

She nodded, wide-eyed and watched him intently. She always did like a good story.

"How young?" she asked.

"Err, about thirteen. Anyway, I was living in Bodden Town," he continued.

"How long ago was that?" she interrupted.

"It was back in '25," he said, ready to continue.

"But Gerald, that would make you forty-four! You're so old!" she snickered.

"Do you want to hear the story or not, Anna?" he softly scolded.

"Yes, sorry," she apologized.

"Anyway, that was the year the Northern Wars began. I was working in the stables when the first siege of Bodden occurred. Back then, the Keep was not as well fortified as it is now. I huddled into the cellars with the women and the other children. The siege was bad, they broke through the wall and entered the central keep. They rushed in, killing anyone in their way. We heard them coming towards us, and then there was a commotion in the hallway. They were yelling that they had found the women. The door burst open, and a man stepped in. He was huge, at least to me, and his axe was dripping with fresh blood. He grabbed Meredith, and she screamed. He was twisting her wrist and forcing her to her knees."

"What did you do?" an enthralled Anna asked with bated breath.

"I had nothing to protect myself with, but the man had a dagger, and in those days I was quick. I stepped forward, then grabbed the weapon from the man's sheath."

"And you killed him?"

"No, he turned on me, knocked me to the floor with a vicious backhand."

Anna was on the edge of her seat. "What happened next?"

"He turned back to Meredith, and I was overcome with anger. I struck with his dagger and sliced into his arm."

"Did he let go of her?"

"Oh, yes, but then he turned on me. Here I was, a young boy armed with nothing but a knife, while this towering man with an axe was getting ready to kill me."

"And then you killed him?"

"No, I backed up, but I tripped and fell. It was one of the scariest moments of my life. I was sure I was going to die."

"But you're alive now, so what happened?"

Gerald blushed, "Meredith saved me."

Anna's brow knitted, "So let me get this straight, the girl, Meredith, kept you safe? Did she kill the man?"

Gerald cleared his throat, "No, it's a bit more complicated than that."

"So what happened, exactly?"

"Meredith jumped on his back, and it threw him off balance. He fell forward, onto the knife I was holding."

"And that's when you killed him?"

"Yes, that's when I killed him."

Anna stared at him for a moment, "You know, that's not the most heroic account, Gerald. Is there a point to this story?"

"Yes. Even though I was scared, petrified even, I still tried to fight. I knew it was the right thing to do. Sometimes you have to do what you think is right, regardless of your fears."

She nodded wisely, taking it all in.

"I know what I have to do, Gerald," she said earnestly, "but I have to do it properly. Will you help?"

"Of course, Anna, tell me what you want me to do."

"All right," she began, "first you have to tell Sophie…" the instructions were clear and, to Gerald's mind, very well planned out. He didn't know where she got her ideas from, but she spent some time finalizing every detail.

Sometime later, Renfrew arrived at the clerk's office, summoned by a servant. The door opened, and the groundskeeper invited him in. He walked in, his back straight, expecting to see a recovered Hanson, or perhaps his successor, sitting behind the desk. Instead, an unexpected scene presented itself. Princess Anna was sitting behind the desk appearing impossibly tall, or was it his imagination? The groundskeeper, Gerald, pulled out the chair for him, and Renfrew graciously accepted the invitation. To his surprise, as he sat down, he fell a little farther than he had expected. The chair was smaller than usual and had shorter legs. He suddenly realized why it was a tight fit, he sat in a child's chair! He made as if to stand up, but a growl erupted from the side of the desk. He turned to see the massive dog sitting on the princess's right. The groundskeeper's firm hand was placed on his shoulder to keep him seated.

He was infuriated but acquiesced. He was about to say something when the princess suddenly put her finger to her lips and shushed him.

"Mister Renfrew," she began, "I am going to tell you what's going to happen and you, in turn, will listen carefully. When I am done, you may have your say, agreed?"

Renfrew was about to speak again when the dog growled, a low rumbling sound that shook him to his very bones. He nodded nervously.

"During your time here, you have taught me very little that I didn't already know. You have taken me away from my friends, and you have mistreated me. That will cease immediately. In fact, your services are no longer required. I would dismiss you, but another replacement would likely be sent in your place, so I'm going to give you an alternate arrangement. You will continue to take your place here at Uxley as Royal Tutor, but I will have nothing to do with you. You are free to come and go as you please and live a life of relative luxury commensurate with your position here. I will even give you a slight raise. All you must do in return is write your regular reports and glowing recommendations about how well I am progressing as your student. Is that understood?"

Renfrew nodded, but a devious look crossed his face. He was about to speak again.

Anna looked briefly at Gerald for steadiness. He smiled, she was doing well.

"If you do not," she continued, "I shall write a letter to the king, about your callous disregard for my well-being." She stumbled a little at some of the words but grew more confident the more she spoke. "I needn't tell you the king is not known as a man who takes criticism of the Royal Family well."

Renfrew paled at the thought. The king indeed was not known as a merciful man. His justice was often brutal and quick. He gulped, then nodded.

"Now," she continued, "you may have the rest of the day off. Here are two crowns, consider it a bonus. Go into town, have a drink, maybe a meal, but I warn you, if I learn you have double-crossed me or slighted me in any way, your punishment will be permanent."

He stumbled out a, "Yes, Your Highness. Thank you, Your Highness," before being hustled from the room.

Gerald closed the door as he left. They heard the tutor almost running down the hallway. He was so proud of her. She had stood her ground and dealt with the problem. He turned back to see Anna, still standing behind the desk when he noticed her trembling. Tears were starting to form in her eyes, and she was shaking even as she stood there, oblivious to her surroundings. He cursed to himself. He had pushed her to do this, telling himself it was the right thing to do, but now he had doubts. It wasn't worth it to see her in such turmoil. He walked around the desk, enveloping her in his arms.

"It's all right, Anna, it's over now!" he soothed.

She clung tightly to him for some time, until she stopped trembling. She straightened herself back up.

"Look at me, I can't even do this without falling to pieces!" she said in self-disgust.

"It's all right, Anna. When I was in Bodden, I didn't stop shaking for two days."

He looked at her with a straight face until they both burst out laughing. She would survive this.

SEVENTEEN

The Ambush

SUMMER 957 MC

⌒

I t was a warm summer's day as Gerald finished harnessing the horses. He had decided to head into town with the wagon to pick up some supplies for the kitchen. He looked forward to having a light lunch, and maybe an ale or two, at the Old Oak Tavern with Sam. It was still relatively early in the day. He spotted Anna off to the side of the Hall, playing with Tempus. She looked over and, noticing him, ran to see what he was doing.

"Are you going into town, Gerald?" she asked.

"Yes," he replied, "I need to pick up some supplies for Cook. We're running a little low. I'll be back just after lunch."

"Can you do me a favour?" she requested.

"Certainly, what is it?"

"Well," she considered her words before speaking, "I'd like some pastries from the bakery. Can you wait a moment while I go and get some coins?"

"That's all right. You can pay me back later. Do you want to come along?"

She thought about this before answering, "Much as I would like to, I need to bathe Tempus. He's starting to stink up the house and Cook is getting a little upset."

"Then I'll leave you to it. See you this afternoon."

He waved goodbye, then climbed up into the wagon, giving the horse a gentle snap of the reins. The wagon lurched forward, the familiar sound of horse's hooves striking gravel greeting his ears. He manoeuvred onto the main entranceway heading towards the gate.

Anna and Tempus ran towards the wall that lined the road, the better to wave to him once he exited the gates to start his trip to town. It was looking like a beautiful warm day with just a hint of a breeze to help overcome the heat of the summer.

Once through the gate, which was always left open, he turned to the right, down the winding road that led into the village. The wheels were creaking, as they always did and the horses occasionally sniffed the air. He drove parallel to the wall, and noticing Anna and Tempus leaning on the wall waving, he waved back.

He had only gone a few hundred yards when he heard a sound, and suddenly his leg exploded in agony. He looked down to see an arrow protruding from his thigh, very near his old wounds. A scream of distress erupted from his lips. He saw two men step out from the trees at the edge of the road. They held swords, with a third man, just behind them, holding a bow.

The first one stepped forward raising his hands to stop the horses.

"Hand over your coins, old man," he demanded. "We know you're going to town with an empty wagon, and I'm guessing you've got some coins on hand to pay for goods. We'll gladly relieve you of them."

Gerald was in a great deal of pain but still held onto his wits. He dropped the reins and nodded, reaching below the seat to where the strongbox lay. He waited while the second one sheathed his weapon and climbed onto the wagon, then Gerald made his move. Lying beside the coin box was his cane, and he grabbed it and struck while he had surprise. The cane hit the brigand on the side of the face, causing him to lose his footing and fall back into the wagon bed.

Gerald lunged towards the back of the wagon, intending to throw himself on top of the man while grabbing for his opponent's sword, but the arrow in his leg caught on the seat as he dove, snapping loudly and painfully. He felt blood flowing freely from the wound as he desperately threw out his arms to grab the prostrate man. The bandit now struggled to draw his blade free while lying prone. He had half withdrawn it before Gerald was upon him, grabbing for the hilt as well. They were both trying to gain possession of it, each knowing it was a life and death situation, but Gerald had fought many times before, and the wars had taught him how to survive. He brought his right knee up to smash into the man's groin causing a loud groan of pain from both of them, for the action had done worse damage to an already injured leg. He felt something give in his leg and knew it was now useless, but it had given him the initiative, and in that desperate second, the bandit let go of the sword. Gerald pulled it from the scabbard and struck without hesitation, bringing the hilt crashing down on the man's face. Again, and again he struck, desperate to kill his opponent before the other came upon him.

He heard one of the others yelling, and the wagon shook as someone climbed aboard. Gerald flipped onto his back to face his attacker, and everything spun. His leg was hemorrhaging blood in such great gouts he knew the arrow must have hit an artery. Seeing the second bandit stepping towards him, he struggled to hold onto the sword. He stabbed, but his opponent blocked his weakened blow, knocking the sword from his hand. The bandit stood over him grinning, straddling his body and raised his sword overhead for a two-handed blow that would finish him. Gerald did the only thing he could think of. He sat up, grabbing for the man's sword belt, and pulled him forward. The bandit, poised for a downward strike, was unbalanced and tumbled to the wagon bed, falling heavily on Gerald. The sword flew out of his hand and Gerald, with his remaining strength gripped the man by the throat. Now, they entered a terrible test of strength as his attacker struck back, beating him across the face and arms in an attempt to loosen his grasp.

He could feel himself getting ready to pass out, the wagon bed now slick with his blood. It felt like his life was draining from him. At last, his attacker passed out with a strangled gurgle and fell slowly to his side. Everything around him swung about like a spinning top, and then he saw death coming. The last attacker had mounted the wagon, but he stood in the front, his bow drawn and his mouth curled back in a nasty sneer.

The bandit was about to loose the final gift of death when Gerald heard a loud growl, and suddenly a monstrous blur passed before his eyes blocking his sight. Then the last opponent was gone, horrible screams erupting from him somewhere on the ground. Gerald tried to sit up, but it felt like a weight was pushing him down, and then he fell, almost lifeless, back into the wagon bed. Then finally, the blessed darkness took him away.

Gerald saw himself lying there, his body covered in blood. He heard a wolf howl in the distance. Was this a portend? Perhaps a calling to the Afterlife? He saw Sally, sitting beside him, holding his hand and waiting to guide him to the spirit realm. He tried to call out to her but had no voice. Struggling to move towards her, it took all of his efforts to get closer. Then her dark hair turned blonde and her face transformed from Sally into Anna right before his eyes. He looked on in shock, then felt himself being drawn back into his body.

Gerald opened his eyes to see he was in a well-appointed room. The tableau shifted, and he clung to the bed sheets to stop the feeling of vertigo.

A dog's bark made him swivel his head to the side, and he recognized Tempus, sitting on the floor beside Anna, who was seated in an over-sized chair. She rose and moved towards him saying something, but he couldn't understand the words, so clouded was his mind. She grabbed his face with both hands and stared into his eyes, mouthing something. At first he heard only a ringing sound in his ears, and then, ever so slowly his hearing began to return, and he finally understood her.

"Thank Saxnor you're awake, Gerald. I was so worried about you!" The tears were running down her face. He was touched by her caring. "Now, don't you worry," she continued, "I've sent for the Royal Physician. He should be here in a day or two."

Gerald struggled to get the words out, "How long have I been under?"

He tried to move, to sit up in the bed, but even the small movement sent agonizing pain through his leg. It felt as though his entire lower torso was being roasted over a fire.

"Don't move!" Anna ordered him. "You have to lie still, you've been unconscious for almost two days."

"What happened?" he asked, through gritted teeth. "I saw something flash across my eyes before I passed out."

"Tempus saved you! We heard the fighting and Tempus ran to save you. The last man was going to shoot you with his bow. Tempus jumped clean over the wagon and took the man's face off. There was ever so much noise from him. It's all right though, they're all dead. Now, you need to rest."

She turned slightly to the side, and he heard her wringing out a cloth in some water, then she placed a cool compress on his forehead. He was sweating so profusely that the bed was soaked. Looking down, he saw the sheets were stained red around his right leg, and the pain was excruciating.

"Drink this," Anna prompted, holding a small mug to his lips. Gerald sipped the concoction, and the effect on his throat was instant. He felt the warm liquid, some herbal tea, soothe his ravaged throat, and he realized how thirsty he was. He gulped the tea down, almost choking on it. The pain slowly eased, and he relaxed back into the bed. Anna was bending over him, wiping his face with the cloth, a concerned look on her face. He lost focus on her as his vision failed. He fell back into a fit-full sleep.

Red hot fire erupted from his leg, and he was thrust awake, screaming in agony. The room was lit only by candlelight. He saw an older man, clean cut with a neatly trimmed beard, leaning over his leg. He held a small metal rod, and once again he poked it into Gerald's wound releasing another tortuous spasm of agony. He saw Anna standing nearby, nervously wringing her hands while Tempus, ever alert, watched her with great concern.

The old man was speaking, "I'm afraid there is little we can do, the corruption has already set in. I shall flush it of course."

He reached into a bag, withdrawing a small bottle which he proceeded to pour onto the wound. A new wave of torture struck him. He could have sworn the man had set him on fire. The man then squeezed the wound, and surprisingly, this did not hurt.

"You can see here that the pus is oozing out. There are probably fibres in the wound turning it necrotic."

Anna's voice spoke up, seeming so child-like in the presence of what he had to assume was the Royal Physician.

"What about warriors moss, would that help?" she pleaded.

"I'm afraid not, Your Highness. Oh, warriors moss might stop it from leaking so much, but nothing will fix the rot that has embedded itself in this poor fellow's body."

Anna's voice was trembling as she spoke, "What if you amputate the leg? Would that work? You must save him!"

"My dear," the physician spoke, sounding very condescending, "I'm afraid you must say your goodbyes, this man will die. There is nothing more you, or anyone else can do for him."

Gerald watched her face set and her visage became angry.

"Get out!" she shouted. "Get out and never darken this Hall again!"

"But, Your Highness-"

"How dare you come here with your overbearing attitude and tell me there's no hope. I will not give up while he still breathes. Get out of here and pray I don't report your failure to the king!"

These were the last words Gerald heard before he once again succumbed to unconsciousness.

When next he opened his eyes, he was so weak he could barely move. It must have been the middle of the night. The light of a lantern suffused the room with a yellow glow. He turned his head to the side to see Anna on the floor. She had books spread around her, and she was examining them intently, each turned to a different page. She looked up at the door, and Gerald was shocked to see her face. It was gaunt and sallow, looking as if she hadn't slept in days. She barked out an order to some servants who were standing in the doorway.

They didn't appear to react, and suddenly Anna shouted, "Mary!"

The young girl turned to face Anna, dragging her eyes away from Gerald's deathly pallor. The poor girl was in shock and didn't seem able to do anything. Anna turned to one of the others.

"Sophie," she commanded, "go and get some beef broth from Cook, not too hot, and bring a spoon."

"Yes, Your Highness," Sophie responded, and pushed her way past the other servants.

Gerald closed his eyes. He wanted this nightmare to end. It was destroying him to watch Anna devolve before his very eyes. Better for him to die quickly and put an end to it.

He woke sometime later. His leg felt cold, and he wondered if he had lost it. Sophie was holding his head and, with the help of Charles, was lifting him, tucking pillows behind his back to prop him up. Anna came forward with a bowl and started to spoon a warm, filling broth into his mouth. He felt some strength returning to him. She finished feeding him and set the bowl down on the nightstand. She had dark circles under her eyes and looked ragged.

"Anna," he finally got out, "it's no use, I can't last much longer. Please, get some paper, I want to dictate my will before it's too late."

"No," she said firmly, "you will not. You are not giving up on me, Gerald Matheson. I've put warriors moss on your leg and sent for the Royal Life Mage from Wincaster."

"It's no use," he said again, "he won't come, I'm a commoner."

"I commanded him," she said triumphantly. "He can't refuse a royal command, even from me!"

Her voice began to crack, and she turned away, but not before he saw the tears forming in her eyes. He closed his own eyes and fell into a fit-full sleep once more.

He awoke later, to feel a tingling in his leg. He opened his eyes and looked down to see an old, gaunt man he didn't recognize. The gaunt man had gently placed two hands on Gerald's leg and, with his eyes closed, was muttering something he couldn't quite understand. He realized with a shock that he was no longer in pain, and, though weak, felt quite well.

The man stopped his strange litany of words and raised his hands from his leg. To Gerald's surprise, no sign of his leg wound remained. Not only that, but not even his old wounds, which had plagued him for so long, could be seen.

"I see the patient has awoken," the old man said, turning to look at Gerald. "How are you feeling?"

Gerald blinked a few times before answering, "I feel weak, but I'm not in pain anymore."

"Of course, I have repaired the flesh, but the spirit will still have to heal. You'll need to stay in bed for, let's say, three days." the old man said, looking with interest into his eyes.

"I don't understand. What just happened?" Gerald's question hung in the air.

"Simple," the man explained. "I healed you using the Arcane Powers that I have learned. Allow me to introduce myself, I am Andronicus, the Royal Life Mage."

So this was the mysterious life mage he had heard so much about. The same life mage that Marshal-General Valmar had refused to allow Gerald to visit when Fitz had shipped him to the Capital. He couldn't believe how good he felt. His smile was infectious, and it was as he was looking around that he saw Anna. She looked tired, and dishevelled, but much more relaxed with the beginnings of a grin on her face.

"You're a lucky man," continued the mage, "if the princess had not used the warriors moss on you, you'd have been dead before I arrived."

He turned to face Anna. "Where did you learn such things, Your Highness?"

Anna looked back at Andronicus and smiled, "Gerald taught me about the moss, and then I looked up the rest in the library here. I read a lot."

The last was added almost as an afterthought.

"Well, it seems," continued the mage, "that we have a budding scholar in the Royal Family. Would you like me to send you some more books on the subject?"

"Yes, please. It proved to be ever so useful."

Andronicus rose from his seat and slowly walked over to Tempus, who was lying on the floor.

"This fellow," he noticed, "has seen a lot of fights in his time. Do you mind if I help him a little?"

"Of course not," replied Anna, "but what's wrong with him?"

"Oh, nothing too bad, I'm just going to freshen him up a bit."

With these words, the mage placed a hand on the dog's head and Tempus relaxed. Then the mage starting an incantation and the dog's face seemed to grow fuzzy. It took a moment for Gerald to realize what was happening. He was regenerating Tempus' skin, and even as he watched, the scars disappeared.

"That ought to do it!" said the mage. "Now," he continued, "remember my instructions. You," he pointed at Gerald, "are to rest for three days and you," he turned to look at Anna, "go and get some sleep. As for me, I am a busy man. I'll take a quick look at the steward, and then I must get back to my studies." He bowed gracefully to Anna, "I am ever at your service, Your Highness."

Gerald watched him walk out of the room. The Mage appeared to glide along the floor.

Sophie stepped into the room, and spoke to the princess, "I'll look after Gerald, Your Highness. You should go and get some sleep."

Anna nodded and turned one last time to smile at Gerald, allowing the other servants to guide her from the room.

Two days later, Gerald was feeling much better. He had Sophie and Anna nearby while he tried to stand. Much to his surprise, he found his right leg completely healed and it was as though he had never been wounded at all. He felt younger than he had in years. He was very pleased with his progress, prompting him to attempt to walk from one side of the room to the other. He was soon feeling faint, for though the mage had mended his limbs, he still had to recover his energy. He was tucked back into bed for more rest. Over the next few days he was allowed the briefest of exercise until, five days later, he could walk without getting dizzy. He was soon back to his old self, better actually, since he no longer had the limp that had plagued him for so long.

By the time he returned to the cottage, he was as fit as can be. He took the walking stick that Anna had given him and placed it on the wall along with his chainmail. It was a memento now, a reminder of his past.

EIGHTEEN

The Birthday

AUTUMN 957 MC

It was October the Eleventh, Anna's birthday. Gerald had decided to surprise her, so he made his way to the Hall for breakfast, like he would any other day. The weather was a little cool for the time of the year but not so cold as to require heavier clothing.

As he entered the servant's dining hall to sit down for his morning meal, he nodded to Hanson, who had resumed his seat at the head of the table. The old man was not very active these days and still suffered from his condition. Andronicus had been unable to heal him, for even magic had its limitations. He was permanently afflicted with a limp arm and a face that didn't quite work properly on one side, but his presence brought a calmness to the table.

Anna took up her seat at the opposite end, with the food being served by Mrs Brown. Thick warm toast to go with fresh bacon and eggs, lovely scones on the side and a delicious apple cider which she had flavoured with something called cinnamon, a rare spice brought into Merceria by Westland traders.

Anna appeared particularly pleased with herself this morning, thought Gerald. Apparently, she was expecting some recognition that it was her birthday. Gerald decided to play innocent.

"How are you today, Anna?"

"I'm very well, Gerald," she replied politely. "Isn't it a grand day?"

"Why would you say that?" prompted Gerald. "Is it a special day or something?"

The look she gave him was priceless. He had convinced her that he had forgotten her birthday! The look of shock was too much for Gerald to bear, so he decided to change his tactics.

"Oh, yes, it's your birthday today, isn't it?" he remarked.

"Yes," she replied with a big smile. "I'm ten years old today."

"Well," he continued, "I suppose we should do something special today. How about a trip to the village?"

Tempus, who until this time had been quiet on the floor, sat up and barked. He was far too smart for a dog and had learned to recognize the term 'village'.

Anna grinned as she responded, "I think that would be an excellent idea."

They ate their breakfast rather quickly, much to the consternation of Mrs Brown, who had been awake for hours in the kitchen preparing the meal. They all but rushed from the room, still carrying a slice of toast and jam as they made their way to the stables. Of course, Gerald had already prepared the wagon, and Anna gave him a look that said she realized he had planned this all along. Shortly after, they were on the way to town with Tempus lying in the back of the wagon.

Since the attack, Gerald had taken to wearing his sword on his trips into town. While they were driving Anna watched him adjusting it slightly when it rattled against the seat.

"What was it like in Bodden?" she asked quite unexpectedly.

"The town or the Keep?" he replied.

"The village, was it a lot like Uxley?"

"No, they built the village at Bodden inside the outer bailey. The whole village is essentially walled."

Anna was thoughtful for a moment then asked, "Do they grow the crops inside the walls then?"

"No," he continued, "the farmers grow their crops in the area away from the Keep. The baron doesn't want any buildings just outside the walls, it aids the enemy during a siege, so the farmhouses are all some distance away."

"But what if an attack comes?" she asked.

"Well, there's a keep at one end that's much higher than the walls, and there's a signal fire at the top. If an attack is imminent, a fire is lit, and that's the signal to rush to the Keep. Normally there would be outposts with signal fires as well, but during the first siege, back in '25 the raiders bypassed the signal fires and got into the inner keep."

"It must have been terrible."

"Yes, there were a lot of deaths. After that siege, the baron re-organized the watch system to avoid the same mistake. He was a fast learner, and he wouldn't get caught unawares again."

"What was it like being a soldier? What did you do when you weren't fighting?"

"Mostly I trained. I was driven in those days, the loss of my wife and daughter had hurt me deeply, and I swore to kill as many Norlanders as possible. I was a soldier when I married, but after their deaths, I became a man obsessed. Every spare moment was taken up in training."

"Did you fight a lot?" asked Anna.

"Yes, the frontier was a volatile border, with Norland raiders coming across the river on a regular basis. They made a big push the next summer and laid siege. Lord Richard became the Baron of Bodden when his brother died. When he was named the new baron, he made me his Sergeant-at-Arms.

"What's a Sergeant-at-Arms do?" Anna seemed extremely interested in every little detail of his frontier life.

"He's the senior soldier in the garrison. The baron would give the orders, and I would make sure they were carried out. That included seeing to the men's training. Eventually, he also made me the weapons master."

"What's a weapons master do?" she prompted, absorbing his every word.

"It's like a senior sergeant. I had to look after the weapons, properly train the soldiers, and so on. I was even asked to teach the baron's daughter, but that's a whole other story."

They rounded the corner that led to the village, and the familiar structures that collectively made up Uxley were not far off. They would be arriving soon. The view was quite picturesque, and they shared a moment of silence.

"What was it like fighting? Was it scary?"

He thought for a moment and then replied honestly.

"It was terrifying. A battle is not all clash of arms and ringing horns. It's blood and guts and sweat. It's entrails and shit clogging your movement and swamping your nose with smells. It's wild moments of fear, but an experienced soldier can harness that fear, and as long as you don't break, you'll win through. The baron hated killing, but he was a good leader. We had a chance to obliterate the Norlanders, but he wisely chose to let them escape. He said that if he killed them all, the entire country would rise against us, yelling for revenge. He's a resourceful tactician."

"What are the Norlanders like? Are they really wild men in furs?"

"No, they're much like us, even speaking the same language, though they have some words that are slightly different. If you were to dress one as a Mercerian, you wouldn't be able to tell the difference."

They were coming into the village proper, and Tempus sat up. Off in the distance, they heard Jax barking, and Tempus knew it was play time. He leaped from the wagon, shaking it with his sudden movement, and before they knew it, he was running ahead, barking in glee.

Sam Collins came out to meet them. They unhooked the horses from the wagon and stabled them. The saddle maker was always happy to see them. They exchanged pleasantries and headed for their usual haunt, the Old Oak Tavern. Jax and Tempus followed along, running circles around the trio as they made their way across the bridge and up to the tavern's entrance. Gerald stopped at the doorway and opened the door for Anna, who dutifully stepped forward to enter. Making her way through the opening, she was greeted with a tremendous cacophony, as all the people inside yelled, "Happy Birthday."

Sam and Gerald stepped up behind her. She had stopped and held her hands to her mouth, utterly surprised by the villagers. A table was set for them at the end of the room, near the fire. In the corner, the local blacksmith was playing the flute with some skill. They brought drinks to the table and then Mrs Babbage, the local baker, presented a large bowl of the sweet apple pudding that Anna liked so much. It was steaming with rich cream poured over it. The smell alone made the entire room echo an appreciative, "Mmmmm."

Gerald was enjoying the experience. He noticed even Renfrew sitting at a table raising his mug in salute to the princess. Cheers were raised, songs were sung, and the party-like atmosphere was infectious.

They were chatting amongst themselves when a red-haired stranger entered the tavern. The room went quiet as he made his way to the bar. A rough-cut green cloak covered his dark chainmail. He walked with an air of importance and leaned on the bar.

"A drink of ale, my good man."

Arlo Harris, the tavern owner, glanced over at the new patron and, with a look of disgust on his face, poured him an ale.

Anna was confused, and asked, "Who's that?"

Gerald sized the man up quickly.

"That," he said quietly, "is a King's Ranger."

"Don't they patrol the king's roads?" she asked.

"Originally, they did, now they just travel around enforcing the king's will. There are still some honest men and women who are rangers, but mostly they take advantage of their position to enrich their own pockets at others expense."

The man drained his tankard and banged it on the counter, the universal signal for a refill. Arlo looked at him, expecting to see some coins.

The man reached into his tunic and brought forth his mark. Each King's Ranger wore a medallion around his neck with the symbol of the rangers on one side and their number on the back. It was a sign of their power. The man held it out as if it were a magic talisman.

"Rangers drink for free," he said loud enough for all to hear. "If you disagree, you can send the bill to the king."

"That's not true," Anna burst out, incensed at the ranger's attitude. "There's no such law!"

She sat up, angry that he was taking advantage of the villagers, her villagers. The ranger looked at the table and wandered over in a slow, calculated manner.

"Well, well, well, what do we have here? An expert in the laws of the kingdom?"

The room was still quiet, watching the story unfold before their very eyes. No one dared upset a King's Ranger, it just wasn't done. Anna stood up in an attempt to make herself bigger. She was scared but dared not back down now. Gerald immediately stood, placing his hand on the hilt of his sword.

"We don't want any trouble," he said, keeping his voice as neutral as possible.

"King's Rangers don't get to take what they want!" Anna declared, defiantly.

Tempus perked his ears up.

She was cut off abruptly. "Shut up," the ranger yelled, "or I'll cut that tongue from your mouth!" He turned to look at Gerald who stood, calmly, waiting for his next move. "You have the appearance of a soldier. You ever served?"

"Yes," Gerald replied, "in the Northern Wars."

The ranger eyed him carefully before he spoke again, "I say you're a deserter. You look fit enough. No one leaves the army till they're dead or infirm."

Gerald took a step forward to place himself between Anna and the ranger. No one in the room moved, so spellbound were they by the confrontation. Anna put a hand on Tempus to calm him. The last thing they needed right now was the dog attacking a King's Ranger.

"Hear me!" the man spoke in a loud voice. "I am Osferth of the King's Rangers, and I arrest this man as a deserter."

He moved to draw his sword, but Gerald's hand was quicker. It shot forward, and he gripped the man's wrist, holding it tight in a vice-like grip.

"Get your hands off me, you filthy deserter!" Osferth snarled.

"I think you are mistaken, friend," Gerald said, trying to soothe the man. "I work at the Royal Estate."

"A likely story," Osferth said. "I don't suppose you have any proof of this?" He glanced around the room.

Surprisingly, it was Renfrew who spoke up. "It's true," he offered, "he's the Royal Groundskeeper and that young lady," he pointed at Anna, "is Her Royal Highness, Princess Anna."

His words were slightly slurred, a testament to the alcohol he had consumed. He rose, albeit unsteadily to his feet and moved slowly over towards the ranger, who watched him warily.

"Of course," Renfrew continued, "you could arrest or kill Gerald here at your discretion, but I would have to report that to my immediate superior. Perhaps you know him, Marshal-General Valmar?"

The name struck fear into the ranger's eyes. Everyone knew that Valmar was the king's closest confidant. Gerald slowly relaxed his grip on the man's wrist. He was aware that Osferth would not like this humiliation, but now he needed a graceful exit.

It was Arlo who diffused the situation.

"Come," he said, "finish your drink my ranger friend, and let's forget this whole thing."

Osferth stared at Gerald. It was as if there was a test of willpower going on.

"I'll remember you," he said at last. "You'd best hope that our paths don't cross again."

The ranger turned back to the bar and quickly drained the tankard again. He wiped his mouth on his sleeve and then strode from the bar. A collective sigh of relief emanated for those watching as he left. Anna walked over to the bar.

"Here," she said, "let me pay for the ranger's drinks."

Arlo surprised her. "No, Your Highness, it's just part of doing business in Merceria. You keep the coins for other things."

She turned to face Renfrew. "Thank you, Renfrew, for your service."

"Don't thank me, Princess," he said, "I'm merely being selfish. I've grown quite accustomed to this new lifestyle, and I wouldn't want anything to interfere with it."

She watched him wobble a little as he tried to stand still, then he turned slowly and trod back to his seat, waving at the tavern owner to get another drink.

. . .

It was late afternoon by the time they were ready to leave the party. Gerald checked outside to make sure the ranger wasn't around to cause any trouble before he would let Anna out. They made their way back to the wagon and Gerald hitched the horses. Tempus was very alert, looking out for danger and Anna clung to the loose skin around his neck.

They said their farewells to Sam and Jax, then headed back towards the estate. They would be home by dinner time, but neither one was hungry. They had eaten heartily, but the confrontation prevented the food from sitting well. After some moments, Anna turned to Gerald.

"I was scared, Gerald. Why would that man be like that?"

He carefully considered his answer. "I'm afraid that the king is not known for his hospitality. He can be a cruel man, and the people that enforce his rule can be brutal. They're not known for their manners, unfortunately. Men like Osferth like to abuse their power, to make other people look weak."

"It's all because of the king," she stated with a resigned voice. "No one likes the king, all they ever do is fear him."

He felt sorry for the young girl, she never really had to deal with her father.

"I'm afraid that's true, Anna, but that doesn't mean you have to be like him. You're free to make your own decisions in life."

"I wish that were true," she said with a wisdom that belied her age.

"It is true," he reiterated. "You can do anything you want."

"Really?" she said, putting her hand to her chin.

She had seen Gerald do this on more than one occasion and now mimicked his mannerism.

"Really!" he assured her.

She looked straight at him as if to size him up. He kept his eyes on the road, but he couldn't help but feel that Anna was still measuring him somehow.

"You've taught many soldiers before, even the baron's daughter," she stated.

"Yes, that's true," he agreed hesitantly, knowing something else was on her mind.

"Would you teach me to defend myself? I don't need to be a knight or anything, just the basics of keeping myself safe."

He turned to look at her, to gauge the depth of her commitment.

"All right, I will," he finally acquiesced. "We can start tomorrow, but it will take time."

She smiled and sat up straighter. "Yay," she celebrated, "I can't wait to start."

For the rest of the trip, Gerald listened with a smile on his face as Anna described how she would become a mighty warrior princess, vanquishing evil and bringing peace to the land.

They started training the very next day. Gerald, carrying a large sack, took Anna out to a field, away from the view of the Hall. It was a warm day for autumn, and the sun had decided to come out, reflecting its glory on the leaves of red and yellow. Anna was eager to start, waiting impatiently while Gerald looked around. Satisfied that he had found the best place to begin, he drew his sword and presented the handle to Anna.

"Here," he suggested, "try holding this. Get a feel for the weight of it."

Anna complied, grasping the hilt, but when he let go of the other end, the heavy blade fell to the ground. She struggled to lift it, but her small body was just too light to hold the heavy weapon.

"It's too heavy," she objected through gritted teeth, still determined to give it her best try.

Gerald gently removed the sword from her hand.

"One day, you'll find it easy enough to wield, but for now we need to build up a little bit of muscle. To start our training, I have two things for you."

He reached into the sack and pulled forth a slim dagger in a leather scabbard.

"This," he said, handing it to Anna, "will be your dagger. I'll show you how to use it eventually, but first, you must learn to care for it. Each day you will need to clean it and oil it, but I'll show you how. The second item I have is this." In a smooth motion, he reached into the sack and pulled forth a stick, about three feet long. "It'll feel a bit awkward at first, but it's much lighter than the sword."

He walked over and handed it to her, presenting it by holding it much like a staff. She took the stick in both hands and examined it. It was a pretty ordinary stick, though it had been trimmed to be smooth and there were no rough edges on it

"What do I do with this?" she seemed perplexed.

"We're going to go on a walk, and you're going to swing it. Pretend it's a sword, try to take the top off the weeds, that sort of thing. Once you've gotten used to carrying the weight, we'll go through some basic drills."

"So, you're going to teach me how to use a staff?" she asked him.

"No, you're going to learn to use it as a weight trainer. For you, it will be a mighty great-sword that you can use to slay dragons!" He was enjoying himself.

She contemplated the stick, then picked the end that appeared easier to hold. She gripped it with both hands, one above the other and tried swinging it. It appeared clumsy in her hands, and Gerald knew it was an unnatural movement for her. She moved it left and right and tried to twirl it over her head, but she almost hit herself.

Gerald, who had been standing back while she swung, moved closer.

"Try to spread your hands apart a little, it will give you more control over the stick." He placed her left hand at the bottom of the stick, gripping it firmly and then moved her right hand up farther so that there was about a hands-width between them. "Try it again," he said, " but this time a little slower and more deliberate."

She swung again and found it easier to control. The smile on her face told Gerald everything he needed to know.

"Now, we are surrounded by the enemy and must fight to the last."

He dramatically drew his sword, holding it up in front of him like a flag.

"Death to the enemy!" he shouted, and then swung the weapon in an arc slicing through the long grass of the field.

Anna joined in the fun.

"To Victory!" she shouted and swung with all her might.

Later, with the enemy soundly defeated, not a single thistle stood where shortly before there had been a veritable army of them.

They sat down together, and he noticed that Anna was already feeling the weight in her arms.

"Such a victory shall be sung about by the bards for many years. Let us hasten back to the castle, my lady, for a victory toast!"

"Onward Captain," she laughed as she continued, "lest the enemy return!"

Gerald liked to make the training fun, so for the next few days, they carried on with attacking weeds. Anna's arms grew more comfortable swinging the stick, and after a while they were not quite so sore in the evenings. After each day's activities, when Anna retired for the night, Gerald would return to his cottage where he would pull out his knife to continue making a wooden training sword for her to use. He presented this to her on the fourth day. He even had a rather crude scabbard that he had convinced Sophie to sew up for him.

She strapped the new sword to her waist, and Gerald realized he must teach her another skill, walking without tripping on one's scabbard, for she was still quite short and it had a tendency to hit the ground when she walked.

By the second week, she was getting used to it, and it became a symbol of pride for her to walk around with her sword. They were heading out to the field again with Anna deep in thought. She looked at Gerald and then spoke after organizing her thoughts carefully. He could always tell when this was the case for she had a habit of furrowing her brows just before she turned to face him.

"What weapon did you use during the wars?" Anna began.

"Oh, I've fought with many. Axe, mace, longsword, hammer, pretty much everything."

"But did you have a favourite?" she probed, a pensive look on her face.

"Primarily a Mercerian longsword, but when I was in a shield wall, I would use a short sword or a long knife. A much better option for stabbing."

"Aren't all longswords the same?"

"They're similar, but Mercerian longswords tend to be a little shorter with a slightly wider blade. In Westland, their swords are thinner but longer, a very elegant weapon."

"What do the Norlanders use?" She was certainly inquisitive today.

Gerald thought about this before answering, "They use pretty much anything. They seem to favour axes when on foot, but their horsemen use swords."

Anna pondered this for a moment before continuing. "What's it like to be in a battle?" she asked at last.

He had to think on this.

"Most of the time," he started, "you stand around waiting. The actual fighting doesn't last long. I remember a stand-up battle we had near the river once."

"What's a stand-up battle?" Anna seemed to have a question prepared for each of his answers.

"More of a formal battle, where both sides form up before the fight. Sometimes conflicts happen when two armies blunder into each other, but occasionally both sides are ready to fight, and we refer to those as a stand-up battle."

"Do they happen very often?" she continued her interrogation.

"No, it takes some skill to move an army into a position where the enemy has to fight, and we spent most of our time chasing raiders. We chased them once to the river, but it turned out to be a trap. They were waiting for us with their troops already deployed."

"Did you fight?"

"Oh, yes. The baron deployed the men with the footmen in the middle and archers on the flanks. He kept his knights in reserve for the final push. I can still remember the cold. It was an early winter, and the frost was forming on our armour. Chainmail can get very cold, and we weren't moving right away. It was a relief when the baron ordered us forward, I can tell you. I can still hear our feet crunching the icy snow as we strode along. I was a sergeant then. My job was to keep the line straight as they advanced while the archers fired from the flanks. The enemy was using their shields to protect themselves from the arrows, so they were holding them over their heads. When the arrows stopped, they suddenly realized we were coming."

The story entranced Anna. "What happened next?"

"I ordered the men into a run, not a full out run, mind you, more of a jog. We hit them before they could properly form a shield wall and punched right through their line."

"Did you kill them all?" she prompted.

"No, when a line is broken, the army generally falls apart. Their leaders in the back tend to panic, and the whole command breaks apart. They broke and ran for the river, and we let them go."

"What do you mean you let them go? Why would you do that?" she said, surprised.

"Our knights moved in and herded them using the flats of their swords, but not before we'd managed to capture their leader."

"And you brought back the prisoners in triumph!" she said.

"No, actually, the baron made them promise never to invade Merceria again, and then let them go on their honour."

She looked dumbstruck. She had not expected this.

"But why didn't you kill them?"

"Killing them," he continued, "would only have made the other survivors thirst for vengeance. Fitz had the right idea for they didn't trouble us for years after that."

"But the Northern Wars continue," she prompted.

"Yes, but those leaders and their men were never seen again. I learned a valuable lesson that day. There's more to being a great leader than just fighting well, you have to apply the mind and the heart to it."

She took her time thinking about this before speaking again, "I think I understand. War is something to be avoided if at all possible, isn't it?"

He was surprised by her easy acceptance of the logic.

"Yes, war is the last thing to have, and only when all other avenues have been exhausted."

"There are all sorts of books in the library about war, and fighting and glory and such, but none of them talk about war like you do."

He looked at her in earnest. "Of course not, those books weren't written by people who were there! You'd be surprised, I think, to talk to real soldiers. Perhaps one day you'll meet the baron, and he can tell you."

"Do you think that I should learn other weapons as you did? Should I know how to use an axe, spear or mace?"

"Well," he said after some thought, "that would be difficult since we don't have those weapons here."

"We could order some from Wincaster," she suggested. "You give me the name of an armourer in the Capital, and I'll send some coins and have them delivered here."

"And how would we get the coins for them?" Gerald asked.

It was her turn to smile, "That's easy, there's plenty of coins in the strongbox. I've been looking over the books. Uxley Hall has a large budget, and we're only using a tiny part of it."

Now it was Gerald's turn to be surprised again. "You've been going over the books?"

"Yes, I've been taking care of the estate's ledgers, and then I get Hanson to sign the letters going to the Palace."

He should have known that this small child would see it as her duty to keep her home running efficiently. It wouldn't be the last time he was surprised by her, but it was certainly one of the more interesting things he learned.

"All right," he said at last, "let's get to the clerk's room and write up a letter and see what it gets us. With luck, we'll hear back in about a month."

They headed off to the Hall to draft their strange request. Gerald wasn't sure if it would work, but since coming to Uxley, he had learned at least one thing, strange was the new normal.

NINETEEN

Fitz

AUTUMN 957 MC

~

E very year, just before winter set in, King Andred IV liked to call all his nobles to court. It was not that there was anything important to discuss, but he wanted to wield his authority by having them obey the summons, bringing him a feeling of absolute power.

It was for this reason that Lord Richard Fitzwilliam, Baron of Bodden, found himself following Marshal-General Roland Valmar as he inspected the troops on the parade square behind the Palace. The king, in his infinite wisdom, had not seen fit to send additional troops to Bodden, despite the baron's repeated requests, but had insisted that he follow the marshal-general on his monthly inspection to see the calibre of the forces that the kingdom boasted.

As he followed along behind the marshal-general, he was appalled at the poor state of the soldiers. It was clear that Valmar did not place great reliance on his infantry, for they were poorly turned out, with weapons dull or unused and chainmail that was patched in random places. Fitz didn't care much what a soldier looked like as long as he could fight, but rusty mail and dull weapons did not bode well for the troop's morale. The marshal-general, for the most part, ignored the men lined up in two ranks but spent great effort to be cordial to the officers, whose well-bred back-grounds were quite evident. The only exception was the Wincaster Bowmen. These troops, known as 'The Greens' for their distinctly coloured surcoat, were led by Captain Harold Wainwright, a commoner, as was usual for all missile troops. Wainwright's men looked battle-hardened and lethal and yet the marshal did not even deign to talk to their captain. Fitz fell back from the group as they passed, allowing him to speak with the captain. Captain Wainwright looked surprised. He was used to being ignored.

"An exemplary body of men, Captain," said Fitz.

"Thank you, my lord," Wainwright responded professionally.

"How long have you been in Wincaster?"

"Only six months my lord," he replied, once again in a very neutral tone.

"And where were you before that?" Fitz asked. "Your men looked hardened."

The captain, still standing stiffly at attention looked directly at the baron.

"We were in Mattingly, my lord. We recruit from the villages of Mattingly and Wickfield, with a few Hawksburg men thrown in."

The baron leaned in conspiratorially to talk in a lower voice, "Keep them the way you have them, Captain. Companies in the capital tend to get lazy and lose their edge. I know Valmar doesn't give you much credit, but the greens are an important part of a combined army, remember that. Good work, keep it up."

"Aye, my lord," the captain replied, stiffening his shoulders.

Fitz, finished with the conversation, increased his pace to catch up to the marshal-general, who had now reached the last unit, the knights. These elitist troops were the kingdom's pride and joy and, Fitz had to confess, they made an impressive show. They were the heavy troops of the realm, with glittering plates of steel attached to their chainmail which had been polished to a high degree. Impressive to look at, but Fitz knew that most of them were useless. They were all nobles, born to an elite ruling class, but very few could take orders correctly. He had carefully trained the few knights he had in Bodden, breaking them of their old habits, but this bunch seemingly considered their appearance more important than anything else. They had the most expensive horses, impressive to see, but as somewhat of an expert in horseflesh, Fitz knew they would not have the stamina for a campaign. No, here stood parade troops. The only saving grace was the fact that no other kingdom in the land had such a contingent, and even the Norlanders had been quiet of late. He fervently hoped that things would stay that way for some time and that these men would not have to ride into battle.

The marshal-general finished his inspection, having spoken to a number of the knights in person.

He turned to Fitz and asked, "Well, what do you think, Baron? Do they impress you?"

The baron replied diplomatically, "They are quite a sight, marshal-general, quite a sight indeed."

This appeared to placate the marshal who smiled.

"Indeed, they are," he agreed. "Come, let us return to the Palace for some refreshments."

Without waiting for a reply, he strode back towards the Palace. Fitz followed, but as he approached the Palace, he noticed Lord Brandon coming out of the building and raised a hand to get his attention.

"I will be with you in a moment, marshal-general," said Fitz, "I just need to take care of something first."

"Don't be long or all the wine will be gone!" Valmar laughed as he spoke, disappearing into the Palace.

Lord Robert walked over to the baron.

"I hope I'm not interrupting anything?" he said, a slightly worried look on his face.

"Not at all Robert, I've always got time for you. Something important?" Fitz asked.

"Not so much important," Lord Robert continued, "as puzzling."

"You have me intrigued," the baron responded. "Let's talk as we walk, I need to change. Do you mind?"

"No, not at all, Richard. You remember that business with Uxley I told you about?"

"Yes," replied Fitz, "I remember it well. I sent a letter to the estate. Did anything ever come of it?"

"Oh, yes. The very next letter apologized for the inconvenience and said that everything had been resolved satisfactorily, but that's not what I wanted to talk to you about."

"Indeed?" said Fitz. "Now, you have me even more interested."

"Well," continued Lord Robert, "it seems the estate is making some rather strange requests of late."

Fitz stopped in his tracks and turned to look at his friend. "What kind of strange requests?"

"It seems they want some weapons."

"Weapons?" asked Baron Fitzwilliam. "What do you mean, they want 'weapons'?"

"Well, they're not raising an army, if that's what's worrying you. They asked for some weapons, two of each to be exact. Maces, axes, swords, spears and so on."

"Did they say what for?" asked the incredulous Richard.

"No, but they did include the funds to pay for them. They even had the name of a weaponsmith in town, a man by the name of Simon Graves."

Fitz thought for a moment before speaking, "Yes, I know the name. He supplies weapons for some of the infantry companies stationed here. I suspect our favourite groundskeeper has provided the name. He would certainly be familiar with it."

"So what should I do?" asked Lord Robert. "Do I send the weapons?"

Baron Fitzwilliam stared off into the distance thinking, then turned back to his friend. "I tell you what, write back and let them know you are working on it and they can expect them to arrive within, say, two weeks. I have to return to Bodden soon, so I'll escort them to Uxley myself."

"Splendid!" replied Lord Robert. "I will leave things in your capable hands."

Baron Fitzwilliam let Robert depart and put his mind into organizing mode. He had much to do; he must wrap up his affairs in Wincaster, and then visit Uxley Hall. He didn't know what to expect when he arrived, some disfigured forgotten royal offspring no doubt, but why the request for weapons?

Anna swung her sword with her right hand. His quick parry stopped her blow, so she twisted the blade and swung in an arc over her head, using a backhand slice. A defensive move blocked this as well. She took a slight step forward and repeated her actions. They had been at it all morning. First, she would advance and swing, then she would back up, performing the blocks as Gerald took his turn attacking.

It was very repetitive, but her movements became more natural to her. She reached the end of the practice area and put her blade point down to the ground, the sign of surrender. They took a break and, despite the cold day, they were both sweating. The yard at the side of the house was flat and, thanks to Gerald's efforts, nicely grassed. They had given up on trying to hide the training. Everyone at the Hall already knew what was going on and this way they were close to the Hall and fresh water.

Anna took a seat on the small wooden bench that was placed against the wall for just this reason. Tempus, who had been watching the practice with a calm demeanour, immediately got up to go over and sit with her. Gerald was wiping the sweat from his face when he heard the distinctive sound of a horse and wagon in the distance.

"Hello," he called out, "it sounds like we have visitors."

"We're not expecting anyone. Who do you think it is?" Anna asked.

Gerald moved so that he could view the roadway.

"It looks like a wagon, but there's also a rider with it. Can't tell who though. They're bundled up against the cold weather."

"I'd better get inside and change," remembered Anna, who had taken to wearing old clothes for practice.

"Good idea. I'll go and see who's here."

He leaned his practice sword against the wall before making his way to the front of the house. He rounded the corner in time to observe the wagon pulling up in front of the entranceway. The rider dismounted effortlessly and then took a moment to stroke the horse, talking to it softly. Gerald watched as the stable master and two stable boys ran out to take care of the horses. As he neared, the cloaked man turned to him, removing the scarf from his face to be heard.

He then called out, "Gerald, old boy! So good to see you!"

Gerald was stunned. Lord Richard Fitzwilliam had come to Uxley Hall!

"My lord," he stammered out at last, "what brings you to Uxley?"

"I've come to check up on you," he smiled.

Gerald was at a loss for words. Fitz extended his hand in a manner of greeting and Gerald shook it heartily, still the firm grip that he remembered.

"So good to see you, my lord," he said finally.

"That's enough of that, Gerald. You must call me Fitz, everyone else does."

"I wouldn't dream of it, Lord," Gerald responded.

"I'm told you've been rather busy here of late," the baron shared.

"According to whom?" Gerald responded with suspicion in his voice.

"Lord Robert Brandon, you remember him? He oversees the Royal Estates now. Oh, don't look so worried, Gerald, you know he's an old friend of the family. You're not in trouble. I was on my way back to Bodden for the winter, and I was informed the estate ordered some weapons. Expecting trouble?"

Gerald was relieved. "No, my lord, those are for training. I have a new... pupil who wants to try different weapons and get a feel for which one they like."

"Typical. I send you to the middle of nowhere as a groundskeeper, and you end up arming the peasants." The tone was serious, but the smile on his face was genuine. "So, tell me, who is this mysterious apprentice?"

Gerald wasn't sure how the baron would react, so he responded neutrally, "Oh, a local type who just wants to be able to defend themselves properly."

As they were talking, Anna appeared from around the side of the house, having changed into something a little nicer. Fitz saw a young girl, about ten, and smiled.

"And who do we have here?" he asked, expecting it to be a servant's daughter.

Anna did her best curtsy. "Anna, my lord," she responded.

The baron smiled, but before Gerald could say anything, Fitz began talking again.

"Listen, Gerald," he said, "I have it on good authority that there may be a royal around here somewhere. Have you seen anything strange? Perhaps a room that no one enters? I think they may be disfigured in some way."

Gerald couldn't help but chuckle slightly, "Oh, aye, there's a royal here all right, and the disfigurement is quite real, I think you might even say shocking."

The baron's interest was piqued. "Do tell," he prompted.

"Well," began Gerald, not quite sure where to start.

"She's disfigured," burst in Anna, "and she has a limp."

"Yes," added Gerald seeing the situation with amusement, "and she has a hunchback."

"And she covers her face," Anna added, quite pleased with herself.

"Truly?" asked the baron, looking at Gerald for confirmation.

Gerald was sweating, not sure how long he could deceive the baron, but he persisted.

"Perhaps," he said at last, "young Anna here could go and inform Her Highness that she has a guest. She does so love visitors for she doesn't get them very often."

"Yes," Anna agreed, "she likes to meet people in the trophy room. Why don't you have His Lordship taken to the drawing room and I'll send Sophie to let you know when she's ready to receive visitors?"

"An excellent idea. My lord?" Gerald looked to the baron.

"By all means, lead on my good man."

The baron appeared intrigued by the forthcoming meeting. Anna ran off to make preparations, while Gerald escorted Baron Fitzwilliam into the drawing room.

They had only gone a few steps when the baron caught his arm, "You're not limping!"

"No, my lord, I was healed."

"The Royal Mage? I thought he only worked for the king."

"I was lucky, he was passing through Uxley and heard of my injury."

"Perhaps my letters to Valmar weren't wasted," Fitz mused.

"I don't believe Valmar knew anything about it."

The baron wore a surprised expression.

"I suppose we will never know for sure. Shall we continue?" he indicated the entrance.

"How are things in the Capital, my lord?" Gerald stalled to give Anna time to prepare herself.

"As uneventful as ever, you know how it is. The king loves to have the nobles beg and scrape for attention. Valmar inspects that group of men he calls an army, and the nobles continue to grumble. Basically, nothing has changed."

"And how fares Lady Beverly?" asked Gerald.

"Nice of you to ask. She's doing well. I had her in service to the Earl of Shrewesdale for a while, but that didn't work out very well. I made it up to her by sending her to the household of Robert Brandon."

"I do remember him," said Gerald. "I met him on a couple of occasions, I believe. He's your brother-in-law, isn't he?"

"Yes," Fitz replied with a sad look on his face. "Lady Evelyn was Robert's older sister, but, as you remember, she died in childbirth. How brief a time we have here before we travel to the Afterlife. Still," he continued, cheering up slightly, "my daughter does me proud."

They entered the drawing room to find Owen placing a tray with some glasses and three bottles of wine on the sideboard. His responsibility discharged, he bowed politely, exiting quietly. Gerald made his way over to the tray to examine the bottles. He noted the presence of a Hawksburg red, holding the bottle up for Lord Richard's inspection.

"A little of the red, my lord? I believe it's one of your favourites."

The baron was all smiles at the prospect, "Excellent choice, I see that being a groundskeeper has not dulled your sense of sophistication!"

They both laughed, for it was a running joke between them. Fitz liked Gerald and ignored his rustic manners. He was more interested in what a man could accomplish than what family he was born into, and he had relied on Gerald for years to keep his men at peak readiness.

Thinking back to his time at Bodden, Gerald asked, "How are the men? Are they still keeping out of trouble?"

"After you left, I had to pick a new sergeant, so I picked Blackwood."

Gerald smiled, he knew William Blackwood well. They had joined up at the same time and had become inseparable. He was a stalwart companion, both on the field of battle and at the taverns.

"A good choice."

"He's turned out well enough," continued the baron, "though he isn't you. He doesn't quite think as fast as you do, but he's good at keeping the men in line."

He sipped his glass of wine, letting the fragrant aroma tease his taste buds before swallowing. His enjoyment of the drink was interrupted by a light knock on the door, which then opened, revealing Sophie.

"If Your Lordship would be so kind," she spoke somewhat timidly, "Her Highness has sent for you. If you follow me, I'll show you the way."

Fitz drained his glass and placed it gently on the table. "By all means, lead on."

They fell into step behind Sophie. From the drawing room, it was a short walk until Sophie was lightly knocking on the door to the trophy room.

"Your Highness," she said, "your guest is here."

Only a muffled reply could be heard, then she opened the door to allow them to enter. The heavily curtained room boasted a newly lit fire. It was the only light source present and the flickering flame threw dancing shadows around the room, lending it an eerie presence. A chair had been set near the fireplace. Looking at it, they could discern it was a high-backed chair with thick arms, but the seat itself was enveloped in shadows.

A voice rasped out, "Come to the fireplace where I can see you."

Baron Richard Fitzwilliam trod quietly as if any sound might upset the solemnness of the room. He stood just in front of the fire, his back towards the heat so that he might face the person in the chair. The small figure in the chair was wrapped in a dark cloak which concealed their face. The baron was unsure of what to make of this diminutive figure. Gerald stood off to the side, waiting to watch what would transpire.

"And you are?" squeaked the voice.

"Lord Richard Fitzwilliam, Baron of Bodden," replied Fitz

"And why have you come?" posed the voice.

"I have come to offer my service to you, Your Highness, to do whatever I can to assist you," the baron offered earnestly.

A giggle escaped the cloaked figure and then a cough to cover it up. A small hand was extended out of the hooded cloak and was held out to Gerald.

"Gerald," she commanded, "would you mind introducing me to His Lordship?"

She rose from her chair as Gerald began to speak.

Gerald took a step back and bowed. "May I present to you Her Royal Highness, Princess Anna of Merceria," he said, sweeping his arms to indicate Anna. "I do hope you don't find her blonde hair too offensive."

Anna threw off her cloak revealing herself. Baron Fitzwilliam was a hardened soldier having fought on the frontier in many campaigns, yet never, in all his years, was he so surprised as he was at this moment. Anna was now laughing out loud, and even Gerald failed to suppress a chuckle.

The baron stood there for what felt like an eternity and then recovered his wits. He extended a leg and bowed deeply, his hands out behind him.

"Your Highness," he solemnly replied, "I am truly honoured to meet you."

Anna held out her hand, and the baron took it in his and kissed her knuckle. She took a good look at Lord Fitzwilliam as he straightened up. He was older than Gerald with the same hardened look, but where Gerald was a commoner, the baron was every bit a noble, dressed in the finest of clothes without being ostentatious.

Conscious of perhaps insulting a noble, Anna apologized, "I trust, my lord, that you do not take offense at our little jest?" She seemed a little less sure of herself.

Fitz smiled warmly, "Of course not, Your Highness. But if I might enquire?"

Gerald knew where this was going. "She's not disfigured, my lord. Only the colour of her hair marks her in any way."

Now, after all the years of mystery, Fitz understood. The entire royal line, stretching back to the founding of the kingdom, were dark haired. A blonde child could only mean one thing. No wonder the king took pains to hide her away. He felt a wave of sympathy for the child. It was a situation not of her making, yet to be hidden away forever and denied even the comfort of a family, it was almost too much to bear. As he looked from Anna to Gerald, he recognized the bond that they shared, and now he understood Gerald's devotion. She was like the child he had lost, and he was like the father she never had. He felt proud that he had sent Gerald here, though he had no idea at the time how things would develop. His thoughts were interrupted by the princess.

"Are you travelling alone, Baron?" she asked.

"No, Your Highness, I have an escort, but I felt it best to leave them in town. I didn't know what to expect here and, well, I thought it best to keep it as quiet as possible."

"Gerald," requested Anna, "would you mind opening up the curtains, I think now that our little charade is over it might be nice to have some light in here. Will you join us for dinner, Baron? We have a well-stocked pantry," she added.

"I would be delighted," he grinned, as he responded to her invitation.

Cook prepared a meal fit for a noble while they gave the baron a tour of the estate. The ride was pleasant, though the cooler weather had set in, and by the time they had returned to the delicious meal that awaited them, they were quite chilled. The three of them ate in the dining room, a ridiculously large room, but Anna defied convention by having them all sit at one end. They talked all through the meal, Fitz filling them in on what was transpiring in the kingdom, and Gerald and Anna telling him about the things they had done.

Fitz envied them. It had been many years since his daughter had been this young, and he remembered with fondness how the small red-headed child had stolen his heart so readily after her mother died. He was impressed by how intelligent the princess was. She appeared to have a wealth of information within her small head and could conjure forth facts and figures with ease. She veritably absorbed anything he told her like a sponge. In the end, Anna insisted he stay overnight at the Hall, so notes were sent to his escort in town not to expect him until morning. He was put up in a well-appointed guest suite.

Early the next morning, after a hearty breakfast, they escorted him to the front of the Hall. His horse was waiting for him, held by a stable hand.

"It has been an honour to visit you, Your Highness," said Fitz.

"The honour was all ours," said Anna, Gerald close beside her.

Fitz mounted his horse with the ease of a man bred to the saddle. He looked down at the princess one more time.

"If ever Your Highness needs anything," he promised, "I trust you will remember that I am at your disposal."

"Thank you, my lord. I shall remember that," she humbly accepted his pledge.

The baron waved one last time and rode off, leaving Anna and Gerald watching him until he passed through the estate's gates. Anna looked up at Gerald who returned her look.

"First one back in gets the rest of the bacon!" she yelled and then ran inside, her old friend following behind.

TWENTY

The Grotto

WINTER 957/958 MC

⌇

The winter of 57/58 was the harshest they had ever experienced. Cold winds blew in from the north, and the ice and snow covered the land in depths never before seen. So cold was the weather that the princess seldom went outside. Even Gerald struggled to make it back and forth from his cottage that year, and in the end, Anna insisted he stay in a guest room in the Hall, rather than tread through the heavy snow every day.

The Hall was warm and cozy, but the firewood would only last so long. On at least three occasions, when it looked like the weather might let up for a few hours, a whole troop of servants, led by Gerald, ventured forth to help chop wood and cart it inside. The stacked cords of wood, thoroughly wet from the ice, became frozen together and in the end, it was decided to bring the wood inside, stacked in the great hall until needed.

So desperate did the need for firewood get that Gerald ventured out one day wearing three layers of clothes. Even so, the cold seeped through the layers and in short order his fingers were numb, and his legs shivering. He persisted, and brought down a small tree, trimming its branches and dragging the trunk back to the Hall. By the time he was at the door, he was faltering, and it took Ned and Owen to pull him inside. They hauled the trunk in and began splitting the wood in the great hall.

Gerald, quite naturally, considering the circumstances, managed to acquire a wicked cold and was sentenced to bed rest. Spoon fed an herbal tea that Anna arranged to have brewed, he recovered quickly, and when he asked about it, she told him that Andronicus, the Royal Mage, had sent her some books on herbal remedies.

Once he recovered from his cold, he and Anna resumed their training. The Hall now became their battleground, and she was developing a quick blade. Being small in stature, she could never produce a heavy blow, but they decided she should use her speed to her advantage, striking quick but light thrusts whenever possible.

They were practicing in the Hall, just after midwinter and Anna was trying out her new shield. It was a light wooden construction, made for her size. Gerald stood opposite with practice sword and shield in hand. He advanced towards her, and she held the shield up, as she had done many times before. This time, however, instead of thrusting with his sword, he used his shield to strike hers, the force sending her tumbling. She got up and dusted herself off.

"That's not fair," she complained.

Gerald relaxed his weapon and looked at her.

"What do I always tell you?" he asked.

"I know, nothing is fair in combat, but how am I supposed to stop that?"

"Come at me with your shield, and I'll show you," he explained

He stood with his shield in his left arm, facing her. As she moved forward and pushed with her shield, he stepped slightly to the right and angled his shield to the left. It was enough to throw her off balance, and she staggered forward. He tapped her lightly on the backside with the training sword.

"That," he said triumphantly, "is how it's done. Now, you try it."

It took her a couple of tries at it, but she soon got it down. Gerald knew the trick would never work on her again. She was fun to teach, and her excitement was infectious. When she wanted to understand how a shield wall worked, he roped in several servants to help. He showed Anna and Sophie how to hold a shield and interlock them, then the three of them made a small wall. The other servants tried to push their way through. It was quite entertaining. Anna had to convince them to try harder to break through. In the end, the servants could drive them back as the floor was rather slippery, but they could not break the wall. Anna was deliriously happy and had the cook prepare a special meal for everyone that evening. The servants joined them in the big dining room for a feast. They were sitting at the table, having finished their dessert when Anna brought up a new subject.

"Gerald," she said in a rather serious manner, "what do you know about kingsleaf?"

Gerald looked at her, once again amazed at her knowledge.

"Kingsleaf is a rare herb, used for the treatment of many symptoms. Chiefly pain management I believe, but it's notoriously difficult to find."

"I've been reading up on it," she said, "in one of the books Andronicus sent me. I think we might be able to find some here, on the estate."

Gerald doubted that but one never really knew, and throughout his time at Uxley, he had learned not to discount things so quickly.

"What makes you think that?" he asked.

"Well," she said, warming to the topic, "according to the books, it grows in marshy areas, and I know the northwest corner of the estate is marshy. You know, down by the grotto."

Gerald knew where she meant. They had often talked about exploring the mysterious grotto, but they had never actually made it down there.

"Well, I suppose it's possible, but we'd have to wait until spring. Anything down there now would just be frozen and covered in snow and ice."

"Exactly," she said triumphantly, "and so I propose Operation Kingsleaf!"

He thought about it for a moment. "I suspect there'll be more than just kingsleaf there. Perhaps we should choose a different name."

She absently tossed a pastry to Tempus, who was lying at her side. The huge dog deftly caught the treat and chewed it quietly.

"You're right. How about Operation Grotto!"

"Very good, Your Highness." His voice took on the 'official' tone, "We shall begin mustering the troops at once."

"Excellent," she declared. "You can be the marshal."

"Who will that make you, then?"

"Why, the queen of course, or maybe the empress? That sounds far more grandiose."

"And what shall our empire be called?" he prompted.

"The Empire of Uxley of course, and Tempus will be the duke!"

"Well then, Your Empress," said Gerald, rising from his seat, "perhaps the duke will join us in the drawing room to discuss our coming campaign."

He knew Tempus would follow her anywhere, the two of them were inseparable. In the evenings, they would retire to sit in front of a roaring fireplace. Gerald would sit in a comfortable armchair, but Anna would always sit on the floor, using Tempus as a backrest. Sometimes she would rise to get a hot drink, and the dog would look forlorn, waiting for her to return.

Anna rose from the table, Tempus dutifully rising from his place beside her and they made their way to the drawing room. They got themselves comfortable, Anna once again using her dog as a backrest. She had a book of herbs from Andronicus in front of her. It was an illustrated guide with beautiful hand-drawn sketches of the various plants. Gerald was sitting comfortably in his usual chair with a hot cider beside him and was perusing a book about swords.

"Gerald," she asked almost absently, "what would kingsleaf be worth, to sell I mean?"

He had to think about that for a moment.

"Let's see, I remember getting some in Bodden once, cost about half a crown per leaf if I remember."

"Half a crown! If we could find one and plant it, we could make a fortune!"

"I don't think it can be done, it's only found in the wild. I don't think anyone's ever been able to grow them in a herb garden," he explained.

"Don't be silly," she said, engrossed in her book, "of course it can be grown, it's a plant, isn't it? It just means we would have to create the right conditions for it to thrive, much like a marsh. Plenty of water I suspect would do the trick, and maybe some loose soil?" She was musing now, thoroughly caught up in her idea.

By the end of the evening, she had come up with a plan and had roped Gerald into helping. They would make a special area in the garden that would be swampy and use soil they brought back from the grotto. Little did they realize what they would find come the spring.

The bitterness of winter had finally passed, and the warmth of spring enveloped the land. The mountains of snow took an interminably long time to melt. The fields turned to mush with the runoff, and the operation could not be started until the melting snow had had its chance to drain away.

Finally, after several weeks of waiting, they mounted their expedition. They wore long boots, for the mud in the grotto would most likely cling to their legs. They took food, packed into backpacks and Tempus carried, in his saddlebags, jars to fill with samples.

The trek to the grotto was lengthy, and it was over a full bell's toll by the time they approached it. According to the maps at the Hall, the grotto consisted of a small cave in a large rock that was surrounded by a pool of water. At some point in the past, an estate owner must have decided to make a little place to escape away to. They didn't know what to expect, but they were prepared for anything. Gerald brought his sword, in case they should run into bandits or dangerous animals, and Anna was still carrying her dagger, which was now her pride and joy. Tempus, of course, didn't need a weapon, his mouth was full of teeth which he was quite capable of using, should it be necessary.

The grotto lay in a depression in the extreme northwestern corner of the estate. They had to travel through some thick woods to find it. There must have been a trail at some point in the distant past, but it had long since grown over with weeds and underbrush. As they cleared the tree line, Gerald paused for a breath of air. Anna, always eager and full of energy, ran ahead and stopped short.

"Oh, it's beautiful," she avowed, awe filling her voice.

Gerald pushed himself forward to stand beside her. Tempus, ignoring the view, decided to lie down and eat some weeds. Below them, they saw a pool of water with weeds and long grasses clogging the bank. There was, indeed, a large rock, so out of place but it took up the northern bank of the pool. The pool itself must have been about thirty yards in length and about the same width, though the actual banks were hard to determine due to the dense growth of reeds. The water looked clear, and as they watched, the sun came out, sending a cascade of shimmering light across the surface.

They made their way down to the grotto, quickly discovering another interesting fact, the ground was very muddy. It clung to their boots in great chunks, and almost immediately they were struggling just to move. The muck made sucking sounds as they pulled each foot out and tried to move forward.

Anna quickly found herself stuck in the mud and Tempus charged forth. Instantly he was covered in the stuff too, but the great beast struggled desperately to get to her. As soon as she could grasp his collar, the huge mastiff pulled her free, dragging her from the grip of the muck and mire.

They retreated to a dry spot to reconsider their plans.

"It appears," remarked Gerald, rather obviously, "that our plans will have to wait a few more weeks for the sun to dry this out a bit more."

Anna, who by this time was sitting on the ground catching her breath, was a sight to behold, for she was covered in mud from head to toe.

"Yes, I think you're right," she replied breathlessly.

Tempus rose suddenly and started sniffing around, his tail wagging.

They both looked at him, then Anna said, rather needlessly, "Looks like Tempus found something."

She rose from her spot on the ground and wandered over to where the great dog was sniffing. She placed her hand on him, and he sat obediently. She looked intensely at the ground.

"Gerald," she beckoned, "come over here and look at this."

The interest in her voice coaxed him to rise. He walked over to where she was examining the ground. She had pulled out her dagger and now used it to point to something on the ground. Gerald knelt to get a better view of a depression in the mud, a footprint, but a print the likes of which he had never seen before.

"What do you make of it?" Anna asked, intrigued by the strange marks.

The prints were slightly smaller than Gerald's hand but showed a three-toed foot of some type. His first thought was a bird, but it was too large, and the toes were more substantive, like a lizard. The single print did not reveal much more. Gerald stood up and placed a foot beside the strange depression and put his weight on it, then withdrew his foot.

"What are you doing?" asked Anna.

"I want to estimate how much weight made the print. You can see my foot went farther into the mud, so it probably weighs less than me. You try it on the other side."

Anna deftly placed a foot on the opposite side, putting her weight on it and then withdrawing. She leaned down and looked at the result.

"My prints are about the same depth," she said after careful examination, "so, whatever it is, is probably about the same size as me. Any idea what it might be? I've never heard of anything that would leave a print like this, have you?"

Gerald thought. He had seen lizards scurrying about near Bodden, but they were much smaller and left more of a slithering trail as their bodies struck the ground. It was then that something occurred to him.

"I think it was walking upright. There's no dragging of the mud on the forward edge of the print."

Anna took off her backpack and rummaged around inside. Moments later, she withdrew a notepad and charcoal and began sketching the print. She had just finished when Tempus barked, and suddenly they were surrounded by a thick fog which appeared out of nowhere.

Anna panicked. "Gerald!" she cried out.

Gerald, who was only a few feet away, stepped towards her to see her shape loom out of the fog. It was mystifying. Only moments before the day had been bright and sunny. He called Tempus, and the big dog appeared through the fog. Gerald played through their actions in his mind. He was confident that if they walked directly away from the way they had been standing, they would be heading towards the tree line.

He grabbed Anna's hand. "This way, don't panic, keep alert."

"Wait," she said, "I haven't finished putting everything away."

She struggled with her pack, almost blind from the fog and Gerald waited nervously, not knowing if anything was about to loom out of the fog.

"I've got it!" she said, and he began moving in the direction he hoped would lead them to safety.

They trod cautiously, testing the ground lest they become stuck in the mud again. Time seemed to pause as they made their way slowly, painfully, towards safety. Suddenly, the fog began to thin, and Gerald could see the tree line in front of them. They staggered out of the fog into the daylight. They made their way up, out of the grotto and turned to look back the way they had come. The thick fog was just beginning to disperse, but it still covered the entire pool.

"That was close," said Anna.

"A little too close, I think," agreed Gerald. "We need to do some research before we come back here. Maybe your books will give us some idea of what made those imprints."

Anna was familiar with every book in the library.

"I don't think any of them mention marks like that. I'm going to write to Andronicus and include a copy of my sketch. We shouldn't do anything till we hear back from him."

"Agreed," said Gerald.

They began the trip back to the Hall, both rattled by their encounter with the fog. They stopped halfway back to get their breath and Anna, turning to Gerald, began to laugh.

"What's so funny?" he asked.

"You! You're all covered in mud!"

He laughed, "You think that's funny, wait till you see yourself in the mirror!"

They laughed all the way back to the Hall and Tempus, always willing to join in the fun, barked and howled as they went.

TWENTY-ONE

The Courier

SUMMER 958 MC

Although Anna had written to Andronicus immediately after returning to the Hall, they had not heard anything in response. They decided against returning to the grotto until such time as they had a better idea of what they were dealing with.

It was later in the summer, and they were in the village, sitting at a table under the old oak tree by the tavern. The sun was hot but a nice breeze cooled them while the tree shaded them. Tempus, as usual, was lying in the sun, trying to absorb it all. Anna was eating a pastry while Gerald sipped cider. The villagers waved or hailed them to say hello as they passed. It was very relaxing, and Gerald soon found himself beginning to doze off, the only thing that stopped him from doing so was the appearance of a rider.

He was coming down the road from Wincaster covered in dust and dirt. The road through Uxley led to the north, and dispatch riders were not an uncommon occurrence. This time, however, the rider dismounted, talking to some villagers nearby. One of them pointed towards Gerald and Anna. The traveller began leading his horse in their general direction. Gerald smiled as he came closer.

"Well, as I live and breathe, Edgar Greenfield! What are you doing here, you old dog?"

The courier stopped short and gazed over at his old friend.

"Gerald Matheson?" he said in disbelief. "I ain't seen you for years. How are you?"

Gerald stood, and moved forward to shake his friend's hand. It had been years since he had seen him.

"I'm good, living the life of a civilian now. How is it you've come to Uxley?" he asked.

The man smiled, "Work. I've been hired to deliver a message to someone at Uxley Hall. Is that about here somewhere?"

"Depends," responded Gerald, "who's the letter for?"

The man reached into his satchel and withdrew a letter with a wax seal on it. A name was written on the front.

"Someone named Anna? Sorry, that's all it says."

"Well, you've come to the right spot," he turned to the side to indicate Anna. "This," he proclaimed, pointing at her, "is Anna."

Edgar walked over to the table and handed the letter to her.

"Thank you."

She took the letter gingerly in her hands, opening it carefully, making sure not to rip the paper. She glanced over the message.

"It's from Andronicus, and it's quite long. Can you wait to see if I have a reply?" she requested.

"Certainly miss," responded Edgar.

Gerald sat down. "Sit down, man, and tell me what you've been up to. It's been ages since I saw you in Bodden."

Edgar grinned again, "Well, I ain't been in Bodden in a couple of years, I can tell you. I ain't a soldier no more, getting too old for that stuff. I'm an independent courier now."

Gerald thought it over while Anna read her letter. Tempus had absorbed all the heat he could handle and came and sat beside his mistress, trying to see what she had in her hands.

"How does that work, being a courier?" he asked.

"Oh, I runs letters for people, charging by the letter and the mile. It's not a great livin', but I gets by. Luckily, I owns me own horse, so I save coins on that. What're you doing now?"

"Would you believe a groundskeeper? It's a simple life, but it keeps me busy."

Anna looked up from her letter, interrupting their conversation with her words, "Excuse me, did you say you were a courier?"

Edgar looked back at her. "That's right miss, a letter courier."

She looked thoughtful, then spoke, "Would you be interested in supplementing your income?"

"I'm always interested in extra coins," answered Edgar. "Whatcha have in mind?"

"I'm looking for people to write to me about their observations as they travel. You know, who's visiting towns, what's happening in the capital, all that sort of thing."

"You mean gossip?"

"Yes, I mean gossip," she replied flatly. "Would you be interested in writing to me about any gossip you hear? I can pay you in crowns?"

"Well," pondered Edgar, "I certainly hear more than my fair share of gossip. How much we talking about?"

"How about," she paused for a moment, "five crowns a month. Plus, I'll give you a ten crown sign-up bonus, provided you don't tell anyone you're working for me."

Edgar looked shocked.

"Let me get this straight, you wanna pay me five crowns a month just to pass on gossip?"

"That's right."

"When do I start?"

Gerald could see her taking the measure of the man.

"I can speak for his trustworthiness," he quickly vouchsafed.

Anna smiled at this, "Thank you, Gerald, you've just made up my mind. Tell me, Edgar, where are you staying tonight? At the inn?"

"No," he answered, "I'll camp just outside of town, cheaper that way."

"I tell you what," Anna continued, pleased with his response. "You follow us to Uxley Hall, and we'll see you fed and put up for the night. In the morning, I'll want you to take some letters back to Wincaster for me. Would that be all right?"

"Certainly miss, be happy to."

"Excellent, it's settled then. Come along, Gerald. We've work to do."

She rose from the table and Gerald, surprised by her sudden energy, rushed to down the rest of his cider. They headed back to Sam's to get their wagon, Tempus loping along after them and Edgar leading his horse by the reins.

A short time later, they were on their way back to the Hall with Edgar trailing along on his horse. Gerald turned from holding the reins to look at Anna.

"What was that all about?" he asked.

"It occurs to me, that there's little more I can learn from the library at Uxley Hall. What better way to learn about the kingdom than by having a group of private messengers?"

"But gossip? What good will that do you?" He was trying to understand where she was going with this.

"I already know about how the kingdom is organized, all about the nobles and so on, but how do the people of Merceria act? What do they talk about? I find it all quite fascinating. Are the people happy? Do they enjoy their lives? I want to know it all," she said, sounding quite passionate about it.

They sat in companionable silence for a little bit. Gerald could see Anna working things out in her head. He let her be for a few more moments, not wishing to interrupt her, then spoke up.

"What was the letter about?" he reminded her finally.

"Oh, I almost forgot," she smiled. "Andronicus thinks we may have found a Saurian."

"What's a Saurian?" he continued his enquiry.

"He says it's an ancient race, sort of a lizard person. He's not familiar with them himself but recommends that I write to some other mages he knows. He sent me instructions on how to contact three of them."

"Three mages? I didn't know the kingdom had that many," responded Gerald.

"We don't. At least one of them is all the way over in Westland." She dug the letter out of her pocket. "One's called Albreda, and she lives in the woods near Bodden. Have you ever heard of her?"

"I believe Fitz had some dealings with her, but I don't know much about her."

"And then," she continued, "there's another one near Mattingly named Aldus Hearn. Apparently, he lives in the woods near there. The third one's called…" she read the name off the page, pronouncing it slowly, "Tyrell Caracticus, he lives in Southport, in Westland. Andronicus says if anyone knew about the Saurians, it would be one of them."

The information was fascinating to Gerald. Other than short trips across the border into Norland, he had not travelled much, certainly not as far as Westland.

"Mages," he murmured, more to himself than to Anna, "you can never tell whether to trust them or not, or so they say."

"So who says?" quizzed Anna.

Gerald was taken aback by the question.

"Well, you know, they! No one knows who they are." He paused for a moment. "Well, I guess I answered your question, there isn't a 'they' is there?"

"Probably not. It's most likely just an old wives' tale."

They arrived at Uxley Hall, and Gerald handed the wagon off to the stable master. They entered the Hall, and Anna called for some food for their guest. Gerald found the meal to be simple, yet filling. Cook had prepared some delicious stew for the three of them, and together with some fresh bread, the meal was quite satisfying. They spoke little during their dinner, but Anna finished eating first and was just waiting for Edgar to complete his meal so that she could ply him with questions. He had just finished his last morsel of bread when she spoke up, taking him by surprise.

"So tell me, Edgar," she began her inquisition, "how did you meet Gerald?"

"Well," he started, "I was a soldier up in Bodden Keep. It was during the siege, you see, the first siege that is. A bunch a Northerners had gotten into the Keep. The little beggars managed to bring down a section of the Keep wall. It collapsed just as it got dark and they had launched an attack from the opposite side to distract us. They was into the courtyard before we knew it." He grabbed his mug, downing a swig of cider before he continued. "Anyway, Fitz, he organizes everyone, and we pushes them back out, but then someone says that a few of them got into the main keep. He gathers me and three others, and we heads in, leaving the rest to shore up the wall with whatever they could."

Anna was engrossed. "Did you find them all?"

"Finding 'em was the easy part, left a path of ruin behind them. They was too interested in looting. Anyways, we follows them down into the cellar and comes across a Northerner lying on his stomach, not moving. Underneath him, you see, was Gerald here. He couldn't have been much older than you are now. He'd stuck a knife into the man's gut. He was all covered in blood."

"It must have been horrible," prompted Anna.

"Oh, it was," Edgar provided, "but after that first siege, Fitz made sure it never happened again. He built an outer wall and set up extra doors inside the Keep to funnel any attackers into a death zone."

"A death zone?" Anna was intrigued to learn more about what Fitz had done.

"Yes, they'd all be led to a courtyard where they'd be trapped, and archers could pick 'em off. Course we never needed it, 'cause Bodden weren't never breached after that, though they tried again, but that was years later."

"So you knew Gerald when he was a child?" She had a smirk on her face as she continued, "What was he like?"

Edgar pulled another sip on his cider and looked at Gerald, who had turned slightly red in embarrassment.

"He were much like any other youngster really, nothing special to speak of. Though I remember that young lady taking a shining to 'im. What was her name, again?"

Now, it was Gerald's turn to speak.

"Meredith," he said, the name dripping off his tongue like honey.

His face was lit up for a brief moment and then, inevitably, came the feeling of loss as he remembered her death.

"Whatever happened to her," Edgar asked, unaware.

"She died," he said quietly.

Anna, seeing her friend suffering from the memory, decided to change subjects, "So how long were you at Bodden?"

"Well," he recounted, "let's see... I was there back in '24, that were my first year. I remembers the cold that year, it was 'orrible. Mind you, back then, the Northerners weren't much of a problem. An occasional bandit made his way across the river to raid, but no serious threat. 'Course, back then, Fitz's older brother was the baron."

Anna was shocked. "You mean Baron Fitzwilliam wasn't the baron? Why is that?"

"Well, if you'll pardon me for saying, there were a Baron Fitzwilliam, just not Lord Richard. He had an older brother, you see, named Edward, who was the baron."

"What happened to Edward?" she prodded him to continue his recollection.

"He died in the second siege in '33. Last we seen him, he were in the breach. He was overrun with Norlanders, must've been killed in the fighting. Afterwards, we looked for him, but we'd used fire bundles to light the breach and most of the bodies, well they was badly burned."

"Wouldn't he be recognized by his armour, or sword or something?" she asked.

"Aye, but the raiders, they'd stripped anything of value from the bodies. By the time the sun was up, we couldn't recognize nobody."

"So then, Richard became the baron?" she suggested.

"Yes miss, he was the only member of the family left, but he had us searching for days to try to find his brother's body."

Edgar tried, unsuccessfully, to stifle a yawn.

"My pardon, Edgar. I can see you're quite tired after your travels and here we are keeping you from your sleep. I'll have one of the servants show you to your room."

Edgar looked at Anna as he rose from the table.

"You're most gracious miss," he said.

Later that evening, after Edgar had gone to bed, Gerald and Anna sat in front of the fire in the trophy room. It was Anna that broke the silence.

"I have an idea, Gerald. Tell me what you think."

"All right," he responded, guarding his words, for her last idea had ended in her hiring a personal courier. "Let's hear it."

She sat up, as she always did when she was planning.

"The budget for Uxley Hall includes thousands of crowns just for my wardrobe, but I can get the dresses sewn in town for a fraction of the cost, so I'm going to use the funds to build up my information network. I want to find old soldiers, men who can no longer fight, who are trustworthy, but they have to be able to read and write. We'll start with Edgar, and if he comes across any other old soldiers that he trusts, he can send them here to Uxley. Eventually, we'll have a whole company of private couriers travelling the land and sending me reports."

He looked at her intently, trying to seek out the meaning behind this latest plan.

"To what end?" he finally asked, choosing to be blunt.

She almost cut him off, so quick was she to respond, "I want to know all about the kingdom. I may not be able to travel, but I can travel through letters. It will be so exciting!"

He had to admit the plan was solid enough, and he made a mental note to check the credentials of anyone they might hire. They must be sure only to recruit the most trustworthy of men, he thought. He retired for the evening with visions of a huge network of couriers stretching, spider web-like, over the kingdom.

The next morning, he joined Edgar and Anna for breakfast. The courier was well rested and had been fed. They escorted him to the front entrance-way, where a stable hand was waiting with his horse. While Edgar mounted, Anna turned to Sophie, who had been following along behind. Sophie gave her a satchel, and Anna passed it, in turn, up to Edgar.

"This satchel," she began, "is to be delivered to Andronicus, the Royal Mage in Wincaster. Also, I've three letters here that require delivery, though I fear it will take you some time. One is near Mattingly, one near Bodden and the last requires you to ride across the border to Westland. Can you do that for me?"

Edgar looked at her directly as he spoke, "Yes, miss."

"Excellent," she responded. "I have a purse here to cover your expenses," she tossed him the coins as she spoke. "There's also ink, quills and paper so that you can write your observations down. I look forward to reading your reports. Oh, and don't forget to wait at each location for a reply. You should be able to be back here before winter sets in, but don't take any chances.

Hole up in a city if the cold comes too soon, I don't want you risking your life."

Edgar nodded, "I'll see you back here, miss, before the first snow."

At the conclusion of this statement, he spurred the horse forward, trotting off. The man rode high in the saddle, as though he had just been given a new lease on life. He was to be the first of her couriers.

Anna and Gerald rode into the village on a pleasant summer's day. Anna had been anticipating today because it was the day of the festival, and she was impatient for all the sights and sounds that awaited them. Their wagon rattled as it travelled down the roadway and Tempus, lying in the back, shifted his weight slightly, then stood up, making his way to the front of the wagon. A moment later, his monstrous head poked between Anna and Gerald, who was driving.

Anna pet his head. "Tempus is excited about the festival."

"More likely he's excited for all the food people will be dropping," replied Gerald.

Anna laughed.

"Well, that's true," she admitted, "but he's always eager to go into town, aren't you boy?" She scratched the dog's chin, and he leaned in closer to her. How he didn't knock her from her seat, Gerald couldn't figure out. "Now," she continued, "the first order of business will be the food tasting."

"Are you sure that you're qualified to judge the baking?"

Anna looked at him, miffed by his statement. "I'll have you know I am the leading expert on baked goods."

"Why do you think that?" he egged her on.

"On account of I've eaten more than anyone else. How else do you become an expert?"

Gerald laughed. He was sure this would be a fun day, and Anna was going to enjoy herself immensely, as she always did when going into town.

They dropped the horses and wagon off at Sam's, making their way to the commons. They noticed that the field was already getting crowded as the locals made their way to the festivities. They saw people practicing with their bows on the southern side of the field, where straw targets had been laid out. Word of the archery competition had travelled quickly, and many had come from miles around to compete for the chance at the prize, which Anna had generously put at a respectable twenty crowns. They even recognized Renfrew, trying to charm a couple of the local women.

Anna made a beeline directly for the food pavilion where the villagers had placed tables under a huge awning they had erected. These were now chock-full of pies, rolls, tarts and all sorts of other treats. She had graciously agreed to judge the quality of the cooking, and soon all the local women descended on her, the better to ingratiate themselves. She was delightfully swamped with copious samples of tasty tidbits. Tempus was nowhere to be seen, no doubt busy sniffing the ground for morsels that had been dropped. Gerald wasn't worried, for although Anna was surrounded, she couldn't have been safer in a castle. The villagers adored her, making a fuss of her anytime she came to town. They weren't sucking up to her, they genuinely liked her.

Gerald watched her make her way along the tables, the villagers handing her tarts and slices of pie to sample. He gazed off towards the archery field to see who was competing. The usual assortment of farmers had brought out their bows. There were one or two youths that Gerald didn't recognize, but they were accompanied by some of the locals, so he relaxed. His eyes wandered down to the butts, and he absently watched the arrows strike their targets. He could even hear the occasional thud as they hit.

After a bit, he heard a slight commotion over by the crowd watching the archery. Looking over, he saw three arrows hit one of the targets in rapid succession and remarkably, they were in a very tight grouping. Gerald wondered who had made such an exceptional display. He turned back to the assembled archers, immediately struck by a mild attack of loathing. There, stringing another arrow, was the red-headed King's Ranger, Osferth. Gerald remembered the last time they had met, it had not gone well. Now, he feared that Osferth, an exceptional shot, as were all rangers, would easily win the archery competition. Nothing could kill the festive mood quicker. He began to think through all the possible rules and see if they could disqualify him.

"No," he thought out loud, "that wouldn't be fair. Like it or not, the competition must be fair."

His thoughts were interrupted by a voice, "What wouldn't be fair?"

He turned to see Sam, who had just walked up beside him. Jax rushed past, heading straight for the food pavilion where Tempus was still sniffing around.

"Take a look," Gerald nodded towards the competitors, "see anyone you recognize?"

Sam looked over the crowd, then sighed.

"Only the presence of a King's Ranger could suck the life out of a party. Still, I suppose you're right, we can't just disqualify people because we don't like them."

"No, I suppose not," Gerald commiserated. "Well, it'll be interesting to see if anyone can compete with his skill.

Sam watched them practice before speaking, "I'm finding that doubtful, though I hate to admit, he is very good with the bow. I never realized just how well trained the rangers are."

He turned to look at Jax, who was now chasing Tempus. They were running around the Pavilion, barking, and Sam and Gerald, who had also turned to look, both smiled.

"It seems that someone's fun has not been dampened by the presence of the ranger!"

They watched a small group of children chasing Jax. It was quite a circus; Tempus would rush forward, for a large dog he was incredibly agile, with Jax trailing him and the children following along in an attempt to catch them both. He could swear that Tempus was playing with them, deliberately waiting for his followers to catch up before bursting forward once again.

"I think," interrupted Sam, "that you've lost Anna."

Gerald looked over to the pavilion to see Anna seated at a table with plates of delicious smelling food being placed in front of her.

"She's in good hands," he said, after noticing the tavern keeper watching over her. "Let's go talk to some of the other competitors. Maybe someone will surprise us."

They walked over to the practice field, steering ever so slightly away from Osferth. They chatted with a few of the locals. The consensus was that Clayton Green was reckoned to be the best shot in the area, but even he appeared intimidated. The overall mood of the competitors was bleak. The ranger, for all his attitude, merely shot arrow after arrow into his target, striking each time with precision. This would likely not be much of a competition, more like a slaughter. Gerald was about to say something to this effect to Sam when he overheard a familiar voice.

"Now," the voice was saying, "I always believed that it was easier to draw the bow than the string."

Gerald turned in the direction of the voice to witness an elderly man talking to a young village lad who was having trouble handling his bow. A wide grin crossed his face.

"Wilfrid Hodgeson!" he called out in greeting, genuinely pleased. "I haven't seen you in years!"

He walked towards the man who, looking up, grinned sheepishly, extending his hand in greeting. The two clapped hands as Gerald turned to Sam, who had followed.

"Allow me to introduce you. This is Wilfrid Hodgeson, an old friend from Bodden. Wilfrid, this is my good friend, Sam Collins, the local saddle maker."

The two shook hands while Gerald continued, "What brings you here? You weren't hoping to win the archery contest, were you?"

"No, bless my soul. I haven't used a bow for more'n ten years. I'd hardly know how to handle one these days," he grinned as he answered the question. "I'm here 'cause I ran into a mutual friend of ours, said there might be some work hereabouts."

"Work?" asked Gerald.

"Aye, Edgar Greenfield said to mention his name. Seems you're looking for trustworthy people?"

"Yes, but we'd best not talk about it here. Come up to the Hall after the festivities are over, and I'll fill you in."

Sam looked quizzically at Gerald. "Trustworthy people? Work? What's that all about?"

Gerald was slightly embarrassed. "Oh, er, well, Anna wants to hire some people for some courier work, nothing you'd be interested in. It requires a lot of travel." Sam appeared to relax at his explanation. He hated not telling his friend the truth, but it was not his secret to share. "Listen, let's head over the Old Oak, and the three of us'll have a drink, for old time's sake."

"What about Anna?" Sam gently reminded.

"Tell you what, I'll go collect her and see you back at the tavern. Can you show him the way, Sam? I'll be along as quickly as I can."

Sam and Wilfrid headed off for the tavern, while Gerald tried to make his way through the press of people to where Anna was mowing down on another pastry. Jax and Tempus had finished their game, and now the two of them were lying beside Anna's chair, one to each side. They were quick to grab any treats that 'accidentally' fell their way.

"Anna," interrupted Gerald, "I've got someone I'd like you to meet."

Anna waved her hand. "Not now, I'm busy with these delicious pastries."

"But I wanted you to come over to the tavern. There are some things to discuss," he persisted.

"You go on, I'll be safe here," she mumbled as she stuffed yet another pastry into her face.

He finally gave up and made his way over to the tavern.

The archery contest was scheduled to begin at noon. Just before it started, Gerald made his way to the seats that had been set up for judging the competition. Anna was already there, looking slightly uncomfortable. As he approached, she belched, trying unsuccessfully to cover her embarrassment.

"Are you all right, Anna?" He tried to sound concerned while he had an amused look on his face.

"I think I may have overeaten," she replied. She looked at him with a serious face, "Don't you dare say it!"

He suppressed his laughter. Now was not the time to say he told her so. He took his seat beside her, seeing Tempus laying in front so that her feet were resting on him. The competition began with the elimination rounds. These were interesting to watch and, until Osferth shot, things looked close. The ranger shot in the third round, easily beating the competition and securing a berth into the finals. After five rounds of elimination, there were ten people selected to compete in the final round. Not even one of them had shot half the points that Osferth had. Convinced the ranger would win it handily, people were talking amongst themselves. They hoped that one of the locals could at least put up a good show.

The ten archers took up their places, waiting for the master of the bow to drop the handkerchief, signifying that they were to commence.

Suddenly, out of the throng of observers, a lone voice welled up, "Wait, stop!"

The villagers turned, and Gerald wondered what was happening. The crowd parted revealing a young woman with dark brown hair, tied off in a ponytail, stepping up towards the judge's stand. She wore a long green cloak and carried a well-worn longbow in her hand. She strode confidently forward and stopped before the stands.

"I beg your pardon, honourable judges, but I ask permission to compete."

Anna leaned forward in her seat, and asked, "Who are you?"

"I am Hayley Chambers," she announced in a loud voice, "a King's Ranger."

The villagers, as one, suddenly let out a loud gasp. A King's Ranger was a rare thing these days, but to have two show up on the same day was almost unbelievable. Gerald could tell Anna was intrigued by the way she sat forward in her chair, her discomfort all but forgotten.

"The competition is in the final round, how is it that a King's Ranger cannot find their way here in a timely manner?"

"I beg your forgiveness," the ranger continued, "but I was delayed by the execution of my duties. I had to return unexpectedly to Tewsbury after I arrested some bandits. I'm afraid the delay cost me a lot of time as I had to wait for a magistrate there."

Anna looked confused, and she turned to Gerald, asking, "I thought that rangers doled out the king's justice on the spot?"

"Not always, Anna, there are still some that follow the rules of the land."

"What should we do?" she asked. "We can't just let her compete. She should have gone through all the elimination rounds."

"Why not have her shoot right now? If she scores as good as the others, you can add an eleventh shooter to the final round. We have enough targets."

"Excellent idea!" She turned back to the new arrival. "We have deliberated and decided that in the interest of fairness, we will have you shoot ten shots. From your performance, we shall determine if it is fair for you to compete in the final. Is that agreeable to all?"

She asked the crowd this. The response was instantaneous, as a horde of cheers erupted. Gerald could tell she was playing to her audience, and they loved it.

"Take up your position, and make your shots."

The young ranger walked to the line taking her place. Removing an arrow from her quiver which hung from her waist, she then stood for a moment, looking at the target. She wet her finger and held it up, testing the wind, then placed the arrow into the ground in front of her, followed by eight more. She drew the tenth arrow, putting it on the bow, drawing it by pointing it upward, then extended her arm as she brought it down in front of her, using the extension to add draw power to the bow. Holding it for only a moment, she then let it loose.

There was the briefest of sounds as the arrow tore through the air, impaling the target very near the centre. In rapid succession, she drew the arrows from the ground, and with a machine like precision, they whistled through the air to strike the target. The crowd cheered as her last arrow hit the bullseye solidly, the third of the ten to do so. The judges examined the target, then walked to the stands to give their report. She had scored higher than all the other competitors, save for Osferth. Anna stood slowly, and the crowd grew silent.

"It is the opinion of the judges that the Ranger Hayley Chambers be allowed to compete in the finals."

The crowd went wild with cheering, but Osferth stormed over to the princess.

"I object, Highness. The final ten have already been determined and she," he looked at Hayley with disdain, "does not merit inclusion, once the competition has begun."

"I am afraid that I have been told that one cannot refuse a King's Ranger's request to participate in a competition." Anna turned to examine the other townsfolk sitting nearby, searching for Renfrew. "Isn't that right, Renfrew?"

Renfrew, ever the obedient servant now, stood to answer, "This is accurate, Your Highness, as I instructed your brother Prince Henry himself. A King's Ranger cannot be refused entry to an archery contest, for it is part of their charter that they be the finest archers in all the kingdom."

Osferth, knowing he had been out-manoeuvred, stomped back to his position in the shooting line. Hayley retrieved her arrows and took up a position at the end of the line. The other contestants looked on with interest.

The shooting commenced, but it was soon apparent that the real contest was between the two rangers. Osferth shot with tremendous force, his arrows often sticking out the back of the target, while Hayley shot with swiftness, often being the first to loose all her arrows, which appeared to strike their target unerringly.

Third place was eventually awarded to Clayton Green after the others bowed out. So close were the scores of the two rangers, that it came down to an elimination round to determine the winner. They would both shoot one arrow at a time to their targets until one outshot the other. The crowd was holding their breath as the two archers prepared. Osferth shot first, striking the centre of his target. Hayley loosed her missile which impaled her target dead centre as well. Osferth delivered his second shot, a solid hit which touched the bullseye, but not dead centre. The crowd gasped as Hayley shot, her arrow striking her target so close to her previous hit, that they thought she had split the arrow.

It was only when the judges examined carefully, that they saw the two arrows side by side, buried in the exact middle of the target. The judges strolled over to Anna and spoke to her quietly and then she stood to pronounce the verdict. The crowd was hushed as she stood.

"The winner of this competition is," she paused for dramatic effect, "Ranger Hayley Chambers!"

The crowd erupted in applause and surged forward, lifting the winner onto their shoulders in her triumph. Gerald watched Osferth steaming in the background, now being ignored by everyone. The ranger would not forget this, he thought, and perhaps one day he would return to exact some form of revenge for this supposed insult.

TWENTY-TWO

Return to the Grotto

SUMMER 958 MC

~

G erald strode into the kitchen to grab something to eat. He had been working all morning, trimming the trees. Anna was sitting at one end of the table in the kitchen, while around her the staff worked. She was nibbling on some pastry, reading a letter that she held in her hand.

"What have you got there?" Gerald asked.

Anna looked up. "It's a letter, from Westland, from that mage," she looked down at the page again, "Tyrell Caracticus. Funny name, isn't it?"

"Yes, well, I suppose all mages have unusual names. It's not as if Andronicus is an ordinary name."

"Is that how you know if you're destined to be a mage," Anna mused, "being born with a funny name?"

"I doubt it." Gerald grabbed a pastry from the cook's tray before continuing, "They probably pick their mage name when they become an apprentice."

"I suppose that makes sense," she said absently. "I never really thought about it before."

"So what does the mage with the funny name have to say," he asked, before stuffing the food into his mouth.

"Quite a lot. He confirms the race is called Saurians, and they are one of the ancient races."

"Ancient races?" mumbled Gerald around a mouth full of food.

"Yes, the races that predate us Humans. Apparently, there were many civilized races before the coming of mankind, but only three survive to this day; the Elves, that are rarely seen; the Dwarves, who spend most of their time in the mountains; and the Orcs, who he says have degenerated into a savage race. At least that's what he writes."

"I don't know that I would call the Orcs savages," Gerald ruminated over a tart as he spoke. "I've seen one or two of them. They're primitive, but not necessarily savage."

"Be that as it may," she continued like a tutor, "at one time it's believed the Saurians had a vast trading empire. All the other races valued their goods, and they commanded high prices."

"Does he mention what these Saurians looked like?"

"Yes, they were about four and a half to five feet tall, slim of build, but very agile. They were said to be very wise, and their knowledge was known to surpass even the Elves. Are Elves known to be exceptionally wise?"

"Well," replied Gerald, "they certainly like to tell everyone else they are. Most of us seem to think the Elves are a bit high and mighty. Then again, I can't say I've interacted with them much."

"They do live a long time. I suppose when you live that long you could learn quite a lot. I wonder if the Saurians lived a long time?" she wondered aloud.

"Does he say anything else?" he prompted.

"Yes, the Saurians were an old race before the others came along. Some people believe they were the very first race, but by the time mankind arrived, they had all died out, or so it's believed. He thinks they may have been a race of mages too. Not much detail, but it sounds interesting, don't you think?"

Gerald knew what was coming next, so he pre-empted it. "I suppose this means you want to head back out to the grotto and have another look?"

"Yes, but I have an idea. I want to take some wood with us," she stated.

"Wood? Whatever for?" He had thought he knew what she planned, but once again she had surprised him.

"For a raft. I can float along holding onto the wood and get closer to the cave."

"I don't remember a cave," he said, looking at her quizzically.

"Oh, I found a reference to it in one of the old books about the estate. There's a cave only accessible from the pool, but the pool was supposed to be smaller. When they made the grotto all those years ago, they didn't take into account the way the water drains off the grounds, so the pool's deeper than they had originally planned."

"Are you sure it's wise going into a cave that might be inhabited by something?"

"Don't be silly. If there was something there that was dangerous, it could have killed us last time we were there."

He had to admit she had a point. The last time they went to the grotto, they had been stuck in the mud while surrounded by the fog. Anything could have taken them out.

"All right," he agreed with a determined expression, "let's get going and see what we can discover."

They ended up using the top to an old mahogany chest, just removing the hinges. They found that, inverted, it floated nicely. It was large enough that Anna could, if necessary, lie on its top, though her feet would be dangling over the edge along with her arms. Gerald fixed a rope to one end with a metal ring, so that he could pull her back if something went wrong. The entire process didn't take much time, and they easily made it to the grotto before lunch.

The grotto was as they remembered it, but this time the summer heat had dried the mud, and it no longer tried to keep them in their place. They carried the raft to the edge of the pool, putting it in the water. Anna lay on it and experimented with using her arms to paddle. It took some concentration, but she soon discovered she could manoeuvre the raft, although slowly.

She paddled out with Gerald paying out the line as she went. Tempus sat watching the entire operation from the bank, relaxing in the sun. Anna moved the raft towards where the cave should be, stopping her paddling as she looked through the water.

"I can see a cave entrance. There's about a hands length above the surface, and the rest is underwater. It looks quite large."

He watched her trying to peer into the cave, her head even with the surface, but after a while, she looked back to Gerald.

"It's no use," she shouted. "I can't make it through with the raft. I'm going to lower myself into the water."

Gerald was about to object, but she acted too quickly, rolling off the makeshift raft, holding onto it with one hand. She disappeared below the surface with her hand still touching the wood, and a moment later, she resurfaced, gasping for air.

"The water seems clear here, I'm going to try again, but I won't come up for a moment or two."

She disappeared below the surface again, this time her hand let go of the raft. Gerald was worried. This was dangerous work, he decided, and she shouldn't be taking this risk. Time seemed to stand still, and he found himself holding his breath, imagining what it must be like for Anna, under the water.

He had never been a fan of water, at least not immersing himself in it. He was all right with baths, but couldn't understand why anyone would want to go swimming for the fun of it. With a splash near the raft Anna resurfaced, grasping for it. She was breathing hard and hanging on with both hands.

"Pull me in!" she yelled.

Gerald immediately began tugging on the rope. It did not take long to pull her back to shore. She was catching her breath but had a big smile on her face.

"What did you see?" he asked, still concerned about her safety.

"There's a cave there, and it's filled with air. But it was dark and I couldn't see much. Only a little light comes through the entrance. We need to return with a lantern of some sort. Perhaps a small one we can float on the raft."

"The raft is only big enough for you," Gerald reminded her.

"I thought we could make a smaller raft. I don't have to ride on it, I can just hang on, and we can set a lantern on it. Then we can float it through the entrance that's above the water. We just need to make sure it's the correct size."

Gerald looked around and found a small stick, which he handed to Anna.

"Take this stick," he said, "and paddle out to the entrance. Break the stick to a length that matches the width of the cave entrance that's above the water level, that way we'll have a measurement for the new raft."

She thought this was an excellent idea, and after catching her breath, she was paddling back to the cave. Once she had decided on the length of the stick, she waved to be pulled back.

This time Gerald had attached the other end of the rope to Tempus. He ran with the dog, resulting in the raft moving with a high velocity back across the pond and onto the bank.

At a sound from behind him, he turned to see Anna yelling, "Weeeeeeeee!" as the raft was pulled in.

"That was exciting. We need to do that again sometime!" she said.

Gerald took the stick and carefully placed it into his satchel. He removed a blanket from his pack and wrapped it around her. Though it was a warm day, the water here was quite nippy. She was shivering, and cold to the touch. They ate while they waited for her to warm up, discussing their progress.

"We need to get you some warmer clothes for when you come out."

"Yes, it's quite cold," she agreed, "but it's all right for short periods of time. I didn't feel cold till I got out."

He gazed out at the grotto as he considered what they needed for their next visit.

"We'll bring you a change of clothes tomorrow and a small lantern."

He was trying to think of a small lantern, but all he could think of was the coach lanterns, and they would be far too big.

"What about an oil lamp?" she suggested. "We could use a small bowl of oil with a wick in it?"

He thought about it for a moment then replied, "No, the oil could get spilled and cause problems, plus we'd have to transport it here."

"How about a candle?" she suggested.

"Yes, that'd work. We'll cut it down to make it shorter. You shouldn't need it to burn for very long. You don't have to light it until we're ready to float it out. You'll just have to be careful not to get it wet." She looked pleased with their combined solution.

They gathered up their things, then made their way back to the Hall. Gerald could tell that the adventure had taken its toll on Anna. She was dragging her feet and was almost falling asleep as she walked. By the time they arrived, she looked utterly exhausted. He carried her up to her room, letting Sophie put her to bed. Once she was firmly tucked in, Gerald entered with Tempus, encouraging the dog onto her bed, his usual place of slumber. The great dog leaped easily onto the large mattress, and Gerald was just turning to leave when she spoke.

"Don't leave, Gerald," she asked tiredly. "Can you read me a story?"

He turned to meet her eyes, then scanned about the room, examining the books that were scattered hither and yon.

"I think you've read every book in the Hall."

"Then make up a story!" she begged.

She was giving him the sad eye treatment, and he couldn't resist.

"All right, but don't blame me if it isn't very good."

He pulled up a chair beside the bed and sat down, thinking through what he was going to say.

"This is a story," he began, thinking quickly, "of a young girl who wanted to be a knight."

"Was she a noble?" she interjected.

"Er, yes, the daughter of a baron."

"How old was she?" she piped up.

"Well, let's see, we'll start when she was eight. That was the first time she knew what she wanted to be."

"Where did she live?" she continued with her questions.

"At Bodden Keep with her father. In those days, the frontier was wild, and Norlanders raided across the border all the time. Her father loved her very much and always included her in his discussions. She'd grown up around knights and soldiers and was loved by everyone. Being the only child of the baron, she knew she would never inherit the title."

"Because," Anna interrupted, "women can't inherit titles, isn't that right?"

"Yes," he responded, "that's the law of the land."

"Isn't that a bit silly?" she innocently commented.

"It's not something I spend a lot of time thinking about, it's just the way things are. I suppose if I was a baron with only a daughter, I might believe it was silly too."

"Maybe I should talk to the king and make him change the law!" she suggested.

"I doubt that would go over very well. Now, are you going to let me finish my story?"

She nodded sheepishly. "Sorry."

"Well, one day this girl was standing in the courtyard watching a group of young boys play at being soldiers. She would watch them fight with wooden swords. What they didn't know, of course, is that she could already use a practice sword, for she had been learning in secret for weeks. In fact…" he trailed off as he gazed at her drooping head and closed eyelids.

It was apparent that she had fallen asleep after the story had barely begun. He gently tucked her blanket around her and patted Tempus on the head, then tip-toed from the room.

TWENTY-THREE

The Prince

SUMMER 958 MC

Gerald rose, as he often did, quite early the next day, making his way to the Hall. As he expected, Anna was also up, ready for the adventure of the day. Together, they went to the kitchen where Cook had food laid out for them. He was just about to finish off his sausage when Anna interrupted him.

"What do you think we'll find in the cave?" she asked.

With a mouth full of food, he found it difficult to answer. His years of soldiering had taught him to eat quickly, and this usually meant he wolfed it down.

He finished his mouthful before replying, "I don't know. I expect there'll be some evidence of something living there."

He speared the sausage and raised it to his mouth, but was once more interrupted.

"Do you think it's dangerous? Maybe I should take a sword?"

"No," he replied, "you said the letters indicated a peaceful race. We're not talking Orcs here, or Humans for that matter."

The sausage entered his mouth but it was not ready to be eaten just yet, as for the third time, he was interrupted.

"What if it uses magic?" she pointed out excitedly.

Gerald sighed and placed the sausage back on the plate. It was destined, yet again, to be delayed.

"If it uses magic, the area will fill with fog. If that happens while you're in the cave, get back into the water and make your way out. Or you can just yell, there's an opening above water, so I should be able to hear you."

That appeared to satisfy her curiosity, but Gerald could still see the gears working by the look on her face. He thought about stabbing the elusive sausage once more but held off, waiting for the next question to arise. The anticipated interruption came from a rather unexpected source as Charles, the servant, entered the kitchen searching for Anna.

"Your Highness, a visitor has been seen coming up the road. He should be here shortly."

The words were like magic for suddenly everyone sprung to life. Anna rushed off to change as a visitor meant she must present herself appropriately. Cook jumped up to prepare snacks for guests, while the other servants rushed about rapidly cleaning and organizing the Hall as best they could in short order. Gerald, having no real requirement to change or any impending work to do, followed Charles back to the entrance to greet whatever guest was arriving.

As he stood by the front door, he wondered who might be coming to Uxley Hall unannounced. It was considered bad etiquette to visit without warning, which meant that either it was someone significant who didn't need to announce themselves, or something had happened that required immediate action and there was no time to send word ahead. His thoughts turned to the latter, and he nervously awaited the rider, which they could now see turning into the estate at the gate. Was the kingdom at war? He thought that unlikely, but being in the middle of nowhere, any news was scarce.

He didn't have long to ponder before the figure came closer. He immediately recognized the young man on the horse. It was Prince Henry, older brother to Anna, and the heir to the throne. He was taken aback at this recognition, for he had never expected to see the prince here in Uxley. As a soldier in Wincaster, his company had been inspected once a month by the nobility, including, on occasion, King Andred and Prince Henry. Though Henry had been only a young lad at the time, Gerald still recognized the man. His face had grown fuller, he had filled out his clothes, and he had grown into an adult, but he was easily identifiable as the son of the king. The faint whiskers marked him as a young man, and Gerald estimated him to be, perhaps twenty or twenty-one years of age.

All these thoughts were swept aside as the prince arrived and dismounted, his horse heavily sweated. Gerald surmised that he had ridden directly from the roadside inn on the king's road. He must have risen early to make the trip. The prince handed the reins to Charles, who dutifully held them waiting for a stable boy to appear. Henry removed his gloves, shook the dust from them and looked at Gerald.

"You must be Hanson."

"No, Your Highness," he said, "the name's Matheson."

He wasn't sure why he didn't use his first name, but his gut was tightening as he spoke.

"Well, Matheson," the prince said nonchalantly, "lead on. I've been on the road for quite some time, and I have a thirst that needs quenching."

"Certainly," Gerald bowed slightly as he had seen officers do on occasion. "If you'll follow me, I'll take you to the trophy room, where we can bring you some refreshments."

He led the prince through the doorway, and into the great hall, steering him towards the south wing.

As they reached the door leading to the hallway, a young voice echoed, "Henry? Is that you?"

Henry turned, a smile forming on his face, "Squeak? Is that you?"

Anna came running down the grand staircase, slowing as her feet met the floor. She had somehow found the time to change into a fancy dress, and now she appeared to float as she walked, adding a graceful touch that Gerald had not seen her display before. He was standing behind the prince as Anna approached.

"My goodness, Sister! How you've grown! You're almost a young lady now."

Anna smiled at the compliment. She was pleased to see her oldest brother but wasn't sure how to behave.

"It's so good to see you, Henry," she said, trying to remain dignified.

Gerald was struck by her resemblance to the queen whom she was trying to emulate. He knew Anna had a pleasant warmth to her features, whereas he remembered the queen as cold and calculating.

"I'm surprised by your visit," she continued. "Is everything all right?"

"What?" he stuttered. "All right? Of course, everything is all right. I'm on my way to Tewsbury, and I'm meeting some friends here. We're going to ride on together tomorrow morning. That reminds me," he turned back to Gerald, "Matheson, make sure the Hall is prepared for three guests, along with a good supply of ale." Without waiting for a response, he turned back to Anna, "Come along, sister. Show me where you keep the wine. I'm absolutely parched!"

Gerald turned towards Anna. "If Your Highness escorts the prince to the trophy room, I'll have the drinks brought in," he said, trying to emulate the dutiful servant.

Anna and Henry disappeared through the door, heading to the trophy room, leaving Gerald to assemble and organize the servants. Once that was complete, he arrived at the trophy room with Charles, who was now carrying a tray with decanters on it, along with two glasses.

He held the door while Charles entered, and then announced, "The drinks, Your Highnesses," in the best voice he could conjure.

Charles placed the tray on the table and Henry helped himself to a glass, pouring some of the stronger looking liquor. Henry grimaced as he drank the brew.

"Saxnor, give me strength, that's awful stuff!" he exclaimed. "Better try some of this other one." Despite the perceived problem of taste, he still downed his first glass. He took the top off the second decanter and sniffed it. "This smells terrible!"

Anna looked on with surprise. "That's our finest," she said meekly.

"Not your fault, Squeak," the prince replied. "This is the same horrid stuff that Father likes. Oh well, it will have to do I suppose, unless there's somewhere else we can get drinks?" He raised his eyebrows and looked towards Gerald. "Come on, old man, you must know where to get drinks around here."

Gerald was caught unawares but quickly recovered. "There's the Old Oak Tavern in the village, Highness, if your tastes are closer to ale and such."

Henry placed the top back on the decanter.

"Excellent! Come on, sister dear, let's go to town." He looked back to Gerald, "Do you still have a carriage and horses here?"

Gerald took a moment to respond. They had a richly decorated carriage in the stables, but it hadn't been used in years. Gerald nodded, but he could just imagine the panic as the servants struggled to clean it up.

"Good, then have them made ready, and we'll head into the village for a taste of the local ale."

Quite a while later, they were on their way. Henry insisted on Gerald joining them, to make it easier to summon the carriage when they were done. For the first time, Gerald found himself sitting atop the carriage along with the driver. It was a marvellous view, for the carriage was very high, built upon a suspension system that was said to be of Dwarvish design. It made for a blocky style, but the ride was incredibly smooth. He tried to imagine the cost of such a carriage, but it was likely as much as a large house.

Arriving at the Old Oak, Gerald dismounted the carriage to open the doors for Henry and Anna. Once they had exited, he instructed the driver to take the carriage down to the stables. He would come and get them once they were done. By the time he had arranged this, Prince Henry and Anna had disappeared into the tavern.

As chance would have it, he needed to relieve himself, so he made his way to the back of the tavern where this was customarily done. He rounded the corner to see three men, gathered rather strangely by the back door. They stood in a small group discussing something in very low-pitched voices. As he watched, they donned hoods with rough drawings of skeletal faces on them.

Gerald was immediately shocked by their actions and instinctively reached for his sword. Even as he did this, the men opened the back door and rushed inside. He ran for the open door, yelling a warning in his loudest voice. As he closed the distance, he heard the sound of shouting coming from within. Upon entering the tavern, he spotted Prince Henry, at the bar along with Anna. The prince had heard his warning and had pulled his sword fast enough to block the first attack. The hooded men, their backs to Gerald, moved to surround the two royals, and even as his eyes took all this in, he noticed another two men with hoods entering through the front door.

He struck without thinking, his sword stabbing into the lower back of one of the attackers. The man fell to the floor, screaming, and Gerald had to tug with all his strength to release the blade. He pulled it free just in time to block the onslaught of a sword. Another of the three masked men had heard the scream and turned his attention towards Gerald. The block drove him backwards slightly, but he quickly collected his wits. He vaguely saw the prince duelling with two of the attackers while the last one couldn't get in close enough. Anna crouched on the floor between Henry and the bar.

Gerald stomped his foot forward and hit his opponent's boot. He was rewarded with a grimace of pain on his victim's face, just before he slashed viciously with his sword, carving a red line across his adversary's stomach. His target staggered back, blood flooding between his fingers, which now clutching his wound. The man fell to the floor, writhing in pain. Gerald stepped to the side to avoid the thrashing man and took in the scene unfolding before him.

It only took a moment for Gerald to analyze the situation; Henry had the skills of a fencer, not a combat veteran judging by the small wounds the men fighting him had received. The prince was graceful and precise but lacked the stamina and raw strength for a brawl like this. Gerald rushed forth to swing at one of the two assailants presently engaged with Henry. The man stepped to the side, avoiding the blow, but as he did so, he yelled with pain. Anna had reached out, stabbing the man's foot with her ever-present dagger. Gerald took the opportunity to deliver a backhand swing at his distracted foe. It lacked force, but struck across the victim's face, leaving a vicious looking slash across his nose. The man staggered back to get out of the way, bumping into one of his companions that had come through the front door.

Gerald spotted more coming in from the kitchen, moving to cut off their escape routes, and he had no doubt that they would soon block the back door.

"The stairs, quickly!" he shouted to Henry and Anna.

Anna got to her feet, and he grasped her hand, pulling her towards the stairs, which led to the upper rooms. Another hooded man tried to block his way, so he used his arm to knock the man aside. Once they reached to the stairs, Gerald turned to face the room they had just left. He moved Anna behind him, but she was still able to see the carnage from her viewpoint. He noticed the prince make a lunge at one of his attackers who wisely backed up, easily avoiding the attack, but Henry took this opportunity and darted to the stairs. Moments later, the two defenders stood side by side, blocking the stairs with their bodies.

The remaining five came in a rush. They were disorganized and looked desperate. Gerald easily parried the first blow, and then struck with a stabbing motion, impaling his target in the soft flesh of the stomach. So close was the man that he could smell his breath. He used his other hand to hold onto his victim, turning him to absorb the blow from the next attacker. He felt the first one scream and tense as his partner's blade stabbed him in the back. Gerald pushed the body off of his sword, using his foot to provide more power. His first attacker, now dead, fell heavily on the one who had killed him, and they both tumbled to the floor. As they fell, Gerald stepped forward, placing his foot on them as he thrust again with his sword, this time against his third opponent.

Beside him, Prince Henry dutifully thrust and parried, doing little damage, but managing to keep his attackers at bay. He inflicted many cuts, but none were deep enough to do more than slightly scar his enemies.

All of a sudden, the fighting ceased. The attackers had backed up. Gerald expected them to rush in a desperate final attack, but their nerve broke. One of them yelled, and the next moment they fled, leaving their wounded comrades behind.

Henry stopped, dropping to his knees, out of breath, but Gerald knew better. He rushed the group, striking one of them down with his sword for they might turn back, and he needed to keep them running. He continued his onslaught, following them out the door. By the time he exited the tavern, they were on their way with no intentions of returning.

He turned his attention back to the interior, making sure Anna was safe. Henry was sitting on the bottom stair, panting heavily, but seemingly undamaged. The tavern was awash in blood. It wasn't until he noticed the looks on everyone's faces that he saw he was covered in blood as well.

"It's all right," he tried to calm them, "it's not my blood."

The crowd, stunned by the suddenness of the attack, had stayed out of the fracas, and for that, Gerald was thankful. Knowing that the locals weren't warriors, he was happy that no innocents were hurt. Someone handed him a tankard of ale, and he downed it thirstily. There were several assailants on the floor, screaming in pain, mixed amongst the dead. There had been eight attackers in total; two of them had gotten away, three were dead, the other three were wounded, with at least one not likely to make it more than a few hours.

Henry was furious but exhausted. He ordered the bodies searched. They found a few coins which were graciously donated to the tavern to pay for the damages and cleanup. The man that Gerald had struck down as he tried to run yielded a more interesting artifact in the form of a letter. It was folded up and shoved rather haphazardly into the man's boot. Molly, the barmaid, found it as the body was being removed from the tavern. Gerald unfolded it carefully, examining the contents. It was rather stained and worn, but the message was easy to understand. It read *'Prince Henry will be travelling to Uxley this evening. Follow him and wait for an opportunity to strike him down.'* The letter was unsigned but carried a strange stamp of a hand in black ink. He gave the document gingerly to Henry, as if its mere existence was a threat.

Prince Henry looked up as it was handed to him, not fully realizing what was going on. Gerald nodded towards the letter, and the prince read through it, his face darkening as he read.

"What is it, Henry?" Anna asked, wanting to know what was going on.

"The Black Hand," he responded, the disgust showing on his face. "The same group that tried to kill you years ago!"

He handed the letter to Anna, who examined it with great interest.

The villagers had finished checking over the bodies and were propping the injured against the wall.

"Stop that!" commanded Henry. "There will be no assistance to these murderers!" He looked to the tavern's proprietor and asked, "Do you have a rope?"

"Yes, Your Highness," replied Arlo Harris.

"Then get it and follow me. These villains will pay for their crimes immediately!"

The villagers helped take the surviving attackers outside where Henry had them hanged. It was a pitiful thing to see. It would have been far more merciful to have put them out of their misery with the sword, but Henry appeared to relish the thought that they should suffer for their crimes.

Anna watched the whole affair with a blank look, even seeming to enjoy the spectacle. Gerald was troubled. Her father, the king, was known as a ruthless and sadistic ruler, and now he wondered if she had the potential to be the same. As he pondered this very thing, Henry went back to the bar, ordering up drinks for all. Anna remained outside watching while the life choked out of the last of the attackers. They hanged the man without compassion, and now, instead of a broken neck, he was slowly strangled to death by the rope. It was a terrible way to die.

Gerald thought back to Bodden, and all the fights he had been in, and how they had affected him. He suddenly felt a sense of loss. It was as if the old Anna had been washed away to be replaced by the ghost of her father. Without him noticing, Anna walked over, and suddenly she launched herself at him, grasping him tightly around the waist as she began crying and he felt her shaking. He knew at that moment that he had overreacted to her apparent indifference. His Anna would never be like Henry or the king, and he vowed to take care of her, no matter the cost.

The trip back to the Hall was uneventful, leaving Henry sleeping the entire way in the comfort of the carriage, while Anna sat quietly. As they pulled up towards the Hall, Charles came running out to talk to the prince. While they were in town, two friends of Henry had arrived and now waited in the trophy room. The prince, awakened by this news, insisted on being taken there immediately. Anna, on the other hand, wanted only to go to an early bed. She asked for Sophie but was informed by Charles that Sophie attended the guests.

Gerald immediately became suspicious. He knew about the calibre of friends that Henry had and was worried for the young maid.

"I think that we should go and fetch Sophie for you, Anna. It might be difficult for her to leave the prince's company without permission."

Anna, evidently too tired to resist at this point, agreed, and they proceeded to the trophy room. Anna was used to having the run of the house, so when they arrived, rather than knock, as Gerald would have done, she just opened the door. What she saw shocked her. Henry sat in one of the lounge chairs, his leg over an arm, holding a drink in one hand as he was laughing and looking towards the fireplace at his companions. His two friends stood to one side of the fireplace and had cornered poor Sophie, who looked terrified. One was running his hands through her hair, while the other was grabbing her waist with two hands. Anna was so shocked she didn't know what to say. Gerald noticed a slight rip at the top of Sophie's dress.

Before anything worse could happen, something must be done, so Gerald spoke up in a loud voice, clearing his throat to get their attention. He must be careful, he thought, it would be dangerous to upset the prince.

"Sorry to interrupt your lordships, but the young lady is required by the princess."

"Who cares," uttered Lord Spencer, "she's just a maid, and we are having some fun. Go find someone else!"

Gerald was about to speak again but took a moment to calm himself. Letting his anger get the best of him would do no good. While he stopped to collect his thoughts, it was Anna who spoke next.

"Sophie's not just a maid," she said in a very stern voice, "she's MY servant!"

Lord Spencer was about to speak, but Henry cut him off.

"Let her go," he commanded, "my sister has that right."

The young lord knew better than to contradict Henry. No one dared go against the wishes of a royal these days. Sophie all but ran to the door in fear, stopping just the other side of Gerald who, at least for the moment was at a loss for words.

"I think," Gerald finally found the courage to speak, "your lordships must be tired after such a long trip. I'm sure the king will be pleased that your visit was such a success. If you come with me, I will show you to your rooms."

He stood to the side of the door, holding it open and waiting for them. At the invocation of the king's name, the two nobles complied meekly. Gerald had gambled, and fortunately, the gamble had paid off for he had assumed that these two young nobles were mere followers. He had seen their ilk from time to time, trying to act like officers in the army. Typically, a firm hand by a sergeant was all that was needed, and he was pleased to see this technique work here.

As the two young men sheepishly approached the door, he turned to Anna and said quietly, "Send Charles and another male servant up to the guest rooms. Keep the women away from that area tonight."

Anna nodded and then took Sophie's hand, leading her away. The young woman looked forlorn, and it was quite touching to see the smaller girl lead the older one away with a gentle pull of her hand.

Prince Henry and his two friends left early the next morning without much fanfare. Anna and Gerald watched them ride away. He looked down at Anna who had a firm look about her features. He could tell she was upset that her brother had laughed as his friends attempted to assault Sophie. He knew she would have questions, so he waited in silence for her to get her thoughts in order. The riders reached the gate and turned onto the road. He could see Anna's shoulders finally relax.

She kept staring towards the gate while asking, "Why are men that way?"

He had expected something of the sort, and so found himself prepared for once.

"Not all men, Anna. There are many who would never treat a woman that way."

She looked up at him and continued, "I know that, of course, but why do some men think they can take any woman they want? Have you ever taken a woman against her will?"

This was far more shocking than he expected, but he was quick to respond, "No, of course not! No man in his right mind would do such a thing."

"But it happens in war quite a bit doesn't it. That's what books say. Oh, and they talk about it as if it's no big thing, but it's quite barbaric."

"Agreed. I remember an occasion when we followed a raid back across the river and tracked down the attackers to a farm. One of our men decided to have his way with the local farmer's wife."

A look of disgust crossed her face and then she spoke, "What happened to him?"

"Lord Fitz had him hanged on the spot! He didn't put up with that sort of behaviour in his army," he said.

"What happened to the woman?"

"Luckily, the man was stopped before he got too far. He had just ripped her clothes. The baron felt so bad about it. He was very apologetic and had the troops leave some food for the farmer and his wife."

She appeared to think this over before resuming the discussion, "So how do you prevent this type of thing from happening?"

"Discipline," he responded. "You need to make people understand that it's not going to be tolerated, and that requires leadership."

"Would you call Henry a leader?"

He mulled this over carefully before responding, "No, he's got authority, but he doesn't know how to use it. There's a big difference."

"I'm never going to allow that to happen again, not if I have any say in the matter."

She turned back into the house with Gerald following. It was going to be an interesting day.

TWENTY-FOUR

Lily

SUMMER 958 MC

⌇

T he visit of her brother seemed to disturb Anna more than she was willing to admit. She was happy when he first arrived, but now Gerald realized she was upset as she moped about the house. He needed something to cheer her up, so he put his mind to the task. It didn't take him long to sort things out, for he remembered that they had planned a trip back to the grotto before Henry had arrived. They had gathered all the equipment they would need the previous day. He had merely to get Anna's attention and convince her it was time to go. The best way to do that was to get Tempus on his side.

The loyal dog was upset when they left him back at the Hall yesterday. Gerald was amused to think how quickly the attack would have failed if only Tempus had been with them. Now, the poor creature followed Anna around the house with the concerned look that only a dog can have. Getting Tempus excited would be the key to his plan for he knew that Anna would do anything for her dog. He only had to convince the dog that he wanted to go outside. To this end, he gathered a nice stick, about three feet long and relatively thick. If there was one thing he knew about most dogs, it was that they could not resist a stick toss.

He found them sitting in the sun room. The large, windowed room was on the back of the Hall and overlooked the grounds behind the building. It offered an excellent view of the hedge maze, though from this height one still couldn't see all the twisted paths that the maze held.

As he opened the door, Tempus looked up. He was a very alert creature, and his tail began to thump. All Gerald had to do now, was start swinging the stick back and forth in his right hand. It immediately had the desired effect. Tempus stood up and, much to his surprise, barked. Anna was startled and looked up, her eyes pulled from the distance into which she had been staring. The effect was startling. Where moments ago was a stern looking young woman, now there was a little girl, delighting in her dog's excitement.

"Tempus says," Gerald suggested, over the echo of the bark, "that he's ready to go back to the grotto. We have a mystery to solve. Do you think you're up to it?"

Her face broke into a big grin as she answered, "Yes!"

She jumped up out of her chair with startling speed and ran over to Gerald, who stopped waving the stick and tossed it to Tempus.

"I'm sorry, Gerald," she apologized in a mild tone. "I've been moping since Henry's visit."

"Really? I hadn't noticed."

She laughed at the remark and hugged him, "Thank you for being patient with me."

"You're welcome," he said and hugged her back.

She stepped back, and he watched her composing herself, straightening her back to present the 'official' princess.

"I had better go and change," she said in a serious tone. "I've got some work to do today."

She walked with purpose to the door, giving Tempus the hand sign to stay where he was. Tempus didn't pay much attention as he was so engrossed with his stick. Gerald watched her exit the room with quiet dignity, then once she cleared the doorway, she ran off into the Hall, reverting to the excited little girl that he realized lay just beneath the surface. Gerald knew she would be all right, but one problem now remained, how to get the stick away from Tempus.

Sometime later, they arrived at the grotto. It was a warm day, but the water would most likely still be cold. Gerald stooped to feel it, and his touch confirmed his suspicions as the icy liquid dripped through his fingers. He guessed an underground spring rose here, but it mattered little. It was but a short swim to the cave entrance.

Anna had found some pants and a shirt that used to belong to a stable boy, a much better outfit to swim in, and so she was changing as Gerald made his calculations. With her announcement that she was ready, Gerald made up his mind. Stepping back from the pond bank, he stripped off his shirt and removed his boots.

"What are you doing?" Anna asked.

"I'm coming in with you," he replied, a determined look on his face. "We don't know what's in the cave and I think I should be there, just in case."

She didn't seem to have any problem with this. Gerald stepped into the water and began to pull their small makeshift raft in with them. Anna opened up the backpack and withdrew the candles. They had picked nice thick ones, the better to ensure they didn't fall over. A few strikes of the flint and steel and she had a small tinder lit, which she used to ignite each candle. She stepped to the edge of the pool, arranging the three candles carefully on the raft.

"Are you sure we need three candles?" she asked.

"Yes, one for each of us, and one to leave on the raft so we can find it easily. Now, let's get into the deeper water and then I can pull the raft." They had affixed a small leather strip to the front of the raft, which was just big enough to hold the candles comfortably, yet small enough to float through the opening.

Gerald waded into the water until it was up to his waist. It was freezing, and he had to catch a breath as it passed the level of his groin, stealing the heat from his body. His face must have betrayed his shock for Anna laughed.

"What's so funny?" he said with a voice that was an octave higher than normal.

Anna looked at him, trying to keep a straight face, "Oh, nothing, it just occurred to me that you just wet your pants."

He couldn't help but laugh. It was enjoyable to see the old Anna returned.

"Come on, then," he prompted, "time to get your feet wet. We'll see how you like wetting YOUR pants."

She tentatively placed her toe into the water then finally, after gathering her breath, stepped forward, until she was up to her ankles.

"Oh, it's so cold!" she complained.

Gerald was getting used to it, "It's not so bad once the shock wears off, better to dive right in," he encouraged.

Much to his surprise, she jumped right in, completely disappearing under the water. She broke the surface a moment later, with a shriek, her wet hair steaming as it hit the warm air. She took a moment to catch her breath and then Gerald, not to be outdone, let himself sink below the surface, and he, too, coming back up with a gasp.

"Are you all right?" she asked.

"I'm all right," Gerald replied. "Let's start moving to the entrance."

He dog-paddled towards the cave entrance, swimming being something he was not well versed in. He was careful not to disturb the surface of the water, holding the leather in his teeth. He held onto an outcropping on the side of the cave as he examined the cave opening. His head was too big to fit through unless he dove under, so he looked towards Anna, and when she nodded, he sank down into the water, using his hands to feel his way through the opening. A moment later, his head broke the surface, and he took in a breath, still holding the leather. He tugged lightly and began pulling the small raft through the opening, and Anna's head broke the surface just behind him.

The flickering light of the candles danced across the room, and he rotated to get a better view. Along the back of the cave was a rock shelf that angled down to the right where it sloped to the surface of the water. He swam towards the shelf and was surprised to find that the slope continued under the water. This ramp made it quite easy to exit the pool. He left the water and turned to offer a hand to Anna, but she had already reached the ramp and was passing him. He pulled the little raft closer and grabbed a candle, giving it to Anna, then grabbed another for himself.

Gerald used his candle to examine some markings on the rear wall of the cave. They appeared to be scratches of an irregular nature, and yet, there were repeated patterns. The thought struck him that it might be some form of writing. He was about to ask Anna what she thought when she interrupted him.

"Up here," she beckoned. "I found something interesting. It looks like a bed or nest."

He moved carefully up the incline which ran across the back of the cave. The top flattened out into a small platform, perhaps six feet square. In the back corner was piled all manner of leaves and twigs and other plants. At first, it appeared rather haphazard, but as he examined it in more detail, he noticed a pattern. He used his other hand to move some of the plants

"Interesting," he thought out loud, "the twigs seem to be woven into a frame, with leaves and such piled on top to make it more comfortable."

Anna was intrigued and eagerly bent over the bed to see it more detail.

"What's this?" she said, gazing at the outer edge, for here was a separate construction, another woven object, this time in the form of a bowl. She brought her candle closer and saw some plant leaves and berries in the bowl. "It appears it likes blueberries, and some herbs," she pointed at a delicate leaf that lay inside.

"That's goldenroot," he said, "it's commonly found in remote regions, like mountains. It's very rare. Perhaps it grows here because of how cold the water is?"

He knew he was just guessing, but the excitement on Anna's face was infectious.

"The poor creature that lives here must be cold, it's quite chilly in here. I can't imagine what it would be like in winter time," Anna reflected.

"Perhaps it hibernates, like a bear?" he offered.

He saw Anna begin to think. It was becoming easier to spot this behaviour, for she had recently adopted the habit of glancing up to the left while her tongue slipped out the side of her mouth. He was going to say something to her, but the flickering of the candle off the stone shifted his attention. On the rock shelf, near to the edge that overlooked the pool, he saw scratches. He knelt down and crawled to the brink, holding the candle close. It appeared as though the creature had used a knife to cut something, most likely weeds or moss. He ran his finger over them leaving a green stain on his fingertip.

"These marks seem like knife cuts," he said, more to himself than to her.

"Oooh, let me see!" she said excitedly. She dropped down beside Gerald to examine the marks. "What kind of knife would make marks like these?"

He spent a moment examining them as best as he could in the dim light.

"I would say a bone knife, most likely."

She looked up at him, and he noticed a distant look in her eye, almost as if she was looking through him, deep in thought.

"I have an idea! Wait here, I'll be back in a moment."

He watched her tread carefully down the ramp to the edge of the pool then she grabbed the leather strap, pulling the raft to the side of the shelf. She removed the remaining candle from the raft, placing it gently on the rock shelf. Next, she lowered herself back into the water, paddling over near the door, keeping the leather strap between her teeth while she disappeared below the surface.

He heard her resurface on the outside and a moment later, the little raft was pulled through the opening back to the outside. He went back to the writing on the wall, searching for more patterns, but, although it resembled writing, it was no language he had ever seen before. He resolved to commit as much of it to memory as he could in the hopes that they would send it to Andronicus, or one of the other mages for examination.

So engrossed was he in his study that he lost track of time. The sound of Anna breaking the surface of the water brought him back from his analysis of the wall. She swam back to the ledge, pulling the raft in once again. He spotted a bundle lying on it, and it wasn't long before it was close enough to identify, for Anna had brought in a blanket. She removed it from the raft, being cautious not to get it wet. She brought it up the incline to where the bed was, placing it with deliberation at the end of the bed.

"There," she said with evident satisfaction, "now we've left a present for her."

Gerald looked at her in amazement, "How do you know it's a her?"

"I don't," she replied, "I just have a feeling. The place is quite neat, and everyone knows that men are messy!"

She laughed at the expression on his face until he joined in.

"We should get going," he decided. "It's still a long walk back, and we don't want to disturb whatever lives here."

"Just one more thing," she said, kneeling carefully by the knife scratches on the ledge, and gently placing her dagger there, its blade pointing away from the bed. "Now, we leave."

They made their way to the water's edge, placing the candles back on the raft, and entered the water once again. It didn't feel as cold this time. Gerald reflected that it was most likely they were just used to it. They swam to the cave's opening and dove once more below the cold, clear water, making their way through the entrance, surfacing on the other side. Tempus had obviously been worried about them and barked when he saw them emerge. They swam back to the shore, pulling the little raft behind them. It had been a successful expedition, and there was much to discuss.

That evening, as they sat in front of the warm fire with hot buttered biscuits and cider, they discussed what had transpired. It would be best, they decided, to wait a few days before they returned. That would give them the chance to see if the creature had used their gifts, or if the cave was, in fact, abandoned.

Waiting for three days to pass felt interminable and by the second day, they could wait no longer! They would once again travel to the grotto to discover what had transpired in their absence. The day was quite warm, and the walk across the estate had them both sweating profusely by the time they arrived. Gerald knelt by the pool, cupping some water, and then splashing it across his face. The coldness of the water was refreshing, and he sat back on the bank, collecting his thoughts. He was contemplating their next move when something caught his eye, a section of long grass that was cut back near the bank. By itself, this was not too surprising, but the cut on the remaining grass was very straight as if made by a long blade. He pulled the grass out by the roots and examined the tips up close. Sure enough, a very sharp blade had sliced through the leaves.

"Anna," he called, "come over here and look at this. It appears that the knife you left behind has seen some use."

Anna came over, her attention transfixed by the sight of the cut grass.

Her eyes grew wide, "It's true! Someone's been using the dagger. I knew something was living here. What do we do now?"

He thought it over carefully before answering, "When we came here last time, no one was home. I'm betting that the creature is probably foraging for food during the day."

"That would make sense," she added. "It probably returns in the late afternoon, or maybe early evening. We should find a place to hide that would give us a good vantage point and wait. Perhaps we'll see it return?"

The plan sounded reasonable enough to Gerald, and so he scanned the area, hunting for a hiding spot with an advantageous view.

"Over there," he pointed, "there's some undergrowth at the wood line that would hide us, but still give us a good vantage point."

Anna nodded in agreement, and they made their way over to the wood line. It didn't take them long to get into position and Gerald, who had led patrols into enemy territory before, set up the area to hide their presence.

The afternoon dragged on with no activity before them. The heat of the day soon had a wearying effect on all. Tempus was the first to fall victim to dozing, with Anna following shortly after. Gerald was determined to remain awake lest they miss the opportunity that had brought them to the grotto in the first place.

It was late afternoon when he saw the first indications of activity. It began with a rustling noise from among the reeds. He lifted his head slightly to get a better view, expecting to see a deer perhaps, coming to the pool to get a drink, but what he saw instead ,surprised him. He spied a head poking out of the long reeds. It was elongated, like a lizard, with an eye on each side of its head. The creature couldn't have been more than five feet tall. As it moved out of the reeds, he saw it had a thin frame, with two arms extending into claw-like hands, and two legs with an extra joint below the knee so that the lower portion of the leg bent forward ending in clawed feet. It was a pale green colour and had a small crest which occupied the back half of the head.

He nudged Anna awake, and she crawled forward to see what was happening. As they watched, the creature moved towards the edge of the pool, stooped, and grasped some flowers that were growing near the bank, using the knife to cut them from their stems. It then took the flowers and placed them into a satchel, woven from some plant fibres, that it had slung across its shoulder. Gerald was frozen in place, fascinated by what he was observing, but Anna moved quickly. She stood up and held her hands in the air as if surrendering. She stepped out from behind their screen and then stood perfectly still.

The creature, hearing the movement, rapidly turned its head in their direction and froze. Gerald was aware of holding his breath and the moment seemed to last an eternity. The creature glanced down at its knife then back to Anna. For a moment Gerald wondered if it meant to attack, but then the creature held out the knife in both hands, palm upwards, looking at Anna.

Anna stepped forward slowly, still keeping her hands in the air. Ever so slowly, she began shuffling her feet forward, getting closer and closer to the being. It stared back at Anna, their eyes locked on each other. It suddenly darted forward, closing the distance between them with startling speed. As it closed the range, it placed the dagger into its satchel, stopping about an arm's length from the young girl. They stood staring at each other, then the Saurian, for that is what Gerald decided it must be, placed its hands out in front, palms up, bending its arms at the elbow. Anna did likewise, and then the Saurian spoke.

The sounds coming from its mouth were unintelligible, but it was obviously a language, for Gerald could hear distinct words and phrases.

Anna responded by pointing to herself and saying, "Anna."

When the Saurian made no further noise, she repeated this action, and then it gestured at her and spoke.

"Ahh-Naa," the Saurian said, and Anna nodded. She pointed back at it, waiting for it to give a name, but the Saurian didn't appear to comprehend.

"I don't think it understands," she said, just loud enough for Gerald to hear.

"Try giving her a name," he offered, not too loudly, "perhaps she'll understand and provide you with something else?"

Anna cast her eyes about, searching for inspiration, and her eyes came to rest on some plants nearby. She turned her gaze back towards the creature.

"Anna," she said again, indicating herself, then she pointed at the Saurian. "Lily?"

It took some time to absorb this, then spoke. "Lil-ee" she responded, pointing to herself.

Anna smiled, and the Saurian smiled back. It reminded Gerald of a dog's smile, the mouth wide open with the lips stretched ever so slightly upward. Anna reached under the collar of her dress and pulled out her necklace. She slowly raised it over her head, holding it out in front of her. Lily stood still, and so Anna took the necklace in both hands and lifted it over the Saurian's head, lowering it around her neck.

Lily grasped the lower end of the necklace and held it up to her eye to examine it. She then let it drop back down. Reaching into her satchel, she pulled out some plants that she had earlier cut. As they both watched, she deftly twisted them together to form a necklace. It took no time at all for her to fashion the ornamental string. Once completed, she placed it over Anna's head, dropping it around her shoulders.

Gerald took the opportunity to study, from afar, the Saurian's skin. It was smooth, not scaly as he imagined it would be. The Saurian was slight of frame, and both he and Anna had assumed the creature was female, though there were no physical signs of any sex whatsoever.

Tempus stirred from his slumber and, sitting up, let out a yawn which the still air magnified. The area instantly filled with fog. The whole scene suddenly erased itself from their view with only a scurrying noise as Lily disappeared from their sight.

Anna called out to Gerald, and, guided by his voice, made her way slowly back to their lookout point. It had been an exciting day, and they had much to discuss. Andronicus and the other mages would be thrilled to know that they had made contact with a Saurian, for they both knew that was what they had encountered here.

As summer wore into autumn, visits to the grotto became more commonplace. Lily proved to be friendly but was easily startled, and in each case, the thick fog enveloped the area almost instantly. By the time the cooler weather came even Tempus could be present without startling the creature. Through careful trial and error, they discovered what Lily ate, and what her habits were. Anna and Gerald would bring her food, mostly roots and berries and although they tried to communicate with her, the language barrier just seemed insurmountable. Eventually, Lily would greet them with their names, but further communication was just not possible.

TWENTY-FIVE

The Trip

SPRING 959 MC

The land had finally shed its winter coat, and spring had struggled its way out of the cold. Gerald and Anna were walking back to the Hall from their weekly excursion to the grotto, and Anna appeared to be restless. Gerald watched her in silence for a while, then broke her concentration by speaking.

"Anna," he said, "what's wrong? You're very quiet today."

Her faraway look was washed from her face as she gazed over at him.

"I'm bored," she stated simply.

"Bored?" he retaliated. "How can you possibly be bored? We go to the grotto once a week and you always look forward to your trips into town."

"I know, and I like doing both those things, I really do, but I want to do something different."

"Like what?" he prompted, knowing full well she had thought this through.

"I want to go to Wincaster."

The statement took him by surprise, and he had to gather his thoughts. They walked in silence for some time before he finally spoke, "Why do you want to go to Wincaster?"

"Wincaster is the largest city in the kingdom, and I want to see what it's like. I've learned everything I can here at Uxley Hall."

"I don't think that's a good idea, Anna." He knew that he had to tread carefully explaining this to her. "It's a dangerous city and... well, no one there even knows who you are."

Anna turned to look at him, "I know that, I'm not simple-minded. The king won't acknowledge me, and I haven't seen my mother in years."

"Don't you think," he interrupted, "it might prove difficult when you arrive in Wincaster. I mean, what will the king do?"

"I've thought of that. I know he likes hunting in the spring, and his favourite place for hunting is down by Shrewesdale. He won't even be in Wincaster when we go, and I discovered that Mother spends all her time these days in Burrstoke."

"How do you know that?" he asked.

Anna smiled and answered, "My couriers told me."

He realized that he could not dissuade her, but he felt very protective of her.

"Where will you stay in Wincaster? The Palace?"

"Yes," she replied defiantly, "and why not? I have a Royal Signet Ring. My mother gave it to me the last time I saw her, and it's been sitting in my jewellery box ever since. If I show that at the Palace, they'll have to admit me, won't they?"

Gerald thought it over carefully. He supposed it was true. for there were always rumours of a royal child as Fitz had intimated. Her presence in Wincaster would bring that out into the open. He was worried what effect that might have on Anna's future.

"Very well," he finally said with a hint of resignation in his voice. "I suppose there's nothing I can do to stop you, but I insist on going with you!"

Anna smiled, "Of course, I wouldn't have it any other way. When we get back to the Hall, we shall have to start planning. I thought we might depart in a day or two. How long does it take to get to Wincaster?"

"By carriage, only two days," answered Gerald. "We'd need to stay at the inn on the way. It lies on the king's road. I understand it's quite large with sufficient stabling."

Anna made a face. "Haven't you stayed there? I thought you came to Uxley from Wincaster?"

"No, Anna, I didn't have the coins to pay for an inn. I came cross-country to Uxley and avoided the main roadway. I caught lifts on wagons and carts where I could. I didn't know what to expect at Uxley Hall, so I had to mind my coins. I camped out under the stars as I did so often in the army."

She looked surprised, but he noticed a look of compassion on her face.

"Well, you won't have to worry about sleeping outdoors anymore. There's more than enough in the treasury to cover the cost of a nice room at the inn. Now, we shall have to decide how many people to take. I suppose I should have some servants, and of course a carriage driver."

"Naturally," he agreed, "as well as a lady-in-waiting or at least a maid."

"Yes," she agreed enthusiastically. "Sophie will be my lady-in-waiting. This will be so exciting!"

By the time they returned to the Hall, they had the beginnings of a well thought out excursion, and Gerald found himself warming to the task.

Two days later, in the early morning mist, they set out. Inside the carriage were Anna, Gerald, Sophie and, of course, Tempus. Owen acted as carriage driver while beside him sat Ned to help with the horses, and occasionally relieve him should he tire. The princess travelled exceedingly light for she did not want to burden the carriage with too much luggage. Sophie had insisted she take some dresses suitable for court, a decision that Gerald wholeheartedly supported. Anna took some plainer clothes, as she wanted to travel about the city incognito for a little while, to get an idea what life was like outside the Palace.

The spring weather was cool and wet, but the roads were clear and in reasonably good repair. Gerald had never travelled inside a sprung carriage before, although he had sat upon the back of one when Prince Henry visited. He found the carriage to be very relaxing. Though he tried to remain alert at all times, he drifted off to sleep, and only awoke when the carriage pulled into the Gryphon's Rest. He was jostled awake by the sudden slowing, and he tipped forward slightly, almost falling out of his seat. Sophie and Anna sat opposite him, and he detected a look of amusement on their faces at his distress.

He saw two stable hands run out to greet them, no doubt alerted to their approach by the sound of the horse's hooves on the king's road. The carriage usually bore the Royal Coat of Arms on each door, but Gerald had suggested they remove these until they were closer to Wincaster, so they arrived in a fancy carriage with no markings. The innkeeper would infer that Anna was a noble of some sort, and would likely respect their privacy.

Gerald waited for the stable hands to open the door, then exited the carriage first. He offered his hand to guide Anna down, then Sophie. One of the stable hands was talking to Owen, while a second began unloading the chests that were tied to the back of the carriage. A rather plump man exited the inn and was walking towards Gerald, no doubt the innkeeper himself.

"My lord," he said, bowing slightly.

Gerald was taken aback by the greeting and flushed slightly. He had never been mistaken for nobility before.

"This," he quickly improvised, "is the Lady Anna and her lady-in-waiting. We shall require some rooms for the night. I assume you have some available?"

"Of course, my lord. I assume a room for yourself and one for the lady and her servant?"

"And the drivers, of course," Gerald added. "Her ladyship wants them well rested for the remainder of the journey."

"Of course, my lord," the man said and turned to Anna. "If your ladyship would care to come and sit in the common room while we prepare your lodgings, we'd be delighted to offer you some food and refreshment."

Anna straightened her back, trying to be as lady-like as possible. "Thank you, you may lead on Master…"

"Master Thomas Draymon, your ladyship. I have the honour of owning the Gryphon's Rest."

The man was about to turn to lead them into the inn when Tempus jumped down from the carriage. Gerald watched the innkeeper's eyes widen with surprise, but to the man's credit, he didn't let the massive beast intimidate him. Perhaps, he thought, he was used to the strange practices of nobles.

The proprietor led them into the common room of the inn. Gerald insisted that Anna follow the man alongside Sophie, as he and Tempus followed behind. As they entered the room, Gerald felt the warmth of the fire, but a thin layer of smoke hung in the air; the firewood must have been wet. Intermingled with the smell of burning wood was the smell of the kitchen, making Gerald suddenly realize how hungry he was. Leading them to a table near the fireplace, Master Draymon pulled the seat out for Anna. He had evidently had to deal with young nobles before. In mere moments, a serving woman appeared with pewter cups and a delicious honeyed wine for the table. Gerald sniffed this cautiously, then gingerly tasted the concoction. It carried a pleasant odour, and the wine slid down his throat easily. He pronounced it to be suitable and the woman, who had been waiting for his approval, poured wine into the other cups, then disappeared back into the somewhat crowded room to see about some food.

Anna was looking around the room with great interest, taking it all in. Gerald enjoyed the look of excitement on her face. This was all new to her, he thought, and so much different from the Old Oak in Uxley Village. Here, there was a sense of wealth, of influential and well to do customers, very far removed from the simple homespun crowd back home.

Anna leaned in towards the table slightly to speak without being overheard. "This is so thrilling!" she said. "Is this what it's like in Wincaster?"

Gerald cast his eyes over the other customers. "I suppose it's what you might find in some places in Wincaster, probably more the richer areas, close to the Palace, but it's not the kind of place that I would be familiar with."

Their entrance had caused the volume in the room to lower temporarily, but upon taking their seats, the voices returned to their previous level. It was strange, Gerald thought, to be in such an establishment. He felt out of place, like an imposter, nervous that someone might discover his ruse, and turn him out. Their table was quiet as the server brought them food. He noticed both Anna and Sophie straining to hear what other people were saying.

The arrival of the food broke their silence. Soon, all three were tucking into their plates. Gerald dropped some meat to Tempus, who had lain down beside the table, only to discover that Anna and Sophie had both done likewise. The look of surprise on his face must have been evident for Anna laughed, then quickly tried to cover her mouth with her hand, lest she bring attention to herself.

The food was exceptional. Gerald found himself eating more than his usual share. The inn was generous with its portions, and it was quite evident that their customer's expected it to be so, but far too much in Gerald's opinion. He felt guilty leaving remnants on his plate, but so full was he, that he couldn't eat another bite. Even Tempus had had his fill and was now lying on the floor with odd bits of meat nearby, uneaten.

Gerald washed down the meal with more honey wine and soon felt lethargic. The feast and the wine were having its effect, and he found his eyelids drooping. He snapped them open only to see Anna in a similar predicament. Sophie, who had not eaten as much, sipped her wine slowly and didn't appear to be as affected. As he watched Anna struggle to stay awake, he began to discern individual conversations in the room. Most were simply uninteresting, but one, in particular, seemed to grab his attention, for he heard the words 'the king' and his eyes were drawn to a table nearby. Anna heard it as well, and out of the corner of his eye, he saw her turn in the same direction.

The man speaking was younger, in his early twenties, while his companion was an older man, perhaps his father or uncle, based upon the resemblance in their faces. The younger man was intent on toasting the king, for he held a cup up in the air waiting for his companion to acknowledge the toast. The older man had a twisted look of disgust on his face.

"I'll not toast the tyrant!" he refused. "To the Underworld with him."

"Come now," said the younger man, "it's customary to toast the king, surely it couldn't hurt?"

"Not after Wincaster," the older man replied. "There are far too many deaths at his hand. Remember the riots back in '53, that was bad business, that."

"You can't blame that on the king," interjected the young man, "it was food shortages, and a bad harvest, that's all."

"His Majesty certainly didn't suffer from a lack of food," roared the old man. "He was holding lavish parties and feeding his noble friends, while we starved. No, I'll not toast the king," the last word was almost spat out such was the distaste the man showed.

Gerald turned to Anna, who, like him, had been listening. She had a look of shock on her face. She turned pale, and he wondered if she might swoon, but she simply reached for her cup to take a sip. Her whole body seemed to shrink as if she was trying to disappear.

"I think," he started, "that perhaps it might be a good idea to retire for the evening. We want to leave early in the morning so that we arrive in Wincaster before they close the city gates."

Anna was relieved to be given the opportunity to vacate the room and stood, perhaps, a little too suddenly. The effect of the wine was noticeable, and she swayed unsteadily on her feet. Sophie was quick to make her way to Anna's side to steady her, and Gerald took her other arm. They escorted her towards the stairs where the innkeeper met them with a ring of keys. He lead them upstairs, where Anna and Sophie were given the room at the end of the hallway with Gerald and Tempus in the room next door. The two drivers, they discovered, were already ensconced in their room having taken their food with them.

Gerald made sure Anna was all right and left her in Sophie's care. Tempus said goodnight and followed Gerald into his room. The sounds of the common room were dull echoes in the background, but it took little time for Gerald to fall asleep.

He must have slept soundly, for he awoke to Anna opening his door, or rather he awoke to Tempus barking when Anna opened the door. The sun was just coming up, and a thin stream of light penetrated the shutters of his room, casting their rays against the opposite wall. Anna and Sophie, both dressed for the day, brought Tempus down to the common room, while Gerald promised to meet them in a few moments.

By the time he came down the stairs, Anna and Sophie were seated with fresh eggs and ham laid out in front of them. He was greeted by the sweet aroma of freshly baked scones, a particular favourite of his and Anna's. He had first eaten scones back in Bodden and had immediately fallen in love with them. He noticed the heat coming off the ones on the table. Sophie was spreading freshly churned butter across one of them as he sat down. He was mesmerized, watching her delicately spread the delicious topping and then, much to his gratification, she handed him one. He bit into the fresh biscuit, letting out a moan of satisfaction. Anna giggled, and he realized he was making a fool of himself, but he didn't care.

"This biscuit is delightful."

"Funny," said Anna smiling, "I always took you for a bacon or sausage man. I thought I was the pastry lover."

He grinned back, "Well, I do like bacon, and nothing beats a nice sausage, but these scones remind me of Bodden."

"Here we go again," she teased, looking at Sophie, "another story about Bodden."

Her words mocked him, but her face was kind. Gerald tried to keep a serious face, but the whole situation was just silly.

The food had disappeared from their plates by the time Ned came in from outside, letting them know the carriage was ready. They could depart whenever it suited them as the trunks were loaded.

Gerald settled the bill using the funds from their coin box, and they made their way to the carriage. Anna insisted on tracking all their expenses, so they pulled out a small ledger they had brought with them and recorded the coins they had spent. They left the Gryphon's Rest well prepared for the day's journey, with a packed luncheon purchased from the inn.

The first part of the trip was quiet as they all sat in companionable silence. The day was sunny, and the wet roads had dried nicely. The carriage made good time, and soon the rhythmic clacking of hooves on the cobblestones settled into a regular tapping noise. Gerald looked across at Anna. Today she was sitting with Tempus, who had his head laid on her lap.

"What did you think of your first stay at an inn?" he asked her.

"It was fascinating," she had a gleam in her eyes when she answered his question. "I've never really stayed anywhere other than Uxley Hall. Are all inns like that?"

"I don't know about all inns. I haven't stayed at a lot, but I believe the Gryphon is one of the nicer ones. I remember years ago I had to march to Tewsbury to pick up some soldiers that were coming back to Bodden. We were put up in a place, I think it was called the Rose and Sword or something like that. It was horrid. All the men got lice and scratched for weeks."

"That sounds terrible. How do you treat lice?"

"You give them a Dwarf bath," he replied.

"A Dwarf bath?"

"Yes, you light a fire using wet wood to create lots of smoke, and then you smoke your clothes. You stink for days afterwards, but it gets rid of the lice, or at least most of them."

Anna had a look of disgust on her face, "That sounds… terrible. But why is it called a Dwarf bath?"

"Dwarves like fire and smoke and always smell like a furnace, at least that's what they say, anyway. I've only met a few Dwarves in my time, and I can't say they smelled that way, but that's the old saying. No doubt a Dwarf might call it a Human bath. I have no idea."

Anna was amused, and a smile creased her face.

"I was a bit shocked to hear what that man thought of the king. Is he really a tyrant?"

Gerald was not sure how to respond. On the one hand, he wanted to tell her the truth, but on the other, he didn't want her to feel ashamed. In the end, he decided to be honest but tried to put it in diplomatic terms.

"Your father," he started, searching for the right words, "is a man of great power and responsibility. Kings often have to make decisions that will affect many others for good or ill."

"Is it true," she interrupted, "that he held lavish parties while others starved?"

He paused but then decided she needed to be told.

"Yes," he finally said, "I'm afraid it's true. Your father, King Andred, is well known as an excessive spender, and a man who sets the finest table in the kingdom."

"I can understand," she continued, "that he's wealthy and would eat well, but to do so when others are starving just seems so… unjust."

"Wise words," he replied, "but we can't tell others how to behave, especially the king."

"If I was in charge," she said, with a determined look in her eyes, "I would only hold parties if others were fed first. Isn't it the obligation of the nobles to look after the commoners?"

He was startled by her observation, though he shouldn't have been. He often saw the young girl and forgot her more serious side, and then she would surprise him with such an adult concept.

"Those are wise words from one so young," he said, adopting his wise and thoughtful face. "Where, if you don't mind, did you read that?"

"In 'The Noble's Obligation' by Baron Victor Brandon. I think it was written years ago."

"Victor Brandon?" Gerald thought out loud. "Wasn't he Robert Brandon's father?"

"Yes," she added, "he was."

The discussion soon turned to the noble families of Merceria, a topic with which Gerald had only a passing familiarity. He knew that Robert Brandon was the brother-in-law to Lord Fitzwilliam, for Fitz had married Brandon's sister. She had, unfortunately, died in childbirth, producing Fitzwilliam's only offspring, his daughter Beverly. Of course, Anna knew them all, at least by name. He found it fascinating that she could remember so much and yet she pushed him for any details he could supply, for she had never met any of them in person, save for Baron Fitzwilliam.

The morning soon passed into afternoon, and once they had stopped to eat and water the horses, they continued on their way. The countryside here was very flat with farms dotting the landscape. Soon, they passed cows out in the pasture, and farmers tilling the land, planting their seeds for the crops that would grow. The roadway was very straight, and it was when it twisted slightly to the south that Anna first saw Wincaster, its high walls almost erupting out of the ground.

Wincaster was a large city, the largest in the kingdom, and the seat of royal power. Four main gates allowed entry, each named for the points of the compass. They now approached the West Gate, and the carriage slowed. There were other travellers on the road, wagons hauling goods, farmers coming to town, perhaps to buy seed, and other country folk waiting to enter the city.

He knew that the West Gate was the largest structure Anna had ever seen. To either side of the gate were large round towers and a towering portcullis that was visible in its raised position. Two bored guards stood to either side of the road, stopping each traveller, in turn, asking questions. More guards were stationed farther back, closer to the inside of the wall, and at least two archers manned each tower. The line moved slowly. Gerald swore it would be faster to walk, but eventually, the carriage made its way to the gate.

One of the guards came over to the wagon, yelling up to the driver, "Who comes here?"

"A noble of the realm," Owen responded, and Gerald heard the distinctive sound of a coin being flicked through the air.

From his vantage point in the carriage, he watched the guard catch the coin in his hand and look at it.

A quick, "Pass friend" was uttered, and the carriage slowly lurched forward. They passed under the portcullis and entered the city proper. Gerald was rewarded by seeing Anna's eyes open wide at the sight that befell them.

"Welcome to Wincaster, Princess," he said.

TWENTY-SIX

The City

SPRING 959 MC

The carriage rumbled slowly along the narrow streets, the two and three-storey buildings towering over it as it made its way through Wincaster. Anna had never seen anything like this before, so she sat close to the window, peering out at the foreign landscape. To Gerald, it brought back memories of the filth and corruptness of the city. He did have a few good memories of the place, and so he sat silent, letting her enjoy her adventure.

Anna decided she would like to go straight to the Palace, so they stopped the carriage to affix the Royal Coat of Arms to the doors. Gerald then waited outside while Sophie helped Anna change into something more appropriate. With all these details squared away, they were now ready to resume their journey.

The road continued directly eastward, past the Great Library and Gerald pointed it out, for it towered over the shops that surrounded it. Anna promised to visit it later, but she was eager to keep moving. Once past the library, they turned left, heading north towards the Palace itself. From here, the road was arrow straight and only halted at the Palace entrance. The massive iron gates and high walls were easily visible some distance away. As the carriage trundled north, the buildings became larger, with richly appointed spaces of green surrounding them.

At the Palace, the road ended in a T junction with the road turning either left or right, both cutting across the Royal Gardens and to the wealthier estates of the nobles. Directly in front of them, stood the ornately decorated iron gate, guarded by two inattentive soldiers. As the driver brought the carriage to a halt facing the guards, one of them spied the coat of arms on the side and hollered something. One soldier turned and ran for the Palace, while the other, suddenly standing much straighter, moved quickly to release the latch on the entrance. He swung the enormous iron gate easily, for it was a well-balanced superior design. Owen eased the carriage forward slowly, leading the horses through a loop, bringing it parallel to the front of the immense building. The guard closed the gate, taking care to set the latch before returning to his station.

They sat waiting, for none of the group knew what to expect. They were rewarded with a scurrying of feet as the front door of the Palace opened, and servants and guards flooded out to take up their positions. They lined up in a well-ordered manner with servants to the right of the door and the guards to the left. A meticulously manicured man servant stepped lightly forward to the carriage door, deftly opening it, cautiously swinging the door to the side. A young boy ran up behind him with a small step and placed it gingerly in front of the doorway. The elegant man stepped back and bowed deeply, allowing those inside to emerge.

Gerald looked across at Anna, who stared back at him with a confused look on her face.

"What do we do now?" she whispered.

"We get out," he said in a matter of fact tone.

"Yes, but what's the protocol? Who gets out first?"

Gerald stared back. "Don't you know? I haven't the faintest idea!"

He looked at Sophie, but she shrugged her shoulders.

"Am I supposed to get out first," Anna considered out loud, "or am I meant to get out last?"

"Again, I have no idea. I suppose it doesn't matter. After all, you're a royal, you can do what you want!"

She smiled back at him, before making her decision, "Good point. You get out first, then I'll follow with Sophie just behind me."

With the order of egress decided, Gerald moved to exit the carriage. He felt very restricted within the close confines, so he held his sword tightly to stop it from catching on anything or anybody. The last thing he wanted to do was trip while exiting.

He stepped purposefully out and lowered himself to the ground, surveying those that stood lined up. He was suddenly aware of the threadbare nature of his clothes and the worn state of his chainmail which he had chosen to wear. It was all an act, he knew, and he was sure they would see through his false facade. He nodded slightly to the well-dressed servant and turned, offering a hand to help Anna out of the carriage. She stepped down gracefully, elegantly extending her hand as she did so, making it all look so effortless. He marvelled at her calm demeanour, but then noticed the perspiration starting to form on her forehead, she was as nervous as he was.

The elegant servant bowed deeply, his right leg extended, while he swept his hand forward in a well-practiced manner.

"Welcome, Your Highness," the servant said, keeping his eyes to the ground. If he did not recognize her, he gave no sign of it. "If it pleases Your Highness," he continued, "I shall introduce the staff."

Anna followed him as he took her down the line of servants. Gerald and Sophie fell in line behind her. The head servant rattled off their names as each bowed or curtsied, and before they realized, they were walking through the great doors which led into the Palace itself.

The building was massive, built of a type of white stone that Gerald did not recognize. The doorway led into a courtyard, surrounded on all four sides by the structure itself. The courtyard was set with smooth bricks that had the look of long use. It was three stories tall. Three very tall stories, for as they entered the building proper, he was amazed to see the ceiling was a full twelve feet above him. He wondered at the sheer elegance of the work and speculated that there was perhaps an Elven or Dwarven influence.

If he thought the outside of the building was impressive, he was overwhelmed by the interior accoutrements. Rich tapestries, thick carpets, carefully lacquered wooden tables and solid, decorated chairs with thick cushions were all on display as they passed. They ultimately entered a large dining room in which a long table rested. The servants had used their time wisely setting the table, and as they entered the room, food was laid down.

Anna turned to face the elegant servant who had led them in, "Please see to the wellbeing of the drivers. My lady-in-waiting will dine with us."

She sat down at the end of the table, indicating with her hands that Gerald and Sophie should sit to either side. Tempus padded in behind them, causing concerned looks from the army of servants. She called him over, and he obediently sat down beside her, his massive head looming above the table. She inspected the spread thoroughly, daintily selecting a piece of cheese, and passing it to her faithful canine. He took it gently, and with a collective sigh of relief from the servants, they rushed forward to fill the wine glasses.

The trio was hungry from their trip, but ate sparingly, trying to appear sophisticated. To Gerald's mind, they were only partially successful in this, but the servants didn't appear to mind. He wondered what the king's eating habits were like, but then dismissed such thoughts from his head. Anna must make her own way here.

The food was delicious and the wine tasty, with a hint of something he couldn't identify, that gave it a slight tang. The servants all stood behind them in line, waiting to jump at a moment's notice to refill a glass or take away an empty plate. Gerald felt as though he was being inspected, as if he must pass some test. Looking around, he came to the conclusion he was largely being ignored by the servants, whose main focus was the royal in the room.

At last, Anna dropped her napkin over her plate, signalling the end of the meal. The servants moved in to clear away the table.

She turned to the elegant servant, "If I may…" she started.

"Bailey, Your Highness," he offered.

"If I may, Bailey," she continued, "I should like to see our rooms."

"Certainly, Your Highness," he responded, "if you'll follow me, your baggage has already been seen to."

"Thank you. you may lead us. I should also require an adjoining room for my lady-in-waiting, as well as a room on the same floor for my bodyguard."

"Of course, Your Highness," Bailey responded and led the way.

As they moved off, he made hand signals to the other servants. No doubt they would be scrambling to see to the extra accommodations.

They escorted Anna to her room. She was up on the third floor with a balcony that overlooked the front of the Palace. Anna was thrilled to see a giant bed which Tempus lost no time in testing out. The great dog leaped onto the bed and sprawled on his back, leaving Anna with a big smile on her face. The servants appeared mortified but refrained from comment. Sophie's room was adjacent to Anna's with an entrance to her suite, while they billeted Gerald at the end of the hall. All of the rooms were immense, in his opinion. He had a hard time realizing that his room was easily twice the size of his groundskeeper's cottage back in Uxley.

Once in his room, Gerald stripped off his armour and changed into more comfortable clothes. He used a water bowl to wash up and was in the final stages when a light tap on the door proved to be Sophie, coming to get him. They made their way back to Anna's room, where they found her sitting on a large couch with Tempus stretched out beside her, as much as his size would permit, his head on her lap.

Gerald and Sophie sat down opposite her, on two padded chairs. Even the bedroom chairs here were opulent, and he was worried he might somehow damage them.

"What do you think? Isn't it amazing? I never, even in my wildest dreams, thought the Palace would be so nice, did you?"

"I have to say," admitted Gerald, "that I didn't expect the Palace would be so richly decorated and so large!"

He noticed Anna was about to speak when the door suddenly burst open. He turned to tell a servant what he thought of the interruption, but was cut short by the sight that befell his eyes, for there, in the doorway, stood a young woman, perhaps fifteen or sixteen, with dark brown hair that looked like a younger version of the queen.

"Sister!" she said, and strode across the room, suddenly stopping when she caught sight of Tempus.

Anna stood up quickly, leaving Tempus sitting up on the couch.

"Margaret?" she asked.

Now that she was standing, Princess Margaret continued forward, embracing her younger sister with a heartfelt hug.

"I heard you had arrived, but I couldn't believe it. You finally came to Wincaster!"

Anna beamed then collected herself.

She turned slightly to introduce her companions, "This is Sophie, my lady-in-waiting."

"You mean lady's maid, don't you?" Margaret corrected.

Gerald noticed the look of triumph on Margaret's face and saw Sophie's face fall slightly at the demotion.

Anna ignored her and continued, "And this is Gerald, he's my... bodyguard."

Margaret scrutinized Gerald. He could feel fresh sweat making its way to the surface again. Strange how he could feel so intimidated by a fifteen-year-old girl.

"Isn't he a little old?" she teased. "He looks like he would fall apart in a fight. You need someone younger, I've a knight or two I could spare. Shall I send one over?"

"No," Anna quickly returned, trying to sound nonchalant, "Gerald has served me well for many years."

She looked at him, and he could see her eyes pleading. He nodded back and saw her relax a little.

"How long are you here for?" Margaret asked. "We must find time to do some shopping. It will be such fun."

Anna appeared overwhelmed by the sudden need to please her sister.

"Of course, we shall go shopping tomorrow, but it's been a rather long trip, and I'm fatigued."

Margaret took Anna's hands in her own and looked at her with all her fifteen years of wisdom.

"Of course, poor thing," she said, sounding remarkably like the queen. "I should have realized. I shall make the arrangements for tomorrow and let you rest. I am looking forward to showing you Wincaster!"

She turned and left the room with a spring in her step. Both Gerald and Sophie found themselves letting their breath out after the whirlwind exchange. Tomorrow would indeed be an interesting day. Anna had already been disappointed by her brother. He hoped her sister would not have a similar effect.

Gerald had dropped onto his bed in an exhausted state, and fallen into a deep sleep. He woke to the realization that he had not bothered to undress, and so now he had to wash and change. He was surprised by the mirror which adorned his dresser. It was large and of a clarity that he found fascinating. He usually used a small hand mirror to trim his beard, but now he saw himself in crystal clear detail. He noticed for the first time, how old he looked. His beard had an excessive sprinkling of grey mixed in among his normally brown whiskers. His skin was weathered and worn, but his eyes were still alert and clear. He shrugged it off and used a sharp razor that had been provided to trim his beard, eliminating the stray strands of hair that perpetually nagged him. Feeling fit for the day's activities, he made his way down to Anna's suite.

He knocked on the door and was greeted by Sophie, with Anna in the background. She was looking at herself in a full-length mirror, wearing an elegant dress that he didn't recognize.

"Margaret sent it," said Sophie in response to his questioning gaze. "It was her dress when she was younger, and she thought it would fit Anna."

Anna looked over, saw them at the door, and came towards them.

"Time to be off. We have to get some breakfast in before the trip into town."

They made their way down to the dining room with some assistance from a passing servant. Margaret was already eating a sparsely populated plate, while two young men in immaculate armour stood nearby. Gerald had never seen it polished so brightly, and wondered if enemy soldiers might find them amusing.

"Come on, Anna, there's food here for you," Margaret insisted. "Oh, you won't need your lady's maid where we're going, I have arranged a couple of bodyguards for us."

As she made this last statement, Gerald spotted one of them smirking, a breach of discipline that he found unsettling.

"I should like to bring my bodyguard," Anna insisted. "I hope that won't be too inconvenient?"

"If you like," Margaret said, trying to sound indifferent, "but Sir Edward and Sir Edgar here, are all we really need."

Gerald was taken aback, these bodyguards were knights? He examined them closer, forgetting about the food on the table. They wore chainmail, over which was fashioned, in the new style, the breastplates that had become more common. He compared this to Lord Fitzwilliam, whose breastplate was badly scratched and dented from years of use. Even Lady Beverly wasn't so full of herself that she would shine her armour to such a brilliant form. The whole idea felt repugnant to him, but he supposed that life at court, far from the wildness of the frontier, was a much different place. Perhaps here, they valued manners and finesse more than fighting skill. He remembered the fury of his last battle in Bodden, where his leg was wounded. That same campaign had seen Lady Beverly knighted due to the desperate fight that ensued. To see here, an untested youth in shiny armour mocked her achievements.

"Excuse me, Your Highness," Gerald found himself saying to Margaret, "but if I may be so bold, have you ever thought of a female bodyguard?"

"No thank you," Margaret replied. "I had one of those a few years back. All she did was give the other knights dirty looks. Besides," she smiled coyly, "I like having these handsome gentlemen around. It reminds me of the finer things in life," she giggled slightly, and it reminded him of Anna's laugh.

Gerald never did get his breakfast, for so involved was he in his examination of the knights that he didn't realize how much time had passed. The next thing he knew, they were whisked out of the Palace to the courtyard, where Margaret had arranged a carriage. Unlike the one they had used from Uxley Hall, this one was open topped with a small standing platform on the back for the knights. Gerald glanced around, then decided the best option was to sit by the driver, so he climbed up, gave the driver an apologetic look, and sat down beside him.

The carriage made its way out of the Palace turning west and heading towards the richer merchant district. The streets here were wider than they saw yesterday and the feeling of being enclosed was gone. Anna appeared to enjoy having the breeze across her face, for the day was warm, with the sun rising high in a cloudless sky.

They had only travelled a few blocks when the carriage pulled off to the side of the road. Gerald observed other people walking the street and the occasional rider, all of which were either elegantly attired or in armour. Margaret was constantly talking, and Gerald tried to ignore her most of the time. She mentioned that the barracks were nearby, and he wondered if any of his old friends were still in Wincaster, then realized that anyone here would remember his disgrace. Best if he didn't run into anyone he knew.

They travelled on foot for most of the morning, in and out of shops, while the carriage kept pace. The knights would bring out the newly purchased goods and place them in the carriage, or arrangements would be made to have them delivered. Anna bought pots and pans for Cook, some new aprons for the servants at Uxley, and all manner of mundane items. He saw how thoughtful she was and how thankful she was for all the servants back home. Margaret was somewhat put off by her purchases, and insisted they visit a jewellery maker and a lady's dress shop.

They had wandered through fully half of the merchant district when Anna caught sight of a sign that instantly grabbed her attention.

"Look, Gerald," she noted, temporarily forgetting her sister, "Bloom's Herbalists. We must go and see what they have!"

Gerald opened the door for Anna, and a small bell rang. They stepped into a brightly lit room with clay jars and pots lining the walls, each sealed, with names painted on them. A counter stood against the far wall where an older woman, perhaps in her late thirties or early forties, stood. She was marking in a ledger of some sort and looked up as the bell rang.

"Can I help you?" the woman said.

Anna was the first to respond, "Do you have any kingsleaf?"

The lady behind the counter was surprised, "We do, my lady, but it's expensive. Might I ask what you want it for?"

"Oh, I don't want to buy it, I was just curious how expensive it was."

The woman came out from behind the counter and led them over to one of the shelves. She reached up to the top shelf and took down a glass jar which had a wooden stopper in its top.

"This is kingsleaf. It is a very rare herb and has some unusual properties. It sells for one and a half crowns per leaf."

Anna stared at the delicate looking leaf in the bottle as her eyes widened.

"It must be hard to find to be so expensive. What would you pay if someone could supply it?"

The woman looked at her in surprise, "I would pay fifteen shillings a leaf if the quality was good."

"That's a very nice markup, almost double the investment," Anna noted.

"Yes, but it can sit on the shelf for some time because few can afford it. If I could get it in quantity, I would reduce the price and make more coins on volume."

Anna responded with a smile, "I think I can offer you that deal. I happen to know where I can acquire a quantity of kingsleaf that would suit your purposes."

They returned to the Palace for lunch. Margaret made sure a full meal was provided, consisting of the finest of ingredients. If they thought they were going to spend the afternoon resting, they were sorely disappointed, for Margaret had decided to take them on a carriage tour of the city. They left the Palace as soon as they were done eating and travelled east, through what turned out to be the richest section of town. The street here was wide, with carefully tended sidewalks and neatly trimmed trees and bushes lining the road. The grand houses showed off their wealth in a flurry of stone and marble. There were two-storey mansions, complete with small towers on the corners, all the way to single-storey estates, spreading their floors across the ground in seemingly random patterns. There were houses with domed roofs, square entranceways and balconied entrances. They even saw a house that was like a fortress, complete with a portcullis in the entranceway.

Margaret talked the whole time, mentioning how the Earl of Shrewesdale had imported marble for his mansion in the capital, while the Earl of Eastwood preferred the darker brick typical to the Eastwood. She showed them some squat, single floored dwellings with ornately carved entranceways and she explained how they were built in the Dwarven style. Gerald had his doubts. Fitz had told him once that Dwarves, despite their short stature, preferred vaulted ceilings towering above them. The houses here had ceilings no higher than normal.

Anna's sister appeared to be able to talk endlessly, and the trip soon became a blur to him. He found himself beginning to drift off to sleep, despite the constant sound of hoof beats on cobblestones. He shook himself awake and looked back into the carriage. Margaret was still talking, pointing out points of interest to Anna who, much to Gerald's amusement, appeared to be in the same state as himself.

They circled about the luxurious houses, then made their way back to the Palace using the same street that began their journey. Gerald noticed an odd-looking house on the south side of the street which had avoided his attention on the way out. It appeared to be a two-storey building with a single tower built into the front corner, but instead of having the typical battlements on the top, which was the custom, this tower had a peaked roof and a large window built into it. This type of window was more common to a house, rather than a keep.

The whole structure looked rather ramshackle and did not fit the neighbourhood, which consisted mainly of large mansions and well-kept grounds. He turned in his seat to look back at the princesses.

"Whose house is that?" he asked, indicating the strange looking house.

"Oh," said Margaret with disdain apparent in her voice, "that belongs to Andronicus, the King's Mage. The man obviously has no sense of class."

Anna was immediately interested and explained, "I met him. He was good to me. Is he home? Do you think we can visit him?"

"No," her sister replied, "Andronicus is the King's Mage. Wherever the king goes, so goes Andronicus. Besides, he's peculiar, he gives me nightmares."

Gerald wondered why she would have such a negative view of the old man, but then again Margaret only appeared to take pleasure in lovely things, and he would not describe Andronicus as 'pretty'.

He pondered if he would be treated with such disdain when he was old, then remembered his face in the mirror and realized he already was. The cold hard truth was that he had lived many years, and had little to show for it. He was starting to feel sorry for himself, but glanced at Anna in the carriage and realized he was lucky to have her as a friend. Perhaps he had more accomplishments in his life than he realized.

Their sojourn ended, they pulled back into the Palace where Anna was quick to make apologies for she was exceedingly tired. They retired to their rooms for the rest of the day and Anna arranged for food to be brought to her suite so they wouldn't have to endure her sister's chatter more than necessary.

The food was carried in on trays and laid out on tables for them and even dining chairs had been brought in to make them more comfortable in the room. The food, as usual, was delicious and Gerald wondered if he would have to purchase a larger belt.

Their meal concluded, the servants cleared away the plates, leaving them to snack on small cakes and sip their drinks. He found himself getting used to the pampered life. He could easily spend the rest of his days in such comfort, but he knew it wouldn't last. Soon, they would have to return to their lives at Uxley. He was mulling this over in his mind when Anna spoke up.

"Gerald," she said slowly, "what's it like going around town without an escort?"

"Pardon?" he said, not quite understanding the question.

"I know we were shopping today, but we were accompanied by guards and dressed as royals. Everyone was nice, and all the shopkeepers deferred to us."

"As well they should," he said, "you're both royals!"

"Yes," she persisted, "but what if I wasn't important? What would it be like for someone who wasn't wealthy?"

He thought this over before replying, "Why don't we find out tomorrow? You can wear the other clothes you brought from Uxley, and you and I will go shopping." Anna smiled and was about to say something, but he cut her off. "But you can't take a carriage, and we will only take a small number of coins. If we're going into town as commoners, you'll have to act like a commoner."

"Agreed!" He could already see the gears starting to work in her mind before she spoke again, "So when we go shopping tomorrow I will be a commoner. I shall be Winifred Hart, the daughter of a wealthy merchant."

"No, I think not," he corrected. "How about you are Anna, the daughter of a retired soldier."

She grinned, "All right, I suppose that's an easier role to play."

"You're not playing a role, just be yourself, minus your title of course. Now, unless you have something else you want to go over, I'd like to get some sleep, I'm rather tired."

"All right, goodnight… Father."

TWENTY-SEVEN

Commoners

～

The next morning, Anna and Gerald left the Palace by the servant's entrance. They arranged to meet Sophie at a nearby tavern, in case they had trouble convincing the servants to let them back in. They took their time walking, for this was all new to Anna, and she loved taking in the view. Even the mere fact of so many people out and about was exciting to her. They saw young children being walked by their parents, older children running around with no apparent supervision, young couples holding hands and older folks. Well-dressed nobles along with well-to-do commoners mingled with the middle class, and even the odd beggar was visible. These were frequently young children who were often yelled at, then chased off by the town watch.

Anna had never seen the town watch before and found them fascinating, but Gerald paid no attention to them. He had to explain that they were here to keep the peace, but were not soldiers. Yes, they had to be able to fight, but no, they would not stand in a line of battle or march to war. Uxley was too small to warrant a town watch and usually the locals who formed the militia dealt with any rowdiness. Here in Wincaster, they seemed to spend their time eyeing strangers and giving them dirty looks. Gerald had never trusted the town watch here. They had a reputation of being corrupt and lazy, but they were a reassuring presence for the locals as they went about their day.

They walked past a few stores, with Anna examining their windows to see what was inside. The first one she decided to enter was a gown shop.

They stepped inside to an ill-lit interior where they saw dresses hanging on hooks and bolts of cloth laid out beneath a worktable. A tall, thin woman was at the table, cutting material with a pair of elegant scissors. The shiny fabric reflected the light and Anna, entranced by the material, made her way over to watch. She reached out, touching the silky material before her eyes looked up at the woman. She was shocked to realize the face looking down at her was not Human. Gerald chuckled as he remembered that Anna had never seen an Elf before.

The woman looked down at Anna, with a smile coming to her face as she responded, "Is there something I can help you with, miss?" The woman's voice sounded as silky as the material she was cutting.

Anna gazed up at her, not seeming to know how to react. Gerald had interacted with Elves before, but he was aware that for Anna, this was a new experience. The woman appeared Human in general shape but was much taller and thinner. Her hair was a dirty blonde colour, tied up in an elaborate series of braids. Her most startling feature was her ears, for they were longer than Humans and slightly pointed at the ends. Gerald watched Anna overcome her initial discomfort.

"I'm sorry," she said at last, "I didn't mean to stare, only I've never seen an Elf before. Sorry for being so rude."

"That's quite all right," the Elf responded. "I'm used to it, there aren't many Elves in Wincaster. You can call me Ellian. Is there something I can help you with?"

"I'm fascinated by this material," Anna said, fingering the cloth. "Is it expensive?"

"I would think," the Elf said, looking Anna over, "that it might be a bit beyond your means. May I suggest something a bit more practical?" She led Anna over to another shelf piled with bolts of cloth and withdrew a roll of deep green material, placing it on the table. "This is a very sturdy material that we bring in from the Darkwood. It's very durable and well-made."

Anna studied the cloth, feeling its softness as she spoke, "It's remarkable. I've never felt such a soft material. Would this work as a cloak?"

"Oh, yes," said Ellian. "I use it most often for outer garments. Very popular with some rangers. It can handle the inclement weather, and it's quite warm."

"I would like to get it, but I'm not sure how much I'd need."

"That's easy enough to figure out," the Elf said. "We can sew it up for you, or we can take some measurements, and you can do it yourself."

Anna thought it over before coming to a decision. In the end, she decided to have Ellian make it, and so they spent some time while the Elf took her measurements. Since it would not be finished before they departed the capital, Anna insisted on paying in advance to have it shipped to Uxley.

The visit ended up taking a large portion of their morning, and by the time they left, Gerald was feeling peckish. This turned out to be advantageous, for no sooner had they left the dressmakers than they happened to come across a bakery. Anna insisted on entering, and for the rest of the morning, they examined the delicious treats that lay inside. They sampled a wide variety of goods and purchased some small meat pies which they took with them with the intention of eating later. So tempting was the delicious aroma, however, that they broke down and ate them right away.

Now, fortified by their treats, they proceeded farther down the street. They passed by a candle maker, smelling the paraffin as the wicks were dipped to make the candles. They made their way down the street and turned up Wilson Alley to see a cobbler working at a cramped stand. They purchased apples from an apple cart, while a young troop of girls wandered by who appeared to be on their way to church. The alley led to the adjacent street where they realized they had travelled to a street full of blacksmiths, carpenters and other workmen. Gerald led her to an armourer where the constant pounding of metal spilled out into the street. Displayed in front was a basket full of old swords, and Anna drew one out, examining it. The wooden handle was rather basic, but the elegantly embossed blade appeared to have runes of some type.

"I see you have an eye for swords," said a voice.

Gerald saw her jump, so engrossed was she in examining the blade.

"Yes," she said at last, "it's very nice. Are all your swords like this?"

With the sound of something dropping loudly onto a work table, the proprietor came out front. The smith, it turned out, was a Dwarf, one of the ancient races that dwelt in the land long before the Humans came. He was very Human-like, but short of stature, perhaps only five feet tall, and broad of girth. The smith smiled at Anna, and his toothy grin was bright against his soot-stained face, for he had been in front of the forge for hours. He was grimy and stained with sweat, giving off a rather unpleasant aroma which Gerald perceived had just been detected by Anna. The Dwarf was about to speak when he noticed Gerald, standing just to the side.

"Well, I'll be," the smith said, "if it isn't Sergeant Gerald Matheson himself."

Gerald was pleased the smith remembered him, "Good to see you Herdwin. How's business?"

"Oh, not so bad," Herdwin replied. "You know how it is. When the people are unhappy, the army buys more weapons. Good for me, not so good for the people."

Gerald looked at Anna, "Allow me to introduce Anna. Anna, this is Herdwin Steelarm, one of the finer weapon smiths hereabouts."

"Pleased to meet you," said Anna. "Did you make all these weapons yourself?"

Herdwin looked at the basket. "What, these? No, those are rubbish. I have those for customers that can't afford decent weapons."

"How can you say that?" asked Anna, holding up the blade for his inspection. "Look at the work on this, it's fascinating."

"Hold right there," the Dwarf said gruffly, "and I'll show you workmanship." He disappeared for only a moment behind his stall and returned with a short sword, handing it to Anna. "Now, that," he said proudly, "is the type of work that I do."

Anna took the blade, and Gerald watched her examine it. The handle, a richly polished, dark coloured wood with strips of red leather carefully wrapped around it to make it comfortable, fit easily into her grip. The elaborate cross-guard reminded Gerald of vines of ivy, while the incredibly light blade seemed to catch even the smallest morsel of light and reflect it back tenfold. All along the length of the sword was a series of small runes, forming a column that went from handle to tip. The edge appeared razor sharp, and Anna moved the sword around to look at it from all angles.

"It's incredible," she said in awe. "How did you get it so sharp?"

Herdwin laughed, "I can't tell you all my secrets, now can I? Go ahead, wave it around a little, and get a feel for it. Have you ever used a sword before?"

She swung it around, using practice swings to get a feel for the blade. Gerald was pleased. She had proved to be an adept student and did him proud. She would never be a warrior, but she could protect herself when needed, and that was enough in his book. He hoped that she would never have to use it, but was confident in her ability. The Dwarf appeared surprised to see such a young girl wielding a sword with apparent skill.

"My, you're just full of surprises, little one." He turned to Gerald, "Is she yours?"

"Er... yes," Gerald stumbled on his answer, "my daughter."

"Daughter? Well, I'll be a blank stone. I never knew you had a family."

"It's a long story," said Gerald, "perhaps you'd like to join us for a drink. I believe the Herald is nearby?"

"A tempting offer, but I've work to do." He looked at Anna who was still swinging the short blade like a pro. "I'll tell you what we'll do young Anna.

You take that. Consider it a birthday present from one of your dad's old friends."

Anna looked up at Gerald and smiled, "Can I, Papa? Please?"

He tried to keep a straight face while Anna was hamming it up terribly.

"Sure," he said, "but you must let us buy you a drink. How about I send a jug over from the Herald?"

Herdwin's teeth made another appearance as he grinned from ear to ear, "Deal!" He extended his hand to grasp Gerald's in a firm grip. "Now, you get on over there, oh wait, before I forget," he started rummaging through another basket. "Here's a scabbard for you, and a belt. These are just cheap mind you, I don't make them, but if you're interested in something nicer, there's a leather worker just down the street named Strickland who does some excellent decorative stuff."

Anna took the belt and scabbard, putting the blade carefully away. "Thank you Herdwin," she curtsied dramatically.

"You're quite welcome, lass," the old smith replied, then disappeared with a wave, back behind his stall to his waiting forge.

Gerald and Anna started down towards the Herald to wet their whistle.

"You're quite lucky," said Gerald as they walked, "it's not everyone who gets a Dwarven blade."

"Is it magical?" she asked with wonder.

"No, but very well made. Dwarven smiths know the secret to making their metal light but durable. You'll find that blade much easier on the arm than the one you have back at Uxley, and the blade will stay sharp longer."

"A perfect weapon for a warrior princess," she said proudly.

They took a quick break at the Herald Tavern to fortify themselves, and Gerald made sure to send a jug down to the Dwarf. They left shortly after that and wandered through the maze of side streets, poking their heads into stores, examining carts loaded with goods and generally just observing the townsfolk.

They stopped in at a leather worker where Gerald purchased a belt pouch. He had finished buying the new item and was carefully attaching it to his belt when he noticed Anna. She was hunting for a scabbard for her dagger, and a young lad, only a little older than her, was moving towards her. He felt alarmed and moved quickly to protect her. The young boy sidled up to her, placing his hand lightly on her behind and Anna suddenly squeaked. She turned abruptly and saw the boy, who was grinning from ear to ear. Her face turned red, and just as she was about to speak, Gerald caught the young lad by the ear, dragging him to the doorway.

"Out with you," he said, releasing the boy and assisting him on his way with a boot to the rear end.

The boy veritably flew from the establishment but landed on his feet, scampering off down the street with a look of fear on his face. He kept looking behind him to see if he was being followed.

All of this amused the patrons of the leather worker, and Anna rapidly turned an even brighter shade of red. Gerald took her hand and led her from the building, moving away from the direction the boy had taken. They stopped half a block away, and he watched her fighting to regain control.

She calmed herself, and then said, "Well, that was… interesting."

"I'm afraid that sort of thing is more common than you might think," he said. "I hope you didn't find it too unsettling. Of course, you could have him flayed alive for touching a royal that way."

She turned swiftly towards him and was surprised to see his face was serious, "No, it's fine. He didn't know I'm royal. I must learn to behave as a commoner if I'm to pass as one. No harm was done, but I won't let it happen a second time."

They walked on in companionable silence, then Anna's attention was diverted by a commotion down the street, where they spotted a brightly dressed man standing on a box. He was engaging the crowd with his recitation of a poem. As they drew closer, the crowd broke into applause, and just as they came within earshot, they heard the man speak.

"Be sure to come down to the Grand Theatre this afternoon for the matinee performance of the King's Mistress. We still have seats available."

"What's that man doing?" Anna asked.

"He's one of the actors down at the Grand. They have a play running, a comedy I think."

"A comedy?" she asked.

"Yes, you know, a play with humour. Usually, they poke fun at those in positions of authority. It's all fun and games, no one takes it seriously."

"Can we go see it, Papa?" she said, giving him the well-practiced doe-eyed look, holding her hands in a pleading motion.

He grinned as he answered, "Of course, my daughter, but I must warn you that some of the humour can be… adult. They'll likely poke fun at the king and the other royals."

"That's all right," she said, "I'm just a commoner. It will be interesting to see what other people think about the king."

They decided they should see the play, giving them a timetable for their afternoon. They were told the play would begin after the bells sounded two, so they made their way haphazardly towards the Grand, looking in stores along the way. They had fun. Gerald found himself relaxing and enjoyed seeing the joy on Anna's face each time she discovered something new.

The Grand Theatre was a rather grandiose name for such a modest venue, but it was large enough to have two box seats, one on either side of the stage. They decided it would be safer, considering the earlier encounter with the young lad, if they splurged and bought box seats. As it turned out these were not too expensive, and they settled down for the show.

All the lamps were extinguished save for the lit candles on the front of the stage. Metal was placed around them to direct the light onto the cast members as they assembled on stage. They were dressed in all manner of clothes, some as nobles, some as soldiers and some as servants. They stood in a line across the stage while one man, a host of sorts, strode forward to address the crowd, which fell into a hush.

"Ladies and Gentlemen," the man began, "I introduce to you a tale of a king and the mistress that held his leash."

The audience chuckled. Anna sat quietly then looked at Gerald for an explanation.

He leaned close and whispered, "It's said that the king's mistress controls the king by... favours."

"What do you mean, favours?" she asked innocently.

"Er... well, she gives him favours... in bed. That is to say-"

"Oh, I get it, say no more," she said, cutting him off with a slightly embarrassed look.

The man's introduction complete, the acting troupe scuttled off the stage and the curtain rose revealing what appeared to be a Royal Throne Room. The king, or rather the man playing him, wore an over exaggerated crown that was too large for his head. The play proceeded to tell its story, which mainly consisted of people finding the king in compromising positions with his mistress every time something important was happening. Gerald found the story to be almost non-existent, but some of the scenes were outrageously funny. Anna was laughing uproariously, and even blushed several times due to the rather vulgar, and sometimes overt situations.

The play had been running on for quite some time when a commotion started. The setting on the stage was a Royal Bathing Room and the mistress, played by an overly endowed woman who was not shy about showing her assets, was lounging in the tub, hanging her legs over the edge. Suddenly daylight entered the building from the front of the theatre, and several members of the audience near the door started complaining. The sound of stomping feet began to drown out the performers as soldiers entered the building in two ranks, splitting to move up either side of the room towards the stage.

"In the name of the king, this play is hereby closed, and all within are under arrest for sedition," a voice boomed.

In an instant, a panic started. The room went from almost deathly quiet to sudden screams and yells. The room was still not properly lit, and Gerald couldn't see much detail, but he had seen enough fighting in his time to understand what was about to happen. He grabbed Anna's hand.

"Come with me, quick," he urged, and they fled the box. Just outside the box was a stairway and he turned to head upstairs.

"Where are we going? The exit is that way," Anna yelled.

"They'll have the exits blocked so we'll have to make for the rooftop."

Anna followed obediently. Some of the actors who had not been on stage soon joined them on the stairs. The group arrived at the top and went through the door to the rooftop, which was uneven and angled. They made their way across it carefully, lest tiles work loose and they slip. Gerald heard a commotion on the street and looked down. Fighting had broken out, and he recognized swordplay at work. One of the actors indicated a path to the south, and the troop made their way across the roof. The buildings here were close together, and it was only a narrow gap, no more than the length of his boot, to make their way to the next rooftop.

"Keep going," urged an actress, "we have to get across two more rooftops, then we can cut across to Cutler Street. It'll be safe there."

They heard the sounds of pursuit from a couple of guards as they made their way around a chimney. The rooftops were not all the same height, and the next building was half a storey higher. They had to use a drain pipe to climb up to it. Gerald urged the others on, telling Anna to meet him back at Herdwin's. He saw a worried look cross Anna's face and then the actress took her hand. Gerald turned to see the pursuing soldiers and waited until they saw him. He strode across the rooftop, angling away from the route the others had gone. The soldiers took the bait, and he heard them trailing. He saw a door leading down into the building and made a snap decision. He paused in front of the door then kicked it open. The door opened with a gratifying bang, and he stopped it from bouncing back and hitting him. He heard the footsteps getting closer and knew they would be on him in just a moment. He ran to the side of the rooftop and lowered himself over the edge, holding on with both hands.

He held his breath as best he could and waited. Sure enough, one of his pursuers shouted and then he heard their footsteps echo as they entered the doorway and descended the steps. With some effort, he hauled himself back onto the roof and retraced his steps to join up with the others. After waiting to ensure there was no pursuit, he cut across to Cutler Street. By the time he reached the ground, he spotted the group, with Anna. They were catching their breath and laughing at their close escape.

Anna saw him and exclaimed, "Gerald!" then ran over to him, embracing him in a hug.

It was far too much excitement for one day, he thought, but he had to admit it was quite a story. At Anna's insistence, they took the survivors to a tavern and purchased them a round of drinks. They were entertained by the actor's stories of adventure and derring-do, for thespians earned little and had to resort to other pastimes to make their living. Anna was entranced. Here were people who lived for excitement and passion, who had a zest for life she had not seen before.

Eventually, the excitement wore off, and the young girl emerged, exhausted and ready to sleep. They bid farewell to their new friends, making their way back to the rendezvous to meet up with Sophie. They only made one stop along the way, and when they arrived at the Hogshead Tavern, near the Palace, they saw Sophie sitting at a table, Tempus at her feet. The great beast had proved invaluable, for Sophie had not been bothered, and now, as they sat down, Anna rubbed her dog's ears and gave him the bone she had picked up on the way back.

Upon meeting up, Anna had a burst of energy as she related all that had befallen them during their foray. Sophie was completely enthralled, and he realized how lucky Anna was to have her, for she was much more than a servant, she was a friend. It was dark before they finally made their way into the servant's entrance of the Palace and up to their rooms. It didn't take Anna long to fall asleep once they were back. Indeed she was half asleep before she was even through the door and Gerald carried her to her bed. She was so tired they decided to let her sleep in her clothes with her valiant hound snuggled up against her on the bed.

TWENTY-EIGHT

The Slums

SPRING 959 MC

G erald stretched luxuriously in the large four-poster bed. He glimpsed sunlight trying to peek through the curtains, leaving a thin line of bright light that threatened to creep ever closer as the sun rose. He had slept peacefully, so well that even now the bed threatened to pull him into sleep's tender embrace once more.

He knew he had things to do and so, reluctantly, he dragged himself out of bed, making his way to the dresser to wash up. As he began to move about, his stomach reminded him that he had not eaten in some time, so he dressed quickly, eager to obtain some food from the kitchen.

In a thrice he was ready and made his way down the hallway. Best, he thought, to check in on Anna and Sophie, and see how they were doing. He knocked quietly on the door and was beckoned to enter. Inside, Anna and Sophie sat together at a small table, sipping on herbal tea of some sort, and eating mini cakes. They had apparently been up for some time, for the remains of a breakfast lay on their plates nearby.

He wandered in, noticing the bacon and sausages that still lay on the serving tray, tempting him with their aroma. His stomach made a gurgling noise, and he apologized. Anna insisted he help himself, and not wanting to appear churlish, he took up a small plate and placed the food on it, being sure to grab a fork.

He was fascinated by forks. They were said to have been invented by the Elves, but everyone used them, even Orcs were known to favour the pronged implement. Most Human forks had four prongs, but he was aware that Elves preferred three. He wondered, as he ate, if there was some significance to that and then stopped, half a slice of bacon in his mouth when he noticed that Anna was speaking to him.

"I'm sorry," he said, trying to finish the bacon quickly, "could you repeat that?"

"I was saying that I'd like to take a carriage to the poor section of town today."

"The slums? Why would you want to do that?" he asked in amazement.

"I know how the rich live, and now I've experienced briefly how the middle class live, but I want to see how the poor live. Does that make sense?"

"I suppose so, but we should take some extra guards. It's a dangerous area of town," he paused for a moment before continuing, "and I should like to avoid the area near Walpole Street. It has some unpleasant memories for me."

"That shouldn't be a problem," Anna agreed. "I'll arrange to get, say, four soldiers to act as an escort?"

"I would suggest four horsemen and two foot soldiers on the carriage, just to be safe. It's not unheard of for mobs to swarm carriages."

"Very well, I thought we might head down that way just after noon."

"How much time does that give us until we leave," he asked, polishing off another sausage.

Anna smiled, "Enough time for you to finish eating, I should say."

The look of surprise on Gerald's face must have been plain for all to see, for both Anna and Sophie laughed. He sheepishly downed the last of the sausages.

"I'll just clean up a bit after my breakfast... or lunch and be ready to go. Shall I meet you downstairs?"

"Yes, I'll send word for the soldiers. I expect it will take them awhile to get ready."

He headed back to his room to get into his travelling clothes. This time he donned his suit of chainmail and strapped on his sword. He looked at his reflection in the mirror and noticed how battered his mail was. It had been patched and repaired over the years, and you could tell from looking at it where new links had replaced the old. If he were returning to service, he would fix that, but the prospect of combat seemed remote. He was now a peaceful man, a simple groundskeeper, but he would still take care to protect Anna. He tucked his helmet under his arm and made his way downstairs.

The carriage was already waiting with four soldiers on horses nearby. As he approached, one of them dismounted and came towards him.

"Sergeant Matheson?" the man enquired.

"Yes?" Gerald answered.

"I'm Barret, and these men are Hansuld, Wiggins and Blackburn. We'll be your escort today."

"Thank you, Barret. What company are you with?"

"The Wincaster Medium Horse, Second Company."

Gerald looked them over with a practiced eye.

"Ever been in combat?" he asked.

"Blackburn is new, but the rest of us have fought before, and I've spent some time on the northern border."

He knew what that meant. You couldn't serve on the northern border without seeing a fight or two.

"Glad to see you're with us. I believe we're waiting on a couple of foot soldiers?"

"Yes sir, the Third Foot Company is sending a couple of men. They should be along soon. We passed them on the way to the Palace."

Sure enough, as if summoned by his very words, two foot soldiers arrived, their thick leather jerkins making them look slightly overweight. They reported in as soldiers Buckley and Collins. They looked ill-disciplined, and he was disappointed by the condition of the armour, but he supposed they would do. Hopefully, they would not be needed, and all these extra precautions would be for naught.

The unmarked carriage would have to make its way to the southernmost district of the city to reach the slums. The first part of the trip was pleasant enough for the main thoroughfare led directly south from the Palace then turned west, covering the majority of the route. It wasn't until they turned back to the south that the signs of poverty became more apparent to them. The streets here became narrower than those they had travelled through. Filth was dumped from windows, and some of the roads had no paving stones, only dirt or, more usually mud, which caused thick ruts to impede their progress. Even the buildings here were run down, showing signs of neglect. Many had broken shutters or ill-fixed holes in the wall.

People began to take notice of the carriage, and wherever they went, people stopped to watch. Two of the horsemen had ridden ahead of the carriage with the other two bringing up the rear. Now, the road became quite narrow and the two in the lead had to move forward to remove a blockage. Someone had a stall or barrow that had spilled onto the roadway and the owner was struggling to pick up his goods. Gerald had a suspicion of something more sinister, like a trap, but the way was cleared relatively quickly. As they were sitting, waiting for the horsemen to finish their task, someone knocked on the carriage door, and Anna looked to see a young child, begging for coins. Gerald watched her pull forth a silver shilling and slide the window down, dropping it into his waiting hands. The child grasped the coin as if his life depended on it and ran off into the background. Gerald's eyes followed the child's route as others stepped forward, eager for coins. Soon, Anna was handing out silver back and forth, but Gerald's trained eye caught sight of the first beggar. He had made it to an alleyway, and as he watched, the lad dropped the coin into the hands of an adult. Other children soon joined him, and it became painfully obvious to him that all of these youngsters were turning over their profits to the man.

Anna was genuinely pleased with herself at helping these poor children. He didn't want to disabuse her of this but felt he had to say something.

Before he could act, however, he heard someone yell, "There's a swell over here, with lots of coins."

Abruptly the carriage was rocked as a press of people rushed forward, adults this time, not children. Gerald acted fast. He pulled Anna away from the carriage window and slid it shut. Even as he did this, he had to push arms back out of the way. The carriage began to rock violently, and they heard a scream. A moment later, the two foot soldiers were pulled from the carriage, their bodies driven to the ground. The yelling intensified, and then the whole carriage was in danger of being pushed over. Next, he heard the driver being pulled from his seat, and for just an instance Gerald was glad that they had not brought their own driver.

Something had to be done, and quickly. He looked to Anna and Sophie, thankful that both of them were keeping their wits about them. He drew his sword knowing there was some work to be done. Anna copied his actions, drawing her new blade, holding it towards the window. A stone broke the window and shards of glass scattered about the cabin.

Gerald yelled out, trying to be heard above the din, "Stab with the point at anything that pokes through the window!"

He held his sword in both hands and drove it into the ceiling of the carriage. As expected, the blade quickly pierced the thin wood and canvas, and he began sawing back and forth, desperate to gain a means of exit. The other door was pressed close to the wall, but even so, the mob was trying to gain entry. Out of the corner of his eye, he saw Anna stab and heard a scream of pain as someone withdrew their arm. Sophie was pressed back against the other door, but the rocking of the carriage suddenly resulted in the glass window shattering behind her. She let out a scream of surprise but kept her head. She picked up a shard of glass carefully and cut some material off her dress, using it to create a handle to hold the glass as a weapon. A hand reached around through the window on the left side, and she sliced down with the glass leaving a trail of blood. The hand disappeared, and she gasped for breath.

He cut harder, trying to make an escape route. He heard the soldiers fighting, but at least one of them one was down while a horse whinnied in pain. Finally, Gerald finished the cuts and braced himself beneath, ready to push open the newly constructed hatch. Sophie was watching him, and he handed her his sword then braced his legs against the bottom of the carriage, his hands resting on the panel above him. The small, roughly cut panel came loose when he heaved with all his might. Sophie quickly gave him back his sword, and he started climbing through the hole. He was thankful for his choice of mail, for as he struggled to the top, a man already there struck him with a cudgel. The armour made it little more than an inconvenience, and he pulled himself through the hole, and then attacked the man with a vicious backhand blow, sending him toppling from the roof.

He glanced about quickly, and saw the two horsemen in back, still mounted. They were slashing left and right with their swords, but the crowd was keeping its distance. Ahead, a horse down, its rider bludgeoned to death by the crowd around him. A peasant was trying to climb up the back of the shaking carriage, while it was bouncing around violently. He saw Sophie looking up from below, and braced himself, holding a hand out to her. She caught his arm in a vice-like grip, and he pulled her up to the top in one smooth motion.

The left side of the carriage was up against the side of the street, and Gerald noticed an awning beside them. He pointed to it, and Sophie carefully climbed off, using the canopy as a stepping point to get onto the roof of the building. He swung a vicious cut at another man trying to climb up and almost lost his balance as the carriage rocked back to the right. He saw Anna, coming out of the hole and shouted at her to get to the roof.

She paused half-way out, and he wondered what was happening. He heard a shout from below and realized someone must have tried to enter. She sprang up all of a sudden, having used her Dwarf sword to free herself. The carriage suddenly lurched forward as one of the horses went down, its weight dragging them forward. He saw Anna make the jump and unexpectedly, she was hanging from the awning, it having ripped as she landed on it. Sophie, seeing Anna's predicament, helped her up to the safety of the roof.

Gerald heard men yelling, "Heave, ho," trying to get a rhythm to the rocking of the carriage.

He fell to his knees with the motion, and suddenly one of the wheels broke, causing the carriage to tilt to the side. Suspecting it was about to topple over, he hastily turned and launched himself towards the rooftop. He flung his sword through the air as he leaped, hearing it bounce on the clay tiles at the same time as he reached desperately for the roof. He landed on the corner with a force that drove the air from his lungs, causing him to struggle to find his grip. Gerald felt himself slipping, the weight of the chainmail working against him. At the last moment, his fingers caught the brickwork, and he began to pull himself up. The crowd roared with anger at their perceived loss, but it was too late, he had made it onto the roof. He rolled over on his back gasping for air, the pain in his chest telling him he was still with the living. He would be battered and bruised come morning, but he was at least alive to feel it.

He forced himself to his feet and cast his eyes about, searching for his sword and finding it only a few feet away. Sophie and Anna came over to him, and then they made their way back up the street by going over the rooftops. He was thankful for their adventure the previous day as he now knew he could find a safe passage for their flight from the violence below.

The sound of fighting had attracted attention, and now the town watch was responding. They came down the street in a group, their weapons drawn and ready for a fight. It was all over in a little more than an instant. The malcontents had no real strength, and they fled quickly, leaving a number of dead behind. Seeing Barret, his horse covered in blood, Gerald saluted him with his sword, and the horseman returned it. This had been a bloody day and an unmitigated disaster. There would be a price to pay, and he knew who would get the blame.

Gerald had seen his fair share of luck over the years. Soldiers often live by chance, but today he was sure his luck had finally run out. He was waiting, along with others, in the great hall of the Palace. The king had returned to Wincaster even as they were leaving to go and visit the slums. Now he had heard of the slaughter, and he was not amused. He had ordered the Royal Guard to punish the attackers. As retribution, they had made their way through the poorest districts, indiscriminately killing and damaging property. They must be taught their lesson, the king had said, and he was ruthless in his punishment. It only required the king to pass judgement on Gerald to finish dealing with the problem.

He was brought forward before the king, and he bowed deeply. The king had a stern look, while Anna, with Sophie behind her, stood to one side, the tracks of tears still evident on her face. Marshal-General Valmar, the self-styled Hero of Merceria, stepped forward from the king's side and moved towards Gerald. He grasped the neck of his tunic and pushed him to the floor so that he lay prone.

"Get down dog, until the king says otherwise!"

Gerald felt the cold stone pressed against his face and went still, sure that his execution was only moments away.

"Lift him up, Valmar," the king said, sounding bored. "I would see his face."

He was hauled roughly back to his feet by the marshal-general, his hands held behind his back.

"You have," the king lectured, "by your actions, put the life of a member of the Royal Family in jeopardy. By all rights, I should take your life, but it has been pointed out to me that your actions also saved my daughter's life, therefore it behooves me to be merciful."

Gerald heard Valmar's grunt of disgust, and then his arms were pinned even more uncomfortably behind him.

"I shall, therefore, spare your life. It is our command that you be discharged from your position and that you leave the city immediately. The Princess Anna will return to Uxley Hall under a heavy escort, and from this day forward shall always be accompanied by guards. Marshal-General Valmar, please see to the disposition of the guards and see that this individual is escorted to the gates of the city."

"We are not without mercy," the king continued. "See to it that his belongings are returned to him at the gates to the city."

Valmar nodded and turned, passing Gerald to two knights who were standing nearby.

"I'll remember you," he said threateningly.

Gerald felt relief as he was passed off to the knights. He was familiar with Valmar's reputation. Chances are by tomorrow, he wouldn't even remember Gerald's name.

As they escorted him from the room, he glanced back at Anna to see her standing tearfully behind the king. She turned and buried her face in Sophie's shoulder. Gerald thought it was the last he would ever see of her.

The journey to the gate was difficult. The guards kept tripping him, and more than once he was pushed violently, sending him to the ground. When they arrived at the west gate, they shoved him roughly pushed outside with his armour and sword tossed on the road. The Royal Guards returned to the Palace, and he was left to gather his belongings. The gate guards looked on with some sympathy. No one liked the Royal Guards these days. They had become nothing more than Valmar's thugs. As for Valmar, Gerald's

prediction had come true. The mighty marshal-general was far too important to escort the prisoner in person. For that, he had to thank Captain
Dayton of the Royal Guard, a name that he would not soon forget.

Fortunately, they had seen fit to throw a sack his way, and now he
pushed the chainmail inside it, tying it up and heaving it over his shoulder.
He looked to the west to decide on his course of action. He had no coins to
speak of, the guards had seen to that. He had his armour, his helmet, his
sword and the clothes on his back. He was banished, again, from Wincaster,
and had nowhere to go.

He started walking. He had no idea where he wanted to go, but the road
went west, and thus, it was his only choice. The more he walked, the more
the soreness left his body and soon he felt almost normal again, at least
physically. He felt a great loss and realized how much he would miss Anna.
She was like a daughter to him, made him smile, laugh, made the day worth
living.

The farther he travelled, the more he thought about her, and like a bolt
of lightning, his mind was made up. They ordered him out of Wincaster,
removed him from his position as groundskeeper, but they had not barred
him from Uxley. He resolved to return to Uxley Village. He knew the
townsfolk there and was sure he could find something to keep him busy.
Sam would, no doubt, look after him until he was settled. He might even be
able to farm, though it had been some years since he had done so. It was the
spring and with a little luck and some help, he ought to be able to get some
crops into the ground. His pace picked up, his mind racing as he marched.
He could even keep an eye on Anna, for he was fearful for her safety. He
knew that Valmar was now responsible for her protection, and he didn't
trust the marshal-general one little bit.

TWENTY-NINE

Friends

SPRING 959 MC

I t took all of Gerald's skills and experience to make his way back to Uxley, for, with no supplies and no coins, there were only his abilities to keep him alive. He decided to cut across the country and live off the land. He had operated deep in enemy territory before so he knew what he could eat and what he should not. He spent time setting up some snares and managed to catch himself a hare. It slowed him down, but he drew inexorably back towards the little village that was calling him. He thought briefly of returning to Bodden, for he was sure the baron would take him back into service, but he knew he had made a vow to protect Anna, no matter what. He couldn't think of her being surrounded by enemies, for make no mistake, Valmar was no friend.

It took him a week to get back to the village, and by the time he arrived, he was leaner and more fit that he had been in years. He met up with Sam, and they walked over to the Old Oak Tavern to catch up on the news. Sam was shocked to hear what had transpired. The princess had returned several days ago, her carriage running straight through the village without stopping. They entered the tavern and sat down at an empty table.

Arlo Harris, the owner, came over with a jug of cider and looked at Gerald. "Tell me, what's happened?"

Once again, Gerald recounted his story, and soon all the villagers gathered around to hear the tale. He talked between the mouthfuls of food that they placed in front of him, for which he was grateful. The story finished, the patrons returned to their seats to discuss the matter in more detail. It was then that Arlo came over and joined them.

"Mind if I sit?" he asked.

"By all means," said Gerald, looking at him with some surprise.

Arlo looked at him for a moment as if trying to make up his mind.

"Are you a noble?" he asked cautiously.

"Me?" Gerald replied, genuinely shocked. "No, why would you think that?"

The tavern owner leaned in conspiratorially and talked in a quiet voice, "A few years ago a noble came in here asking for you. I told him you were up at the Hall and then he left. The next day he shows up again looking for me, if you can believe it." He reached into his apron and withdrew a sealed letter. "He gives me this letter and says that one day you might need it, and would I hang on to it till then. I have no idea what it is, but I think this is when you might need it."

Gerald gingerly took the letter, carefully breaking the seal and opening it up, holding it to the candle to see it better. He recognized the handwriting instantly. It was from Baron Fitzwilliam.

12 November 957

My Dear Gerald,

I have just now returned from my visit to Uxley Hall. I am pleased to see you in good health and spirits and must congratulate you on your friendship with the young lady. I am convinced that you have her best interests at heart, but we cannot tell what the future might bring.

To that end, I have made arrangements with some of the locals to assist you should the need arise. I have left this note with Arlo Harris, to deliver to you when he deems it necessary. I have purchased a house and plot in Uxley Village in your name, the deed held by Brother Clarence at the church. He also has, in his possession, a purse to the tune of 100 crowns for you to utilize as you see fit. He has been suitably rewarded for this task, so don't let the beggar tell you otherwise. If you should find more funds are necessary, you may contact me in Bodden, though I dare say it might take some time.

. . .

My hopes go with you for a prosperous future, and I hope I shall see both of you again.

Your friend,

Richard Fitzwilliam,
    Baron of Bodden

As Gerald read the letter, tears came to his eyes. He rubbed them, quickly complaining about the cheap candles. He was a lucky man. He had friends he could count on. He would have a place to live and make a livelihood while keeping an eye on Anna.

He thanked Arlo with all the warmth he could muster and promised to reward the favour tenfold. He looked around the room and saw one of the local farmers, Edwards. He pushed the letter into his pocket and strode over to the man.

"John?" he said, extending his hand.

The huge man shook his hand, "Good to see you've safely returned, though I must say I'm surprised, considering everything that happened. I would have thought Uxley was the last place you'd like to be."

Gerald grinned, "Hardly. I've grown rather accustomed to this location. I was wondering if you might be able to do me a favour?"

"Consider it done," the big man responded without hesitation. "What is it I just agreed to do?"

"The estate still buys their grain from you, doesn't it?"

"Of course."

"I was wondering if, next time they pick up some, you might slip them a letter to take up to the Hall."

"For the princess?" assumed John Edwards.

"No, I think the guards might intercept that. I want to send a message to her maid, Sophie."

"Clever. I can see you're not just a pretty face." The large man laughed at his own joke, with Gerald joining in.

He called for a quill and ink, which Arlo was pleased to provide.

Two days later, Gerald had moved into his new home. The house was similar in size to the groundskeeper's cottage at Uxley Hall, though not nearly so well furnished. He used some coins and favours to obtain seeds, and he was soon working feverishly planting cabbages, peas and other vegetables before it was too late in the season. It was a kind of work that he had done years in the past, and though it took many hours, he found it rewarding. It was mindless, and he had plenty of time to think things over, to evaluate what he needed to do. He wanted to make sure that Anna was doing well. That was his priority, but he also needed to know how they were treating her. Was she a prisoner? Was she mistreated? Was she under the thumb of Valmar? He had no clue.

It was mid-afternoon, and he had been back in Uxley for a number of days. He was planting again, though half his time was spent removing the weeds that had infested the place since it was abandoned. He moved down the line he had etched into the dirt, digging small holes and placing the seeds within. So engrossed in his work was he that he didn't notice he was being watched until a familiar voice barked. He looked up to see Tempus, his front legs on the simple fence that marked his property. He cast his eyes about searching for Anna and saw, off in the distance, a carriage. She was stepping down from it as a group of soldiers looked on. The armed soldiers looked grim, and he sized them up. They looked more like thugs than soldiers to him with their armour mismatched, and their weapons a mixed collection you would expect a raider or a bandit to have, rather than the uniform arming of Royal Guards.

Anna, hearing the bark, turned to see Gerald and ran over, leaving the guards to trail along behind her. He saw the discomfort in their faces. They had probably not expected to be protecting someone so active. She rushed towards him, oblivious to the dirt which covered him and ran into his arms, throwing hers around him with no care at all. She held on to him while he tried to keep the tears from his eyes. Tempus started running around in circles, barking, joining in the happy occasion, an act which put the guards ill at ease, for they were obviously nervous around the great beast.

"I missed you ever so much, Gerald," she said with tears of joy in her eyes. "I'm so sorry for telling you to take me into the slums. I should have known better."

"It's all right," he promised. "I'm all right, and look, I'm a farmer now. You can come visit me anytime you want."

"I shall come every day," she declared. "I don't care what the guards say."

He eyed the guards warily. None of them appeared to be in charge, and he wondered where their leader was? There must have been someone given the task of handing out the duty roster and so forth. He held Anna an arm's length.

"Let's get a good look at you," he beamed. "Why, you must have grown a half a head taller since I saw you in Wincaster."

She laughed, and it eased his mind. If she could be happy, surely things were not too bad for her?

"Who's in charge of your guards?" he asked.

"They're sending someone. These men," she absently indicated them with her hand, "are just the first group. There are ten of them in total. I always have to have two guards with me, four when I go into town."

"How are they treating you?" he asked, the look of concern on his face obvious.

"I'm fine," she insisted. "They still have to follow my orders, but I have to submit to their guarding of me. The rest of the staff is fine." She leaned in close and whispered, "Good idea, sending the note to Sophie. They read all my letters. I think they feel it's their right."

"Doubtful," Gerald noted. "I suspect your father doesn't know anything about that. I think it's Valmar's doing. He wants to know as much about you as he can."

"Well," she said with a smile, "that will backfire. I've started writing letters to non-existent people talking about all sorts of strange things. That should keep Valmar busy for years."

He laughed, and suddenly everything was put to rights. Still Anna, still plotting and planning as usual.

"I'll need you to do me a favour, however," Anna said. "I don't want to go to the grotto and risk them finding out about Lily. Can you visit her?"

He assured her he would, and they moved towards the front of the house, where they sat on a bench talking, while the guards stood around looking uncomfortable. They began to play a game, to see how long the guards would remain. Several times the guards suggested that she return to the estate, and on each occasion, she just refused. By the time the light was failing, Gerald and Anna had partaken of a snack and drunk some cider, all while the guards fidgeted with no recourse but to wait for her command. Anna even suggested the guards go up to the tavern, but they refused. Valmar must indeed have been strict with his orders.

Finally, she decided it was time to return. She called Tempus, and together they made their way back to the carriage. With a final wave of her hand, she left, and he watched her disappear up the road to the estate.

Over the weeks that followed Anna visited every day. The guards eventually bowed to the inevitable will of the princess and started to disappear into the tavern upon escorting her to Gerald's. This gave them the chance to talk in private and discuss things. He fit in a visit to the grotto once a week and kept her apprised of how things were going. Lily proved to be comfortable around him and would often meet him on his way now that he was on a regular schedule. Each time the Saurian would ask after Anna with that same musical lilt to her voice.

On her subsequent visits, Anna brought work clothes with her, and once the guards disappeared she would change into a simple skirt and help with the farming. It was like the old days, cleaning out weeds while Tempus rolled around in the dirt. The faithful hound was the perfect guard, for if anyone showed up, he would warn them with low growls. He even got to visit Jax once or twice when they dropped by. It became the worst kept secret in the village, as the locals soon learned that the princess was visiting daily. The baker would often 'just happen by' with some pastries to sample, and more than once Aldo of the Old Oak dropped by with a jug of cider for their consumption. It was, thought Gerald, a most idyllic life, a life that he could happily continue until the day he died.

One day, late in the summer, they set up a stall in front of the house. The vegetables had come in rather well, and now the carrots, cabbages, turnips and beans had been hauled out of the ground to be made available for sale. The townsfolk were rather a pragmatic people, and everyone used the honour system. A local might need some cabbage and would take a head, to replace it later, with a coin or some item of trade. It was a good system with honest folk and Gerald shared in the level of trust these people had. The two of them were sitting out front one day when Farmer Edwards stopped by to pick up some carrots. After exchanging some words, the man left, with a promise to drop off some fresh meat he had. Gerald looked at the stall, and, realizing they needed more carrots, rose from his seat and proceeded round to the back. Anna, still eating a pastry, watched the stall while Tempus dozed at her feet.

He was digging up a new batch of carrots when he heard talking coming from out front. Curious as to what was transpiring, he crept around the side of the house to get a look.

An opulent carriage, without any coat of arms, had pulled up and a well-dressed merchant had disembarked. He was looking over at the stand while Anna was talking.

"And we have all manner of vegetables," she was trying to sound like a commoner, "as you can see."

The man, whose wealth fairly dripped from his clothes, hummed and hawed, then looked at one of the cabbages.

"That," proclaimed Anna, "is not just any cabbage."

"Indeed?" the man said. "Why is that?"

"Those are special cabbages, Royal Cabbages."

The man sneered, "Royal Cabbages?"

"Yes. Are you familiar with the effect of blueseed?"

The herb she mentioned was likely to be known, of course. Any man who wanted to improve his virility was aware of the properties of blueseed, though Gerald suspected it was all a load of rubbish.

The man looked intrigued. "Go on…" he prompted.

"Well," she continued, "Royal Cabbages are said to possess the same characteristics. You're lucky you came along when you did, we're almost out. You know there's a Royal Estate near here, don't you?"

The merchant's face was blank as he looked at her. "Yes, what of it?"

"Well," she leaned in a little closer as if imparting a great secret, "the king himself uses these 'Royal Cabbages', and you know what they say about him and his mistress."

He saw the merchant's face change. It was as if a torch had been lit behind his eyes, as if he had just discovered some arcane ancient secret.

"How much?" the man said suddenly, almost too eager for the sale.

"Oh, they're normally quite expensive, but I'd let this one go for, let's say, a crown?" she offered.

"A crown! How ridiculous, I'm not going to spend that much coin on a cabbage!"

"Suit yourself, sir, it makes no difference to me. I know nobles who have no compunction about the price."

The man looked at her, indecision wracking his face. Gerald could tell he was under her spell, and he suppressed the laughter that threatened to erupt from within, in danger of destroying the strange tableau before him.

A slender, feminine hand snaked its way out of the carriage window and beckoned him.

"Hurry up," said a woman's voice, "it's getting late, and I'm longing for a warm bed."

"DONE!" the man bellowed while working feverishly to pull a golden crown from his purse.

He looked around to make sure no one was watching then took the cabbage, trying to hide it under his cloak. Anna remained calm as a cucumber and took the coin without even flinching. The merchant climbed back into the carriage and tapped the side with his cane, signalling his driver to move on.

As the carriage disappeared down the road, Gerald came, and asked, "What was that all about?"

"This," she brandished a golden coin. "I have just sold the kingdom's most expensive cabbage."

The smile on her face said it all, and he couldn't help but laugh.

"Well, this calls for a celebration. I suggest we take this newly acquired wealth and put it to good use at the Old Oak. I hear they have venison this evening."

Tempus barked in agreement, and so the trio headed off to the tavern, eager to put their newly found wealth to use.

Summer was almost over and the cooler days of autumn threatened to come early. Gerald made his way to the Old Oak before Anna arrived. He was anticipating a pleasant breakfast, as had become his habit, and smelled the bacon cooking even as he approached the door to the tavern. He entered, to be greeted by the regulars, for the sun was only just up, and they would often gather to gossip before going about their business. He sat down at his usual table, the server, Molly, bringing over his customary hot brewed cider.

"The usual?" she asked, and he replied in the affirmative.

It was nice to have a routine, he thought. He took a pull of the cider, and he felt the warmth travel down his throat. Life was good, he mused. He had perhaps never felt so content, at least not since he lost his family so long ago. Soon, the plate came out, and his nostrils detected the aroma that his stomach so craved. He dug in, eating the bacon with gusto but taking time to taste the fresh bread that came with the meal. It didn't take long for him to finish, but he took his time with the cider, savouring each mouthful. He sat back in his chair and stretched his legs out. The chair beside him was pulled out, and he looked up to see Sam, his dog Jax, now a little grey around the muzzle, standing beside him.

"Mind if I sit?" he asked.

"Of course not," Gerald replied with a genuine smile. "You don't have to ask."

"I see you've demolished another pig. At the rate you're eating bacon, we'll run out!"

"Ha, ha, very funny," he replied. "Seems to me, I've seen you eat your fair share."

"True enough," Sam paused.

It appeared to Gerald that Sam wanted to say something but was, perhaps, unsure of how to say it.

"What's up, Sam? I know that look."

"I don't want to spoil your day," Sam said at last, "but someone's been asking around about you."

"And by someone you mean...?"

"A stranger, not from around here. The man had closely cropped hair and no beard. Looked like a soldier to me."

Gerald sat up, no longer relaxed, "Tell me more."

"He's been doing his rounds. He showed up here last night, talked to Arlo, the servers and anyone else that would listen, trying to be discreet about it."

"What was he asking about?" Gerald's danger sense was becoming active after being dormant since coming back to Uxley. He suddenly had a bad feeling in the pit of his stomach, and he wondered if perhaps his travails in Wincaster had caught up with him. Had Valmar sent someone to finish him off?

"He wanted to know who you were, where you're from, that sort of thing."

"What did you tell him?" he asked.

Sam laughed, "That's just it. I didn't tell him anything. In fact, as far as I know, no one talked. Must have been pretty annoying."

"Did he say who he was?" Gerald asked.

"No, but I'll keep my eye out for him, let you know if he shows up again."

"Thanks," said Gerald, "I appreciate it."

They chatted on for a while longer, and then both headed off. Sam had work to do, and Gerald needed to get back to the house to meet Anna.

As it turned out, he needn't have worried for Anna was late. While sitting out front, waiting for her to arrive, he began to get nervous, that pit in his stomach seemed to grow, and he knew something was up. Sometime later, her carriage finally came. He heard it cross the bridge and then saw it as it passed by the Old Oak. Something looked different, and it took him a moment to register the details. It had the customary four guards, but they were more professional looking. They appeared to have been inspected and gone through a good scrubbing. Their weapons were now clean and well-kept, and so were their faces. Gone was the customary stubble for these men had recently shaved. The carriage pulled up in front of his house, as it always did. Anna waited while one of the soldiers dropped down and opened the door for her. He detected more deference in the guard's actions and wondered what had happened.

Anna exited the carriage, followed by Tempus. The guard dutifully waited until the great beast had exited, keeping his distance all the while. As Tempus trotted after Anna, the man closed the door. At this point, he typically would have signalled to the others, and the four guards would have trotted off to the tavern while the driver took the carriage back to the Hall. This time, much to Gerald's surprise, the guards dismounted but took up positions overlooking the house. Owen, the carriage driver, started the horses moving again and left in his usual manner, waving to Gerald as he did so. Something strange was going on here, but he waited patiently, sure that Anna would reveal all.

Anna came over to him, giving him a friendly hug then said, rather gruffly, "Let's go inside."

He looked at her in some surprise but followed her in. Anna ordered Tempus to guard the door, and the great dog lay across the threshold, his front outside and his rear just inside the door. It would be difficult for anyone to step over him and he looked vigilant, most likely picking up on his mistress' disposition.

He looked from Tempus over to Anna to see her marching back and forth across the room, fuming. He had been with Anna for many years now and knew her well, but he could still be occasionally surprised by the little girl that was still in her.

"Well?" he prompted, expecting her outburst to begin.

"They've seen fit to give me a new nursemaid!" she burst out.

"Nursemaid?" Gerald was confused with what she said, but not with her tirade.

"No, not really, but it might as well be. They've sent a new captain to oversee my guards."

"That doesn't seem so bad. You knew they had to send someone eventually," he offered.

"He's trying to tell me what to do, said I wasn't allowed come into the village, to see you," her eyes pleaded. This had struck her hard.

"Let me get this straight," Gerald tried to organize his thoughts. "He said you weren't allowed to see me?"

"Not precisely," her voice softening a little, "he said it wasn't a good idea, coming into town all the time."

"Did he order you not to come?" he asked.

"No," her voice was beginning to calm down, "not really, he merely suggested it might not be a good idea."

"What did you say?" he prodded.

"I told him I would do what I want and that he can't stop me."

That sounded like the Anna he knew. "What did he say to that?"

"Oh, he said I could do as I wish, but he would make sure the guards would do their job."

"So basically, he agreed with you."

"Well... yes, I suppose so." She hesitated, then continued, "But of all the nerve!"

"Let me get this straight," Gerald said, smiling as he talked, "he told you that you could do what you want, but the guards would stay with you?"

"Yes."

"And why does this upset you?" he prompted.

He could see the turmoil on her face. She wanted to be mad and fume, but the logic was obvious. She let out a big sigh and sat on a chair.

"Oh, I guess you're right, nothing really changed. I suppose it's not horrible, it was just unexpected."

Gerald peered out the door over Tempus' head.

"Well," he admitted, "not everything is the same. I suspect the guards won't be tearing off to the Old Oak anytime soon." He wandered back over to Anna and sat down in another seat. "So there's a new person in charge of your guard?"

"Yes, his name is Arnim Caster, Captain Arnim Caster. Wincaster sent him. He has orders signed by the marshal-general."

Gerald, who was starting to relax abruptly felt his stomach tighten again.

"Valmar? Not the king?"

"The orders said it was in the name of the king, but it was Valmar's seal at the bottom."

"When did he arrive?"

"He came late last night, but I didn't meet with him until this morning. He kept me waiting while he talked to the guards, that's why I was late." She stifled a grin, "He insisted on inspecting them himself, even told some of them to shave, said they were a disgrace."

"Apparently this Captain Caster doesn't like shabby looking soldiers," Gerald mused. "Probably likes them nice and shiny like those in Wincaster."

"I don't know, Gerald, he looks like he can handle himself. He's not like the knights that my sister uses. He also asked a lot of questions about you."

"What kind of questions?" There was that stomach again, telling him something was wrong.

"He knew I visit you all the time. He wanted to know who you were, where you came from, what you did, pretty much anything."

"What did you tell him?" he asked.

"I informed him you were my friend, and if he wanted to know anything else he'd have to ask you."

He mulled this over. He couldn't make up his mind if this man was dangerous or if he was just doing his job. Perhaps, he thought, he should invite this captain to have a chat and find out for himself. He was lost in thought when Tempus suddenly yawned and stretched, breaking the silence.

"I tell you what," he said at last. "Tell this new captain I'd be pleased to meet him. Now, let's get this sorry excuse of a dog here outside to get some exercise. I think we could all use a walk, and besides," he looked at Anna mischievously, "I believe if we walk briskly we can make the guards sweat."

Anna answered back with a grin on her face, "An excellent idea."

The day turned out to be enjoyable despite the rough beginning, and he soon lost the knot in his stomach. Things didn't seem that bad after all. The guards attempted to keep up, and he almost felt sorry for them. They had had it easy for quite some time, and now they had to work. They walked cross country and climbed over fences, the soldiers huffing and puffing with the exertions until they took pity on them and decided to rest for a while. The weather held, and Tempus was kept amused while they tossed sticks for him.

Eventually, they made their way back to the house where Gerald made them some food. By the time the light was beginning to fade, Anna was getting tired. The carriage arrived at sundown to pick her up, and she and Tempus climbed back inside for the ride to the Hall. She promised to give his invitation to the new guard captain and then waved goodbye as they drove off. Gerald, not quite ready to turn in for the night, wandered down to Sam's house and they sat out front sipping some ale, enjoying the good weather.

It was getting late by the time Gerald returned home. He was just starting to prepare the fireplace when a knock came at his door. He put down the kindling and crossed the room, opening the door to reveal a man standing there. He was tall, with a beardless face and closely cropped hair that was dark in colour. The man was dressed in a tunic but wore no sign of armour, though a sword hung from his belt. Gerald took a moment to commit the man's face to memory.

"Captain Caster, I presume? Would you like to come in? I've been expecting you."

The man entered, producing a bottle from behind him.

"Thank you. I thought we might share some wine while we talk." He said, passing the bottle to Gerald.

Gerald looked at the bottle. It was a sweet wine, common among the middle class, not some pretentious wine of the nobility. He was suitably impressed.

"Let me get some cups," he said, moving into the kitchen area.

It only took a moment to fish out tankards, then they sat down near the fire. He passed a filled cup to Arnim, who nodded his thanks, and then waited silently while he filled his own.

Gerald was the first to talk, "So, tell me about yourself. How did you come to be the new captain of the guard?"

A wry smile crossed the captain's lips, "I was a member of the town watch in Wincaster. To be truthful, I am a bit of a stickler for honesty. I was known as a man who couldn't be bribed. I think this promotion was just an excuse to get me out of the watch. I had made some enemies."

"Who hired you, then? Someone must have offered you the job?"

"I was summoned to the Palace by Marshal-General Valmar. He told me what a stellar job I'd been doing and said he had a job that would make more use of my talents."

"Guarding the princess?" Gerald prompted.

"He didn't mention that at first, he was rather vague. He said he had a special assignment that required someone of my skill set, told me he was looking out for me. I asked what he meant by that, but he just said that someday I might be able to do him a favour in return." He paused to take a sip of his wine, then continued, "Of course, I don't like being beholden to anyone, so I was a bit hesitant to accept. That's when he mentioned it was a bodyguard detail. It was when I pressed for more information that he revealed I would command a Royal Bodyguard, at a substantial increase in pay. I didn't know it would be here until after I'd agreed. My first inclination was to think I'd be guarding Princess Margaret."

"Interesting," Gerald mused. "Did he mention Princess Anna by name?"

"No. He said a member of the Royal Family had recently gotten into trouble and needed extra protection. She was just coming of age, he said, and therefore needed a proper guard detail. I wasn't given her identity until one of the knights gave me my written orders. That's when I first learned her name. I'd heard of her, of course, there was that riot back in the spring when she was attacked in the slums. It was when I got my orders that I thought to do some research. I asked about the riot, and that's where I heard your name. You were there, weren't you?" he asked in a non-accusatory manner.

"Yes," Gerald replied, "though I wish I had talked her out of it. I lost my position because of that riot."

"Listen," Arnim explained, "I don't hold it against you. From the accounts I heard, you saved her life. I can't fault you for that, but I am curious how you came to be with the princess in the first place."

"I was a soldier," Gerald said, pulling up distant memories, "and, I think, a damned good one, at least I thought I was. I served up in Bodden, on the frontier."

"Did you see much action?"

"Oh, yes, more than my fair share. I was good, but not so good as to avoid getting wounded. The baron sent me to Wincaster with a note for the Royal Mage to heal my leg. But the mage wouldn't see me, so I was reassigned to the barracks in Wincaster. Have you heard of Walpole Street?"

"The Massacre? Everyone's heard about that, a nasty business."

"I know, I was there. The captain made a wrong decision but managed to get himself killed. As the next ranking soldier, I was the scapegoat. They cashiered me. I only ended up at Uxley Hall because of a personal recommendation by Baron Fitzwilliam. I was a farmer before I joined the army, so they made me a groundskeeper."

Arnim's ears picked up, "That's interesting. I was born a farmer and my parents have a farm in a small village near Wincaster. It appears we have something in common."

Gerald nodded in agreement, "Well, two things, actually. We both want the princess to be safe."

"Look," Arnim knitted his brows in confusion, "it's obvious you two get along. I don't know why Valmar didn't just appoint you as the bodyguard? It would have been simpler."

"Marshal-General Valmar," Gerald paused, choosing his words carefully, "likes people he knows in these positions. My mentor Baron Fitzwilliam, he and Valmar have a long-standing, what's the word, feud."

Arnim nodded his head, "Well, that doesn't bother me. I don't care if Valmar likes you or not. The townsfolk are very protective of you, so you're all right in my book. If I might suggest something, however?"

Gerald, watching his face, nodded slightly.

"I might suggest," he continued, "that occasionally you visit her at the Hall, rather than having her brought to the village all the time. It makes scheduling the guards a little less challenging."

Gerald smiled, "I can agree to that, and perhaps in exchange, your guards can be a little less conspicuous?"

Now, it was Arnim's turn to smile honestly, "I can agree to that."

The wine gone, Arnim stood up, "It's time for me to get back to the Hall. Sorry to have taken up your time."

"Not at all," Gerald offered his hand. "It was good to finally meet the man who's been asking so many questions."

They shook hands, and the captain left, leaving Gerald watching him as he disappeared. Apparently, he preferred to walk, though perhaps he had a horse at the stables. The man had seemed honest and forthright, maybe the new captain of the guard would not be so bad after all. He turned in for the night and fell asleep quickly, the knot in his stomach finally gone.

THIRTY

Osferth Returns

The cooler weather had finally arrived. It was fast approaching Anna's thirteenth birthday, and she wanted to visit the grotto before winter came. Gerald met up with her at Uxley Hall, then they made their way across the estate. Tempus ran in front, occasionally jumping over the tall grass, but otherwise, just pushing it aside with his bulk. Behind them, two guards followed at a discreet distance. The ground started to slope downward as they approached the grotto, and they told the guards to remain behind while they descended into the shallow bowl that was the grotto.

Lily was there, waiting for them, and chattered excitedly when she saw them. She presented them with three fish, and in exchange, Anna gave her some leather she had purchased from the village. They had seen evidence of Lily's skill with a needle and thread before, for she had always worn a type of loincloth. They still could not communicate beyond names, but Lily, now quite at ease with her visitors, sat down on the ground, pulling her satchel around to the front. She looked through it for a few moments then withdrew what Gerald assumed was a needle most likely made of bone. She also produced a thin thread and attached it to the needle by pushing it through the eye. In no time at all, she was cutting the leather with the sharp dagger that Anna had given her, and shortly after that, she began sewing.

They sat and chatted, though neither side could understand what the other was saying. Lily appeared happy to chatter away sitting next to Anna. Things were peaceful until one of the guards approached. Suddenly the air filled with fog, and she could barely see the nose in front of her face. The guard panicked, but Gerald and Anna were used to Lily's behaviour. They told him to stay where he was and keep talking. A short time later, they found him and led him out of the fog, ignoring his questions about the origin of it. They decided they had visited long enough and began their way back to the Hall. It was just past noon, and Gerald's thoughts were turning to food when Anna spoke.

"I'm a little worried about Andronicus," she said without preamble.

"How so?" he prompted.

"I haven't heard from him in some time, not since last year, and I've sent him plenty of letters."

"Strange," Gerald mused, "perhaps he's travelling?"

All thoughts of further discussion on the subject were interrupted when they saw a man running towards them, waving his hands excitedly. While they closed the range, they recognized that it was another guard by the name of Royce. He was nearly out of breath as he approached them.

"You have to go to the village immediately," he gasped out.

"Why? What's happened?" a concerned Anna asked quickly, her eyes shifting to look in the direction of the village.

"They're looking for a fugitive in town, turning out all the houses," he blurted out.

"Who is?" asked Gerald.

"A King's Ranger. He came to the Hall to get some help. The captain called out all the guard to assist him and then sent me to fetch you. We're to meet them in the village."

Hearing that a King's Ranger was there could only mean one thing in Gerald's mind. Osferth had returned, and that meant bad news.

They hurried to the village as fast as they could, reaching the tavern breathless and panting. The townsfolk were on the street, and there was a lot of murmuring and complaining. The soldiers of the guard were searching through people's houses hunting, the ranger had said, for a fugitive. Gerald was sure they would find nothing. No fugitive in his right mind would still be indoors during a search like this. He was mulling this over, trying to figure out what was going on when two soldiers came out of his house. One of them held something up in one hand, brandishing it like a trophy.

"What is it?" called out Osferth, perhaps a little too melodramatically.

The guard walked over, and Gerald saw the man was clutching a hood. It suddenly crystallized in his mind, and he saw the whole setup in front of him, unfolding itself like a bad nightmare.

"We found this in the house, sir," the guard held up the hood. It was a bag that somebody had cut to make eyeholes. The damning evidence was the skeleton face painted onto the erstwhile hood, the tell-tale mark of the Black Hand. Osferth looked at it, leaving it in the guard's hands. He called over Captain Caster, who came to examine the hood.

"Do you recognize that?" the ranger asked.

"It looks like the Black Hand," the captain responded.

The ranger continued his pompous demonstration.

"There is only one punishment for possessing this," he dramatically paused, waiting to announce the sentence, "and that is death!"

The crowd, shocked at such an announcement, began to complain, but Osferth would have his way.

"Have your men seize the prisoner," he commanded, pointing to Gerald.

It was useless to run, there was nowhere to go. Two of the soldiers seized him by the arms and walked him towards Osferth, a look of satisfaction on the ranger's face.

It was Anna who stepped out from the crowd.

"Stop this at once!" she shouted.

The ranger looked over to her, "Your royal status has no bearing here, Your Highness. The mere possession of this hood calls for the death sentence."

She looked desperate, and Gerald had to admit it looked grim. He was going to die because he had made Osferth look bad. He had known this day would come, but he had not foreseen its manner. Now, he was hopelessly condemned, and would likely be hanged from the nearest tree.

"Wait," demanded Anna, "where's the proof?"

Osferth turned to the man holding the hood.

"Did you find the mask yourself?" he asked.

"Yes sir," the man answered, "and Tomkins here witnessed it."

"And where did you find it?" the ranger asked, loud enough for everyone to hear.

"We found it hidden under the bed, sir," the man replied.

"I don't believe it," the princess roared. "You planted it."

"I didn't search the house, Your Highness, your guards did!" Osferth provided this bit of information with satisfaction.

It was a little too convenient for Gerald's liking. He knew the evidence was planted, but couldn't see a way out. No one could call a King's Rangers a liar and get away with it.

Anna stepped forward, emboldened.

"Let me see the hood," she commanded.

The crowd was hushed as the girl stepped forward. He saw her shaking, and she put her hand on Tempus' neck to steady her nerves. The big dog, sensing her anxiety, stayed close. She walked over to the two guards, put her hand out, waiting for the evidence to be given up. The guard looked over at Osferth, who nodded his assent, and the man dropped the evidence into Anna's hand.

She stared at it as if it was some vile creature that might bite her. She looked over at Gerald, and he recognized the inner turmoil. He knew she believed in his innocence, but he was at a loss as to how to prove it.

She turned back to the guard. "Sawyer, isn't it?" she enquired.

"Yes, Your Highness," the man replied meekly.

"Show me where you found this." She turned towards Captain Caster who was standing nearby, "Captain, I order that no action is to be taken against this man until the investigation is complete."

Captain Caster bowed slightly to acknowledge the order, then turned, giving a suspicious eye towards the ranger. Sawyer led Anna back to Gerald's house, and they disappeared inside, with Tempus following behind. Osferth looked over at Gerald.

"You're a dead man," he said, the slightest hint of a smirk on his face. The ranger turned to one of the other soldiers, "You there," he commanded, "get a rope ready, we'll be needing it shortly for the hanging."

"Belay that order," Captain Caster instructed. "No man shall take action until I say so. Let the princess have her say."

The crowd uttered their support, and the ranger carried it no farther.

A moment later, Tempus appeared with Anna following closely behind. The great dog was sniffing the ground, following a scent and Gerald realized that she had told him to track the scent from the hood. The dog was going back and forth in front of the house, then, with a loud bark, ran up the street, stopping erratically to sniff the ground again. Anna followed, clutching the hood in her hands.

Tempus got closer and closer to Gerald, and he wondered if the dog was simply following his scent, but then he realized, as did the assembled crowd, that he wasn't heading for Gerald, but for Osferth, who was standing near him. Sure enough, the great dog ran straight up to the man and then starting barking.

"Get this beast away from me!" the ranger hollered. "This proves nothing."

Anna simply smiled. She told Tempus to sit. The great beast followed her orders but growled menacingly. She looked over towards Captain Caster.

"Captain?"

"Yes, Your Highness?" he replied.

"I believe you were once in the town watch in Wincaster. Is that correct?"

"Yes, Your Highness."

"Would you come here and examine this?" She was holding the hood carefully as if she might break something. Captain Caster moved across to where she was standing.

"Would you tell me what you see here?" she pointed.

The captain examined the hood before replying, "It appears to be a hair, Princess."

"And what colour hair is it?" she prompted.

He extracted the hair and held it up to get a better view, "It appears to be a red hair princess."

"Would you please tell me what colour is Gerald's hair?" Anna asked with a smile.

The captain looked across to Gerald "Why, I do believe it used to be brown, Your Highness, but there's a lot of grey these days."

Anna looked around triumphantly before continuing, "Would you tell me who, here today, has red hair?"

Captain Arnim Caster looked about the crowd, taking his time.

"I would say there is only one person here with red hair, Your Highness, the ranger Osferth. Shall I take him into custody?"

"Yes please, Captain, and have your men release Gerald Matheson."

Osferth looked like he was going to explode, but he knew he had been defeated. Then his eyes grew wild as he realized he would surely die, for he had carried the forbidden hood. Suddenly, he turned and sprinted, in a desperate attempt to get away. It looked like he might accomplish this task for he startled everyone with his actions, but he needed to push through the crowd first. It all happened in a blur from Gerald's perspective. As Osferth starting to run towards the villagers, Anna called for Tempus to attack. The ranger was desperate and shoved his way past a few of the onlookers. The crowd was of course against him, and as he tried to move past the towns-folk, someone put out a foot, and the ranger tripped, falling in the dirt. Moments later, Tempus was upon him, tearing him apart. Osferth screamed in agony and Anna was about to stop him when Captain Caster spoke quietly to her.

"It's better this way, Your Highness," he said simply. "No ranger would be found guilty of such a crime. This way, justice is done."

The man's screams didn't last long for the strong jaws of Tempus broke his neck. The deed done, the great dog released the body. No one was sad to see the ranger dead. As soon as it was over, some of the townsfolk began getting shovels. Best to bury the body quickly and say no more.

Captain Caster interceded and set some of his men to see to the ranger's burial, while Anna went over to hug Gerald. He noticed the look on her face. She had not shed a single tear over Osferth's death. She had almost revelled in it, and it gave him a slight shudder. She had a dark side to her soul, he thought, and he realized the king had a similar personality. How alike the two were in some respects. Tempus sat down beside them, back to the lovable hound, so unlike the vicious beast that had been unleashed mere moments before. Gerald was glad he was here and patted the dog's head.

Anna looked up at Gerald, "I'm so glad you're unhurt Gerald. I don't know what I would have done if he'd hanged you."

Gerald looked over as two guards dragged the body away.

"Remind me never to annoy your dog, Anna," he said with wry amusement.

The captain came over to them with a sombre look on his face.

"I feel I should apologize to you both. I must obey the law, and a ranger outranks me by a substantial degree. I had to allow him to take command of the men, but I had no idea what he was up to."

Anna did not look impressed, "You are the captain of my bodyguard now, Caster. As such, you will only take orders from the king or me."

The captain recognized her look of determination, "Yes, Your Highness."

"Your men, do you know them well?" she asked.

"I'm afraid I didn't have much choice in the soldiers I was assigned to lead. I was told to report here, but Marshal-General Valmar picked the men."

"I would suggest that perhaps you should hire one or two guards at the least, men that you can trust. I happen to know of an ex-sergeant who is entirely trustworthy," she said, turning and smiling at Gerald.

Captain Caster looked at Gerald.

"The marshal-general did give me leeway to hire on extra help. An excellent idea! He is obviously skilled and has the best interests of the crown in mind. May I offer you the position of sergeant in the Royal Guard?"

Gerald looked surprised but was pleased with the thought.

"I would be honoured, though I fear we've some work to do to get these men into shape."

"Don't I know it!" Arnim agreed.

Anna beamed, "And I should like to insist that Gerald be one of my personal guards, not some drudge to man the gates."

Captain Caster had a look of resignation on his face, "Of course, Your Highness. Anything else?"

"Time will tell, Captain. Time will tell."

Gerald smiled. This day had ended much better than he had thought it would.

"Now," continued Anna, "I think it only proper that we should go to the tavern to celebrate your new position." She looked over at Tempus, "And perhaps wash off Tempus, he's got blood all over his face. Come along, Captain, you're invited too."

THIRTY-ONE

The Duke

AUTUMN 959 MC

Anna had just turned thirteen and to celebrate, she and the servants organized a party in her honour. They held a fair in the gardens with invitations sent out to all the townsfolk. Uxley Hall had not seen this many visitors in a score of years, which created a festive mood throughout. Game stalls were set-up and staffed by the servants, while impromptu races happened on the front lawn. The weather remained clear throughout the day, despite that the cooler weather had started moving in. Cook insisted on feeding everyone, so the great hall was set up for a feast. They had searched throughout the attics to find enough dishes and cutlery for such a huge crowd. The townsfolk also brought along food of their own to add to the feast, overburdening the tables with a heavy addition of pastries and pies, the princess's favourite. The whole village enjoyed themselves immensely, there was genuine affection for the princess in everyone's face.

The cleanup of the grounds took nearly a full two days to accomplish. Some townsfolk came up to help, and soon the Hall was back to its former splendour. Gerald remembered how unkempt and run down the Hall was when he arrived all those years ago. How things had changed! He was supervising the cleanup when a fancy carriage appeared at the end of the driveway. Four jet black thoroughbred horses pulled the heavily lacquered black and gold carriage. The two servants upon the driver's seat matched the two at the rear. It wasn't until it turned in the circle that Gerald spotted the coat of arms that bedecked the side. He had no idea who the mysterious visitor was, but he knew they were most likely a noble. Leaving Charles to supervise the final bit of the cleanup, Gerald ran for the Hall, only to find that Anna had already been alerted. He fell into position behind her, following her out, Tempus trotting along behind, as he usually did.

The carriage halted, then a servant sprang from the rear seat to open the door, placing an elegant step upon the ground to allow the occupants egress. Gerald observed Anna trying to see who was visiting while she stood and waited as was proper. She was quick to notice the appearance of a rather large individual who stepped from the carriage, dressed in a richly appointed coat with his fingers dripping in rings. His face was puffy, his complexion red as if the very act of moving was tiring to him. He bowed slightly as he cast his eyes upon Anna.

"Your Highness," he addressed her. "Allow me to introduce myself. I am Lord Reginald Anglesley, Duke of Colbridge."

As he spoke, another, younger version of him stepped from the carriage, "And may I also introduce my son, Lord Markham Anglesley, whom I hope you will get better acquainted with."

Gerald immediately noticed that the duke's son appeared to be only a little older than Anna, perhaps sixteen or seventeen, and wore the same bored expression as his father. Where the father was overweight and red-faced, the son appeared somewhat fitter, which was due mainly to his lack of age.

"Pleased to make your acquaintance, Your Grace, though I must admit to some surprise at your visit. Is it not common in Colbridge to tell your host ahead of time that you will be arriving?"

The duke waved off the criticism, "Pish posh, such things are trivial when the king visits."

"The king?" she asked suspiciously.

"Why, yes, we're here to join the king's hunt. He's coming here to Uxley for the autumn hunt. Did they not inform you?"

Anna looked around at her servants, but none had an answer.

"The king is coming here?" she asked incredulously.

"Yes, he will be here in two days' time, I should think. Now, have your servants take our things. We have important business to discuss, you and I."

The duke walked forward inviting the princess to take the lead, and they entered the Hall, Master Markham following behind. Gerald followed them, keeping Tempus with him so as not to excite the duke.

"Now," the duke was saying, "I come from a long and distinguished family and our house has always been faithful servants to the Crown. I understand you have just turned thirteen?"

"Yes," she answered, "only two days ago."

"Excellent," he continued, hardly waiting for her response, "then you must consider your future. You are of an age now, Your Highness, where you need to think about your prospects. Marriage into a wealthy family with your father's interests at heart would be most beneficial to you."

Anna sputtered, and it took all of Gerald's self-control not to laugh. Was this man serious? He watched as she struggled to regain her composure.

"My lord," she spoke at last, "you flatter me, but this is, perhaps a little premature, is it not?"

"Nonsense," the duke persisted. "I mean to ask your father for permission to announce the engagement this very week. After all," he looked her up and down in a decidedly condescending manner, "you appear to be prime breeding material. Pity about the hair colour. Still, dark hair runs in the family, isn't that right, boy?" He directed this last comment at Markham, who nodded meekly, seeming lost.

"I shall take the queen's room, I think. She won't be showing up, and I know that the king has ample room in his chambers for the royal mistress." The duke grinned as though he was one of the privileged few with the king's confidence. "You can have the servants take the chests up directly. Markham and I will require some food and wine, of a decent vintage. I believe you have a trophy room if memory serves. We'll take it in there." He looked Anna up and down again, and Gerald realized it was making her uncomfortable. "We'll give you some time to pretty yourself up, and then we can get down to business."

The duke wandered off, without another word, heading for the trophy room, his son following dutifully behind him.

Anna waited until he left the room before turning. Gerald saw her face instantly go from a polite smile to a scowl.

"Who the blazes does he think he is?" she fumed. "Am I some chattel to be sold off to the highest bidder? And what about that son of his, he looks like he can barely put two words together?"

"I think," Gerald interrupted, "that perhaps there is a more pressing business than your possible future fiancé. He said the king is coming in two days."

Gerald was slightly amused to see the change in expression once again, this time she went from a scowl to shock.

"You're right. We must get people moving. We're never going to be ready in time. How are we going to handle this?"

"Relax, Anna," he said soothingly, "you just planned a massive birthday party. It's almost the same thing, just a bit grander."

"How am I going to handle all this AND deal with the duke?" she asked in desperation.

"I should think we can get some help from the town. In the meantime, we need to get into planning mode. I'm afraid the duke will have to wait."

Anna smiled, "Oh, Gerald, you always know the right thing to say. Please give my condolences to His Grace and explain that I am far too busy planning for the king's arrival to entertain any serious discussion at this time."

"How did that just become my responsibility?" he asked incredulously.

She smiled at him and simply said, "Please?"

"As Your Highness requests," he surrendered with an exaggerated bow.

The duke turned out to be a demanding house guest, seeking constant attention and expecting the servants to be at his beck and call. Captain Caster was forced to provide him with two guards for carrying out tasks, which mainly consisted of going into the village to acquire more wine or pastries for him.

They sent word to the village, and the sudden influx of eager townsfolk swamped the Hall. Anna insisted on paying them for their service, creating an enjoyable atmosphere. It took a lot of work to get the Hall the way Anna thought the king would want it. Despite being an invalid, Hanson had many ideas. He had served the estate for countless years and remembered the king's habits well, from when the family used to vacation here in the summers.

They had much to do and not much time to do it. The linens must be freshly washed and dried; cups and plates that befitted the king's station must be brought out of storage and polished and cleaned; food bought from town to enhance the pantry and the cook, Mrs Brown, had to create a menu worthy of a king.

They had no idea how many people would be coming with His Majesty, and that only made things worse. It was difficult to guess the number that would descend on the Hall, so they had to improvise. Anna examined all the books she could find to discover what etiquette would be required. She pored over the Hall's ledgers from years ago for clues as to numbers the king had brought previously. Luckily, she found that the king had held a hunt here three years before her birth, so she estimated the numbers from that information.

The grounds were in good shape due to the supervision of Gerald, who although no longer the groundskeeper, oversaw the staff in their maintenance. Anna and Gerald walked through every room inside and the grounds outside the Hall looking for any possible improvements. Tempus was trotting along nearby, smelling the grass and perhaps a scent or two of a hare. Servants pulled out the parts of a large tent from storage to assemble, for it was said that the king liked sitting outside, particularly before a hunt. They had even marked off two large fire pits that would be ready to roast whatever beasts were hunted down.

As they oversaw all this, Tempus wandered around the perimeter on the lookout for killer squirrels that might interrupt the festivities. After examining the tent, Gerald gave up on how to assemble it. The entire structure was a mess. He turned back to Anna and was about to speak when he noticed someone riding on the roadway.

"Who's this?" he said, more to himself than to her.

Anna turned around. A lone horseman was coming through the gates. The man was wearing robes, perhaps he was a member of a Holy Order? Tempus, disturbed from his hunt, looked up, and, noticing the horse approaching, began trotting towards the visitor to see more. Gerald and Anna watched, waiting until the traveller was closer so that they might recognize him. As Tempus closed the distance, the stranger stopped his horse and dismounted. Suddenly, he began moving his hands in the air in a strange pattern, and Tempus unexpectedly dropped to the ground, as if his very life had been taken from him. Anna screamed and ran forward.

"Tempus!" she howled in desperation.

Gerald ran behind, drawing his sword, for he feared this would not end well.

"Guards!" he shouted, getting the attention of two that were nearby.

Anna ran over to her loyal dog, sure that the interloper had murdered him. Gerald came up behind her, keeping his sword out and facing the intruder. The now dismounted rider was unconcerned by all the activity. He was young, in his early twenties, and sported a shaved head. His robe was mostly undecorated but looked to be of a nice quality.

Upon further scrutiny, this man held no holy title. Gerald briefly looked down, trying to keep the individual in his peripheral vision. Tempus lay on the ground, drooling. He suddenly realized the dog was sleeping, for the great beast could be heard gently snoring.

"What have you done to my dog?" Anna demanded through her sobs.

"Relax," the man replied nonchalantly, "there's no need to worry. He's just taking a nap."

She looked at Tempus' side to see that he was, in fact, still breathing.

She stood, angrily demanding, "And who are you to decide whether he should nap or not?"

"I'm Revi Bloom," he presented himself calmly, a slight twinkle in his eye. "I'm the Royal Mage."

Anna was speechless for a moment.

"That's not possible," she finally said, "Andronicus is the Royal Mage."

"He's dead, I'm afraid," explained Bloom. "I was his apprentice before he died."

"How is it," she persisted, "that I never heard of you? Andronicus and I corresponded a lot over the years."

"I'm afraid I'm at a loss to explain that, but I must tell you that Master Andronicus was... not himself in his last year. I'm afraid his mental state deteriorated quickly. He finally passed, peacefully, in his sleep, a little over two weeks ago."

She was devastated by the news, and Revi Bloom looked on with sympathy in his eyes.

"I've been told to come here to report to the king as the new Royal Healer. Might I ask who you are?"

It was Gerald who spoke up first, "This is Her Royal Highness, Princess Anna of Merceria."

"Pleased to make your acquaintance, Your Highness. I am so sorry I put your hound to sleep. I honestly didn't think it would work."

"What do you mean 'you didn't think it would work'?" she said, baffled by his confession.

"It's a relatively new conjuration for me, and I didn't think I could generate enough power. I thought I would just make the dog tired. I had no idea I could put him to sleep."

"You had no idea?" she asked incredulously. "What kind of a wizard has no idea what his magic does?"

"I'm afraid I must confess," he said, his face turning red, "you see, um, Andronicus never got the chance to complete my training. By all rights, I should have been his apprentice for maybe two more years. Instead, I'm only partially trained. I've been going over his books and scrolls, but it's just not the same thing." The mage looked to Gerald, "And you are?"

"Sergeant Gerald Matheson, the princess's-"

"Trusted advisor," Anna interrupted. "Did you say your name was Bloom?"

"Revi Bloom, yes."

"Are you any relation to Bloom's Herbalists?" she asked.

The mage smiled as he answered, "As a matter of fact, they are my parents. Why do you ask?"

"Oh, nothing important. I did some business with them recently. Do you share the family interest?"

"You mean do I know about herbs and such? Yes, I do, though I find myself rather busy to keep up with it."

Gerald interrupted, "So apart from sleeping large dogs, what else can you do? Magically speaking, I mean."

"Well," the young man said, "primarily I can heal wounds. I'm learning how to regenerate, but it's taking its time. Unfortunately, I have to interpret the spells, and the notes from Andronicus are notoriously difficult to decipher."

"What happened to Andronicus? We haven't heard anything from him for months," asked Gerald, knowing that the princess would want to know about her friend.

The mage's face turned serious at the change of topic. Apparently, he was taking some time to formulate an answer.

"I'm not entirely sure," he said at last. "I know he had been working on a new spell for some time, but he was having trouble with it. I think he might have been experimenting and encountered some permanent effects. For the last few months, he was mostly rambling. I jotted down everything I could, but up to now, I haven't been able to make sense of it. His last words to me that made any sense were for me to learn tongues."

"Tongues?" asked Anna. "What's that?"

"It's a spell. It allows the subject of the spell to speak a particular language."

Anna was suddenly very interested, "Any language?"

"Well, there has to be someone nearby who speaks or understands the language, but yes, pretty much any language, though only at a rudimentary level."

"You are saying that if you ran across a man or a creature that spoke an unknown language, you would be able to understand them?" she asked.

"Yes, but once again, only at a most rudimentary level. You would be able to get across basic ideas, but you wouldn't be able to communicate complex topics."

Gerald looked at Anna and could almost see the gears turning in her head again. She was thinking the same thing as he was. With this spell, they could finally communicate with Lily.

Anna smiled, "We shall have to talk more about this later, Master Bloom. Will you require a room?"

"Any spare bed will do, Your Highness, thank you."

Gerald called over a nearby servant and instructed them to find the mage a bed somewhere.

He turned to Anna, "This day," he said, "is getting more interesting by the moment."

Later that day, Gerald was overseeing the erecting of the tent, as he had finally figured out how to assemble it. It stood covering a long table, a suitable outdoor venue for the type of meal the king would expect. He looked upon his handiwork with some pride, and then turned to Anna, rather pleased with himself, only to realize that she had disappeared somewhere. He made his way around the grounds, asking about her, only to discover that she had retired indoors. It took some searching of the Hall to find her, for she was in the clerk's office.

He opened the door to see her sitting at the table, her head in her arms. He was about to say something to her about sleeping on the job when she looked up, and he realized that she had been crying. He entered the room, closing the door quietly behind him.

"Anna," he gently asked, "what's wrong? Are you all right?"

"No," she said through held back tears, "I'm not all right. I'm to be married to some buffoon, and paraded around like a prize racehorse."

"The duke can't make you marry his son," Gerald said indignantly.

"No," she agreed, "but don't you see, I'm a daughter of the Royal House. The king decides who I will marry. If not this duke's son, then it will be someone else. I wish I had never been born a royal."

He walked over to her, kneeling to put his head at her level.

"There there, Anna, you'll be fine."

"No, I won't," she insisted, "don't you see? They'll take me away from here, from you, and I'll never see you again."

He felt a lump form in his throat, and he couldn't speak. He couldn't imagine her not being around. It was as if his whole life had changed and he hadn't even realized it. He had never thought about what would happen when she grew up, and now he underwent an immense sense of loss. He felt the emotion washing over him, threatening to engulf him.

"I love you, Gerald," Anna declared. "You're a father to me in every way, but name, more of a father than the king ever was or will ever be. I don't want to leave you!"

Tears came to his eyes, and he leaned forward to hug her.

"I love you too, Anna," he said in a wavering voice, "and I won't let anything happen to you." He held her until he felt her relax at last. He released his grip and sat back to look at her. "We'll deal with this one thing at a time, all right?"

She nodded through her tear-stained face.

"Now, first things first. We need to either discredit the duke in the eyes of your father or convince him it's an undesirable match. The king will never consent to a marriage if he thinks the man is a buffoon, not that he'll need much convincing." He made a face as he talked and she broke into a grin. "What else can we do?" he asked.

She was looking at him, and then the answer just sprung from her lips, "We can run away!"

He was surprised by the sudden outburst, but at the same time, touched.

"We can't run away, Anna. We'd never get very far. What do you think would happen if a Royal Princess decided to flee? Half the kingdom would be looking for us."

"I suppose you're right," she admitted, "but I can still dream. I'd love to be just ordinary Anna, living the life of a free commoner."

"I admit, it's a nice thought, but best we put it to bed for a while. We've far too much to keep us busy, at least for the short term."

"All right," she smiled, "but promise me you'll think about it, even just a little?"

He nodded his assent, for he was too choked up with emotion to say it out loud. He had to keep his mind on the work, or he would fret over their situation. Perhaps, someday, they might be able to enjoy a more 'normal' life, but that time was not now, especially with the king's coming visit.

At her insistence, he left her in the office, allowing her time to compose herself. He headed out into the hallway, making his way to the front hall, where decorations were being laid out for the royal arrival. He headed up the great staircase, hoping to have a better view of the preparations. At the top landing, he ran across Master Markham Anglesley. The young man was leaning against the railing, watching those working below. He held a goblet in his hand, swirling his wine around slowly as if he had a purpose. Gerald was going to ignore him but saw an opportunity to find out more about the young man. He wandered over to the railing and leaned beside him.

"Master Anglesley," he greeted the lad.

The youth appeared rather bored but looked back at him.

"You're the bodyguard, aren't you?" he asked.

"Yes, Gerald Matheson."

"Shouldn't you be guarding or something?" disdained Markham in a slightly irritated tone.

This time, Gerald resisted the temptation to bite back for diplomacy was the answer, not confrontation.

"So," he said at last, "I hear your father wants you to marry the princess. How does that sound to you?"

Markham sniffed his wine and took a sip before answering, "I suppose it doesn't seem too bad. I suspect she'd be a bit of a frigid log in bed, but that's what mistresses are for, aren't they?"

Gerald was sure the look on his face betrayed his anger.

"She'd be what?" he finally stammered as if he misheard the man.

"Frigid, you know, not very enjoyable. But I'd only have to do it enough to get an heir," the youth smiled cruelly. "Maybe I could put a hood over her head," he laughed at his own words.

Gerald snapped. He grabbed Markham by the throat and walked him away from the railing, pushing him against the wall. The young man let out a small yelp and then his eyes bulged in fear.

"Listen here, you little weasel," Gerald threatened, "if I hear you say anything demeaning about the princess again, I will rip your heart out where you stand. If you treat her in any way that I perceive as rude or condescending, I will personally remove your manhood. Is that clear?" He had not intended to sound that menacing, but now he saw the look of fear on the young man's face. "And if you utter even a word of this to your father, I will see to it that the new mage makes you permanently impotent. Do you understand?"

He had no idea if such a thing was even possible, but it had the desired effect. The youth gurgled a yes, and Gerald let go of him. He fell halfway to the floor, landing on his behind in a sitting position, his drink spilled onto the expensive carpet. Staring down at his handiwork, Gerald channelled all his hate and frustration at Anna's predicament towards him.

"Get out of my sight!" he spat.

Young Markham half crawled, half ran down the hallway, so eager was he to depart the scene. Gerald was shaking. He clutched his hands and tried to take a deep breath. He was worried, he had lost his temper once again and may have caused more problems than he intended. He turned around, ready to descend the stairs and saw Sophie standing there. She was carrying a tray with some food on it along with a bottle of wine. His eyes met hers, and he felt shame for his actions.

"It's understandable," said Sophie, showing wisdom beyond her years. "He had it coming to him, and I didn't see anything." She moved forward to pass him and stopped, "I think you need this more than the duke," was all she said as she handed the bottle to him.

She then disappeared down the hallway, heading towards the duke's room.

THIRTY-TWO

The King

AUTUMN 959 MC

The king arrived with great fanfare. He was late, as befits a king, and was accompanied by far more people than they expected. The first sign of them was when a troop of soldiers, mounted on jet black horses, appeared on the road leading to the Hall. These were the King's Royal Bodyguard, hand-picked knights who were the finest in the land. Their highly polished breastplates reflected the sun, sending beams of light in all directions. Gerald was not normally one to take note of such things, but even he had to admit they looked impressive mounted on Mercerian Chargers, massive horses and a breed only seen in this kingdom. The mere presence of one was said to inspire terror in the enemy. He had only ever seen one in combat, for Lady Beverly Fitzwilliam had such a mount. He knew first-hand they could be fearsome troops if used correctly. The thought was quickly driven from his mind as they rounded the bend and came through the gate. Following them was Marshal-General Valmar who looked more like a popinjay than an army commander. He was wearing a magnificent cape with a feathered plume attached to the top of his helmet. Gerald had nothing but disdain for Valmar but kept his opinions to himself. The other servants seemed in awe of him as he trotted behind his men.

In the wake of this ostentatious show, one would think nothing could compare, but the Royal Carriage was the most ornate and expensive in the kingdom of Merceria, in any kingdom for that matter. It looked as though the entire conveyance was embossed with silver and gold. Six black horses pulled the carriage, with six servants in fancy dress riding on the top. When it turned onto the estate's road, the servants and townsfolk in attendance gave a cheer. He could barely make out the face of someone at the window until it drew closer, then he was able to see a mature woman with dark coloured hair and a pale-face ensconced within. It could only be the king's mistress, Lady Penelope Cromwell.

Behind the king came more mounted troops, mostly knights and men-at-arms, trailed by foot soldiers. Next came a legion of followers, including lesser nobles enjoying the hospitality of the king. The parade looked to go on forever, and Gerald wondered if the other end of the line was still in Uxley Village.

The guard trotted into the loop, passing in front of the entranceway and halted leaving space for the carriage to draw even with the front door. One of the carriage servants deftly leaped from his perch to open the gilt handled door, and slowly lowered the fold up step.

The servants lined up in front of the Hall. Anna stood in front of them, Tempus at her side, with Gerald slightly behind her. The first to appear from the door was a woman's foot with a stylish shoe decorating it. The dark-haired woman descended the step, standing to the side to allow the king room to exit. King Andred the Fourth was a tall man, requiring him to stoop slightly as he stepped out of the carriage. Immaculately dressed in expensive clothes, his delicately embroidered material glinted in the sun. He held his hand out, and Lady Penelope clasped onto it as they stepped towards Anna, who curtsied, and the king nodded.

"Daughter," he said in his deep baritone voice, "I'm glad to see you're well." He looked around as if examining the Hall for the first time. "I see you've done an excellent job preparing for the festivities. I look forward to the hunt."

As he was talking, Marshal-General Valmar walked up to the king's other side and scrutinized the staff up and down. Gerald was worried he would be recognized, but if he was, neither the king nor Valmar gave any evidence of it.

"What do you think, Valmar?" the king asked.

"Well done, Your Majesty. It seems the hospitality of Uxley Hall has managed to shine once again."

The king looked directly at Anna, "Would you care to introduce the staff?"

Anna walked down the servant's line, the king at her side, making introductions. Gerald kept just behind her, avoiding direct scrutiny. He found himself walking beside Valmar as the introductions ensued while Lady Penelope had chosen to wait by herself. He avoided looking directly at the marshal as they reached the end of the line.

"And this," Anna was saying, as Gerald's attention returned to the task at hand, "is Master Revi Bloom, the new healer."

The king looked at the young mage. "Healer, eh? How much Life Magic do you know? You look a bit young."

The young mage looked nervous but answered, "I studied under Andronicus, Your Majesty. I was his apprentice for years."

The king turned to Valmar, "What do you think Valmar? Think he's got what it takes?"

Valmar grimaced, "I doubt it, Your Majesty, he still looks wet behind the ears."

The king turned his attention back to Master Bloom, "Can you heal people? Have you managed to master that, at least?"

Revi Bloom nodded, and the king turned his head back to Valmar. "What do you think, a demonstration?"

A rasp of steel rang out as Marshal-General Valmar drew his sword, and suddenly all eyes were on him.

"Anyone in particular, Your Majesty?"

The king waved his hand absently as he said, "Doesn't matter, you pick one."

Valmar turned to view the servants. Each was nervous and full of fear, for no one knew quite what to expect. Valmar struck suddenly, thrusting his sword forward. Gerald felt it enter his stomach and instantly pain shot through his body as the blade penetrated, coming out the other side. He was literally impaled. His legs gave way beneath him, and he fell to his knees clutching his stomach. Valmar withdrew the blade and watched him fall back onto the ground. Gerald heard Anna scream, and saw the mocking look on Valmar's face as he enjoyed the spectacle.

The king stepped forward to take a look, "I hope you didn't kill him outright. Even a healer can't bring back someone from the dead, Valmar!"

The king laughed, and Gerald felt the life begin to leave him. He heard Marshal Valmar laughing along.

"Come on, young healer, let's see you in action," the king commanded, and the mage ran across to where Gerald lay in a rapidly expanding pool of his own blood.

Anna was there, crouching by his side, desperately trying to hold his wound, as if she could stop the blood from spilling out. The mage concentrated and began his incantation, but nothing happened. He started again, panic gripping his face. Gerald's view was starting to blur, and everything was becoming unfocused as his lifeblood fled from his veins.

He thought he heard Anna's voice commanding the mage, "Concentrate, put all else from your mind. Ignore the distractions. Feel the healing."

Gerald suddenly felt a snap, there was no other way to describe it. No sound, just a sudden feeling of... change. He knew something was happening, his mind cleared, and the pain began to dissipate. He sensed a transformation inside him as if skin and muscle were reattaching themselves. The wound began to close, and he blinked, trying to clear his vision. Revi was standing over him, covered in blood and Anna, who was sitting on the ground beside him, was still clutching where his wound was no more. Blood was everywhere, but the only other remaining evidence of his injury was the sword cut on his tunic. "Marvellous," the king said. "Nice to see magic at work."

Valmar offered his opinion, "Too bad it didn't seem to work right away, Your Majesty. Perhaps the young man needs to practice his craft a bit more before he brings it to the Palace."

"Good point as always, Valmar," the king agreed. "We must make sure Mister Bloom has more time to perfect his art before we need his services."

The king, still chuckling, quietly took Lady Penelope's arm and entered the Hall, Valmar right behind him.

"Good thrust there, Valmar," he was saying, "you've developed quite a good technique. You'll have to show it to my guards."

"Thank you, Your Majesty," Valmar answered. "I would be delighted."

Revi Bloom was drenched in sweat but looked relieved.

"I thought I'd lost you there," he said, almost out of breath.

Captain Caster had come over and was now helping Gerald to his feet.

"What kind of man stabs someone just to test a healer?" he asked incredulously.

It was the thought on everyone's mind. What kind of monster was the king?

Even though Revi healed him, Gerald missed most of the first day's festivities for he had suffered a massive amount of blood loss and was noticeably weak. Anna insisted he lay down and rest, even putting Tempus to watch over him. Revi checked in on him several times during the evening, and even Cook came to visit, bearing him some special soup to make him feel better.

Later that night, Anna came to tell Gerald what had transpired. She was furious with the king, but when she had tried to tell him so, he wouldn't listen. He spent most of his time flirting with his mistress and chatting with his lackeys. The guests included many nobles, and they all but destroyed the great hall, so dirty and messy was it by the end of the evening, Anna was convinced there had been a war enacted in there. She had needed to send word to the village once again, asking for help and even now, at this late hour, there were dozens of people trying to clear up the debris. She told Gerald that he hadn't missed much and he admitted he was feeling much better.

The next morning the hunt began. Dozens of horsemen, all noblemen, were ready to chase down any deer that might cross their path. The king had insisted that Anna accompany them, for it was fitting, he said, now that she was a young lady, to learn what her future husband did in his spare time, whoever that might turn out to be.

At this, Lord Anglesley spoke up, "Have you considered my offer, Your Majesty?"

The king turned to the duke and answered, "Give it some time, Anglesley, she's only just turned thirteen. Besides, I may have other offers."

The king looked knowingly at Valmar, who was mounted on a horse beside him and winked. Gerald paled at the thought.

Gerald was sitting on a horse beside Anna, Tempus between them. Their horses, being from the Uxley stable were used to the big dog, but the knight's mounts nearby were nervous. Gerald looked on with amusement. The knights were well mounted, their horses big and powerful, but they showed a lack of skill at controlling them. Typical knights, he thought, probably had servants to look after their horses. A real soldier should care for his own mount. The sound of the horn drove these thoughts from his head. The hunt was about to begin.

The king had sent riders out early in the morning to track down the deer. Now, they signalled the location and prepared to beat the bushes to chase them in their general direction. The riders surged forward in a mob. Gerald held Anna back to avoid the crush of horseflesh. He watched as the visitors rode forward in a haphazard manner tearing up the ground as they went, destroying the lawn and leaving naught but mud and clumps of stray grass.

The king expected every able-bodied man to ride, at least everyone who wasn't a servant, and so Master Revi Bloom and Captain Arnim Caster were trotting along at the back of the pack. They fell in beside Gerald and Anna. None of the quartet seemed the least bit interested in the hunt, but the weather was unseasonably warm for the time of year, so they rode along at a relaxed pace.

The day's activities took them all over Uxley's large estate but, thank-

fully, nowhere near the grotto, for its marshy land was not a favourite spot
for deer. All morning they followed the hunt. Occasionally, there would be
a shout of triumph, and suddenly a bevy of horsemen would rush to one
side hoping to get off a shot. The favourite weapon for the hunt was the
crossbow for it was shot easily from horseback and required less skill than
the longbows employed by the army. The quartet was, collectively,
disgusted with the laziness shown by the hunters, for none of them bothered to dismount, to look for tracks or to sneak up on the prey. They would
yell out and charge, loosing bolts with wild abandon. It was a wonder that
people didn't get injured.

As noon approached the king called a halt, and an army of servants
began setting up a tented pavilion. They erected a table and then served the
food. Lady Penelope was not in attendance, having remained at the Hall
along with the few other women that had accompanied her. Anna was,
therefore, the only female in attendance, a fact that escaped the attention of
most of the party, for they soon settled down into talks of female conquests.
Gerald steered their small party to the edge of the clearing, and Captain
Caster went and retrieved some food, which he brought back and shared.
Tempus lay on the grass, Anna rubbing his belly, while the group quietly
enjoyed their meal.

The luncheon finally complete, the horns sounded again. This time the
mob broke into smaller groups, each going along different paths to try their
luck. Gerald saw at least one group heading towards the grotto and pointed
it out to Anna. They immediately rode to stop them, riding as fast as they
could, with Caster and Bloom following along behind, unaware of the true
nature of the problem. Once they caught up to the hunters, it was simply a
matter of informing them that they were headed for a swamp and fresh
deer tracks had been found to the east.

By now there were riders all over the estate, and so Anna suggested they
make for the northern border. It was near the Sandlewood farm, and she
suggested they might be able to water their horses there. They rode
sedately, taking their time. The weather was pleasant, and the sounds of the
hunt were far off in the distance.

It was Captain Caster that first saw it, a dark smear in a small gully.
Riding closer, they noticed that the runoff from a recent rain had created a
slight depression where the ground was torn up. Horses had been here at
some point today, likely from the hunt.

The captain called a halt, "I suggest you wait here, Your Highness, and
let me have a look. It might be dangerous."

Gerald saw Anna bristle at the suggestion, but sensed that Caster was
concerned about something.

He pushed his horse forward, "I'll give him a hand," he explained as he passed her.

They rode forward, the gully being only some fifty feet or so away from them. Arnim stopped his horse just short, standing in his stirrups to look over his horse's head. Gerald moved his mount slightly, turning his head to view what had caught Caster's attention. Lying in the ditch, covered in mud, was a body. They both dismounted and slowly walked towards it, careful not to trip. The ground had been ripped up by horses, making it slippery and difficult to navigate. Mud clung to his boots in great clumps making it hard to move. They stepped closer, observing that the body was a young woman. She was wearing or had been wearing, a simple dress, but it was now ripped, and blood stained the water pooling around her.

"Bad business, this," said Arnim.

Gerald made his way closer to the girl. The stench was overpowering. Urine soaked the clothes and pooled on the ground. He feared what he would find upon further inspection. He searched the body carefully seeing blood pooled beneath her.

"She's been stabbed through the heart," he grimly observed as he turned over her body. "Whoever did it knew what they were doing, they thrust up from the stomach into the heart to avoid the ribs."

"And she's been... abused," Armin said through gritted teeth. "Can you identify who it is?"

He carefully used his hand to wipe the mud from her face.

"It's Molly Sandlewood," he said fighting back the tears, cursing. "She was only fifteen. The farm we were on our way to is owned by her father. She served me drinks at the Old Oak on occasion."

Arnim started walking around the site, searching about for clues. He crouched down and looked at the ground thoroughly.

"What do you make of this?" he asked.

Gerald lay the girl's head back down gently, making his way towards the captain. There were numerous horse prints on the ground, as well as some boot prints. He had spent years tracking down raiders, and he knew what to look for.

"These marks," he explained after some examination, "belong to a military horse. I would suggest a knight or a Royal Guard. They're far too heavy to be a standard riding horse."

Arnim nodded his agreement, "That narrows down the potential candidates by a large degree."

Gerald looked around some more, crawling on his hands and knees, examining the ground. It didn't take long to find what he was after.

"I have some boot prints here, come and have a look."

Captain Caster made his way over, careful not to destroy any evidence.

"See here," Gerald pointed with a small stick he had taken from the ground. "These prints are from military boots. Notice how they use nails, common for soldiers, but there's one set that has a stitched sole, from someone more affluent. The footprint is deep indicating someone who is, perhaps a little heavier than average."

"During my time on the watch," Arnim shared, "I had to deal with this sort of thing on a number of occasions. We need to examine the body."

He stood up and beckoned for Revi to come over. Gerald walked back to talk to Anna, to tell her what they had found. He broke it to her as gently as he could, but she was heartbroken. She had met Molly on more than one occasion, and she was a regular at the fairs. Now, she would never again bless this place with her presence. Arnim and Revi finished examining the body and walked back to them.

"I'm afraid it's worse than we thought," said Arnim, "it looks as though there were a number of them that participated."

They all stood in silence as the information sank in.

"Who's responsible?" Anna demanded, barely controlling her wrath.

Gerald piped up, "There can only be one logical answer, one well-off person who has access to a Mercerian Charger, and who has guards that follow him everywhere."

"Marshal-General Valmar," Anna spat out the name. "What can we do about it?"

"I'm afraid, that for the moment, Your Highness, we can do nothing," Armin seemed as frustrated at the circumstances as Anna did.

"Nothing?" she fumed. "Don't tell me we can do nothing!"

"Marshal-General Valmar has the confidence of the king," Arnim continued, despite her outburst. "We can no sooner accuse Valmar, as we can accuse the king."

"This woman," Anna was making a visible effort to control her voice, "this young girl was terrorized, brutalized, murdered and pissed on, in an act of barbarism perpetrated by the vilest and most disgusting creature ever to take a breath. I vow that he shall one day pay for this… this assault."

She was sitting on her horse, her hands clenched on the pommel.

Gerald stepped over and placed his hand on hers, stating, "I pledge not to rest until we bring the people responsible for this heinous crime to justice."

Another hand appeared on top of his, "And I," said Arnim, "pledge likewise."

"Me, as well," added Revi, stretching to place his hand over the others.

Tempus barked, a deep throated bark, which seemed to echo the sentiment.

"Thank you, everyone. I think we should see to the body. The family will want to hear the news, unpleasant as it may be."

The sadness in her eyes remained, but she knew she had a responsibility to the Sandlewoods.

"What will we tell them?" asked Revi.

"We say that there's been an accident," said Gerald. "There's no sense in causing more grief. We all know what's at stake here. We'll do what we can to see to it that justice is served."

They all nodded their agreement and got to work and moved the body, trying to make it more presentable. It wouldn't bring her back to life, but at least it didn't look like she had been murdered. Arnim rode back to the Hall and returned sometime later, with some old servant's clothes that they would use to dress the body. While he was gone, they moved Molly to a nearby stream where they washed her.

The hardest part of all was bringing the body back to her family. As soon as they were spotted, Molly's mother ran from the house, inconsolable over her daughter's death. The official story was that a hunter had accidentally ridden over her and killed her. Telling a lie made Gerald feel terrible, but he knew that the true story would shatter them. They promised to try to find out who was responsible, and it was Anna who spent the most time with Mrs Sandlewood.

It was nearly dark by the time they finished at the farmhouse. They rode back to the Hall, not over the grounds, but by taking the road that led around the perimeter of the estate. The mood was black and little was said, but as they got closer to the Hall, their tempo picked up a little.

"I am going to join the festivities," said Arnim, much to everyone's shock.

"How can you think of such things at a time like this?" demanded Revi.

Arnim turned to look at the young mage as if it were obvious.

"One thing I learned in the town watch is that people that perpetrate crimes like to brag about it. With all the wine that's flowing in there tonight, I'm bound to hear something."

Gerald was impressed with Caster. This was something that was way out of his comfort level.

"Good idea, we should all keep our ears open. Arnim, you've conducted investigations before, you take the lead."

"Remember," said Anna, "Valmar might be untouchable now, but one day he'll be vulnerable. We'll document everything so that when that day comes, we'll put him in his place."

. . .

Later that night, as Gerald was finally ready to turn in, he was summoned by a servant who told him the maidservant Sophie needed him. He went to Anna's room where Sophie was trying to comfort Anna.

"She's having nightmares," the distress was evident in the young maid's voice.

Gerald sat down on the edge of the bed and Anna hugged him. Even Tempus snuggled closer as if aware of the stress she was experiencing.

"I want to be away from this horrible place," cried Anna. "Please let us leave this nightmare, I can't bear it any longer."

She cried in great racking sobs, and Gerald held her tightly. This house, this Hall, had become her prison, and now he felt the weight of her future on her shoulders. He thought such a young girl should never have to witness such depravity. He must get her away from here, or she would break. Perhaps it was already too late, maybe she was already past saving, but he must try, he must try to save young Anna from the future that awaited her, here in Merceria.

The next day the king left with little fanfare. The guests dribbled out in small groups after the king's departure. King Andred had praised Anna for the effort and invited her to return to Wincaster at some point in the future. The king was off to Shrewesdale, he said, and would probably not return to the Capital until next summer. Anna played the dutiful daughter, but Gerald knew that the king was dead to her now. She lost whatever small measure of respect she might have had for the man when Arnim had reported his findings from the last evening's festivities.

It had been hard for Captain Caster to make his report, and he had spoken to Gerald before the princess, for he knew the information he gathered would hurt her deeply. He had overheard Valmar bragging to the king about his 'tryst' with Molly Sandlewood, even going so far as to go into a detailed description of what he and his knights had done. Hearing his tale, the king roared with laughter, and when told she did not survive, he merely muttered that it didn't matter, she was only a peasant.

Captain Caster had stayed at the gathering throughout the night trying to pry information out of drunken knights. He was successful in his investigations, revealing six names.

After sharing his report with the princess, her only comment was, "Please add their names to the list, Arnim. One day they will all pay dearly for what they have done."

Epilogue

THE SWORD OF THE CROWN

Spring 960 MC

⌇

The inevitability of winter is that it often comes unbidden and it felt like no sooner had the king left than the cold weather came with a fury that seemed to punish the land for its imagined transgressions. The winter of that year was severe, and Gerald found himself once again abandoning his home, and taking up permanent residence at the Hall.

It was during a particularly bad blizzard that Anna and Gerald made their decision. Anna could no longer bear the life that she was destined for, under a king she despised. They began planning their escape. She had collected maps, had received information from her 'couriers' whose numbers had swelled, and learned everything she could from the books at her disposal.

To the east lay the impenetrable mountains which formed the natural boundary of the realm. To the south, the land was blocked by the great swamp, thousands of miles of waterlogged terrain inhabited by all manner of beasts and cutting off access to the sea. To the north lay Norland, a land of the uncivilized, a land of warring earls who fought bitter wars against each other and raided into Merceria. A lone pair of Mercerians in Norland would not be safe, so they turned their eyes westward, to Westland.

From her research, Anna learned that Westland was a land of enlightenment. They spoke almost the same language as Merceria, though with slight variations in dialect. It was a Monarchy and was said to have laws similar to

Merceria, but with a significant difference. In Westland, the power of the king was limited by the earls, whereas in Merceria the king ruled supreme. They would travel to Westland in the spring, for the roads needed to be clear of snow for them to get away unhindered. They looked over several maps to decide on a route choosing to avoid the king's road and travel overland. It would take longer, they reasoned, but the chance of being discovered was much less. Once they had picked out their route, they moved on to planning how much food to take. Even plotting out where the hunting might be decent, for they could live in the wilderness for a while if they needed to. Gerald made sure they both had bows, and they practiced all winter long, shooting shafts into snowmen.

Anna's mood was very different this winter. Gone was the little girl who had grown up around him. Now, she was a young woman, driven by her desire to get away from the life she so despised. The only regret that Anna had was that she would never get to see Valmar and his minions get their due, for it appeared the marshal-general was indeed untouchable. He had risen in the king's estimation, and it was now rumoured that a title would finally be his.

It was important to begin the journey as soon as weather allowed, for Anna was worried that she would be forced to marry the man. There was almost a sense of panic to her planning, as she weighed every possibility. She would practice every day with her Dwarf sword. Gerald pitied the wooden training dummy, for, by the time she was done, it was little more than a post with large chunks of wood carved out of it.

Spring finally arrived, and with it, the snow began to melt and the roads cleared. It was agonizing, waiting for the ground to dry, but if they left too early, they would be mired in the mud and too easy to track.

Finally, the sun came out, and the land began to dry. They decided that on the third day without rain they would make their move. They had their bags packed and hidden away in the groundskeeper's cottage for no one used it anymore. Anna had even written a note, leaving some coins for Sophie and letters for the other servants that had been so good to her. Hardest of all was saying goodbye to Lily. Here, at least, they had had some luck, for the mage, Revi Bloom, had stayed on at Uxley Hall, hoping to perfect his magical abilities. It was he that came up with the spell for speaking in tongues.

It was with a heavy heart that they made their way to the grotto, for what would be the last time. Anna, Gerald, Revi, and Tempus of course, left their two guards nearby and descended to the little pool. Lily was cutting weeds, harvesting what they now knew as mistgrass, one of her favourite foods. Gerald heard Lily in the background chattering away as was her custom when they came to visit. Revi turned Anna to face him and began the incantation. He moved his hands around her and Gerald felt the air buzzing, as if there were something present. Anna's face suddenly lit up.

"She's singing," she said. "I understand what she's saying. She's singing!" She turned to face Lily, and strange chattering noises came from Anna's throat. Gerald knew that Lily understood, for the Saurian came running over towards her, chattering back. Anna turned back to Revi and asked, "How long will this last?"

"I'm not exactly sure, Your Highness, so make the most of it," he replied.

The excitement was evident on Lily's face as well as Anna's. She joined her lizard friend in cutting the grasses that she so enjoyed. Soon, they were both singing, a strange sing-song warbling that felt almost angelic.

Anna stood facing her Saurian friend at the end of the visit. Revi told her the spell was about to end, so she bid Lily goodbye. Lily reached into her satchel and withdrew something, handing it to Anna. They hugged each other, and then Anna walked back to the others. She held up the exquisitely crafted dagger to discover the weapon was fashioned out of bone.

They made their way back to the Hall. Gerald saw the sadness on her face, but Revi seemed oblivious. Only the two of them knew that this would be their last full day here at Uxley. They crossed the estate, taking their time. Both Anna and Gerald took in the magnificent view. They would never return here, best to remember it as it was.

It was late in the morning as they came into view of the Hall. Gerald remembered that first day he had arrived, how bad the grounds were and how he had found this little girl that had so changed his life. Those memories would always be there, he knew, but now a new life awaited them.

They walked past the cottage, with its thatched roof and then past the stables. They would enter the Hall through the front door this one last time, he thought. Stopping at the entrance, Gerald turned to look around, to take in the view of the front yard. To his shock, he saw a mounted figure at the gates. He watched as the figure trotted its horse through the gate. There was a second horse behind the rider, tethered by a rope, and he couldn't understand what was happening. Anna came to stand beside him, watching the approaching visitor as well. Soon, Revi too, was looking at the strange rider. Even Tempus appeared mesmerized by the spectacle.

It took only for the rider to draw closer for Gerald to understand. Here was a knight, riding his lighter horse while his warhorse was trailing behind, keeping the heavier mount from using unnecessary energy. Who could this rider be, he thought, and why had he come here, to Uxley?

The rider raised a hand and waved, trying to get their attention. They watched as he started moving the horse into a faster trot. Looking at the armour he was wearing, Gerald felt that something seemed oddly familiar. At last, the rider drew within hailing distance and removed the hood to reveal a mass of red hair and he instantly knew who it was.

"Lady Beverly Fitzwilliam," he announced incredulously.

"Who?" asked Revi.

Anna piped up knowingly, "Lady Beverly Fitzwilliam, daughter to Lord Richard Fitzwilliam, Baron of Bodden, often called Fitz the younger."

"Dame Beverly," Gerald corrected.

"That's right," agreed Anna, "she was knighted by the king."

Lady Beverly rode forward, dismounting as she did so. The action was smooth and practiced. Gerald was impressed by her skill. The young knight came straight up to Anna and, drawing her sword, knelt in front of her, holding the sword point down.

"Your Highness," she said in a solemn oath, "I pledge my life, my sword to your service."

Anna looked at her in some surprise while Gerald smiled. It was inconvenient for her to show up as they were about to make their getaway, but he couldn't help but be pleased.

"I don't understand," Anna's confusion permeated her words.

Gerald intervened, "She's pledging to serve you, offering to become your knight, your protector."

Lady Beverly remained kneeling, holding the sword by the grip.

"Why would she do that?" said Anna, ignoring the knight before her and speaking to Gerald.

It was Beverly's turn to answer, "Long have I sought someone worthy to serve, Your Highness."

"What makes you sure I'm worthy?" she turned back to speak to the knight knelt before her.

Beverly looked Anna in the eye and then turned to look at Gerald, "The fact that Gerald Matheson is here is proof enough for me," she said in all earnestness. "He has always been a loyal servant of the crown."

"But I'm not looking for a knight," professed Anna, "though I'm flattered, of course."

Beverly, for a brief moment, appeared slightly confused and then her face changed. "Have you not heard the news, Your Highness?"

"What news?" Anna appeared to find everything about this knight to be confusing.

"The kingdom has been invaded. An army from Westland crossed the border and a second, from Norland, has attacked Bodden. We're at war!"

Anna looked at Gerald in alarm, and as their eyes met, they both knew what it meant. He was aware what her choice would be, for she couldn't let innocent people suffer. She looked at Gerald, sadness etched on her face.

"It is the obligation of the nobility to protect the people," she said, and he realized that at this exact moment, she had grown into womanhood and accepted her role in society.

There would be no escape for them. Their destiny was inextricably tied up with the fate of the kingdom they called home.

≈

ONTO SWORD OF THE CROWN, BOOK TWO!

≈

IF YOU LIKE THE HEIR TO THE CROWN SERIES, YOU'LL LOVE THE FROZEN
FLAME SERIES
ASHES: BOOK ONE

Share your thoughts!

If you enjoyed this book, I encourage you to take a moment and share what you liked most about the story.

These positive reviews encourage other potential readers to give my books a try when they are searching for a new fantasy series.

But the best part is, each review that you post inspires me to write more!

Thank you!

Sword of the Crown: Chapter 1

BODDEN

Winter 935 MC

The wind howled in from the west, driving the snow into great sheets of white, blocking everything from view. The horses struggled to make their way through the deep drifts, forcing the riders to slow their pace. Ahead, periodically, they spotted the Keep, its beacon lit to guide them home. Another gust swirled around them, temporarily stealing the scene from view. The leader, encrusted in snow and weighted down with the responsibility for his men, pushed on. "Almost home," he yelled, but his voice was carried away by the relentless squalls that stole the very words from his lips.

The wind died down revealing the welcoming gates of Bodden before them. He looked behind him to see his men strung out in a single line, following his trail through the deep snow. The horses were breathing heavily, and he felt the cold seeping through his thick clothes. This was no time to be outside, but even in these severe conditions, the land must be protected. They had come across the raiders by accident, stumbling into them in the worst weather they had seen for years. It had been a quick and bloody encounter, with the enemy fleeing, leaving behind two dead and carrying off three more wounded. Now the patrol struggled to make it back without freezing to death. One of their own, Jack Anderson, had taken a brutal cut to the arm, and now he slouched in his saddle, tied in place with some straps that they had managed to cobble together.

The gate drew slowly closer, and it seemed that winter threw its last gasp at them with a massive crosswind that threatened to blow them off their horses before they reached home. Sergeant Gerald Matheson, the leader of the frozen group, clung to his saddle, his hands growing more numb by the moment. Just a little further, he thought, and they would be safely within the walls.

They passed through the gate, and suddenly the wind dropped. Almost like magic, the sky cleared as if portending some great event. He knew the weather here could be fickle; he had served for years in Bodden and had seen clear skies turn dark with little warning.

He dropped to the ground, taking a moment to shake the snow from his cloak. Ice crusted his thin beard, and he rubbed it, trying to warm his face. He stroked his horse's neck absently as he watched his men trail in behind him, two of them carrying Anderson to the surgeon. They had worked hard today, in harsh conditions to protect this land, now they deserved a rest. With no thought to his own respite, he led his horse to the stables. The stable boys came to take everyone's mounts, but he insisted on taking care of his horse himself. He owed his life to this creature, the least he could do was look after it.

It was late, and darkness was just starting to fall as he made his way into the great hall after tending to his mount. He saw Sir Randolph standing by the fire, sipping a cup of wine, and nodded his welcome.

"Sergeant," the knight said, "how went the patrol?"

"We ran into some raiders, but we managed to drive them off," Gerald replied. "I doubt that particular bunch will trouble us again, but Anderson took a hit."

"How bad?" the knight asked.

"I'm afraid he won't be able to swing a sword again," Gerald paused. Bodden was chronically undermanned, and even the loss of this one man would have far-reaching ramifications. He needed to find the baron. "I must report to Fitz, is he in the map room?"

Sir Randolph held up his hand to halt him and walked over, stopping to fill a second cup along the way. He handed it to Gerald. "I'm afraid," he said solemnly, "that the baron is otherwise engaged."

Gerald took the cup, looking Sir Randolph in the eye. "The child?" he asked.

Everyone knew that Lady Evelyn Fitzwilliam was due any day now. He could only assume she was delivering this evening.

Sir Randolph smiled, but there was a sadness in his eyes. "The child lives," he said, "but Lady Evelyn will likely not see morning."

Gerald grew silent. It had been only three years since the loss of his own family, and he knew the pain that Baron Fitzwilliam must be going through.

Outside the master's bedchamber, the wind was howling and shrieking, but the shutters kept it at bay. Candles dimly lit the room while Baron Fitzwilliam mopped the forehead of the pale woman lying in the bed.

"I'm sorry, Richard," said Lady Evelyn, "I failed to give you a son."

Baron Fitzwilliam's eyes teared up. "You have failed no one, my love. You have given me a daughter."

"But a daughter cannot inherit. You must remarry and have a son."

"Nonsense. I never wanted the title in the first place. If my brother hadn't died, I'd still be a soldier. I shall never remarry. Our daughter will carry on the name." He noticed her strength draining, her face growing paler by the moment.

"But the family name?" she whispered.

"Will remain in safe hands," he finished. "I promise you, our daughter will grow up to be the mistress of this Keep, and she shall remember the great love her mother had for her."

"What shall we call her?" he asked, desperate to keep her with him, if only for another moment.

She smiled briefly, "Beverly, after my grandmother."

Her eyes closed. He saw her take one more breath and then lie still. Outside, as if recognizing the solemnity of the occasion, the wind died down. Lady Evelyn Fitzwilliam, the Baroness of Bodden, was dead.

Baron Fitzwilliam walked over to the midwife, gently removing the baby from her arms, gazing at the infant through tear-stained eyes. The baby looked up at him, squirming in its wrappings. "You," he said, his voice breaking with emotion, "are Lady Beverly Evelyn Fitzwilliam, and your mother was the most wonderful woman in the kingdom. I promise you that I will do everything in my power to make you happy, and one day, when you're older, you will rule Bodden, I will see to it. On your mother's honour, I pledge to give you the life you deserve."

～

Continue the adventure in Heir to the Crown: Book Two, Sword of the Crown, now available at your favourite retailer.

How to get Battle at the River for free

Paul J Bennett's newsletter members are the first to hear about upcoming books, along with receiving exclusive content and Work In Progress updates.

Join the newsletter and receive *Battle at the River*, a Mercerian Short Story for free: PaulJBennettAuthor.com/newsletter

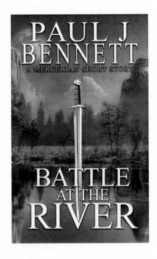

An enemy commander. A skilled tactician. Only one can be victorious.

The Norland raiders are at it again. When the Baron of Bodden splits their defensive forces, Sergeant Gerald Matheson thinks that today is a day like any other, but then something is different. At the last moment, Gerald recognizes the warning signs, but they are outnumbered, outmaneuvered, and out of luck. How can they win this unbeatable battle?

If you like intense battle scenes and unexpected plot twists, then you will love Paul J Bennett's tale of a soldier who thinks outside the box.

A few words from Paul

No story exists in a vacuum, and it is important for a world like Merceria to feel three dimensional. Though briefly mentioned in the book I had to develop extensive notes on all manner of topics for this series, from military organization to religion to the structure of the nobility.

The characters all have interesting tales to tell. Baron Fitzwilliam is an important figure in this first book, for he shapes Gerald much as Gerald shapes Anna. More will be learned about him in the next book, Sword of the Crown, though the story actually follows Lady Beverly Fitzwilliam. Arnim and Revi also have interesting back stories, just hinted at in the first book. These characters will have more of their past revealed as the story progresses.

Many of these back stories are being collected into a short story collection. These stories will be published as Mercerian Tales and will, chronologically, take place between book two and book three of the series.

Heir to the Crown is, at its heart, about Anna and the people that shape her life. Her adventures have only just started; the Kingdom has been invaded, and the crown threatened. It is now time for the Sword of the Crown to take centre stage.

About the Author

Paul J Bennett (b. 1961) emigrated from England to Canada in 1967. His father served in the British Royal Navy, and his mother worked for the BBC in London. As a young man, Paul followed in his father's footsteps, joining the Canadian Armed Forces in 1983. He is married to Carol Bennett and has three daughters who are all creative in their own right.

Paul's interest in writing started in his teen years when he discovered the roleplaying game, Dungeons & Dragons (D & D). What attracted him to this new hobby was the creativity it required; the need to create realms, worlds and adventures that pulled the gamers into his stories.

In his 30's, Paul started to dabble in designing his own roleplaying system, using the Peninsular War in Portugal as his backdrop. His regular gaming group were willing victims, er, participants in helping to playtest this new system. A few years later, he added additional settings to his game, including Science Fiction, Post-Apocalyptic, World War II, and the all-important Fantasy Realm where his stories take place.

The beginnings of his first book 'Servant to the Crown' originated over five years ago when he began running a new fantasy campaign. For the world that the Kingdom of Merceria is in, he ran his adventures like a TV show, with seasons that each had twelve episodes, and an overarching plot. When the campaign ended, he knew all the characters, what they had to accomplish, what needed to happen to move the plot along, and it was this that inspired to sit down to write his first novel.

Paul now has four series based in his fantasy world of Eiddenwerthe, and is looking forward to sharing many more books with his readers over the coming years.

Made in United States
North Haven, CT
26 March 2022

17552404R00188